Other titles in this series

The City of Veils
The Veil of Ashes
The Veil of Trust
The Queen of Veils

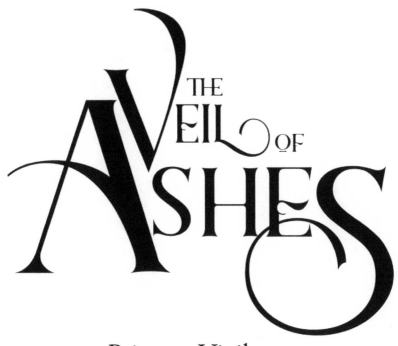

THE VEIL OF ASHES

Princess Vigilante

Book 2

S. Usher Evans

Sun's Golden Ray
Publishing

Pensacola, FL

Version Date: 3/29/22
Copyright © 2019 S. Usher Evans
ISBN-13: 978-1945438264

Cover Design by Jo Painter
Line Editing by Danielle Fine, By Definition Editing

Sun's Golden Ray Publishing
Pensacola, FL
www.sgr-pub.com

For ordering information, please visit
www.sgr-pub.com/orders

DEDICATION

To the girls who make the hard choices

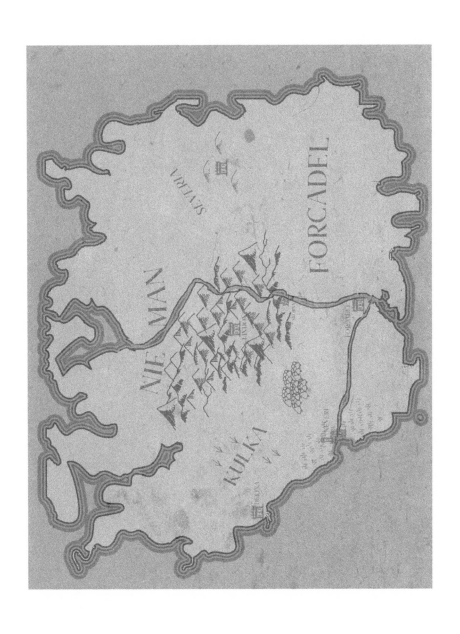

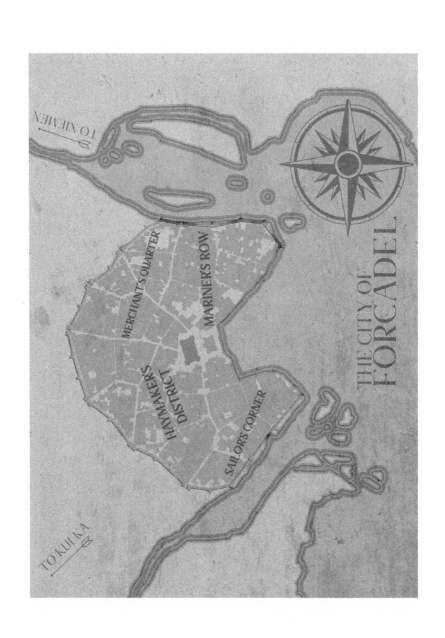

Chapter One

Steel met steel as the two children faced each other. They wore matching expressions of loathing and desperation as they clashed with a sword and a spear. But the girl on the left was more desperate, pulling a stick from her belt and jabbing the boy in the stomach. He lost focus, and she knocked him to the ground, effectively ending the match.

"What did you learn?" I asked the boy, whose name I hadn't bothered to learn.

He was silent, his red face etched in stone.

"Don't trust anyone," the girl parroted, giving me a look not unlike the ones I used to give the trainers when I won.

"Right," I said softly. If only I'd taken that lesson to heart. "Go wash up for dinner."

The two children scampered toward the bathing room, shoving each other playfully as they went. They couldn't have been older than ten—orphans both, if I were to guess. The ones who were here against their will didn't laugh so easily.

They were good fighters. Although the boy had lost, he would still be a useful foot soldier in Celia's army. They'd join the ranks of the children in the trees who scouted the trade road that connected the kingdom of Kulka to Forcadel. It would be a few more years before they were handed real swords.

Dusk had begun to settle, so I cleaned up the discarded weapons and left the small ring where the children were taught. Tall pine trees towered just outside the camp's guard walls, but inside neat little log cabins lined the expanse. Everything was communal, from the sleeping arrangements to the bathing and dining houses. Privacy meant secrets, which was why only Celia lived in her own cabin at the back of the camp.

I didn't mind an audience, because I had nothing to hide. Not anymore.

Celia was also keen on everyone pulling their weight, so I was making myself useful by training the younger kids to survive in a fight. It was hard not to feel that every day was a reflection on my failures, especially as I drilled into these kids the one lesson that hadn't stuck. I'd trusted too many people, and I'd ended up as defeated as the little boy.

With my mind on other things, I walked into the dining hall, which was already filled with the chatter of young and old. Celia accumulated children—some orphaned, some whose parents were in dire need of cash, some just stolen—and kept them until they paid off their debt. Unfortunately, that debt accumulated with every meal and every night spent in the camp, so there were also those well into adulthood, still tethered to this place. After a while, some just adjusted to the yoke.

I sat down in an empty spot at one of the long tables with my bowl of meaty stew, staring at the dark depths of the broth and trying to clear my head.

"Long day?"

I looked up at the kind face of a girl I'd seen around camp. I wouldn't call us friends, but we'd been friendly. She sat down across from me, still wearing the apron and hair tie that marked her as a maid. Her hands were pruny from spending the day dunked in the river, washing the camp's considerable laundry.

"Every day's a holiday," I said dully, pushing a piece of potato around.

"I don't think I've seen you smile since you returned," she said, daintily slicing through a carrot with her spoon. "What's on your mind?"

"At the moment?" I shrugged, not sure why I was talking to her. "Failure."

"The kids seem to be getting better with you there," she said with a small smile. "The other tutors, they train with harshness and threats. You take the time to talk to them."

"Perhaps I should be harsher," I said, pushing my bowl away. To her stricken face, I offered a small shrug. "Sorry, just...not really hungry. Feel free to give my bowl to anyone who wants it."

I left the dining hall, knowing that in the morning I would regret giving up my one meal. For now, though, I was content to take a moonlit walk to clear my thoughts. Unfortunately, I didn't get very far before they were rudely interrupted again.

"Always the giver, aren't you?"

I stopped, inhaling deeply, then turned to face Celia. The woman was in her mid-fifties, but barely looked a day over thirty. Her short black hair hung around her ears and her fiery dark eyes stared down at me with a mix of amusement and scrutiny. At her hip, she carried a bejeweled knife the length of my arm.

"What can I help you with?" I asked, nodding my head slightly.

"Oh, come now. You don't need to bow to me, Your Highness." I winced at the title, and she chuckled. "I figure I should start referring to you as such, since it's clear you've forgotten."

"I haven't forgotten." I wished I could.

"Then, *Princess*, I wonder why you haven't made good on your promise to reclaim your throne?" she asked, knowing full well the reason. "It's been four months."

"I'm working on it," I said, turning to walk past her.

The sound of metal on metal made the hair on the back of my neck stick up, and I moved out of the way just as her blade came within an inch of my shoulder. My hand went to the knife at my hip and I drew it to match with Celia's. I stood there, at an awkward angle, waiting for her to strike next, but she stepped back, sheathing her blade.

"It's clear you aren't still injured," Celia said. "You're wasting your time and mine, Brynna. I'm not running a charity."

"And I'm not asking for charity," I snapped, turning to face her fully. "I'm training people."

"I have plenty of trainers. What I don't have is a queen on the throne." She lifted her chin, her gaze piercing me as sharply as Ilara's knife had. "I suggest you remedy that before I decide you're more valuable to me dead."

She turned on her heel and walked away, leaving her words to settle on the mountain of guilt I'd been carrying. I placed my hand against my stomach, feeling the raised skin of my scar. There wasn't a reward for my capture, as all had assumed I'd perished. But I didn't doubt Celia would run me through and deposit my body on the front steps of the castle if she thought it would get her a king's ransom.

Or queen's, as it were.

Not in the mood for more conversations in the sleeping quarters, I turned in the opposite direction and joined the shadows along the camp's tall walls. Above me, the soft footfalls of the sentries kept me company.

In the darkness between the torchlights, shame and

embarrassment came roaring to the forefront, reminders of how I'd allowed Ilara, the queen of Severia, to walk right into my kingdom and take it from me. She'd played me effortlessly, coming on bended knee and begging for my help. And, like an idiot, I ignored all the advice to the contrary and allowed her to set up her coup right under my nose. I'd never been so completely blindsided in my life. More importantly, people were dead because of my mistake. Innocent people who'd perished just because I was too stubborn to see reason.

I hadn't left Celia's camp since waking up half-dead, but from what the messengers brought back from Forcadel, Ilara's takeover had been swift and absolute. Her power extended from the Forcadel Bay all the way to the borders, which she'd all but closed. There had been a few riots, but from what I'd heard, people had settled into her reign. It appeared everyone in the country was glad to be rid of me, even those I'd considered my closest allies.

A tear fell down my cheek and I brushed it away quickly. Katarine, my sister-in-law, was now Ilara's personal tutor, imparting all the wisdom she'd given to me to her new queen. And Felix...his loyalty was to the throne, not the person sitting on it. He had made it abundantly clear to me that he would always place duty above everything else.

It still hurt to think about how readily they'd thrown out the months we'd spent together. Katarine had called me sister, and Felix had looked at me as a man in love. I'd trusted him implicitly, despite my better judgment, and I'd even allowed myself to become vulnerable with him. Let him see me cry, let him see my joy. Let him taste my lips and hold me like a lover.

"Brynna, that kiss was...a mistake."

I exhaled, staring at my hands. Perhaps deep down, I wasn't really angry with them, nor did I blame them for turning their colors so quickly. I'd been given my chance to do the right thing, and I'd chosen wrong. Queens didn't get second chances. And I certainly didn't deserve one.

Still, I'd have to do something to get Celia off my back. In her own deranged sort of way, she was probably trying to encourage me to take action. I could always return to a life of vigilantism, protecting my city from thieves and criminals. But what had once been a fulfilling endeavor now felt hollow. At this point, it would take more than the threat of death to get me out of the camp.

It would take a miracle.

Chapter Two

Felix

"Captain, why is smoke rising from the southeastern neighborhoods?"

My upper lip twitched as Queen Ilara stood with her back to me, staring out a window at the city she'd taken four months before. She was two heads shorter than me, with a skinny, bony body that belied her sharp mind and sharper personality. Her black hair ran straight down her back, resting atop a shapeless, Severian silk gown that ended just above her sandaled feet.

"Captain, did you hear me?" She turned to look at me, nothing but contempt in her eyes. "Why is my city on fire?"

Because it isn't yours. I cleared my throat and forced myself to look interested. "The citizens seem to be protesting your latest edicts on the curfew."

"By setting their own homes on fire?" She snorted and turned back to the glass. "These people are idiots. Cut off their noses to spite their faces. Tell me you've made progress finding who is responsible."

I bit my tongue and swallowed all the words I wanted to say. "Not yet. For obvious reasons, the citizenry doesn't trust us anymore, so it's been difficult to get information from them. Unfortunately, there are still many who don't accept you as the queen."

She stiffened and cast me a dangerous look over her shoulder. "And do you, Captain, accept me?"

I covered the silver Severian crest at my left breast and bowed. "Of course."

We'd been playing this delicate dance since the day I'd sworn fealty to her. She could very well have me hanged, but then she'd have the entirety of my guard up in arms against her. She needed them on her side, and so she needed me on her side. Alternatively, if I decided to leave my position, there would be no one to protect the guard—or the city—from her capricious whims. I had to stay, even if it made my skin crawl to be near her.

She seemed placated and turned back to the window. I fought the urge to rip the seal off and throw it at her head. If I thought she'd listen, I would've told her that replacing all the symbols of Forcadel with Severian ones was part of the reason everyone hated her. The other, of course, was that she was responsible for destroying the Lonsdale line, including my best friend August and my...my Brynna.

A pang of sadness echoed in my chest, but this one wasn't very harsh. Thinking about it from a distance seemed to help.

"This city should be thanking me," she muttered under her breath.

"If I may," I began slowly, "it might be in your best interests to allow more ships, at least from Neveri, so we can start receiving food shipments from the Kulkans again. Perhaps just increase the tariffs—"

She spun, a deadly look in her eye. "It's not about the *money*, you stupid man. King Neshua has yet to accept me as queen of

Forcadel. So why would I give him what he wants?"

I could've told her that Neshua couldn't care less if Forcadel starved or thrived, but I knew better than to try to reason when her ego was wounded. Forcadel's industry was wholly dependent on trade and shipping, thanks to her strategic position at the mouth of the Vanhoja and Ash rivers from Kulka and Niemen, respectively. But Ilara seemed to think it was better to close the borders to all ships.

"When I want your opinion, I'll ask for it," she snapped, turning back to the window. "I suggest you figure out who set this fire and bring them to justice."

"Of course," I replied, pressing my hand to my chest and bowing. "Will that be all, Your Majesty?"

Her dark brown eyes searched for some excuse to call for my execution. But she flicked her wrist, and I bowed before walking briskly from the room. My mind elsewhere, I almost missed the shadow standing against the wall, waiting for his turn in the throne room.

"Felix."

I stopped mid-step, a smile curling onto my face. Lieutenant Coyle, the sole traitor in my squad, stood to my left. Wisely, he hadn't said one word to me since the Severians invaded, but perhaps he'd forgotten that I wanted to press his face into the bay until the bubbles stopped.

I turned slowly, making sure he saw just how low I thought him to be. "Yes?"

"I have been speaking with Captain Maarit," he said. "She is concerned about your cadets."

I clicked my tongue against the roof of my mouth. Maarit was Ilara's Severian military leader and had made no secret of the fact that she considered my position here a formality. It didn't surprise me that Coyle had thrown his lot in with her. He was good at finding the strongest person and allying himself with them.

Presumably why he'd become so chummy with me and Prince August.

I quirked a brow. "Curious that Maarit would speak with one of my subordinates instead of coming directly to me."

A flash of annoyance crossed his face. "Well, you're so hard to pin down lately. What with your nightly visits to the pub."

"If you know I'm visiting them, why don't you just find me there?" I retorted with a steely glare. "We can have a pint and talk about the past few months."

He sighed and took a step forward, lowering his voice. "I think it would behoove you to watch your tone and who you piss off around here. You aren't invincible just because the cadets worship you, Felix."

"That's *Captain* Llobrega to murderers." His reaction was swift but muted, not at all what I wanted. So I kept digging. "You know, I'm sure it takes a special sort of man to look someone in the eye while plotting their death. Did you feel anything when you put the poison in August's food?"

"I didn't kill him," Coyle said. "I just—"

"Made sure it happened?" I offered. "Whether you slipped it into his dinner or not, you're complicit." I shook my head, disgusted, as I walked past him. "If I'd have known you were so desperate for my job, I gladly would've stepped aside."

"Would you?" he asked softly. "I didn't think anything got between you and your princess."

My steps faltered before I could stop myself, but when I turned to face him, he was already walking away. I glared at the back of his neck, envisioning what it might be like to drive my sword through it. But he turned the corner, and all that was left was my anger and failure.

My princess. She certainly was that. I had no idea when that annoying, petulant, beautiful woman had crawled under my skin. Whether behind a mask or sitting on the throne, Brynna was a force of nature. She was impetuous but also fiercely loyal. Fearless and impossible to tame. And yet smart, methodical, strategic. I had known she'd be difficult when I found her in that butcher's shop, but I hadn't expected her to tear down my defenses and take residence in my heart so assuredly.

And now she was gone.

The pain I'd locked away broke free, and my eyes grew wet with regret and grief. I could almost hear the sound of her sardonic laugh. The quiet whisper of her feet against rooftops. The beating of her heart as I held her close to me during that brief, beautiful moment when I'd allowed myself to believe that we could be together.

I swallowed, clearing my throat. Brynna would've wanted me to continue what she'd started—to keep a close eye on the people she'd sacrificed so much for. But it was hard with Ilara's iron grip on the country. Blockading the border was merely the beginning—she'd implemented a curfew in the city that was stymying business, and the jails were filling with more innocents than not. Her Severian guards, technically reporting to me, were wreaking havoc in the city. The Council was now relegated to squabbling amongst themselves as they fought for Ilara's favor. Only Garwood had chosen to go to jail than swear fealty to her. She was content to let him rot in there, as the few public executions she'd conducted had resulted in riots that lasted for days.

As for the rest of us, we were powerless in most ways, so we did what we could. I remained as a buffer between my cadets and Ilara's demands. For however long she tolerated me.

With Coyle's—and presumably Maarit's—attentions on my cadets, I spent the afternoon with the oldest: twenty-five cadets who by all accounts should have been graduated months ago. But they'd lived through not one but *four* monarch changes during their last year of training. They were as unsettled as I felt, and I worried they might do or say something to earn a reprimand. And unlike the previous three royals, Ilara had little patience with insubordination.

"It has come to my attention," I began, watching the ripple of attention shift down the line, "that there have been some discussions about the queen that haven't been favorable. I know that this year has been difficult for all of you, and we're all adjusting to our new sovereign. But as her royal guard, you have a sworn duty to the crown—and whoever wears it."

A flicker of disgust crossed on a girl's face, but she schooled her expression quickly.

"And more importantly," I continued, choosing my words wisely, "you have a duty to your kingdom. Without its people, Forcadel is nothing. Protecting those people is as important as protecting the one person up there." I pointed at the castle behind me. "As is protecting your guard siblings. You've been together since you were children, as I was with my squad. You are a family, and always will be."

I paused to let my words sink in then began to walk the length of the cadet line.

"Trust, however, isn't easy to come by, it appears," I said, trying not to think of Coyle and what he'd done. "So if you think you can speak freely and poorly of our queen in front of your friend, you might find yourself in the town square sooner than you think. If you have concerns, come to me. If you have disloyalty, then..." I paused. "Then the door is right there. I'd much rather you leave than stay on disgruntled."

And be executed for treason, I finished silently.

"Let me make one thing clear to you: If I find any of you disparaging the queen in any way, I'll have you lashed within an inch of your life then dismissed onto the streets. Is that clear?"

"Yes, Captain," they chanted back.

"You have been given a great honor here," I continued. "I only accept the best of the best in my ranks, and the moment you slip, you will be out of here. Onto the streets or back to your families to live a life of shame."

"Yes, Captain."

"I handpicked most of you," I said, coming to stand in the center. "And I *hate* being wrong. Understood?"

"Yes, Captain."

"Dismissed."

In unison, they pressed their left fists to their chests, void of any crest until they graduated, and bowed. Then they turned to their left and dispersed in an orderly fashion. They said nothing, but I could tell by the way they looked at each other that each was taking a different lesson. I had a feeling the half that could leave, would. And they'd be better for it.

"I *hate* being wrong, hm?"

I turned and a warm smile blossomed on my face. Katarine and Beata stood behind me, arm-in-arm and dressed in blue and purple, respectively. After Ilara had taken over the castle, she'd taken care of announcing to the kingdom that Katarine and Beata were a couple, and everyone was too terrified of ending up dead in the town square to talk much about it. The one good thing Ilara had done since she'd arrived.

"I'll see you upstairs," Beata said, kissing her girlfriend on the cheek. "Don't be too late."

"Out for a stroll?" I asked Katarine as Beata disappeared.

"Since I can't seem to get time with you, I thought I'd meet you out here," she said, taking my arm and walking me toward the barracks. "I miss you, Felix."

I squeezed her arm. "I miss you, too."

"And I'm worried about you," she said. "The guards say you're drinking yourself to sleep every other night."

"They're exaggerating. It's once every three nights."

"She wouldn't want you to do this to yourself," Katarine said in a soft whisper.

She... I tried not to let myself react, but it was hard when my best friend scrutinized me. So I looked away to hide my face.

"Felix, you have to stop blaming yourself for what happened," Katarine said as we walked into the empty halls of the barracks. "It's been months. You have to move on."

I forced a smile onto my face. "Have you?"

"I'm trying to." She shook her head, and a blonde strand fell from her tight bun. "I keep reminding myself I have a duty to this kingdom, and to Beata, to keep moving forward." She turned to me, pressing her hand to my cheek. "And you have a duty to me not to leave me alone with that witch."

"Did you not just hear my rousing speech on besmirching the queen?" I wagged my finger at her.

Katarine smacked my hand away. "Felix, I'm serious. If you drink yourself to death..."

"You're probably more likely to find me in jail—"

"Don't joke about that. I don't think I could handle it if you ended up there, down with Garwood." She cast a longing look toward the castle. "I'm worried. He's become quite ill, and Ilara won't let me tend to him..." She turned back to me. "You're one bad mood away from joining him."

"If something happens to me, you can go back to Niemen with Bea," I said. "I know your sister would take you back."

"Forcadel is my home." She stopped and turned to me, poking me in the chest. "And you're my best friend. So you'd better knock it off before I move you in with Bea and me to keep a closer eye on you."

I softened. Katarine wouldn't willingly give up her newfound privacy with Beata unless she was really worried about me.

"I'm not going to die," I whispered. "Promise."

"There are people who love you," she said. "I don't know what

I'd do if I lost you, too."

I pulled her into a hug, and she rested her forehead on my shoulder. We'd lost so much already—Maurice, August, Brynn, the kingdom. Katarine had been so strong through it all, even though I knew in her private moments, she let herself disintegrate. The last thing I wanted was to add to her pain, so perhaps a little white lie would soothe her in the short term.

"I promise, Kat, I'll be here for a long time," I said, rubbing her back. "And to that end, I'm spending the evening with two soldiers. On duty."

She gave me a look so fierce I almost felt bad for lying to her. But the less she knew, the safer she'd be.

Chapter Three

I rose with the sun, sitting on the edge of my cot and rubbing my face as I considered another day of avoiding my problems. Celia's words echoed in the back of my mind, melding with the ever-present voice of disappointment as I left the sleeping house and headed toward the training rings. My stomach growled unhappily; it would be a long day until I could eat more.

Just as I finished pulling the last sword out of the trunk, a loud clanging echoed across the camp, and sleepy-faced children filed out of the sleeping houses, pulling on their cloaks and blinking in the early morning light. They spread out across the camp to their various jobs—some to till the fields on the south side of the camp, others to work the kitchens and laundry. And those who were able to hold a weapon headed toward the training arenas.

There were no regimented schedules or assigned trainers. Those who were told to learn how to survive in a fight did so or faced the consequences. When I was younger, I'd thrown myself into usefulness, learning every weapon I could get my hands on. Those who'd trained me were still roaming around, but they cared as much about me as I cared for the kids I now worked with.

However, thanks to my apparent reputation for kindness, there was always a queue for training help. A gaggle of thirteen-year-olds shoved each other as they ran toward the ring, assembling in a makeshift line in front of me before I could even say a word. They stared up at me with hopeful faces, knowing that the ones I sent away would get the harsher morning.

I opened my mouth to speak, but a young girl spoke over me. "I should be your student this morning, Larissa. I won my fight yesterday—"

"No, I should," cried a boy. "She should train those who need the *most* work—"

"You had her yesterday and you *lost*," said another girl. "I should—"

"Slow down," I said, nursing a pain in my right temple. "I can only take a few of you."

"Here!" A girl to my left produced a piece of crusty bread. "I saw you didn't eat last night. I bet you're hungry. If you'll train me today, I'll let you have this."

I eyed the bread, processing what she'd said. Then, in a single move, I snatched it out of her hand and took a bite. "Fine. Pick a partner. The rest of you can learn something from her."

"How to bribe someone?" asked a sour-looking boy.

"How to get what you want," I corrected, my mouth full of day-old bread. "Observation, kids, is how you learn someone's weakness. If you're patient, and if you keep your mouth shut and ears open, eventually things work out. Now, go bother someone else."

The crowd dissipated, discussing amongst themselves. Tomorrow, I might see five kids with bread, but that wouldn't be the lesson for that day. Tomorrow's lesson would be on staying flexible to changing requirements. Because I most assuredly would be eating tonight and tomorrow morning, bread wouldn't be the thing I needed.

I turned to my chosen pupil and found her alone. "I told you to pick a partner."

"My name is Elisha. And I did," she said. "I want to fight you."

I shook my head. She couldn't have been more than twelve. "No way. That's not how you learn. I'd beat you before you even had a chance to raise your sword."

"But I don't think you will," Elisha said, bouncing on her toes as if she were a student bursting with the answer. "See, I've been watching you these past few weeks. Your wound has healed, but you're still distracted. You don't sleep. It's not the first time you've skipped a meal."

I actually laughed. "I can tell you don't need the observation lesson. So today, you'll learn another one: how to not overplay your hand."

Her eyes widened.

"You have correctly assessed my current state," I said, smirking as I brushed the crumbs from my hand. "And as it would be quite embarrassing to lose to a kid, I won't deign to train you at all. Goodbye."

"B-but...!"

I turned to walk away, calling over my shoulder, "Thanks for the bread."

⇒⟶

My hunger sated, and my morning now open, I was faced with the choice of either finding another child to work with or making myself otherwise useful. Or, perhaps even planning a trip back to Forcadel instead of hiding in shame. But who was I kidding? I'd stay here until I died at this point.

A flurry of hooves and voices drew me to the front of the camp, where the large wooden gates had been drawn open, and a group of horses and riders came galloping in a cloud of dust and grass. Among them was Jax, a Forcadelian man in a black tunic with a permanent sneer on his face. He was one of Celia's favorites, which was good for him because, as far as I could tell, he was stuck here. We'd tangled a few times when I'd been The Veil, and I'd broken his arm the last time we met. Since I'd been back at the camp, we'd kept a cordial distance; he'd spent most of his time away and I did my best to avoid speaking to him directly.

Today was different. Along with his usual two thugs, he'd brought back a pair of pale-faced, shaking children.

"Who are they?" I asked, walking up to Jax. The two Nestori in the camp—Callum and Nicolasa—arrived shortly thereafter to peel the children off the horses. They had the unenviable task of integrating new children into the camp, checking them for disease and drying their frightened tears.

"Does it matter?" Jax replied, dismounting from his horse. "I don't report to you, *Larissa*. And since you don't wear that mask anymore, you can't do anything about it."

I stared daggers at his retreating back, imagining the sickening crack when I'd broken his arm months before. Jax had probably kidnapped these kids, and he would tell Celia they'd been offered up as payment from someone who owed her money. Celia never questioned as long as she got fresh blood in the camp.

And as someone who lived and worked in the camp, I had no right to question any of this. After all, if it grated on me so badly, I could always leave.

But since I was a coward, I returned to the training ring. Elisha had found another trainer and was practicing with a bow and arrow nearly as tall as she was. I felt her gaze on me as I walked past her, and was surprised her arrow didn't land in my back as I grabbed a young boy and girl who were hitting every target they shot at.

"Where are you taking us?" the boy asked.

"You've mastered the skill of pointing and shooting in broad daylight when you have time to consider your target," I replied, opening the door to a dark hut. "But when you're in the thick of things, you'll need to think faster, be quicker, react with certainty."

Inside the house, I pulled two crossbows off the wall and handed them to the kids. "This crossbow will be your best friend. When I was The Veil, and I needed to neutralize combatants twice my size, I'd use the crossbow with some knockout powder. But in order to get it in the right spot, I'd have to know where to aim."

"Into the big guys," the girl said.

I smirked. "Not always. Sometimes, you aim for the spot between them, so they'll both get a bit of powder. The point is, you've got to be able to aim, focus, and shoot in mere seconds if you want to be successful." To prove a point, I snatched the crossbow out of the girl's hand and shot it at the wall.

"So why are we in the dark?" the boy asked as I handed the girl her bow back.

"There are twelve posts in here," I said, walking to the door. "You have twelve arrows. Hit all of them and I'll let you out."

And with that, I walked out of the hut, shutting and locking the door behind me. In a moment, I heard six shots, one curse, and a lot of shuffling. After the fury died down, I opened the door and squinted into the darkness. As I'd figured, most of the arrows had hit haphazardly against the wall.

"Guess you guys are staying in here," I said. "Get the arrows off the wall and try again."

I chuckled as a smattering of curses echoed from inside and shut the door, staying away from the line of fire. I didn't expect them to be able to hit all twelve; if they managed to get one, I'd be impressed. But it was good training regardless.

"Are you...Larissa?" I turned to see a young girl standing behind me, her eyes on the ground. "Celia is asking for you."

"What does she want?" I said, looking back at the door which an arrowhead had just splintered.

"I-I don't know, I was just told..."

"Go find a trainer named Dudlin," I said. "Tell him there's a pair of kids learning to shoot in the dark here and to check on them every so often."

She nodded and scampered away. I had a feeling Celia was calling either to kick me out or kill me, and I didn't want those two kids to be shooting arrows forever.

I crossed the short distance to the back of the camp, where Celia's small hut nestled against the wall. It was a modest size, but compared to the cramped, shared spaces, it was practically a castle. With a soft sigh of resignation, I pushed open the front door and walked inside.

She sat at her desk, reviewing a map of Forcadel, and didn't look up. Jax was already seated in one of the two chairs, picking at his nails with his knife. Surely, Celia wouldn't gut me in her office. It would be entirely too messy. Still, I remained on guard.

"You wanted to see me?" I said, after a moment.

"Sit down," Celia ordered.

"I'd rather stand when you kill me," I replied evenly. "Or if you're just here for pleasantries, I'll go back to my training ring."

Jax quirked a brow, but Celia sat back, smiling. "I'm not here to kill you, *Larissa*, but I'm also taking you off training duty. I need you to go out on a recon mission with Jax, back to Forcadel."

Of course, I thought moodily. "Fine. What do you need to know? I can tell you right here."

"Unfortunately, the city has changed since the desert-dweller came into power. Doors that were once open to us have been shut. So we'll need a new map of the city."

Instead of arguing that if my knowledge was out of date, she should send someone else, I asked, "What do you mean?"

"Ilara has set up a blockade around the kingdom and the city,"

Jax said. "Unless you have a Severian seal or a lot of money, nobody's getting in or out."

I ran my tongue along my teeth, suppressing all manner of commentary. "What do you want me to do about it?"

"You have plenty of experience skulking around the city," she said. "I'm sure you know plenty of secret entrances we don't. Find a way in that I can use."

The urge was strong to argue—clearly this was a trap—but instead, I nodded. "I'll do my best."

"Oh, and Larissa?" Celia said, leaning on her hands with a smirk on her face. "You may need some extra supplies on this mission, so stop in at the Nestori hut. I'm sure you'll want to make sure you have everything."

The double meaning behind her words wasn't lost on me. Ready or not, my time at the camp had come to an end.

Chapter Four

I didn't have much to gather, but if I was leaving for good, I didn't want to go back to Forcadel unprepared. In the weapons hut, I grabbed a pair of small knives and strapped them to either leg. To my belt, I latched a small crossbow and gathered a few small arrows that I added to one of the hanging slingbags on the wall.

Next, I headed into the Nestori hut, where Callum and Nicolasa were tending to the young ones injured in training. Nicolasa was plucking the petals from a hyblatha flower, a floral herb she used in our calming teas.

"Smells good," I said, walking to the shelf of tins that held the potions and powders.

"We've been using more of it lately," she said. "Lots of unrest in the air. Nervousness spreads."

I wasn't sure if she knew my real name or this new mission, so I chalked it up to her usual Nestori weirdness. I sifted through the tins, finding some pouches of knockout powder and a flashbang, adding what I could to the bag around my back.

"You might want to take one of the newer bags," Nicolasa said, nodding to a rack of them hanging by the window. "Celia asked us to fortify them with beeswax so they're waterproof. She says she's tired of rusty weapons."

Good thing she won't get these weapons back, then. "Is it going to rain?"

"Very much so," she said, glancing at a glass jar on the cabinet that had fogged up.

"Of course it is," I muttered.

My final stop was back to the bed I'd been sleeping in for the past few months. Under the mattress, I'd stashed a second tunic and pants, which I added to my bag, and a leather garment—the cloak I'd worn as The Veil, the very one I'd been wearing when Ilara stabbed me. It was custom made, with pockets that helped me fly off rooftops and for holding a variety of items. It had been at my bedside when I first woke up in the camp, but I hadn't put it on once.

Along with the cloak, I found a strip of black fabric with two eyeholes cut out. It wasn't the mask I'd worn back in Forcadel, and I wasn't quite sure when this one had come into my possession. I toyed with bringing it. On the one hand, The Veil was dead. On the other...

"Can I go?"

I looked up at the sound of a small voice. The girl who'd wanted to be my training partner looked down at me from the other side of the bed.

"You don't even know where we're going," I said, stashing the cloak and mask into my bag with the rest of it.

"Forcadel," she said, scrambling around the bed as I stood up. "You're going with Jax."

I stopped and turned to her. "Celia doesn't take too kindly to people eavesdropping on her."

"I didn't," she said. "Jax was bragging about it at the front gates."

"Of course he was," I muttered under my breath. "No, you can't go. You're a kid."

She puffed out her chest. "So? I can fight."

"I'm not going to fight," I said with a shake of my head as I walked toward the front of the sleeping hut. "I'm going to do reconnaissance. That means staying out of trouble."

"Is it true you were The Veil?" she asked, darting in front of me to stand in my way before I walked out of the hut.

Again, I stopped, resting my hand on the doorframe. "Who told you that?"

"Nobody, I just assumed." She furrowed her brow, staring up at me as if I were her savior. "I met The Veil a couple years ago. She helped me get away from some bad men. There was a rumor in camp that The Veil came from Celia's camp, but she didn't have a brand. And since you're here, and you don't have a brand..."

Instinctively, I turned my left forearm away from her. "Yeah, I was The Veil. Once. I'm sorry I wasn't able to save you from Celia's camp."

"I came here willingly," she said, picking at the wood on the doorframe. "My sister threw me out, so I thought it was the best place for me. At least here, I get food."

"And now you want to go back to Forcadel?" I said. "You can't just come and go as you please, kid."

"Elisha," she said with a look. "And you're coming and going as you please. Maybe if I help The Veil, I can, too."

I sighed heavily. "The Veil is dead. You're better off staying here."

And with that, I left her behind, trying to forget her face and the extra measure of guilt she'd saddled me with.

Celia had ordered two horses tacked for us, so Jax and I set off immediately. Jax rode beside me in silence, but I didn't expect much from him. Perhaps, if I didn't do what Celia asked, Jax had orders to kill me and hand my corpse to Ilara. I doubted he knew who I was; he'd probably just jumped at the chance to finish what Ilara had started.

Celia's camp was a few hours' hard ride from Forcadel on the main road that connected the city with the Kulkan border. The road was open, with scattered travelers and merchants too poor to commission a ship to carry their wares. They ignored us, for the most part, and we did the same to them.

As the sun dipped lower in the sky, we came to the river Vanhoja, which connected the country of Kulka with Forcadel. The brackish water smell rustled my nerves, reminding me of home and all that I'd been avoiding.

I did my best to bury all the emotions fighting to break the surface. If she wasn't trying to kill me, Celia was trying to manipulate me into action. After all, guilt over killing a royal guard had made me leave her camp three years ago and become The Veil. Ilara had used sympathy so she could stay in my city while she gathered her forces. Seeing my kingdom in the hands of someone who didn't deserve it would certainly motivate me if I let it.

But still, what did Celia think I'd do? Throw caution to the wind, pick up my sword and...what? March into the castle and demand the Severians leave? Stab Ilara? I doubted anyone even remembered my name. I'd only been pseudo-queen for three months.

Besides that, acting rashly was what had gotten me into this position. From now on, I wanted to be a cool, rational person who thoroughly weighed pros and cons then took no action.

I snorted at myself.

"What are you laughing at?" Jax barked from beside me.

"Nothing," I said, looking down at the reins in my hands. "Surprised you volunteered to go with me."

He made a dismissive noise. "Nobody volunteers for nothing there. Except you, it seems."

I glanced at the sword at his side, then turned to the front again.

"River's empty," Jax said with a frown on his face.

"What?" I turned on my horse. There were several ships along the river, with their sails billowing in the wind as they ran with the current. Other ships with large paddles pushed them the opposite way. "There are ships."

"Should be ten times these. Sometimes it's so busy, the ships are bow to stern." He shook his head. "Damn queen screwing everything up."

All I could do was nod. Celia had probably told him to point out everything he could to remind me why I should return to Forcadel.

"So what happened to you?" Jax asked, after a moment. "Why'd you give up the vigilante thing? I know you got stabbed and all, but seems like it's time to head back into the city. Doesn't matter who's on the throne."

"Things changed," I said simply.

"Celia obviously thinks they need to change back," he said. "Never seen her so eager to kick someone out before."

"I'm special, what can I say?"

As the sun was setting, Jax turned his horse off the main road toward a small village, and I followed. My stomach was grumbling, so I assumed his was as well. We stabled the horses without speaking a word, and then found the nearest mess hall to fill our bellies.

But unlike Jax, I had no coin on me. So with a scowl, I sat across from him and tried not to gawk at the huge mountain of food he'd plated.

"Where's yours?" he asked, a knowing smile blooming on his face. "Don't tell me you don't know how to nick a silver off a farmer?"

"I do," I said. "But I choose not to."

He grinned, his mouth full of food. "We'll see how noble you are when you're starving half to death."

"It's one meal," I said. But it raised a larger point—what would I do if Celia didn't let me back in the fortress? I could always return to a life of sweeping blood off the floor.

Except Tasha and his family had died in the initial explosions. Nothing left of their butchery but a pile of rocks.

I shifted in my seat, looking around the room and taking stock of the citizenry. There were farmers, mostly, but some merchants in finer clothes. How many had come from Forcadel?

"What do you know about getting into the city?" I asked Jax.

"Nothing. That's why you're here," he said, spearing a particularly juicy-looking berry with his fork.

"Not about getting past it, but about the new defenses," I said. "I'd like to know what I'm up against."

"Well, you know, the rivers make it hard to get into the city from all sides except the northern gate," he said. "And our new queen has a great number of soldiers guarding that entrance. You're out of luck getting into the bay, too. Unless you've got the official seal from Her Highness, you're sunk—literally."

I nodded, crossing my arms as the door opened. My mouth parted in surprise as two soldiers walked in—Forcadelians both wearing Severian uniforms. The rest of the room cast scornful looks at them, and they took their food and ate in the corner. One even removed his coat, ducking his head low as he quietly picked at his meat.

"That's their uniforms now," Jax said, his gravelly voice lower than usual. "Makes me sick to see."

"Didn't take you for much of a patriot," I said, unable to tear my gaze away from them. Was Felix wearing something like that, too? Would I have to suffer through seeing him in another country's colors?

"I just don't like people who take what ain't theirs."

I spun around so fast my neck popped. "Seriously? Have you taken a look at your life?"

"Oh, it's not a big deal when *I* do it," he said with a laugh.

I rolled my eyes and got to my feet. "I'll be with the horses. Let me know when you're ready to set off."

He rested a silver on the table and slid it over to me. "Find someone to give my horse an apple, will you?"

With a glare, I swiped the silver off the table and marched out of the mess hall.

I fed our horses bruised apples from the barrel near the stables, as the silver I decided to save for good use—buying information. After all, I wasn't about to accept charity from Jax. It rarely came without strings attached.

I loitered around the stables, listening for conversations from incoming merchants and hoping they'd come up with something helpful.

"Evening," I said to an older woman who dismounted her horse.

"Evening," she replied with a small nod as she led her horse into one of the empty stables. "Strange to see the city so empty, hm?"

"You said it," I said, patting my horse on the nose. "Are you coming or going?"

"Coming," she said. "Attempted to get into Forcadel City and found myself turned around before I got a word in edgewise."

I nodded. "Know anyone who is getting in?"

"Not us lowly merchants, I'll tell you that much. That Captain Llobrega has the city locked up tight."

I winced in the darkness. "He's a jackass."

"Pretty sure he's just stuck, if you ask me. My nephew's in the King's Guard—the whole lot of them are terrified he's going to be the next one she hangs. But as long as they outnumber the Severian guards in the castle, he's safe."

"And as long as he does her bidding," I said, wishing the thought of Felix and a noose didn't send chills of fear and sickness through my body. "I'm headed that way tonight. Any advice?"

"Yeah," she said with a shake of her head. "Don't."

Jax arrived shortly after she left, patting his stomach and belching loudly. "Mm. That was a good meal, wasn't it?"

"You've got lettuce in your teeth," I said, leading my horse out of the stall. Lightning split the sky above me; Nicolasa hadn't been too far off about the rain coming, and I didn't want to get caught in it.

Chapter Five

We rode hard along the dark road, our only light the occasional flashes from the incoming storm. In the distance, pinpricks of light from torches became visible—presumably the guards standing in front of the northern gate. I slowed my horse as another lightning strike illuminated the road and a queue of carriages waiting to get in.

"We need a better strategy," I said to Jax. "It doesn't sound like we can just waltz right in. And I don't think we brought enough gold to bribe them."

"You could try swimming?"

"I doubt Celia will allow me back inside if I offer that suggestion," I said with a sigh as I sat back in the saddle.

"Do you...really think that's what this is about?" Jax said with a quirked brow. "Or are you just hoping it is?"

"Are you telling me you escorted me all the way to Forcadel just to, what, piss me off?"

"Make sure you got here," Jax said, turning his horse around. "She gave me coin to feed you, too. Shame you didn't use it." He pulled his sword. "Now get off her horse. I have orders to bring her back."

I rolled my eyes and dismounted, making sure to grab my bag before Jax snatched the reins from me and tied them to his saddle.

"Pleasure doing business with you," he said with a tap to his forehead. "Have fun."

With my arms crossed, I watched his shadow disappear into the night, annoyed at myself for many things—not the least of which was not seeing this coming. Perhaps I had, in the back of my mind, but I hadn't thought Celia would go to so much trouble to deposit me back in Forcadel. She could've just thrown me out on my ass.

And just like that, the sky opened up, just as Nicolasa had predicted. Within seconds, I was drenched.

"Fine," I huffed, shouldering my bag and marching toward the high walls. They'd been built to be impenetrable to any enemy ships that made it past the river fortifications, but I wasn't convinced it was impossible. There had to be a grate, a small door, something I could use to sneak inside. But I'd never been faced with this challenge before. All my knowledge was how to get around the city, not to sneak into it.

As the wall circled the city, the space between the river and the stone grew narrower and my path became more treacherous. Eventually, I would run out of path as the wall had been built into the river, but I hoped I'd find something before then. The rushing water below was a constant companion, swollen by the recent storm and sounding more dangerous than it probably was.

My foot slipped and before I could even scream, I plunged into the frigid river. The current was swift as it pulled me lower and I tumbled head over feet. Lungs burning, I kicked myself toward the surface, spitting water and gasping for air as I broached.

The river carried me indiscriminately, slamming me into sticks and small stones that left my body jarred and bruised. With my eyes closed to the brackish water and darkness, I could do nothing but hold my hands out helplessly and pray to the Mother that she would see me through this—especially as the current dragged me under over and over again.

Finally, I tumbled out into the larger bay, and managed to keep myself above water for a few breaths. It was still dark, but the lights of Forcadel were visible. I must've been deposited into Forcadel Bay. My boots were heavy and my bag was probably soaked through, even with the waterproofing, but I paddled and kicked my way toward the docks. My arms ached when I finally reached the rough wooden planks, but I pulled myself onto them anyway. I lay there for a moment, letting my limbs and mind rest from the abuse in the river.

"Oi."

I cracked open an eye to see a dock hand with a patch over his eye. "What do you want?" I asked.

"You'd better not get caught lying here, wet as you are. People might think you're sneaking into the city." He sniffed. "They don't take kindly to that anymore."

With a grunt, I rolled over onto my back and pushed myself to my feet. "Thanks."

It wasn't the most glamorous entrance, but at least I was finally back in the city.

I was still dripping when I reached the end of the docks. It hadn't escaped my notice that all the ships in port flew Severian flags—unlike before, when every country was represented. Anger coursed through my veins but dissipated almost as quickly as it had arrived. I could rage and throw things, but what good would it do? I was still in the same position I'd been in for the past four months: no allies, no armies, no way to do anything about it.

Footsteps echoed in the distance, and I caught sight of two Severian guards out on patrol. Before they saw me, I dashed into an alley, climbing a set of crates to the rooftops before I even thought about what I was doing. I crouched low on the ledge, watching them stroll by with their swords and Severian sneers. I wasn't really trying to get into trouble, but I might as well be prepared.

I sat back on my butt, reaching into my slingbag to see just how poorly my weapons and bags had fared. To my surprise, the interior was still bone-dry, thanks to the brilliant stitching and waterproofing. I attached my weapons belt to my hips and loaded it with my crossbow and knives. I slipped my dry cloak over my arms. It was stiff from weeks of disuse but as I moved my arms in it, it softened somewhat. Finally, with something of a grimace, I rested the mask over my eyes, tying it around the back of my head.

Then, satisfied I at least wouldn't be recognized, I adjusted my slingbag and kept moving.

The city was exceptionally quiet—even in the normally rowdy Sailor's Corner. Here, clubs and bars were usually open all night long, but now every building was dark. It was unnerving. I almost wanted to knock on a few doors to make sure people were still alive in there.

I looked over my shoulder at the large castle visible in the center of the city—illuminated by torches in the central square. More lights reflected out from some of the windows, although the spires were dark. Perhaps Felix hadn't locked Ilara up in the tallest tower as he'd done to me.

The old hurt rushed toward me, as painful and swift as the river. Felix and Katarine were probably very happy in their castle with their new queen. I bet Ilara didn't argue or say mean things to them now. She was probably docile and sweet.

I squinted to make out that tower and wondered if Felix was asleep. At this hour, probably. He didn't have a princess vigilante to follow and annoy until she developed feelings for him. I stared harder at the castle as thoughts of what I might say to him if I saw him again flitted through my mind.

Traitor.

Asshole.

Bastard.

So, mostly epithets.

I turned away from the castle. There were more important matters at hand. I had no money, no food, nothing. I was a woman whose face couldn't be seen in broad daylight. What in the Mother's name was I even doing here?

A soft cry for help reached my ears and I strained to listen. It sounded like a woman, and it wouldn't be out of character for this city for someone to be robbed in the middle of the night.

My first instinct was to go to her, but I hesitated. Two guards had just walked by; surely one of them would hear her. But I couldn't stop myself from walking to the sound of the voice, just to monitor the situation.

I froze. The young woman was being attacked—not by street criminals, but by the two Severian guards. My feet moved before my brain could stop me, and I flew off the roof, landing in a roll and crouching in front of them. I rose to my feet, saying nothing but letting my fury radiate. These men were supposed to be protecting this city, not terrorizing the people.

"Let her go," I snarled, walking forward. "Or I will *make* you."

"The Veil is dead," one said with infuriating certainty.

I allowed a smile to curl onto my face. "Why don't you come over here and see for yourself?"

They released the woman, and she bolted out of the alley. My hand closed around the hilt of the knife at my hip, but I didn't draw it. Neither man was more than a head taller, and maybe twenty pounds heavier than I was. I'd tussled with worse at the camp.

They lunged at once, and I rolled between them, slamming my foot into one's leg and whirling my fist around to land on the others' tailbone. The second cried out as he fell to the ground, but the first recovered, lunging toward me. I ducked just in time, but landed on the second man, who'd also recovered. He grabbed my arm and twisted it behind me, but before he could pin me, I untangled myself.

"You know," I said, panting with excitement, "normally I might've run away by now. But I've got a real hankering to beat the shit out of some Severian assholes, so let's keep going until you bleed more."

They roared in anger and came again, and this time, I was too slow, and they got a hard punch to my jaw. Dazed, I saw the knee coming but couldn't bring my leg up to block it. Pain shot up my body, loosening a cry from my lungs. The blow hurt, but not as much as the pressure on my arms as he pinned me down.

"We'll take you to the queen," he snarled, reaching for the tie on my mask. "See who you really are."

Fear shot through me. Yet again, I'd taken a dumb risk to satisfy my ego and I was captured. But now…now things would be even worse. Forget ever being able to get my kingdom back. Ilara would finally get that public hanging she'd been denied when she stabbed me in the forest.

But the weight on the back of my thighs disappeared. I looked behind me and my jaw dropped. There was a figure fighting off the men. The shadow—I couldn't tell if it was a man or woman—slammed their fist into the first guard's face. Then they pulled the second man off me and made quick work of him.

"Are you—" the male voice started, but I didn't stick around to listen. I scrambled to my feet and took off. It was clear I needed to get out of Forcadel before anyone else recognized me. I'd been in the city all of ten minutes, and I'd already made a giant mistake in pursuit of gratification and something familiar.

I ran as quickly as my injuries would allow, which wasn't very quickly at all, and the man pursued me. I glanced behind me for a second, my eyes playing tricks on me. Was he wearing a mask, too?

The momentary distraction was enough. He grabbed the back of my shirt and threw me into an alley. I stumbled over my feet then moved into attack mode. I had a small knife at my hip, and I unsheathed it in one move, slashing at the man. He knocked it away with his own, larger blade, and I was weaponless, but not defenseless.

I shot my hand out and connected with his stomach then used two hard knocks to the wrists to loosen the knives from his grip. But he was just as quick, grabbing my wrists and slamming me against the wall.

"Who the hell are you?" a familiar voice snarled.

My body went slack.

"F...Felix?"

Chapter Six

The man in the mask dropped my wrists and jumped away from me as if I were on fire. His dark eyes were wide behind the black fabric, sparkling in the moonlight as he gaped. I finally got a good look at him and couldn't help the emotion that welled to the surface. That same jaw line, the dark stubble, the lips that had so passionately kissed me.

I struggled to find the words I'd practiced a thousand times in my mind. Not when he stood before me wearing...wearing *my* mask. Wearing the spare cloak I'd left in the bell tower. Looking at me as if I were the most terrifying and wonderful thing he'd ever seen in his life.

"You're alive," he rasped.

Hesitantly, he took a step toward me. My heart pounded as he raised his hands to my face, gently pushing the fabric from my eyes and over my head. His calloused thumbs remained on my cheeks even after the mask fell behind me, and a tear slid from his eye to disappear into the black fabric on his face.

"Felix, I—"

He closed the distance between us, pulling me to him and covering my mouth with his. For a brief moment, I melted into his embrace, but then I remembered myself.

I shoved him away then socked him hard in the jaw.

"What the *hell* is wrong with you?" I seethed, hating how much I liked his taste. How much every bit of me missed him. It was hard to remember that he'd betrayed me.

"I wasn't sure this wasn't a dream," he said, rubbing his cheek with a dry tone that was so familiar it hurt. "I'm sure now."

"Of course it isn't a dream, why would you think it was?" I snapped, my heart still racing from his kiss.

"Because you're dead," he said roughly, looking up at me from beneath the mask. "You're dead and—"

"No, I'm not." He had all of my weapons—even my bag slung around his back. "Celia found me. Saved my life. For a price, of course."

He nodded, but his gaze was still full awe, wonder, shame, and relief. "You look...good."

"For being half-drowned, sure," I said, crossing my arms over my chest. "What in the Mother's name are you even doing out here anyway? Aren't you supposed to be in the castle with Kat enjoying your new queen?"

He recoiled as if I'd slapped him. "Brynn, I—"

The sound of my name on his lips was a cannon blast to my walls. I needed to remain strong—and angry. "There's nothing you can say that would excuse your loyalty to her."

"You're right, there isn't." His shoulders slumped and he looked away. I'd never seen him so beaten down. Something tugged at my heart, nagging at me to wrap my arms around him and comfort him even as my blood boiled.

"Look..." I said into the awkward silence.

"No," he said. "I failed you in every sense of the word. I should've seen Ilara coming. I should've been more forceful in making you kick her out."

At that, I barked out a laugh. "Felix, we both know I was too stupidly stubborn to listen to you." He wisely didn't respond to that, and silence descended between us again. "But...even still, why are you there with her? You and Kat could've left Forcadel."

"No," he said with a swift shake of his head. "This is our home, and if we left—Brynn, I have no idea what she might do. She started executing people almost immediately. I was worried for my cadets, and Kat was worried for the people. At least with us there, we can temper her somewhat."

Executions. "Who was executed?"

"There was a small uprising—some of the merchants," he said softly. "But when the first round happened, the riots became so bad that Ilara decided against more."

I nodded. More deaths on my conscience.

"I'm limited in what I can control in the castle," he continued. "Every day, Ilara whittles away at whatever power I have left. I knew what was going on in the city, what the Severians were doing. I couldn't just stand around and let them do it. So..."

"So you decided to become The Veil," I said.

"I thought it the best way to honor your memory," he murmured. "Penance for what I did...and didn't do." He looked up at me. "I thought if you found forgiveness in service, I might, too."

The desperate look in his eye was so familiar, I might as well have been looking into a mirror. Despite my best efforts, some of my anger ebbed away. It was hard to stay mad when his self-flagellation was on full display.

"Maybe I should join you out here," I said with a small sigh. "At least it would give me some purpose again."

"You mean...you aren't here to reclaim the throne?" Felix

asked.

I laughed louder than I meant to. "Yeah, me and what army? You're the one who said that I can't fight off an entire armada with one sword."

"I seem to remember you accomplishing quite a lot as one sword."

"Vigilantism isn't the same thing as reclaiming a kingdom," I countered, growing warm at his confidence. "Ilara's got hundreds of soldiers. Even The Veil has her limits."

"The Veil does, but Princess Brynna doesn't," Felix said, taking a step forward. "Because Brynna has allies who would come to her aid, who *do* have armies."

"Does she?" I asked softly as I turned away from him. I couldn't allow myself to be hopeful, not when what he was proposing was lunacy.

He rested his hands on my shoulders, turning me to face him. "She does. In Niemen. Neither Ariadna nor King Neshua in Kulka have accepted Ilara as queen yet. Which means if you show up at their door, asking for help, they might give it."

"And say what?" I asked with a look. "Hi, I'm Brynna and I lost my throne. Feel like helping me get it back?" I rolled my eyes. "Sure, that'll go over well. Especially with the Kulkans."

"It might." He actually sounded optimistic. "Ilara has raised tariffs even more on imports—except, of course, from Severia. She's refusing entry to all the ships from both nations, treating them like hostile actors. But what she doesn't get is punishing them ends up hurting her own people, too. And they will revolt eventually. I'm already seeing signs of it in the city."

I pursed my lips. "I couldn't give a crap about Severians."

"I meant the people here in the city, the Forcadelians," Felix said softly.

Hearing him call my people hers made my stomach turn. "I don't think the Niemenians would help, Felix."

"Maybe so," he said, taking my hand in his. "But if there's anyone who'd convince them otherwise, it would be you. Do you remember what I said about how if I could pick a queen—"

"You'd pick the one protecting the kingdom under a mask," I recited. "Felix, I'm not a queen. I'm not even a great vigilante anymore. I'm just some idiot who got stabbed and left for dead. What you're asking for is way beyond anything I've ever attempted before."

"I have faith in you." He cracked a roguish smile that sent warmth into the pit of my stomach. "Will you come with me? Just for a few hours. If you decide that it's too far-fetched, you're welcome to…well, do whatever else you were going to do. But I think we have a chance here, Brynn."

There it was—that shortened version of my name. I had no idea when he'd started calling me by the moniker, but it set my soul on fire. Against that, his grin, and the hope in his eyes, there was no winning for me.

Despite my better judgment, I nodded.

We dashed through the empty streets and on rooftops when it suited us, making very little sound. My mind reeled from all I'd just learned—that Felix had been punishing himself for my supposed death, that Ilara was even worse as the queen than I'd thought, that there was even the ghost of a chance I could succeed.

A *ghost* of a chance. One that would disappear when Felix came to his senses. Perhaps he was still recovering from the right hook to the jaw.

But when we'd stop to check the streets for guards, and he'd turn to look at me with that brilliant smile, my heart fluttered. It was easy to be here in the shadows with him, and I was willing to play along until the cold light of morning woke us both.

Before long, we were standing at the foot of the church in the town square. Felix moved the pair of loose boards with such ease that I could believe he'd been here for months by himself. He took my hand and led me into the darkness, as I'd once done with him, up the stairs and into the bell tower. He lit a lamp and light dawned in the open space.

My heart ached with the familiarity of it all. My trunk in the corner, the loose floorboards that had once held all my Nestori tricks. The way the small gas lamp cast shadows against the wall. The smell of the oil on the bell above. The echo of Felix's footsteps as he paced the room.

"I can't believe this is all still here," I said after a long pause.

He stopped, swallowing for a moment as uncertainty filled his gaze. "I wouldn't have let Ilara take it."

"Surprised Coyle didn't do it for you."

Felix exhaled loudly at the name of his traitorous comrade. "No one knew about this place except you and me. Even before Ilara had taken over, I didn't want to betray your trust like that. And after...well..." He chuckled humorlessly. "I'm glad the Mother gave me that inclination, because it's the only safe place I have anymore."

"Does Ilara know there's a Veil out here who's grown a foot and become a man? I would think someone might've noticed the change..."

He cleared his throat, the tops of his cheeks turning red. "They might, if it was just me out here. After you... Well, at first, it was just me. But Riya followed me one night, concerned about my health."

"Rightfully so," I said with a small smile.

"And so she and Jo have insisted on taking a shift every other night," he said, running a hand through his short hair. "It helps further the myth that it's not one of us—that someone in the city rose up to take the mantle from you."

I crossed my arms over my chest. "But aren't you captain of the guard? Surely someone would recognize you."

"The Severians don't care enough about me to recognize me," he said darkly. He walked to a small closet against the wall and pulled off his black tunic, leaving me with a view of his bare, muscular back. From the wardrobe, he pulled out his uniform.

No, not his. A Severian uniform.

"Mother," I said, turning away as my stomach came up to my throat. I'd expected as much, but seeing it in person was almost too much.

"Brynna," he said, walking toward me. He slipped a finger under the collar of his brown tunic and pulled on a gold chain until a gold pendant slipped out—the Forcadelian crest.

"Ilara's made us all wear the Severian one on our uniforms," Felix said. "But I keep the Forcadelian seal close to my heart, to remind me of what I've done. Of who I serve."

I gazed into his eyes, my lips tingling with the memory of his kiss. His were parted slightly as his gaze dropped from my eyes to my mouth, and my heart throbbed against my rib cage as his tongue darted to wet his lips.

"I'll be back soon," he whispered instead. "Stay here and keep out of sight."

And then he was gone.

Chapter Seven

"Oh, *Mother!*" Katarine cried out as she walked into the bell tower. I barely got a chance to be surprised as she launched herself at me, enveloping me in a hug so tight it was hard to breathe.

"Brynna, sweet girl." She took my face in her hands, tears springing to her blue eyes. "Is it true? Are you alive? Or is this some Nestori trick?"

"No trick," Felix said, giving me a warm smile from behind her. "Brynna's really alive."

"I am," I said as she poked and prodded at my face. "Promise."

She burst into sobs, her pale face growing red and blotchy as she buried her face in my neck. I awkwardly patted her head, sharing a smile with Felix. "There, there?"

"Give her a minute," Felix said. "It's shocking to see someone come back from the dead."

I let her cry and hold me, thankful that my initial fears about her abandoning me had been unfounded.

"Felix, you *horrible* man," Katarine barked at him, looking over her shoulder. "Why didn't you warn me?"

"I didn't want to chance anyone overhearing us," Felix said. "Because Brynna is going to Niemen to talk to your sister."

"She...is?" Katarine turned to me. "Are you going to launch an offensive against Ilara?"

I wanted to give Felix a dirty look, but in the face of Katarine's hopeful eyes, all I could do was shrug. "I guess? I don't know how or—"

Katarine released me, wiping her wet cheeks and running a hand over her smooth blonde hair. "It won't be easy, of course. But you do have a lot in your favor. Ilara's ruining the country, and she's done her best to spite everyone except the Severians. Beyond that, neither Ariadna nor Neshua—"

"Have accepted her as queen, Felix told me," I said. "But what's to say they won't eventually?"

"Then we'd better act quickly, hadn't we?" she said. "I can write you a letter. That should be enough to get you in the door with Ariadna. Luard is back in Niemen, I hope, so if you can find him, he'll help you, too."

"That's all well and good," I said, clasping my hands in front of me. "But why would Ariadna even entertain the thought of helping me? What does she care what goes on in Forcadel?"

"Because closed borders affect her country, too. Ilara's a nightmare to negotiate with. Besides that, you won't be going empty-handed." She grinned, as if she'd just been struck with a brilliant idea. "You're going to be offering her the city of Skorsa."

"Skorsa? The city on the border with Niemen?" I glanced at Felix to gauge his reaction—he was considering it, but not shocked by the idea. "Didn't you tell me *not* to give up any cities?"

"That was when you were happily on the throne," she said with a small laugh. "Now, you're at a disadvantage, so you need all the help you can get. The Niemenians have been dying to get their hands on the city and control the river gate at the border. All Ariadna needs is an excuse to take it, and she could easily defeat Ilara's forces there."

"That's an odd thing to have prepared," Felix said, eyeing her. "For just finding out Brynn is alive."

"Well." Katarine's pale face grew bright red. "I suppose, when Ilara was being a brat, I perhaps might have thought of how Niemen would invade and de-throne her. Merely as a thought exercise, but in this case, pertinent to your cause."

"You'd have Ariadna sit on the Forcadel throne?" I asked with a nervous laugh.

"No, of course not. She wouldn't take it." Her face was now the color of a tomato. "Before I knew you were alive...it was just a bit of fun. Thinking about revenge, that sort of thing. Now, of course—"

"Sometimes, I don't know about you, Kat," I said with a smile, but only a small one. Either Ilara was often a brat, or Katarine was being a little lighter with the truth than she was admitting.

"I promise." Katarine took my hand. "I desperately want *you* back on the throne. You are what's best for Forcadel. And I would be honored to fight by your side." She kissed my hand and bowed a little.

"You absolutely will do no fighting," Felix chimed in. "You and Beata will—"

"Oh, good, I'm glad I'm not the only one he does that to," I said as Katarine rolled her eyes.

While Katarine drafted and revised her letter, Felix and I prepared my things for the journey out of the city. Most of my weapons and gadgets were exactly as I'd left them. I swapped out the crossbow I'd picked up at Celia's for my old standby and filled my slingbag with whatever I thought I might use: listening cups, twine, and some bags of knockout powder.

"Do you think Celia will care that you disappeared?" Felix asked.

"I think it was clear I wasn't going to be allowed back in the fortress," I replied, plucking a pair of spectacles out from the bottom. With these on, I could see the spores emitted by a special kind of mushroom. But I had no more of the fungus, and so the spectacles were mostly useless. "I still don't know what her end game is. Why save me at all? Why let me linger? Why drop me off instead of just throwing me out?"

"I'm sure she's biding her time until she needs something." He found a few extra arrows and added them to my bag. "How do you think you'll get out of the country?"

"I don't know," I said, glancing up to where the moon was shining in. The earlier storms must've passed. "It was hard to get into the city, I know that."

"There's some extra gold in here," he said, jumping to his feet and heading to the other side of the bell tower. He yanked off a loose floorboard and pulled out a coin purse that sounded full. "Take this on your way."

"I don't think money's going to help me," I replied, but still took it when he handed it over.

"There are always people willing to be paid to bend the rules," Felix said. "I would've thought you knew that better than most."

I ran my fingers along the string of the crossbow. "I don't know much of anything anymore."

"You're still you," Felix said, handing me a black mask. "You're still the same person who protected Forcadel wearing this mask. You just made a mistake. Didn't you once tell me you made those?"

I took the mask but didn't add it to my bag. "This wasn't a mistake, Felix. People died." I closed my eyes to keep my tears from falling. "All because I was too stupid to—"

He covered my hand with his and squeezed. "You and I can sit here and cast blame on ourselves all night long, but it won't change anything. What's done is done, and now we've got to figure out a way forward."

I stared at his hand, the touch of his skin zooming up my arm and making me shiver. He quickly released me.

"I think I've got it," Katarine said, rising to her feet. She carefully folded the letter then chewed on her lip. "It won't have a seal, but I'm sure Ariadna will understand, considering the circumstances."

She handed me the paper and I placed it atop the rest of my weapons. "I hope so."

"Ariadna is very fair. I think you'll like her," Katarine said, her blue eyes growing wistful. "I do miss her terribly. And the rest of my family. Please give them my best."

"I will," I said. "If I make it up there."

"You've got a long road ahead of you," Felix said. "But just take it one step at a time. Concentrate on getting out of the city. Once you're out of the city then it's how to cross the border. And so on."

"Before you know it, you'll be back home with an army and we'll all be sharing a tea back in your room," Katarine said with a teary smile. Before I could say anything else, she pulled me into a hug, pressing me tightly to her.

I wrapped my arms around her and rested my chin on her shoulder.

"I've scarcely had any hope these past few months," she whispered. "But seeing you, it's given me a reason to believe in the Mother again. She will look after you."

"I hope so," I whispered, stepping back, and surprised to find my eyes wet with unshed tears. "Please tell Beata I said—"

"No," Felix interjected with a swift shake of his head. "The only people who can know you're alive are in this room." When

Katarine gave him a pleading look, he softened, but didn't yield. "I know you don't like keeping secrets, but we trusted the wrong people before."

"Bea is—"

"Kat, please," Felix said. "For me."

She sighed and released me. "Fine. I won't tell Bea. You know you're—"

"I know," he said.

They shared another unspoken conversation, one which I could read fairly well and one I wanted no part in. I thought we could trust Beata, but apparently, I wasn't the only one who considered their judgment flawed.

"You should be getting on your way," Felix said, breaking the silent tension. "It'll be dawn soon and harder to move."

I nodded, giving Katarine one more hug before following Felix down the stairwell. It felt as if I'd been there for a thousand days, and yet it was odd to be leaving already. I wanted more time with both of them, to tell them about Celia's camp and surviving, and to hear all of the castle gossip. But time was of the essence.

Still, I paused at the bottom of the stairs, looking up to the lightening sky and listening to Felix's soft breaths beside me. My hand was close enough to his that a flick of my finger would've connected them.

"I feel like I should say something, but I don't know what to say," I whispered, looking at the ground.

"It'll all be fine," he said, and I felt his gaze on me. "I'll worry about the city and keeping things from falling apart here."

"I'm not talking about that." My voice echoed in the silence as my cheeks warmed with embarrassment. "I know I should be focused on getting out of here and getting to Niemen, and I am. But I'm also not sure what I'll find out there, or even if I'll make it back alive, so..." I closed my eyes and took a deep breath. "I can understand why you stayed with Ilara to protect the kingdom, and

I forgive you for that."

"Thank you," he said softly.

"But," I continued, opening my eyes, "when you...when you kissed me then said you didn't want to be with me, that...that hurt more than Ilara's knife. And I don't know how I can get past that."

"Oh." He exhaled a shaky breath. "Would it help if I told you I regretted it?"

"It still happened." I stared up into the darkness. "Maybe I just want to know why you did it. If you regret it so much..."

He was quiet for a long time, so long that I thought he might never tell me. But when he did speak, it was soft and his voice cracked. "Because I'm weak."

Anger flushed my face. "What does that even mean?"

He twisted to face me, wearing a smile that was at once self-deprecating and cocky. "It means that if I got a taste of you, if I allowed myself to love you like I want to, and then, for whatever reason, you couldn't be mine anymore..." He swallowed as he stared directly into my eyes. "I couldn't take it. I'm not that strong."

"You could've asked my opinion on the matter," I said as my cheeks grew white hot at his admission. *Did he just say he loved me?*

"I know what you would've said," he replied, moving closer to me. "You would've thrown caution to the wind and done whatever your heart told you to."

"You're right," I replied, backing up another step and landing against the wall. "And that's what got me stabbed."

He stopped, staring at me with those brown eyes full of indecision. It was a new look for him, and I didn't like it.

"I'm...I'm sorry." He bit his lip then wiped the sadness away from his face. "You should get going."

I nodded, taking a step back and shouldering my bag. I headed toward the open street, my gaze outward, but my heart back with Felix. There was so much more we needed to say to one another, but neither of us could find the words. Perhaps we'd both been second-guessing ourselves in this new reality, and we'd been hoping the other might have some answers.

I turned, walked back to him, and grabbed him by the back of the neck, connecting his mouth to mine. At once, my fears and misery vanished in the bright light of his touch. They would return, lurking in the periphery of my mind like vultures waiting for the dying breath. But for this brief moment, I would cling to the hopefulness I'd been missing for so long.

His touch was feather light on my back, his lips moved against mine as his tongue slipped between my lips. I rested my hands on the nape of his neck, taking all I needed from him and allowing him to kiss me like I'd always wanted him to.

The faraway whinny of a horse made us both jump, and the ever-brightening sky was a signal that our time to part had arrived.

"Take care of my city while I'm gone," I whispered.

He pressed something into my hand—his Forcadelian seal. "Take this with you as a reminder of who you serve."

"Don't you need it?" I asked, looking up into his dark eyes.

"No," he said with a more confident smile. "Because I'm going to dream of you every night until you return."

My mouth parted in surprise, and he captured me in a sweet kiss. "Please be careful out there."

I nuzzled my nose against his. "This doesn't mean I'm not still mad at you, but..."

"I know." He grinned. "But you're always mad at me."

At that, I stole a final kiss and continued out into the early morning.

Chapter Eight

My old mask on my face, and Felix's kiss still lingering on my lips, I felt more like myself than I had in ages. I came to rest on the edge of a building, looking out into the town square and the castle, taking one last mental image and making a silent vow to myself. Felix's pendant hung on its chain around my neck, and I pressed my hand to it.

"Just concentrate on your next step."

The uncertainty died down as I opened my eyes. Felix was right; if I stopped to think about all I had to do, I would get overwhelmed. For now, I needed to find passage to Niemen. And since I had no idea where to begin, it was time to cycle through The Veil's old haunts in search of information.

I avoided Ilara's guards (and a few of Felix's) as I made my way down to the docks. At this early hour, they should've already been filled with ship hands loading and unloading to make room for more ships waiting out in the bay and open ocean. But today, I counted five, all of whom sat on the quarterdecks of a ship smoking pipes and staring off into space. It didn't bode well for my chances of finding someone to get me out of this city.

My final destination was a bar called Stank's, which sat precariously on the wooden docks. The owner, John, was in the business of buying and selling information. If anyone would know how to get out of the city, he would.

Since it was way past last call, I picked the lock on the kitchen door and let myself in. It was odd to be in this place and not see at least one person, or even the bartender, but I pressed onward. I climbed the stairs as quietly as possible, finding a hallway of closed doors. At the end, I assumed, was John.

I opened the door just as a knife landed in the frame inches from my face. I stared at it then at the figure sitting straight up in bed. I couldn't help the breathy chuckle that echoed from my lips. Wearing this mask, having weapons flung at my face, it was easy to remember the person I used to be.

"Is that any way to treat your best customer?" I asked.

"V-Veil?" He ran his hands over his face. "Am I dreaming? I thought you were dead."

"Now who told you that?" I prowled into the room, now sure that he wasn't going to lob any more weapons at my head. "I've just been away."

"Yeah, and from what I hear, there's a bunch of you roaming the streets now," he said, throwing the covers off his legs and standing up. "What are you doing here at this hour?"

"Couldn't wait until tonight," I said, closing the door behind me. "I need to get out of the city—the country, really. Up to Niemen. Know anyone who could help me?"

He winced. "That's going to be a little hard to come by. Most of the ships are off the coast right now, as Her Royal Bitchiness has decreed that only Severian ships be allowed through the two towers at the mouth of the bay. And, of course, no ships can come in from the north because the gates are closed at both rivers."

I chewed the inside of my lip. Jax's quip about me swimming floated through my mind, and I dismissed it. "Surely, some Forcadelian vessels are getting through."

"Some, perhaps." He yawned. "With enough gold."

"I have some gold," I said, but didn't take out the coin purse. John would ask for the whole thing, and I needed it to last. "Who's around that would take me?"

"Your boyfriend, Kieran, was skulking around in here last night," he said with a smirk. "I'm sure he'd take you for a decent price. Thought I saw him docked over on the eastern side of the bay."

Kieran? Finally, some good news. "Thank you. What do I owe you for that?"

After a long pause, he shook his head. "You've been a good customer, so this one's on the house. Maybe one day you'll make it back here and keep protecting this town, hm?"

I rose. "I'll do my best. Thanks, John."

"Hurry back, Veil."

The sun was starting to rise over the horizon as my boots clacked against the wooden docks. The salty, fishy smell was welcome, as was the soft breeze whipping my cloak around my legs. I kept my head down, but no one gave me any notice as I approached a dark boat on the end of the longest dock. A smile curled onto my face as I recognized the vessel, and my heart pounded as I climbed over the ledge and onto the deck.

The woman on the deck, a tall Niemenian with short blond hair, reached for her sword, but relaxed as soon as she took me in fully.

She gestured to the back of the ship. "If you're going to bang, do it quietly," she said, disdain in her voice.

"Nice to see you, too," I replied with a wave as I passed her. The light was on in the captain's quarters in the back of the ship, so I turned the knob quietly and pushed the door open.

Inside was a nicely decorated room with nautical themes and paintings of ships. And a Kulkan man with light brown hair wearing a dark green tunic was hunched over his desk, scribbling on a piece of parchment. I'd known him long enough to not be swayed by his handsomeness, but I still cracked a smile.

"Sarala, I..." He looked up and his eyebrows disappeared into his hair. "Veil?"

"The one and only," I said, walking further into the room.

"Thought you were dead. Are you dead? Is this a haunting?"

"I'm alive," I said with a laugh. "And I need a favor."

"Oh, well, now I know you're alive." He joined me in the center of the room, stretching his arms overhead and revealing a long trail of hair from his navel to his hemline. "What kind of favor?"

"Passage to Niemen," I said, my heart pounding in my chest. Kieran was good, but was he good enough to get past Ilara?

He whistled. "Tall order, Veil. Getting into Forcadel took me forever. Going up the river? That's asking for a miracle."

"Lucky for me, you're a miracle worker," I replied, hoping I sounded more confident than I felt. "Or at least, that's what you told me when we slept together."

"You were a satisfied customer," he replied with a grin that told me he was hoping for more. "Still, as wonderful as I am, the new queen makes things hard."

"I can pay you," I said, allowing a little desperation to fill my voice. "Kieran, this is really, *really* important. To be honest, I don't trust anyone else out here right now."

"What's so important in Niemen?" he asked, eyeing me. "Or are you just a wanted woman and need to lay low for a while?"

I hesitated, swallowing hard. I didn't trust Kieran as far as I could throw him, but among all the sailors in port, he was my best bet. So with a pounding heart, I reached behind my head and pulled the mask off my face. I stared at the floor for a moment, before lifting my gaze to his.

"I need to go to Niemen to ask Ariadna to help me get my kingdom back," I said softly.

He opened his mouth as if to laugh then stopped as his eyes widened and narrowed a few times. "Oh, well." He laughed and rubbed the back of his head. "Should I...bow?"

"No." I rolled my eyes and replaced the mask, feeling too vulnerable without it. "Now do you understand why I have to go?"

"I mean, weren't you stabbed in the middle of the..." Realization dawned on his face. "Celia. You were in her little crew for a while, right? Is that where you've been?"

I nodded. "But this has nothing to do with her. I think Ariadna might help me get back in power."

"That seems...unlikely? I mean, not that I don't want you back in charge, but..." He made an uncertain face.

"My sister-in-law Katarine's sister is the queen, so I'm hoping she'll meet with me," I replied, leaving out that she'd written me a letter. The fewer people who knew that Katarine and Felix were on my side, the safer they'd be. "And I hear Ilara's not making any friends with the other kingdoms."

He worked his jaw. "Sounds like a long shot."

"It's the only thing I have," I said. "Otherwise, the people of Forcadel will suffer, and that bitch will run this country into the ground. I mean, I wasn't doing a *great* job, but at least I wasn't trying to starve everyone."

"True," he said. "I had an issue with your tariff policy, myself, but I suppose we can discuss that when you're back on that golden throne."

I perked up. "So you'll take me?"

"Oh, why the hell not?" He sat up and rolled his shoulders. "I hate having that desert-dweller lording over me, and she's bad for business. At least now..." His eyes glittered. "The queen will owe me a favor. And from what I understand, she's quite good at returning them."

"I can't sleep with you anymore," I said with a hearty roll of my eyes.

"Oh, yes, you were besotted with that handsome captain of yours." He wagged his eyebrows. Felix's face flashed across my mind as my cheeks warmed. "Still in love with him even though he's sworn fealty to the bitch who stabbed you?"

"That, Kieran, is none of your business," I said. As with Katarine's letter, I didn't think it was a good idea for me to tell Kieran that Felix had been moonlighting under a mask. "I have faith that when I return, he'll swear fealty to me. As will many in the castle."

"Did he know you were The Veil?" He continued, undeterred. "And explain to me how Princess Brynna became a vigilante. Because I'm trying to pull it all together and I seem to be missing a few pieces."

"Is this relevant?" I asked with an impatient sigh. "Can't we just get going?"

"Consider this your payment," he said. "Along with the gold I hear in your bag."

I sighed and pulled the coin purse out. "Fine. When I was thirteen, my father tried to marry me off to a prince in Kulka for an alliance. So I ran away. Celia picked me up, taught me how to survive. After a while, I realized criminal activity wasn't for me, so I left to become The Veil."

"Then the line of succession came to you," Kieran said.

"Then it came to me," I said with a solemn nod. "And unfortunately, I was too focused on Johann Beswick to notice that a bitch queen had infiltrated my kingdom until it was too late. So..."

"Hey, we all make mistakes," Kieran said, sitting on his desk with his arms crossed. "Is that why you wouldn't take off your mask when we had our passionate night together? Because you didn't want me to recognize you?"

"Ah." I laughed, my cheeks warming at the memory. "No. I just thought it would be hotter with it on."

"Was it?"

"Absolutely."

He stood. "Well, you know, if that Captain Llobrega decides not to take you back, I'm always around. I've always wanted to be a king." His eyes lit up. "I could be a pirate king."

"I'll certainly keep you in mind," I said dryly. "But I'm not going anywhere near the throne again unless I can get out of the country."

"I'll need a few hours to get prepared," Kieran said. "Call in some favors I'd rather not call in. But for you, Princess Veil, I'll do it."

I cleared my throat at the title. "I do have one more favor to ask."

"Another one?"

"A small one," I corrected meekly. "Don't…mention my real identity to your crew."

He furrowed his brow. "I trust them with my life."

"So did Felix with his guards, and one of them still betrayed me," I said softly. "I just can't be too careful until I know what I'm doing."

He sighed and rested his hands on his hips. "Already making demands. This will be a fun trip."

I spun on my heel, giving him the playful grin I didn't feel. "With you, Kieran, it's always fun."

Chapter Nine

To be safe, I spent the morning hiding in Kieran's quarters while he made his preparations. Although he offered me his bed, I didn't want to invite anything I wasn't ready to give, and it felt odd to share another man's bed so quickly after my passionate goodbye with Felix.

Around noon, Kieran reappeared, looking devilishly handsome in a long cloak that he shrugged off. "Well, my lovely Veil, I had to pull a few strings to get us clearance out of the docks, but I got it."

I actually slumped back in relief. "Thank you. That's incredible."

"And I had to use all the gold you gave me," he said with a grimace. "Sorry."

"Ah, well." I tried not to worry too much, even though I would have no money to purchase food or a way into Linden, the capital city. But Felix's dictum came back: one step at a time. I would worry about food later. "At least you got us clearance to leave."

"Well, not yet," he said, rubbing the back of his head. "One of the inspectors is coming by to see what cargo we're taking out before he signs off on our clearance to leave."

I quirked a brow at him. "Can't you just…outrun the guards? Isn't that what you used to do?"

He chuckled. "Of course, back when things weren't upside-down. But now, your favorite queen has some very nasty cannons pointed right at the mouth of the river. Anyone caught going in or out without express permission…well." He made an explosion sound.

I sniffed angrily. "Same cannons that she set on the city a few months ago?"

"The very same, Veil. The very same. So, c'mon. We've got to stash you somewhere."

I followed him out onto the deck of the ship where his crew milled around, casting me looks with various levels of suspicion. He led me to a door in the back of the ship then down a staircase to the dark belly. I dodged hanging meat and hammocks, stepping over ropes and around crates.

"Anyone ever clean up down here?" I asked, nearly tripping over a section of rope.

"Intentional, Veil. The more shit in the way, the less the inspectors will want to wade through it," he said with a coy grin. We reached the end of the room, and he rapped softly on the wall. A soft *click* and a handleless door appeared. Kieran pulled it open, revealing a small, empty room.

"Surprised you aren't trying to smuggle out more than me," I replied, climbing in and settling as best I could in the small space.

"As it turns out, I've got a nice sum of money to smuggle something in on the return trip," he said, grinning. "Now hush up and don't get caught, m'kay?"

The door closed, bathing me in darkness, and I took a seat on the floor, straining my ears to listen for the inspector. I wasn't sure how long I sat there, or if I drifted off again, but I started awake when I heard voices.

"...shame things haven't gotten any better. People are chomping at the bit to get goods and services out of the city." Kieran's melodic voice carried, probably louder than it should've been.

"Eh, we do what the new queen says," came the gruff voice of the inspector. "And she says we aren't to let anything out of the city."

"Does she now?" Kieran made a noise. "You know, desperate people pay more than they should."

"Yeah? And I got a Severian master staring at me from the shore, so I ain't about to do anything to raise his hackles. Even if you handed me a wife made of gold."

The ship creaked and I placed my hands on my knives, ready.

"Every man has his price." Kieran's voice was smooth and silky.

A long pause followed. "You gotta have enough gold to pay us both off."

"As a matter of fact, I think I have just that sum. Come, my good man."

I exhaled. I sure picked the right pirate to trust.

I must've fallen asleep again, because I jumped out of my skin when the door opened and was halfway to throwing my knife when I heard a breathy chuckle.

"Down, Veil," he said with a fearless grin. "And we've left the docks, so you're free to wander again. Maybe even take off that mask."

"Maybe," I said, rubbing the sleep out of my eyes. "Maybe I'll leave it on, just to be safe."

"You? Play it safe?" he snorted. "That's not The Veil I know."

I could've argued that The Veil he knew was dead, but I left it alone.

"C'mon, I want to show you something," he said.

After being cramped in that small space, it was nice to be out in the open air and daylight again. We'd left the docks, and the Forcadelian breeze billowed the sails as we made our way toward the mouth of the eastern river. But only a large Kulkan man was manning the sail rigging—the rest of them seemed to be assigned a different task.

"What are they doing?" I nodded to two other Kulkans at the back of the ship who were pulling pieces of wood off the hull.

"That's what I wanted you to see," Kieran said. "They're converting the ship. Quite impressive."

"Converting?" I said.

He smirked. "Follow me."

He gently pulled me up the stairs and onto the quarterdeck as the crew sprang into action. The two Kulkans rappelled over the side of the ship to unlock giant white paddles nearly the length of the hull. They tossed them onto the deck of the ship with loud *thumps* that echoed on the nearly empty bay. Then, working in two-person groups, they moved the paddles from the deck and onto the motor on the back until all five were locked in place.

"And now the fun part begins," Kieran said, beckoning me to follow him to a large steering wheel with a set of levers and gauges. They were all foreign to me, but Kieran pushed and pulled them as vibrations echoed through the ship.

"W-what's happening?" I asked, clinging to the edge of the bannister.

"You don't think we can use sails to take us upriver, do you?" he asked with a laugh. "We need a little bit more power. That's the steam engine you feel."

"Better get used to it," his second replied, coming to join us at the quarterdeck. Up close, the freckles smattering her pale skin were visible. "It'll be on until we get to Niemen."

"And there we are," Kieran said, eyeballing a set of gauges near his levers. "Let's be off!"

The paddles groaned forward, and the ship began to move. It wasn't any faster than the sails, but as Kieran said, we wouldn't be moving forward at all if we relied on wind and current.

"Impressive," I said, finally acclimating to the vibrations.

"I'd say so," Kieran said, casting a playful look at the second. "Sarala thinks I should spring for a newer ship. One that doesn't make as much noise."

"Hard to believe we can sneak in anywhere with that thing," she said, pushing him out of the way to take control of the wheels. "Now get off my deck."

Kieran just laughed and walked me to the very front of the ship, now empty of crew members who were still working to keep the newly converted ship afloat. The wind whipped my hair out of the braid, but it felt good. In the summer, sometimes the only place to get relief from the sweltering heat was to stand near the water.

I glanced behind me to where Sarala was guiding the ship, and I could feel her disdain. "Why do I get the feeling she's pissed off?"

"Well, since I had to give away all your money to get us passage, I have no money to pay them," Kieran said. "So I said you and I are screwing as payment. Which, of course, looks great for me. But they also don't get a cut. Unless you'd like to try your hand at sleeping with them."

I should've expected as much from him. "Thanks."

"Hey, you're the one who doesn't trust them," he said with a knowing look. "One word from you and they'll all drop to their knees—"

"No need for that," I said, leaning over the bannister, gazing out onto the kingdom that was once mine.

"They'll know one day," he said.

"Maybe." I looked at my hands, enjoying the splash of the

water as it hit up against the hull. "How long until we reach Niemen?"

"Ah, well, that's a tough question to answer," Kieran said, joining me at the bannister. "Depends on how the currents go, you know? In the summer, the rains come in the afternoon and the rivers swell. Swollen river means stronger current. If it gets bad, we've got to pull into a city to dock until it goes down."

I squinted at the dark sky. "Looks clear to me." But summer storms were common in Forcadel—violent ones, too.

"And even if we don't get any, the stronger the current, the harder the ship has to work to get us where we're going. So it's a crapshoot."

"In your professional opinion, what do you think?"

"One week to the border, then perhaps another five days until we reach the port city closest to Linden," he said. "We can't take you all the way to the capital, I'm afraid. Water doesn't go that far."

"No, I know. As close as you can get is fine." Linden was nestled in the mountains, or so I'd seen on a map.

"What's your plan when you get there?"

"Working on it." I just hoped the letter Katarine wrote would be good enough to get me an audience. It would've been much easier had she been here with me. Or even Felix.

I allowed myself a little smile as I thought about him donning my mask and carrying on what I'd started as The Veil. Perhaps he truly regretted what he'd said to me before the world had gone to hell. Didn't mean I forgave him for the rest of it, but I had faith that he and Katarine would continue to protect my people in my absence.

"What are you daydreaming about?" Kieran asked. "Me, I hope."

"Just thankful that I have people I can count on," I said, running my hands along the ship's smooth railing. "I thought I'd be doing this all alone. I can't imagine people would want me…" I glanced at the crew, making sure they were out of earshot. "Back on the throne."

"Oh, you were beloved," Kieran said, leaning over the railing beside me. "And just wait until they find out you weren't off at art school or wherever they said you were, but you've been moonlighting as the also-beloved Veil. People will throw themselves at your feet."

"This all depends on whether or not I can convince Ariadna I'm worth helping," I said dryly.

"If you ask me," Kieran drawled, turning to grin at me, "the first step in doing anything stupidly optimistic is to believe you can. So, if you already doubt yourself, you won't be successful. And among your many idiotic accomplishments, dethroning a queen seems rather simple."

I barked a laugh. "You think?"

"Well, as I recall, you sank that Niemenian ship last summer," he said with a smirk. "How'd you manage that one?"

"It wasn't Niemenian," I said. "It was actually a Kulkan ship full of produce. I merely commandeered it, put it out in the center of the bay, blew it up, then *told* everyone it was Niemenian."

"Mm. Right under Corbit's nose, hm?"

I grinned, remembering all the work I'd put into it. It had been my first "big catch" as The Veil, when I'd moved from taking on small thugs and street criminals and started working on the criminal underbelly of Forcadel.

"You turned them in to Llobrega, didn't you?" Kieran asked. "Did he know you were The Veil before August died?"

I nodded. "Apparently. He said he was going to arrest me until…well, until he saw how happy I was. And also, I'm sure, because I handed him two notorious criminals."

"But you were The Veil after you returned to Forcadel, weren't you?" Kieran said, tapping his fingers as he thought. "So…?"

"Felix and I had an agreement," I said softly. "I could continue to do The Veil stuff until my coronation." My cheeks warmed. "For a while, anyway. Things went a bit...what did you call it? Upside-down."

"Do you love him?" Kieran asked.

"I..." Something inside me wanted to say yes, but the sound of him telling me to reassign him stopped me. "It's complicated."

"So..." Kieran slid closer to me. "Does that mean we could sneak back to my—"

I barked a laugh and elbowed him. "No, it doesn't. This is a business relationship, Kieran."

"And you and I can get *down* to business—"

I gave him a dry look, and he chuckled. "Fine, fine. I can only suppose you must be choosier with who gets to share your bed. But you know...Pirate King has such a nice ring to it."

I shook my head. "I think that my undying gratitude for your help will be enough." I paused and gave him a look. "But seriously, thank you. I don't know what I would've done otherwise."

"Oh, don't thank me yet," he said. "Favors, favors, Veil. They do add up."

Chapter Ten

Felix

When I awoke the next morning, I thought my short rendezvous with Brynna had been a dream. A beautiful dream that the Mother had gifted to me to torture me further. But the Forcadelian pendant was missing from my neck, so I took comfort that Brynna was alive, mad as hell, and on her way to reclaim the kingdom.

For the first time in months, I had hope. I wasn't merely standing against the rising tide, holding it back until it drowned me. There was something to work toward now, a light in the distance that would grow brighter with time.

I wasn't content to sit around and wait for her to come back, either. Brynna needed all the help she could get; if she was successful in convincing Ariadna to support her, she would need inroads in the city. And I hoped I could make those happen for her.

As soon as I was finishing my breakfast, a messenger came to tell me Ilara had summoned me to the Council room—an odd request from her. I wasn't on her Council, nor was I privy to what they discussed. So as I walked the long hall, my pulse elevated, I prepared myself for anything.

The room was a small space with large windows and a circular table in the center, but of the five councilors, only one was seated at that table. Lady Vernice, an older woman who'd lost much of her sheen in the four months since the invasion, nodded to me.

"Welcome to the nightmare," she said, pulling a flask from her dress and taking a sip. Her hair, which was normally dyed and styled, was now a little looser than usual.

The door opened again and two Severians came in. The one on the right was Tarckza, and he did little more than agree with whatever the queen said. But the one on the left was Captain Maarit. Her opinion of me was clear from the disdain on her face. She'd replaced General Godfryd as Ilara's military advisor, overseeing the Forcadelian navy and army, everything except the royal guard, which remained under my purview. For the time being.

"What are you doing here?" she asked, purposefully taking her seat.

"I was invited," I replied mildly. "What are you doing here?"

She sniffed, the corner of her lip curling upward. "I'm on Queen Ilara's council. Surely you knew that."

I did, but I enjoyed watching her have to explain herself. "Of course. My mistake."

"I suppose Ilara is finally curious why you haven't graduated a class of cadets in months," Maarit said. "Surely the latest crop is overdue to join the ranks out in the city. Coyle informs me they're ready to serve."

"I would hope you'd defer to me to manage my cadets," I replied, casting a long gaze out the window to the dark gray sky outside.

"Perhaps I'm concerned that your management isn't what's

best for your own," Maarit replied. "Perhaps it's time to install someone else in your position. Lieutenant Coyle would be an apt replacement."

"I'm sure he would be," I said. "You are welcome to broach the subject with Queen Ilara."

"Already have," she said with a cruel smile.

The door opened again and in walked a man with slicked-back hair and a too-white smile. Mayor Zuriel had been integral to Ilara's invasion—in what capacity, I still hadn't figured out. Regardless, he was another traitor. It was all I could do not to punch him in his perfect teeth.

"Good morning, good morning," he chirped, clearly not reading the tension in the room. "Ah, Captain Llobrega. Always a pleasure to see you."

Instead of responding, I simply nodded.

"I believe Mayor Zuriel said good morning," Ilara said, walking into the room and eyeing me with her piercing gaze. "Is it not Forcadelian tradition to respond in kind?"

Although every inch of me cried out in protest, I forced the words, "Good morning" through my lips.

"That's better," Ilara said, taking her seat at the most ornate chair at the table. "Vernice, what news from the Kulkans?"

"King Neshua sends his best," Vernice said with a thin-lipped smile. "But...of course, he wishes to know when you'll allow Kulkan ships into Neveri again."

"As soon as he sends his best wishes on my *coronation*," Ilara replied, reminding me of a petulant child who wanted sweets. "Neither the Kulkans nor the Niemenians have bothered to even send *envoys*. Once they decide to accept my role here, I'll let their pretty ships in."

"But my queen," Vernice said, "there seems to be a shortage of goods in the kingdom."

"Like beer and whiskey?" Ilara asked with a quirked brow. "It would serve you well to quit drinking, Vernice. You're losing some of your luster."

Vernice licked her lips, casting a look at Zuriel, who was staring passively out the window. So she continued, her voice growing in strength. "It's not just alcohol, Highness. It's grain in general. If we don't get more shipments in from Kulka, we will suffer a food shortage."

Ilara shrugged. "Then I suggest you send a warning to Kulka to let them know what's at stake." Without missing a beat, her catlike eyes turned to me. "Felix," she said, looking at me with fluttering lashes. "Do tell me you've been able to capture the rebels in the slums? My furrier went up in flames last night."

Her furrier? Most of the fires in the city had been random arson, but to target a vendor of the crown? That was a new development.

"Felix?" Ilara said, catching my attention again.

"No, Your Highness, no news to date," I said, putting this new information in the back of my mind to chew on later. "But I'll have Lady Katarine provide me a list of your preferred vendors, and we'll place a couple of guards at each location. If they try again, we'll catch them."

Maarit chuckled under her breath, and I dug my nails into my palm to keep myself focused.

"I'm starting to wonder if perhaps you just aren't looking hard enough," Ilara said, examining a large grape. "Based on this new information Lieutenant Coyle has brought to me."

My pulse quickened. "Oh? He hasn't shared any new information with me."

"Apparently, a masked person was seen at a bar by the docks," Maarit said. "Some are saying it's The Veil."

Damn it, Brynna. Joella, Riya, and I had taken care to avoid guards in the city, and when we did engage, it was in a dark alley where we wouldn't be recognized.

"It doesn't surprise me someone has picked up the mantle," I said. "The Veil was beloved by everyone in the city, especially in Haymaker's Corner. Perhaps someone noticed the absence and decided to continue protecting the city."

Ilara snorted. "The Veil is as dead as your princess, so I suggest you remind the people of this country that they have a new monarch."

"If I may," Vernice asked. She was sure brave today. "What's so bad about masked vigilantes? The Veil did a lot to reduce crime in the city—"

"Because, you half-wit, The Veil was your precious Princess Brynna, and I want her memory erased from this kingdom," Ilara said, her face growing angry as she rose. "And if the citizenry think they can run around undermining the law, what's to stop them from setting fires and destroying this kingdom?"

"It's as you said," Maarit said. "Brynna is dead. I would release an edict—anyone caught in a mask will be hanged for treason."

"Treason?" I said, quirking my brow. "Seems a bit much."

"Does it?" Maarit said, challenge clear in her eyes.

"Well, considering you're talking about a citizen of Forcadel, yes, it does," I replied hotly. Even if it hadn't been myself and the others, I would've thought treason was too much. "Treason is overkill."

Ilara huffed. "I want to send a message—"

"No one except those in this room know that Brynna was The Veil," Vernice replied calmly. "If anything, someone's merely trying to continue what The Veil started—which was protecting the city from thugs and criminals. I agree with Captain Llobrega, treason is too much."

"Thirded," Zuriel said, speaking for the first time in the meeting. "I would leverage The Veil as a symbol of hope. It might help them—"

"*Enough!*" Ilara screamed, slamming her hands on the table. "I don't care who does or doesn't know. What I want is for that bitch to be erased from the memory of everyone in this city. She's dead, I'm queen, and that's final."

There was a deafening silence that echoed in the room. It was good to know that Brynna's ghost continued to irk Ilara. Especially considering said ghost was weaving her way up the Ash river.

Maarit cleared her throat. "Unfortunately, the three guards who came across this vigilante had differing opinions on what they saw. So until we hear otherwise, I'm assigning Lieutenant Coyle to canvass the city for anyone who might be wearing a hood and mask."

I narrowed my gaze at her. "I didn't realize Coyle reported to you, Maarit."

"Captain, I do believe you have your hands full lately," Ilara said with a dangerous look. "What with retaining your oversight of all the guards, including the cadets, and keeping the city safe in this time of unrest. It would be grossly unfair to add to your burden." She paused, a smile blossoming on her face that sent shivers of fear down my spine. "And speaking of, how are my cadets?"

"Doing well," I said.

She surveyed the nails on her thin fingers. "The oldest group, are they ready to graduate?"

"Not yet," I said, ignoring Maarit's look of triumph. "With the transitions in power recently, I would like to keep them in training for a few more months."

"Maarit tells me you're keeping them to yourself because you're afraid of their loyalty," she said softly. "Or is it that you fear they'll serve me instead of you?"

I had to choose my words carefully. "As I said, with all the leadership changes in their last year of training, I thought it prudent to take extra care releasing them into service."

"Too much care, if you ask me." She dropped her fingers to the table. "You will graduate your oldest *two* classes of cadets, and they will begin their service immediately."

I squeezed my fists behind my back and kept my face passive. One year I could live with; two…she was trying to set me up for something. But there was nothing I could do now.

"Yes, Your Majesty," I replied.

That afternoon, the skies opened in unrelenting rain yet again, and fifty new soldiers entered the King's Guard. Their apprehension was palpable as I handed them what would be their duty weapon, and their restraint was stretched thin as Ilara spoke under a large umbrella about the glory of serving Severia. When she handed them their pins, more than one of them turned a shade of green.

Some of them looked to me for guidance, but I could offer nothing but stoicism. To keep them safe, I needed Ilara to believe I was her servant. Even if it killed me inside.

Chapter Eleven

Sunlight woke me the next morning, and it took me a moment to remember where I was. The sound of the engine was unfamiliar, as was the movement of the bed. But eventually, I came to my senses and sat up in the empty room. After much arguing, and Kieran's solemn oath that he would join his crew's sleeping quarters, I relented and slept in his room. His bed was soft feathers, and the soothing movement of the ship was enough to lull me back to sleep. Instead, I pulled myself together and re-braided my hair.

I went to put my mask back on, but I hesitated. It was one thing to wear it in Forcadel, but we were at least a few hours away now. It might be more conspicuous to wear such a thing. If Kieran hadn't recognized me, perhaps no one else would so far from the main city. So I left it with my things and ventured out into the sunlit deck.

"Good morning, Veil," Kieran called from the quarterdeck. "How lovely you look maskless this morning."

"Seemed a bit odd to keep wearing it in the daylight," I said, coming to join him. Sarala, standing next to him, gave me a cursory glance, then returned to watching the river.

"I trust you slept well," Kieran said, walking down the stairs to join me. "Would you like some breakfast?"

"I can do without," I said, cognizant of Sarala's gaze and that Kieran had told them I was freeloading. I couldn't go the full trip without eating, but I wasn't going to flaunt it in their faces.

"Oh, don't be ridiculous," Kieran said, throwing an arm around me. "We can't have you starving half to death. You're my guest."

Knowing it was useless to argue, I allowed Kieran to feed me a small apple and some salted pork downstairs. While I ate, he flitted around the engine, which was at the front of the ship. He'd test the fluids, check the stores, listen to the groan of the motor and tell me if he thought it was squeaking or not. I couldn't hear any difference from the day before, but if he thought it was making too much racket, he'd open the steel door and poke inside, watching the gears turn.

"What does it run on?" I asked, when he pulled his head out.

"Steam," he said. "We use coal from Niemen to heat sea water which powers the engine. It's an older model—the newer ships get more miles for less fuel. But I don't feel like learning a new ship's quirks."

"I can understand that," I said, downing the rest of the cup of water he'd given me. "I don't want to cause a problem with your crew, Kieran."

"Oh, they'll get over it," Kieran said, as I rose from the small table. "C'mon, I'll introduce you to them all."

Sarala seemed to be the only one discomfited by my presence, as the rest of the crew welcomed me warmly. Eldred was Kulkan, a short, squatty man with dark brown hair and eyes that disappeared when he smiled. He spent most of his time on the sails, watching, adjusting. Dunstan was also Kulkan, but he towered over the rest of the crew. Soft-spoken with a book under his arm, he sat at the bow of the ship, his long legs dangling over the front. Henry, a teenaged boy from Forcadel, seemed fastened to his side, pestering him with questions. The fifth member of the crew was Aruna—who was from nowhere, so she said.

"Sprung out of the ground somewhere along the Kulkan and Forcadelian border," she said, flashing me a smile that was missing a few teeth.

The only country Kieran didn't have represented on his crew was Severia.

"Why would I want them on here?" he asked with a small shrug. "Up until recently, they had no rivers in their country and they had nothing of value."

"What's that supposed to mean?"

"See, I assembled my crew strategically. Sure, Sarala can gut you, and Dunstan and Eldred can intimidate the best of them."

Both Kulkans cast Kieran a dry look over their shoulders and shook their heads.

"But also, when I go into Kulka or Niemen, I can use them to give me cover. Country loyalty can buy you a lot, you know. More than gold, sometimes."

"The opposite is also, sadly, true," I said darkly.

Kieran cleared his throat and lowered his voice so only I would hear him over the wind. "Well, to be fair, you also let Ilara sleep in your castle, so...?"

The anger evaporated into shame. "True."

"She certainly played you, didn't she?" Kieran asked with a coy smile.

"Rub it in."

"I'm not trying to be mean," he said. "They say she killed her entire family to become queen. There were three older brothers who died, and when her father died, she just took over."

I frowned; none of that had come to me. "If I'd known her past history of regicide, I might not have let her in my front door."

"Not a lot of gossip that's not Forcadelian gets to Forcadel," he said with a smile.

"What else do you know about Ilara?" I asked, turning to lean against the bannister.

"It's as I said—she's focused on amassing power, not on what's best for her kingdom. She allows thieves to make money off her people, as long as she gets access to the right people. It's how she got herself into Forcadel without anyone knowing."

I grew silent, trying to keep my mind on the steps in front of me, and not those further down the road. "You know, if you'd asked me four months ago what I wanted most in the world, I would've told you running away from my responsibilities would've been top of the list. Being here with you, on this boat, speeding toward the border." I shook my head. "I would've been thrilled."

"And now?"

I watched a woman paddle downriver in a small rowboat. "Now...as much as I don't want to be queen, I don't want anyone else to be, either. Or at least not Ilara."

"Why don't you want to be queen?" Kieran asked with a look of surprise. "It's the best job in the world! You get to wear fancy tiaras and ballgowns, order people around. Sleep on a pile of gold."

"No gold," I said with a weary laugh. "And it's not really ordering anyone around. It's like playing a game of chess, but instead of playing with pieces, you're playing with lives. If you make the wrong move, people die."

"Oh, don't be so glum," he said, patting my back. "Look, you've had a setback. It happens to the best of us. All you need is to get back under that mask and remember who you are. I'm sure you'll have plenty of opportunities when we get to Skorsa."

The landscape slowly changed from green fields and marshy bogs to brown, dry grass, then dark rock. We passed riverside villages, smoke curling out of chimneys during the day and small fires visible in windows at night. The air grew chillier with each passing day, until the nearly unbearable heat from the Forcadel summer was a distant memory. Now, an icy breeze slid past my skin every morning, and even the midday sun seemed less fearsome than usual.

Seven days after we departed from Forcadel, mountains became visible in the distance, and Kieran beckoned me to his office for a geography lesson.

"See, here's Skorsa, on the border," he said, pointing to a black dot on the western side of the river. "You can't tell on this map, but the river pools into a lake and then narrows on the other side. That's where Niemen begins." He tapped the paper. "There's a large stone wall at the border with an iron gate that can be opened and closed. My sources tell me it's been closed since Ilara took over."

"Maybe I'll just continue on beyond the border on foot," I said, eyeing the distance to Linden.

"Don't be ridiculous," he said. "We've still got five days of river travel before we get to Aymar—that would take you weeks on foot. I promised you I'd get you as close to Linden as I could, and that's what I'm going to do." He grinned. "Besides that, I'm enjoying all these favors I'm racking up."

"Oh, and what are we up to now?"

"Well, so far, I've decided that you should commission a statue of me out of solid gold."

"You'd really want just a gold statue?" I said. "Seems awfully generous to donate all that gold to the people of Forcadel to enjoy in a statue."

"Enjoy? I'd stick it on the front of my ship!"

Around midday, the riverboat sailed into the lake, which was about as busy as a summer day in Forcadel. As Kieran had said, there was a large wall in the distance, stretching across the width of the river. A single, iron gate sat in the center of the river mouth.

"A lever system opens and closes it," Kieran said. "Much less complex than the one in Neveri, but that thing hasn't been closed in centuries. Here in Skorsa, the gate used to go up and down all day, as long as you have the coin to pay the Forcadelian mayor."

The Niemenians have been dying to get their hands on the city and control the border and the river gate. Katarine's words became clear as the gate came into view. There hadn't been any other barrier between Niemen and Forcadel on the river up until now. If Niemen controlled the gate, they'd control access to and from their country. It certainly seemed like an enticing prospect.

Almost as soon as the ship reached the docks, Dunstan and Eldred jumped off to moor it, and the rest of the crew sprang into action to ready the ship for the evening. Kieran spoke with the dock master, paying him another ten gold coins for the privilege of staying the night. I overheard wisps of the conversation, and none of it sounded good.

"One night?" I said as he climbed back onboard the ship.

"That's all we need," he replied with a thin smile. "You're The Veil! A miracle worker. You'll have the gate open in no time and we'll be on our way."

This time, I couldn't stay quiet. "Kieran, that's asking a lot. I don't know a thing about this city, let alone who I can ask to *get* information. I need more time."

"Well, you don't have it, so you might as well get moving." He turned to Sarala, who was throwing bags from the underbelly of the ship onto the deck. "Take The Veil with you and show her around."

She cast me a disgusted look. "Why?"

"Because I said so," Kieran said, quirking a brow. He pulled a silver out of his pocket and tossed it to her. "And make sure to feed her, too. We need our miracle worker to have a full belly if she's going to make magic."

Sarala caught the silver and pocketed it. "Fine, but she gets to carry the bags."

Skorsa was unlike any part of the country I'd ever seen. The Forcadelian crest was present, but on wooden buildings of painted red and orange instead of the more muted colors of the capital city. The windows were all closed—something rare in the Forcadel summers. But here, there was a pleasant breeze that only hinted at summer, pushing the smell of fish and city life out into the rocky fields beyond.

Sarala had clearly been here before as she navigated the strange streets like an expert. Our first stop was the laundry house, where I handed the bags off to a sweaty woman and Sarala paid two gold coins to get the clothes back by the end of the day.

"How often do you guys pass through Skorsa?" I asked, hoping for some conversation. Sarala had ignored me up until this point, but now that I'd carried her laundry halfway across the town, she should've lost her chip on her shoulder.

Apparently she hadn't, because she didn't respond.

So I tried another tactic. "Can you tell me where I should start to find out how to open the gates?"

"Aren't you supposed to be some kind of world-renowned vigilante?" she said, not even bothering to look at me. "Why don't you figure it out?"

I stopped short, the jab hitting a little closer to home than I would've liked. "What's your problem with me, anyway?"

She clicked her tongue against the roof of her mouth. "I don't like freeloaders."

"I'll owe Kieran a favor," I replied.

"And what are the favors of a disgraced princess?"

The blood left my face, and I looked to see if anyone had overheard her, but the street was empty. When my gaze returned to her, she had a self-satisfied smirk on her face.

"Kieran's not the only one who pays attention," she said. "And what I want to know is, what's your business in Niemen? Asylum?"

"If you must know," I said, toying with the leather at my belt as I cast a wary glance around again, "I'm going to ask for some help."

"To?"

"To braid my hair. What do you think?" I snapped. "Now can we quit talking about it in the open where anyone can hear us?"

"Not until I'm satisfied," she replied. "What do you need help for?"

I sighed loudly and stared at the sky. "I'm going to Niemen to ask Ariadna to help me overthrow Ilara."

"Why?"

"Do you really have to ask?" I said, gesturing at the gate in the distance.

"No, I'm not asking about that," Sarala said. "What gives you the right to be Queen of Forcadel?"

I opened my mouth to respond, but found I had no good answer other than *Felix and Katarine told me I should.*

"Things are in upheaval now, but they'll settle as they always do," she continued. "If you walk away from the throne now, you'll be a forgotten footnote in the pages of history. The end to the Lonsdale line and the beginning of Severian rule." She smiled. "Does that grate on your ego, little princess?"

"This isn't about my ego," I said. "This is about the people. They're suffering."

"But will they suffer more if you plunge them into war?" she asked. "Do us all a favor and give up on this mission. Otherwise, you'll be remembered as a war-mongering princess who decided her crown was more important than people's lives."

Chapter Twelve

Sarala's words rattled in the recesses of my mind until they melded with the ever-present whisper of disdain. Nothing she'd said wasn't true. I hadn't really thought about what it might mean to take back Forcadel, really thought about the consequences. About the numbers who would perish in the crossfire, about the upheaval to the city and the country. But once Sarala had opened the door, a flood of unsure thoughts came behind it. The small, steady flame of confidence I'd found after speaking with Katarine and Felix vanished, and I was left with the same inaction that had plagued me for months.

Instead of returning to Kieran's ship, I found a quiet spot on the edge of the dock and watched the ships rock listlessly in the lake. The sunset fanned across the sky in fiery red and orange, which then faded into deep purple, and finally darkness. There was no moon overhead with the twinkling stars, and the only light on the lake was the few pinpricks of torchlight on the far-out boats.

There was a soft *tick-tock* of a clock in my mind, a reminder that Kieran's boat would only be in port until tomorrow morning.

Finally, my stomach gurgled loudly enough to push me to my feet. I couldn't go back to Kieran's ship empty-handed, and I didn't have any coin to purchase a meal. Instead, I took to the streets, wandering through the dark alleys and empty roads with little purpose.

In the center of town, a familiar symbol drew my attention—a church. Back in Forcadel, sometimes Mother Fishen would have a bread basket in the back of the chapel, so I wandered toward the open door and hoped I might find something edible.

Inside, my breath caught at the sight of an entire wall filled with lit candles behind the front altar. I stumbled over my feet then quickly dipped into a nearby pew. It seemed the entire city had lit a candle. It was probably the same way across the entire country. They needed a savior, and I was the only one who could rescue them from Ilara.

"You'll be remembered as a war-mongering princess who decided her crown was more important than people's lives."

I rubbed my forehead, wishing I could erase those words or make them feel less true. I didn't want to disrupt the country, but the country was already in a state of upheaval. I didn't want to be queen, but I didn't want Ilara to be queen either. And unless I got this gate open, I'd never be queen and Ilara would continue her reign of destruction. But if I did get the gate open and somehow convinced Ariadna to help, I would cause even more destruction. But if I didn't... Round and round the thoughts went.

In the left corner of the chapel, the confessional box waited with an open door. Once, when I'd been lost and scared, I'd spoken my fears to Mother Fishen and she'd guided me in the right direction. Fishen was a hundred miles downriver, but maybe her spiritual sister could offer some guidance.

With my head bowed, I walked to the confessional and

unlatched the door. The darkness was at once terrifying and calming, a sense of pure anonymity while being truly vulnerable. In here, there would be no secrets, not from myself at least.

The door to the other side opened, and a soft, old female voice called out, "Is there someone in there?"

"Yes," I whispered.

"Ah, well, let me get settled." Her clothes rustled for a moment, and then she stilled. "What's troubling you, my child?"

"What isn't?" I said with a dry laugh. "I feel a little lost right now."

"Then you've certainly come to the right place. The Mother will guide you."

I chewed on my tongue, unsure of what I wanted to say. "I have this great task ahead of me, and I can't seem to get out of my own head. I want to be successful, but I'm afraid of what success might bring. And I'm not even sure I'll *be* successful. And—"

"Take a breath," she said softly. "Start from the beginning."

I heaved a sigh. "I had something once, a great responsibility that was thrust upon me unwillingly. And while I had it, I didn't really value it. I would've done anything to get rid of it. Then someone stole it from me, and now all I want is to get it back."

"Perhaps it's best to let it go, then."

"But if I let her keep it," I said. "People will suffer. They could die. And if I try to take it back, the same thing will happen. I can't live with myself if I caused harm to others, but in doing nothing, I'll inadvertently cause harm to others. I just... I don't know what to do."

"Which path do you think will bring the most harm?"

"I don't know," I whispered, looking at my hands. "All I want is to help people, to make things better for my countrymen, but I don't know how best to accomplish it."

She chuckled. "Perhaps you should begin by helping one person. You will have made a difference to them, and perhaps that will settle the uncertainty in your heart."

I stared at the grate, wishing I had the words to argue with her. But my heart wasn't just uncertain, it was tired. So I thanked her and went on my way.

The cool night air brushed against my skin as I wandered the empty streets. I reached into my tunic and grasped the small pendant hanging from my neck. Felix had said it would remind me who I serve, but that wasn't the problem. I knew who I served; I just didn't know the best way to serve them. As queen, as a vigilante, or as a footnote in history.

"Stop! Please, someone help me!"

The sound of struggle reached my ears—and my first instinct was to go in the opposite direction. I'd gotten involved with a pair of Severian guards back in Forcadel and nearly been arrested. If I made a mistake tonight, I'd be on my own.

"Ain't nobody coming to save you!"

The assailants sounded more like teenagers than guards, growing my confidence. I came onto the scene of the scuffle in the alley. Their victim was a young boy of ten or eleven, and the bullies were barely sixteen.

I reached into my bag and found my mask, wrapping it quickly around my face and lifting the hood of my cloak over my head. I could do with ten minutes of distraction, and if I couldn't break up a backyard brawl, I'd really be in trouble.

"Let the boy go," I barked, resting my hands on my hips and catching their attentions.

"Who are you?" the one on the right scoffed.

"I'm The V—" I swallowed. "I'm a passing stranger. But if you don't get your hands off that kid, you'll know me better than you want."

They laughed and returned to the boy, striking him hard in the jaw. I cracked my knuckles as I marched toward them. I grabbed the one on the right, a squatty boy with a round face, pulling him back and rearing my knee into his gut. He fell backward just as his partner swung for me. I ducked and swept my leg underneath him, sending him toppling onto his friend.

I bared my teeth as I stood between them and the boy. "Go. Home."

The youths scrambled to their feet and dashed away, the squatty boy limping and casting fearful looks behind him.

"Thank you, Miss." The younger boy sniffed, wiping blood from his upper lip. "But they'll be back. They always come for me on my way home."

I turned to him with a frown. "Aren't there guards who can help you?"

He shook his head. "Things are all wrong since they closed the border. This city's about to blow up, and the mayor don't do nothin' about it. Just sits up there and lets us all tear each other apart."

"Is he Forcadelian?" I asked.

The boy shook his head. "Severian. But he's a crook—my pap was on a ship that tried to bribe him. They wanted five hundred gold coins to open the gate tonight."

I did a double-take. "Wait a minute, they open the gate?"

"Not always, but on a night like tonight where the moon's gone?" He rubbed his bloody nose again, smearing it on his cheek. "I'll bet there's four new ships in port tomorrow. Or prolly, they'll just come through the gate and keep going on their way to the big city down south. Then no one's the wiser. I hear Mayor Kelsor takes the money from the captains himself. My pap said he's the biggest crook of them all."

"Where does he take this money?" I asked.

"Down at the docks," the boy said. "I'll show ya, if you want."

I hesitated. On the one hand, this was exactly the thing I

needed, basically handed to me on a silver platter. But on the other, I still had doubts if I even *wanted* to continue this journey. Getting past the border meant I was one step closer to becoming the war-mongering princess I was determined not to be.

Still...it was hard to argue with a silver platter. I could let this distraction play out a little longer.

"All right," I said, after a long pause. "I'll walk you home and you can tell me where to find this Kelsor guy."

After walking the boy home (and showing him one or two moves to get himself out of trouble), I returned to the docks with renewed purpose. Without the stars or moon, the lake was pitch black, the perfect cover for illegal movement at the border. And I wasn't there for even half an hour before I heard activity on the dark waters beyond.

"Catch the dock!"

I kept low, finding cover behind one of the already-docked ships. It was hard to see, but finally, I made out the schooner that quietly bumped up against the wooden poles. Her crew set to work immediately, tying up the bow and calling out to one another in hushed tones.

"Keep it quiet, you morons," their captain barked. "We're here for one hour then we're going past the gate at sunup. I paid a lot of money to make sure we got past the border."

I peered around the hull, imprinting their faces in my mind. The captain was an older man with a long, scraggly beard. His crew was only three, all Forcadelian.

Footsteps echoed on the docks behind me. A finely dressed man appeared out of the darkness, flanked by two large Severian guards with big swords.

"Evening," he said to the captain, his voice oozing with disdain.

"Mayor Kelsor," the captain replied, jumping off the ship. "Pleasure to be makin' your acquaintance."

"Do you have the money?" he drawled.

The captain procured a large, jingling bag. He struggled as he handed it to the guard on the left then went back for a second bag. "It's all there. I promise."

Kelsor glanced behind him at his guards. They nodded to him and turned to walk away with the gold. Kelsor then pulled something small from his breast pocket.

"Do you have your papers?" he asked.

The captain nodded and handed him what appeared to be an official document from his back pocket—perhaps the permission he needed to get through the gates. Kelsor read through the document just as his goon reappeared with a small candle and what appeared to be a wax melt on top.

Kelsor beckoned the captain forward and bade him turn around. He smacked the paper to the man's back, then dipped his seal into the open wax and pressed it to the man's paper.

"There," Kelsor said with a haughty look. "Show that to the gate master."

"T-thank you, sir," the captain said, still clearly in pain. "Your generosity is—"

But Kelsor was already walking away. And I was in hot pursuit.

Chapter Thirteen

I followed the mayor back to what I assumed was his house overlooking the city. I waited in the shadows while he disembarked from his carriage, berated the guards out front, and entered into the stately abode. And when the lights went out, I made my move.

The large stone wall around the building was easily scalable, and I landed softly on a patch of grass. I listened for the footsteps of passing guards, and when there were none, I moved toward the house.

Going in the front door would be risky, but a mansion this size probably had a servants' entrance or two. Keeping myself close to the house, and keeping an eye out for patrolling guards, I moved slowly until I found a small, nondescript door at the back of the house.

With ease, I picked the lock and slipped inside, finding myself, as expected, in a kitchen. From here, there were really two options for me—hope that Kelsor had an office where he kept a spare signet ring and some papers, or try to lift the seal off him.

I decided to go with option one, for now.

Cracking open the kitchen door, I found two Severian guards standing by the front door with their backs to me. Quietly, I assembled my crossbow and knockout powder then aimed for a spot just above their heads and fired.

The guards looked up, grabbing their swords, but within seconds slumped to the ground. Moving silently, I crossed the main foyer of the house, opening doors until I found one that was locked. I made quick work of the knob, pushing the door open to reveal...Kelsor's office.

"Excellent," I whispered, sliding inside and closing the door behind me with a soft click.

Kelsor's desk was in the center of the room, stacked high with papers and other documents. As quietly as I could, I sifted through the papers, looking for anything that would get the gate open—at least temporarily. If all went according to plan, we could slip through without anyone noticing and be on our way.

Finally, in the bottom of one of the desk drawers, I found a stack of forms that would grant permission to open the gate. Unfortunately, there was a place for a wax seal—but no ring.

Before I could hunt more, cool metal touched my skin.

"What do you think you're doing?" breathed Kelsor behind me.

"Getting passage into Niemen, what do you think I'm doing?" I replied coolly. "Seems to be a lot harder than it used to be."

"Give me those letters," he said.

"I don't think so." In one move, I escaped the knife against my neck and pulled my own, pointing it at him. "You, my friend, have not been a very good mayor of late."

Up close, the Severian man seemed every bit as cunning as I'd anticipated. His dark eyes spoke of a man calculating his chances of survival, and he'd obviously found them to be in his favor.

"Where's the seal?" I asked.

"As if I would tell you," he said. "Or leave it off my person."

"You're fairly lax with these letters," I said, inching backward. In the darkness, I was able to slide my hand into my bag, searching for something of value I could use. "What does it take to get you to sign them, hm? Money? Favors?"

"Who are you working for?" he said, stepping into the space between us.

"The people of Forcadel."

My fingers found purchase on a bag, and without knowing what kind of powder I'd be throwing, I lobbed it toward him. The pouch ignited in a bright burst of light—a flashbang grenade—and I took the opportunity and ran out of the office and then the house.

Behind me, Kelsor's voice echoed into the courtyard, and his guards came running toward me. I flung another bag of something behind me, and the street illuminated in a loud explosion, buying me just enough time.

Shouts and cries of surprise followed me, but I didn't let up. Without knowing where in the city I was, or how I would get out of there, I just kept taking lefts. I needed to put enough space between us so I could find a hiding place.

I turned a left corner and came face to face with three guards, all with swords pointed at me.

"End of the road, thief," the center guard said. "Hand over what you stole."

"Fine," I said, reaching into my bag as if to retrieve the item.

I dug through the bag until my fingers closed around two more pouches. I flung them from inside the bag, the first one landing in the center man's face then turned to lob the other at the men behind me.

My assumption had been correct—all knockout powders. As the guards keeled over, I bolted. This time, I was able to get far enough ahead that I could dive into an alley and hide there until the guards passed. And when I was safe, I let myself exhale and smile.

I'd forgotten how much fun getting into trouble could be.

A voice that sounded an awful lot like Felix's tsked and reminded me how risky my actions had been. But another, stronger voice was louder, saying that we weren't done yet. After all, I only had a stack of signed letters. I needed the wax seal, which was supposedly on Kelsor's person, to get past the gate master.

It was oddly reminiscent of Beswick and his contracts back in Forcadel. Then, I'd snuck into a dance hall and pickpocketed them myself. But all that effort had been in vain—the documents I'd thought would be the proof I needed to finally arrest that slumlord crime boss had been approved by my father.

Something tweaked in my gut, and I forced myself to pause and really consider my next move.

With Beswick, I'd missed the bigger picture. My father had been the one to arrange Beswick's agreement with the Severians, because he was protecting Forcadelian interests. So when I'd presented the contracts to Garwood, he'd not only known about them, but said there was no proof of treason because it had been royally sanctioned. And instead of working rationally—after all, I was to be crowned officially in three days—I'd decided to kidnap Beswick and burn whatever bridges I had left with Felix.

I opened my eyes to the dark alley. Now, I had a similar situation. A man in power, something on his person. This time, I would take the rational route and gather a little more information before I made another move. It was a nice compromise between my earlier paralysis and my reckless idiocy.

I quietly retraced the path I'd taken across the city, but on the rooftops. If Kelsor wasn't out and about, he would be back at his house. Either way, I'd have a chance to eavesdrop.

Happily, my chance came sooner than expected. The man

himself was in the city square, surrounded by a group of guards with varying degrees of interest, based on their body language. The Forcadelians seemed much less engaged than the Severians as Kelsor described the thief who'd been so brazen.

"I didn't get a good look, but I believe it's a woman," he said. "About this high. Forcadelian, I think."

A Forcadelian guard raised his hand. "What did she steal, anyway?"

"Something valuable," Kelsor snapped. "And if you ask any more questions, I'll have you demoted. Just find the thief and bring her to me."

Oh, now that was interesting. One would think Kelsor would tell the guards what I'd stolen, perhaps even send out the signal not to open the gate. That would've been a logical reaction, and yet...

If he was keeping his bribery from his underlings, that might be the exact pressure point I needed to get him to cow to me.

"Patience, Brynna," I whispered to myself. After sending the others away, the only people left in the square were Kelsor and two Severian guards.

"What did she take?" the guard on the left asked.

"I told you, nothing important." Kelsor sniffed. "I just hope these Forcadelian idiots are better at capturing thieves than guarding the city."

I cast my gaze down to the town square, but Kelsor was otherwise unguarded. I pawed through my weapons bag, clucking my tongue when I found no pouches—not even a trace of knockout powder. What I did have was my crossbow, some sticking arrows, and my knives.

Attaching one of the arrows to the crossbow, I leaned over the edge of the roof and aimed. Once I had a good shot, I squeezed the trigger.

The arrow tore through one of the guard's shoulders, pinning him to the wall.

"What the—"

I notched another arrow and hit one of the other guards, the arrow slicing through the outside of his leg and securing him to the wall next to him. That left me with two guards, plus Kelsor.

I leapt off the roof, the air gathering in the pockets of my cloak, and landed in a crouch.

"You again," Kelsor snarled.

"Funny how you didn't want anyone to know what I'd stolen," I purred as his two guards pulled their swords. "Almost like you're trying to hide it. But from whom, is the question."

The guards rushed me, and I parried one with my sword and the other with my knife. I kicked my leg, and it landed square in one guard's gut. The other received an elbow to the jaw and fell backward, out cold. Turning back to the first, I pulled my crossbow out and pointed it directly at his face.

"How loyal are you to him?" I asked with a knowing smirk.

The guard scrambled to his feet and ran off.

And then there was just Kelsor.

"I ain't afraid of you," he said, holding his sword in the air. The slight tremor in the blade belied his words.

"No, but you are afraid of what Ilara might do," I said, lowering my crossbow. "How many ships have you let through, Kelsor? How much money have you pocketed without the express permission of the queen?"

He swallowed hard and his face paled. "S-she gave me—"

"The sweat on your forehead says otherwise," I said, raising my crossbow. "Now, this is going to go one of two ways. The first, you hand over the seal, let me and several ships that have been in port for a while through, and Ilara won't be the wiser."

"What's the other?"

I smiled. "I tie you up, stick you in a boat, and float you down to Ilara to handle. I doubt she'd be as amenable as I am right now."

He reached into his coat pocket and hurled something at me. I caught it just before it hit my face—the wax seal.

"There, take it," he said, rubbing his hands together. "Just leave me alone."

"One more thing," I said, walking toward him. "You will double the number of patrols in the city. These are your people now, and you will keep the peace here. Understood?"

He nodded, and for the first time in I wasn't sure how long, I actually felt like I'd accomplished something.

"I still tied him up," I said, leaning over Kieran's railing as we sailed past the open gates. "Left him for his guards to find."

"Damn, Veil," Kieran said with a shake of his head. "Remind me never to get on your bad side."

"Glad to know I can still strike fear into the hearts of men," I said with a a small smile. Kieran had taken the wax-sealed letter to the gate master, and within an hour, the gates were open and we were making our way into Niemen.

"This won't last, though," I said, watching a Forcadelian ship sail past us in the opposite direction.

"Take the victory," Kieran said, nudging me slightly. "You got us passage. One step closer to reclaiming your throne."

Yeah, that. In all the fun, I'd nearly forgotten why I was getting myself into trouble. I glanced behind me to where Sarala was manning the ship. "Do you think what I'm doing is right, Kieran? Is this—reclaiming my throne—worth all this trouble? Would things be better if I just allowed Ilara to remain in charge?"

"Only you can answer that," he said, catching my gaze. "But if you're looking for a sign from the Mother, it seems you got pretty lucky tonight. Perhaps you should keep going until your luck runs out."

Chapter Fourteen

Felix

The days were moving quickly and I hadn't made any progress on the brewing rebellion in the city—either as The Veil or Captain Llobrega. I had attempted to investigate the fire at Ilara's furrier, but it had been a dead end. There had been neither witnesses nor any warning.

As I told Ilara, I'd received a list of her favorite vendors and had stashed two guards at all of them. Then, once I escaped the castle, I monitored from the rooftop. It was incredibly boring work and more than once, I fell asleep waiting for something to happen.

Unfortunately, something finally did. A tailor, one of Ilara's favorites, went up in flames just as the furrier had. The two Severians who'd been assigned to guard it couldn't tell me how it had happened, so I decided to head out into the city to get answers for myself.

At this hour, the vendor market was already starting to pack up in advance of the dusk curfew. I still received several nods of welcome, but there were more than a few scornful looks. I didn't understand the increased scrutiny until I saw the new wanted posters hanging in the square. Anyone caught masquerading as The Veil would be arrested for treason and executed immediately.

I stared at a poster for a while, glad I was the one out tonight and not Joella or Riya. I would never forgive myself if something happened to them.

"I say we just find a place to drink and say we did our rounds," said a young voice. "Mother knows everyone hates us out here anyway. Not as if two guards could really stop a riot if one started."

I ducked into a nearby alley when two of my soldiers turned the corner. Jorad, the young, black-haired boy with sharp green eyes, was my father's younger sister's son. His partner, Aline, seemed to have some Niemenian in her lighter hair and skin. Both had been part of my recently graduated cadets.

"You're free to go back and tell Lieutenant Coyle, but I'm going to keep patrolling the streets," Jorad replied, adjusting the sword on his belt. "I'm not gonna get hanged for treason."

"He ain't gonna hang us."

"He might. You saw what my cousin did to those kids last week."

"Just overreacting."

Jorad shivered. "I don't envy him. Seems like he's stuck between a rock and a hard place."

"I think he's too drunk to make a decision," Aline said. "He's always swaggering in at midnight, drunk off his ass. He can't even stand upright in the morning."

I sighed and looked to the Mother for help. Had I not impressed upon them the dangers of running their mouths? As they turned a corner, a pang of sadness hit me. It wasn't just the queen they were disparaging, it was their captain. I was failing them as a leader in order to save the kingdom.

And now I was hiding in an alley to avoid being seen by them.

Straightening, I walked out into the street and cleared my

throat behind them.

"Captain!"

They scrambled into a hasty salute, Aline's face growing red and her eyes wide. I responded in kind, glad to see they still showed some semblance of respect in person.

"How are things going?" I asked, resting my hand on my pommel. "Are you settling into your new roles?"

"Of course," Jorad said, even as his eyes told me he was lying. But as a Llobrega, duty came above all else for him, as it had once been for me.

"It's different," Aline said with a bit of a wince.

I laughed. "I'm headed to Mariner's Row to have a chat with the man whose shop was burned down. Would you two care to escort me?"

"Would we ever!" Jorad said before realizing himself and clearing his throat. "I mean, of course. Whatever you need, sir."

As we walked through the emptying streets, we talked about their new roles as patrollers, and things they'd seen on their first rotation the night before.

"It's weird," Aline said as we passed one of Beswick's shuttered clubs. "He's the reason I got into the guard in the first place. He paid my way, and so my folks were..." She blushed. "They had to work for him. But now that he's gone, I guess they don't anymore."

I nodded. "No one's seen him since the invasion, but some of my sources think he's gone up to Niemen."

"I'm grateful to him for giving me the scholarship," she said, looking at her hands. "But he certainly made my parents' lives hell for it."

"He did," I said with a nod. "See? There's some silver lining to the Severians being here."

"I'm a little nervous," she said. "My brother says that I should leave the guard. Says that it's not right after what...well, what happened. But I worked hard to get here and I'm not about to abandon Forcadel because I don't like the leader now." She blushed as Jorad gave her a death look. "With all due respect."

"Quite all right," I said. "Things are much different than they were. But you're right. We owe it to the people of this city to maintain some semblance of normalcy."

"I, for one, am happy to be in the guard," Jorad announced.

Aline rolled her eyes, and I just laughed.

The shop in question had been completely burned to the ground, and with some cajoling, we got the address of the shop owner. He lived on the other side of town in Merchant's Quarter, in a row house that seemed fairly nice, but nothing too fancy.

"Good evening," I said with a forced smile. "Can I talk to you about—"

The door slammed in my face.

I turned to the two lieutenants behind me, both of whom wore nervous looks. I offered them a confident smile before rapping on the door once again.

"Please open up," I said, trying to sound kind and nonthreatening. "I don't want to break your door."

The door cracked open. "I ain't done nothing wrong."

"Of course not," I said with a tight smile. "I just wanted to ask you questions about the fire at your shop last night."

"Aren't you Llobrega?"

"I am." I nodded. "I just want to help find out who was responsible. Can you tell me anything about it?"

"Wasn't there," he said. "But if you ask me, it's retaliation. The queen took a liking to me recently, and gave me a few yards of beautiful silk. I hadn't seen such finery since before Maurice died, and she tasked me with making her a pretty new dress." He sighed. "I hadn't even finished half of it. Now it's ash."

I smiled thinly. "If you can tell me anything about who might be after you, that would really help. Even if it's just someone strange hanging around your shop."

He cast a look behind me. "I ain't seen no one. And if I did, I wouldn't tell you. Don't want them coming to destroy my house, either. I lost my income, but if they destroy my house, I'll lose my family." He bowed. "Sorry. Good day to you."

The door closed, albeit more softly than before, and I exhaled.

"Dead end, sir?" Jorad asked behind me.

"Perhaps," I said. "But we'll keep asking until we find a break. That's what we're here to do. Help the people."

"Psh. You're nothing but a bunch of traitors."

The girl who'd spoken was perhaps younger than even my soldiers, with sharp green eyes and a cruel, unforgiving gaze. She was propped against the wall across from us, her arms folded over her chest as she observed us.

"Excuse me?" I said, after a moment.

"The whole lot of you—nothing but traitors," the girl snarled at me. "You allowed Princess Brynna to die. You allowed that bitch to take over our kingdom. And now you're her lapdog. Wearing her crest like you forgot who you are."

I held up my hand to stop the two behind me from taking action. "I'm sorry that's how you feel."

"Only a matter of time before you get what's coming to you," she said, spitting on the ground in front of us. "Ain't no one in this city gonna mourn for your swinging bodies."

Aline's face had gone pale, and Jorad's eyes were wet as he watched the woman walk away. My heart broke for them—young adults who'd spent their childhoods in pursuit of a purpose that was now being dragged through the mud. I wished I had words of optimism to give them, or that I could at least tell them to hold onto the hope that Brynna would be returning.

But as I could do neither, I turned to the only other salvation I could offer them.

"Come on, I think we need to have a chat."

As we approached the large church in the center of town, the tension on their faces had grown worse. Inside, Mother Fishen was sitting with a pair of older women, speaking in hushed tones. She nodded toward me and I bowed back. But instead of joining her, I led my soldiers to the front, where we took seats at the center of the pew.

"Talk," I ordered.

"Pardon?" Jorad said.

"I want to hear your thoughts on the day," I said. "This is a sacred space. You may speak as freely as you wish without repercussions."

Neither spoke at first, but Jorad was the braver one. "I joined the King's Guard because I wanted to help people. I don't want to be hated."

Aline made a noise. "How can we help people when we're working for...for..."

"Go on," I urged, not tearing my eyes from the candles. "No repercussions."

"That bitch," Aline finished. "She's ruined this city. She's ruining our country. And I feel like I've turned my back on both by wearing this Mother-forsaken uniform."

I gathered my thoughts. "There's forgiveness in service," I began. "When you serve others, you're closer to the Mother. At least, that's what I was taught."

"But are we serving others?"

"Are you?" I asked, tilting my head in their direction.

Jorad ducked his head, but Aline stared defiantly ahead. "I don't feel like we are."

"Then how do we change that?" I asked softly.

Both turned toward me, confusion evident on their faces.

"If we truly want to be of service to the Mother and to our

people," I said, "we have to find ways of making that happen. Perhaps it's standing up to a Severian guard who's bullying an old woman. Perhaps it's protecting a Forcadelian shopowner so they can continue to work in this town." I glanced upward. *Perhaps it's running around as a masked vigilante.* "If we're to survive this, mentally and spiritually, we all need to find ways of coping. Of keeping ourselves together in this world where we can't control much."

They nodded silently.

"I may not be in charge for much longer," I continued. "But know that I'm doing everything in my power to keep all of you safe. I just need you to help me out and not get yourselves into trouble."

"We will," Aline said softly.

"And thanks," Jorad murmured. "Others may not see it, but we do."

We sat there for a while, and eventually both Aline and Jorad rose to light a few candles and leave. But I remained, finding solace in the silence and respite from my thoughts. I had no idea if my words had meant anything to them, but I hoped they had.

I rose and walked to the candles, kneeling on the low bench in front. I ran my fingers along the bannister in front, reminded of the time Brynna and I had come here. When I'd lost my cool and she'd refused to speak to me. And then, like sunlight breaking over a dark sky, she'd smiled and we were back to being friends.

I knelt in front of the row of candles and plucked a match from the bunch. As the flame sparked to life, I touched it to an unlit wick and breathed a quiet prayer.

Please let her be safe. Please let her have found friends to aid her along the way. Please give her strength.

Then I took the flame and lit another candle.

And, if you get time, please send the same to me and my guards.

Chapter Fifteen

Five days after we left Skorsa, I awoke to frost on the edges of the ship and my breath puffing in front of my face. My teeth wouldn't stop chattering as I joined Kieran on the quarterdeck. He laughed and threw his arm around me.

"You'll probably want to buy some warmer clothes for the mountains," he said.

"How cold could it be?" I said, my voice shaking.

"And how far north have you been?"

"I've been as far north as the Kulkan border," I said, adjusting my sleeves down my arms.

Kieran snorted. "You'll want some new clothes."

Aymar grew steadily larger as we approached. It was nothing more than a collection of dark wood buildings on the side of the river, but the snow-capped mountains seemed impossibly close as Kieran's ship sidled up to the dock. Everything was different, even down to the scent in the air. Forcadel always smelled of fish and salt water, but here it was more...I couldn't even describe it. It wasn't home.

"So I suppose this is farewell for now, hm?" I asked Kieran as the two Kulkans put out the gangway. "You guys are continuing up the river?"

He nodded. "Hoping to get to our destination then back through Skorsa before all hell breaks loose. We've got a nice sum of money waiting if we can deliver to Forcadel within the next two months."

I didn't want to ask what he was smuggling; he probably wouldn't tell me anyway. "Any suggestions on how to get to Linden from here?"

"Aymar is the official port for the royal family—see that flag over there?" He pointed out a light blue flag fluttering on top of one of the houses near the docks. "That's their symbol. They say there's an underground road that'll take you under the mountain and reach the capital in a few days."

"That would be convenient," I said.

"They also say the road is for the royal family and shipments only," Kieran said. "Although perhaps if you drop some names, they might let you in. Or, I suppose, you could just pony up some gold."

"Can't really do that," I said, a nervous fluttering in my stomach at the thought of being on my own without any coin.

"Here," Kieran said, sliding a pouch across the wooden bannister. "Take this."

Coins—four gold ones. "Kieran, I can't take more of your money—"

"Consider it buying more favors in the future," he said, closing my fingers around the leather. "It's not much, but I don't think you want to be carrying too much gold. Buy yourself something warm. You'll need it in the mountains."

My eyes moistened as I stared at the bag. "Kieran... I don't know what to say."

"Pirate king is still on the table," he said, his breath puffing in front of him. "I might not be as upstanding as your captain, but we'd surely have more fun."

I laughed, casting a coy look at him. "I wouldn't be too sure about that."

"Be careful, Veil," he said, leaning forward to kiss my cheek. "Niemen isn't Forcadel."

I stood on the docks until Kieran's ship disappeared around the far bend of the river, then remained there until my hands turned blue from cold. Finally, I tore myself from the view, knowing that if I didn't find a pair of gloves soon, I'd lose my fingers. Dock workers—some even in short-sleeves and short-pants—worked and milled around, casting suspicious gazes at me. They were all pale-skinned and light-haired, although their skin seemed rough and leathery from the cold and sun.

As a gusty wind blew off the river and cut right through me, I decided I might be more useful if I was warm, so I ducked into a clothing shop. There was a roaring fire in the corner that defrosted my trembling fingers, and I exhaled as I walked toward it like a moth.

"You're not from around here, are you?" asked a young woman dressing a mannequin.

"How could you tell?" I asked, my voice trembling.

"Forcadel?" she asked, and I nodded. "You all arrive here the same. No cloak, no jacket. Thin boots that slip on the ice. Dressing rubes like you is how we make our business."

I narrowed my eyes, hearing the inflated prices in her words. "I don't have much, so I'm afraid I just need a jacket."

"Suit yourself," she said with a shrug. "But it's a nice summer day here, and it's much colder in Linden."

"You're just trying to make a sale."

"Girl's gotta eat."

I ran my fingers along a wool scarf. "How much does it cost for passage into Linden?"

"Depends," she replied, adjusting the scarf on the model. "I know a man who'll take you to the front gates of the royal castle for twenty gold coins. Make it thirty and no one will know you're there."

And I only had four in my pocket, so walking by foot would have to do. "I'll take a cloak, boots, and gloves."

One gold coin lighter, but a whole lot warmer, I walked through the city in search of a place to find information about the royal road and found what I thought to be a mess hall. I had a silver left, and I used it to purchase a bowl and a tankard—both of which I could refill at my leisure. I settled down at one of the long tables, spearing the potatoes with my fork and keeping my ears open. But the stew was bland and conversations nonexistent. So I'd have to spur some.

"Evening," I said to the man across the table from me.

He cast his gaze upward then back down at his food, muttering something under his breath.

"Is there any salt?" I asked.

He gazed at me once more then stood and walked to another open spot. I might've taken offense, except every other person was eating in silence. Twins three seats down from me were staring into their bowls, ignoring one another as if they were strangers.

It was the oddest thing I'd ever seen. As a whole, Forcadelians weren't the kind of people to close our doors. A little booze, a little smile, and most of us would spill our deepest, darkest secrets to a stranger on the street. Niemen, it seemed, was as closed off as Katarine had been the first time I'd met her.

And that wasn't the only difference. My features—which I'd considered pale from spending my days sleeping and nights on rooftops—were still much darker than anyone else's in the room. They had varying shades of blond hair, some even a vibrant red. A couple of mariners had a smattering of freckles on their face, but with my black hair and brown skin, I stuck out like a sore thumb.

After finishing my meal, I headed out into the frozen streets again, the warmth in my belly from the bland stew disappearing in the first cold wind. The sun was starting to set over the mountain ridges, and although I might find more information at night, I sure didn't want to be outside after dark.

My pace a bit brisker, I continued exploring the city, poking my head into taverns and mess halls alike. All of them—silent inside. It was as if the Niemenians didn't know the first thing about socialization.

"Excuse me," I said, walking up to a Niemenian guard stationed at one of the cross-streets.

He grunted and turned to me. "Whatdya want?"

"I'm looking for information on passage to Linden," I said, holding my cloak closer as a cool wind seeped through my clothing. "Can you help me?"

He rolled his eyes and marched away.

"Seriously?" I said. "Does no one in this city have any common decency?"

I heard a snicker behind me. A pair of young teenaged girls giggled together.

"What?" I snapped, crossing my arms.

"As if anyone would tell a *seaweed* like you anything. Why don't you go back to your own country?"

My jaw fell open as they walked away. Was that they called us up here? Seaweed? As insults went, it was a little laughable.

Apparently, I would have to bribe or beat information out of someone. I returned to the docks, where I'd seen a riverside tavern that appeared to be somewhat livelier than the rest of the city. Inside, the fires roared and several Forcadelian sailors sat around a large table, their bellowing laughs echoing out onto the street. I sidled up to the bar, palming my gold coin and hoping I wouldn't have to show it.

"What are you after?" the bartender asked.

"Whiskey," I said. "And information."

"You got money?"

I grimaced, but I put the gold coin down on the bar. "Will this suffice?"

"Depends," he replied, eyeing it greedily. "What kinda information are you looking for?"

"Headed to Linden," I replied. "How do I get there?"

"That information will cost you more than that," he said with a smile. He was missing one of his front teeth.

I exhaled and placed the remaining two gold coins on the bar. "What about for this?"

"Oh, for that?" He swiped the coins off the bar. "That'll get you out the door."

I chuckled and sat back. Then in one movement, I jumped over the bar, grabbed the bartender by the arm, twisted it behind his back, and pressed my knife to his throat.

"Give me my coin back or I'll take it out of your hide," I snarled.

He cried out and placed the coins on the bar. I vaulted over the dark wood and grabbed the coins, replacing them in my pouch.

"You might've been able to swindle Forcadelians in the past," I said, pressing him harder to the bar. "But now you'll think twice about it."

"Oi!"

The guard I'd seen earlier in the day walked through the door. He yanked out his sword and pointed it at me. "I knew you were trouble, Forcadelian! Unhand him!"

I released the man. "He stole from me."

"Lies!" the man cried. "She just attacked me! Trying to rob my bar!"

"Oh bull—"

The guard stormed toward me. "You're under arrest!"

"Perfect." I heartily rolled my eyes. "I'll just be on my way. No need to do anything stupid."

The guard lunged for me, but overcompensated and slid over the wet surface, landing in a heap on the floor. I took the opportunity and dashed out the door, into the cold night.

In hindsight, it might've been smarter to go to jail.

I kept running until I was far out of town, until my lungs burned from the cold. It was now past dark, and there was nothing on this road but shadows and a bitterly cold wind that blew right through this so-called warm cloak. I'd hoped there'd be a nearby town that might have an empty room, but so far, I was just walking aimlessly.

Panic creeped in at the edge of my mind. Even in the weeks when I'd first arrived in Forcadel and I hadn't had a place to lay my head, I hadn't worried too much. It had been a balmy spring, and sleeping under the stars was something of a blessing. But here in this frozen wasteland, if I didn't find shelter, I might very well die of exposure.

My fingers found the fabric of my mask in my slingbag, and I pressed the cloth against my numb face. My breath dispelled the cold somewhat, but the rest of my body was still trembling.

My foot slipped on a patch of dark ice and I landed hard on my rear. I winced, both from the pain and from the frigid wetness now seeping through my pants. Gingerly, I crept back onto the dirt of the road and glared at the offending patch. My tailbone ached— I hoped it wasn't broken. I officially hated this country.

But just as I was cursing everything related to Niemen, including Katarine, I spotted something in the distance. A small light.

Sending a prayer to the Mother that I wouldn't find more of that northern hospitality, I gathered myself and walked toward it. As I drew closer, I made out the shape of a farm, the light coming from a lantern over the farmhouse.

I approached slowly, keeping my footfalls quiet. The farm itself was modest; a large barn with locked doors sat directly across from the house. A shadow moved, and I nearly fell on my ass again. The cat meowed, gazing up at me with eyes illuminated by the lantern.

"Are your people nice?" I whispered.

The cat turned and walked away, its tail curling around in what was probably a rude gesture.

I blew air between my lips quietly, watching the air blossom upward. Nothing in this country had led me to believe that if I knocked on the door, the people inside would help me.

A horse whinnied from the stable next to the barn, and I smirked. But what the house occupants didn't know wouldn't hurt them.

The stables were also locked, but I managed to find a window I could slide open. I landed in the tack room, where I snatched a few blankets that would surely keep me warm during the night. Quietly, I opened the door and walked down the row of doors. A horse popped its head out and whinnied at me; I cooed to quiet it. Holding out my hand, I wished I had an apple or something, but the horse clomped over to me without it. I pulled off the thick gloves and pressed my fingers to its soft nose.

"Ssh," I whispered, running my fingers down its muzzle. "If you don't rat me out, I'm going to bunk with you tonight. Promise I won't hog the covers."

The horse nudged me again, and I realized it was uncovered. So I unlocked the gate and threw one of the horse blankets on top of the animal and made sure it was attached for the night ahead.

"There, happy now?" I asked, locking the gate again. The stable next to it was clean and mostly empty, save for a pile of hay. I laid another horse blanket on top then sat down and covered myself with my cloak. I was still frigid, but even the cold hay was warmer than nothing. And with some difficulty, I lay back and drifted off to an unsettled sleep.

Chapter Sixteen

"Who are you?"

I yanked my knife and pointed it at the figure in the light. A girl—barely a teenager—stood in the stable doorway, armed with nothing more than a rake and a sliced-up apple, which had fallen from her hand.

"W-who are you?" she asked. "Are you gonna steal our horse?"

"No, of course not," I replied, sheathing my knife. "I'm sorry I scared you. I just needed a place to sleep for the night."

She quirked a brow at me. "So why didn't you come to the door and ask?"

"Because you Niemenians don't seem the most welcoming of people," I replied. The girl, however, seemed nice enough with her rosy red cheeks and bright blue eyes, so I forced my frozen face into a smile. "I'm Larissa."

"Katya." She swallowed hard, coming into the barn but still keeping her distance. "You're that Forcadel woman, aren't you?

The one who threatened Boris? They were talking about you at market this morning."

I assumed there probably weren't any other Forcadelian women wandering around threatening people. "You mean after Boris tried to take my money?"

"He's a brute," she said, offering me a small smile. "I'm... surprised. He described the woman who beat him as much larger. You're nothing but a girl yourself."

"I'm bigger than I look." I gingerly stood and brushed the hay off my rear. If the authorities were looking for me, I needed to leave before they caught up. "How far is the next city from here? Preferably in the direction of Linden?"

"Oh, um..." Katya hesitated. "The next city is over the mountain, in the valley. But if you're going to Linden, you should take the royal road. It starts about five miles north of here."

"I know all about the royal road," I said. "Can't afford it. Know anyone who'd be going that way who could use an extra set of hands?"

"M-my sister might know someone. She's a fur trader, and she goes to Linden all the time. Maybe she can help you."

I hesitated. "Are you going to tell your sister I slept in your barn?"

She grinned. "I don't see how that's any of her business."

I smelled like a horse, but I followed Katya toward the small farmhouse I'd seen the night before. The red door had probably been something in the past, but it was faded and chipped now. The whole estate had seen better days.

"You said your sister is a fur trader?" I asked.

The girl nodded. "Our family has been for centuries. Used to be the most well-known in the country. But you know, when that royal road got put in a few decades ago, people started getting their furs from the bigger cities up the river. And with the wolves..."

"Wolves?" I swallowed hard. Perhaps I'd been luckier than I'd thought the night before.

"They aren't around here," Katya said. "But they're up in the mountains. Brigit can tell you more about them."

I nursed my trepidation as Katya led me into the small house. The kitchen had the same look as the rest of it—faded wallpaper, an old woodburning stove with rusted feet, and a kitchen table that had seen its share of meals and burns.

"Brigit?" Katya called.

"In the back."

We continued through the back of the house and into a small workshop where an older woman was turning a wrench on what appeared to be a wagon wheel. She looked up at me for a moment, then straightened, holding the wrench in a defensive position. Her skin was beginning to wrinkle around the eyes, and wiry gray hair peeked out from her blond hair.

"Who's this?"

Katya hesitated. "This is…"

"Larissa," I said, stepping forward. "I'm in need of passage to Linden. Your sister thought you might know of someone going there."

Her blue eyes scanned me as if she could see inside my soul. "And what's your business in Linden?"

"My business is my own," I said then paused and added, "Just need to meet with some people there."

"Can't write a letter?"

I cleared my throat. "Hardly. This message has to be delivered in person. I'm not here to cause trouble."

She snorted. "I may not be much, but I'm still loyal to Niemen. Don't like foreigners coming into my capital city who can fight like you can."

I rolled my eyes. News traveled fast, it seemed. "I come in peace and…on behalf of Princess Brynna."

"Thought she was dead."

"Not yet," I said. "And she's trying to gather allies so she can get her kingdom back. She's sent me to speak with the queen to ask for help."

Brigit studied me for a long time—so long that I was sure she would throw me out of her house. But surprisingly, she didn't. "As it turns out, I need to make a trip to Linden. Have enough furs that I can sell at the market there. Just need to get the carriage set up and packed. Think you can help out with that?"

"Are you serious?" I couldn't believe my luck. "You'll take me? Just like that? Today?"

"I've been mulling over trip for the past few weeks," she said, averting her gaze. "And you seem like the sort of person who'd get me to the capital unscathed."

The hairs rose on the back of my neck. "What do you mean unscathed? What's in the mountains?" I glanced to Katya. "Wolves?"

Brigit glared daggers at her little sister, who cowered. "Ain't nothing but thieves and regular human monsters. I can't protect my stock and myself at the same time. Be nice to have another sword, especially one so well-used."

Hesitation forced my silence as I quickly considered the pros and the cons of helping this woman. It was clear she was no slouch, but something in the mountains concerned her. Enough to trust a complete stranger. Still, this was my one shot at getting to Linden —and the price was one I was willing to pay.

"Yes, that sounds fine."

Brigit nodded. "Help Katya get the wagon ready. We're leaving as soon as possible."

⇨————

"And when you get to Linden, you must visit the chocolate shops," Katya said from beneath the pile of soft pelts she was carrying. "They bring in the best from Kulka and beyond. They've also got the prettiest jewelry there. Brigit brought me a ring once, so gorgeous it was."

"Was?" I asked, taking the pile from her and assembling them on the old wooden wagon, our transport over the rocky mountain. I wasn't sure how this would go, but I assumed the fur trader had more experience, so I didn't question it.

"I decided to sell it to a passing trader. Things haven't been easy since Dad died last year. It's hard to pay for a trip into the mountains, especially when we're not sure all the stock will get there." She beamed at me. "But with you there to help Brigit, I'm sure you'll get there safely."

I grimaced, which I tried to hide under a smile. "So, these wolves. Your sister said they were human. Are they not?"

She shivered and didn't respond.

"Katya, I need to know what I'm getting into," I replied. "What kind of creatures are they?"

"They're human—I think," she said. "I've heard stories. They say that they're shifters, turning into vicious, bloodthirsty creatures at the drop of a hat." She made a gesture toward the barn. "Bigger than that."

I swallowed hard. Humans, I could handle. But giant wolf creatures? That might be more than The Veil could take. All I had in my bag were vigilante things, a crossbow with a few arrows, rope, and my knives. I would need more.

"What weapons do you have?" I asked.

"Not many," Katya said. "But maybe in the workroom."

The tannery was inside the locked barn and smelled of old blood and drying flesh. Pelts of every size hung along the walls, some stiff with frost, and others seemingly ready to take. A skinned carcass rested on the table—an elk, if the antlers were any indication.

"I have to prepare it," Katya said, glancing at me. "We'll dry and salt the meat for winter."

"Suppose not much spoils up here," I said. "It seems freezing year-round."

She cast me a long look. "If you think this is cold, you should take another cloak. This is summer weather for us."

I stifled a whine as she led me into a back room. There, I found an assortment of knives in a block, a staff, an axe, and various other skinning tools. Swords and weapons weren't my problem—I needed something bigger.

"Like this?" Katya said, holding aloft a bow nearly as big as she was.

"That'll work," I said, taking it from her. "Have any arrows?"

"A few, but there's flints in the mountains," she said, showing me a quiver with two arrows in it.

I nocked one in the bow and aimed for a spot on the wall, releasing it almost instantly. The arrow hit exactly where I'd intended. I pulled it from the wood and checked the tip—still sharp.

"You'll keep my sister safe, won't you?" she asked quietly.

I looked at her. "I'll certainly try."

"If we don't get some money soon, we may lose the farm," she said, her eyes growing misty. "I prayed to the Mother that She would send someone to save us, and then…then I found you in our barn."

As much as my unease bubbled in my stomach, it was hard to say no to Katya's eager eyes. At the very least, I could swear to keep her sister safe, if only to give her some peace.

"I promise," I said quietly. "I'll do my best to keep her and your stock safe."

The little girl beamed.

When we returned to the carriage, Brigit was already seated on the bench and the horse tacked and ready to go. Katya wiped her eyes, trying to remain stoic as she approached her sister.

"Watch the apple trees," Brigit said, ignoring her sister's tears. "There's been some elk out and about, and I don't want to lose our last crop."

"I will," Katya replied. "Do you have the food?"

Brigit nodded. "Well, Forcadelian? Are you ready to depart? Mind the furs when you step in."

I climbed atop the bench to sit next to her, resting the bow and arrow behind me. "Ready when you are."

The elder woman gave her sister one last, lingering look before snapping the reins. The horses jumped and started walking, pulling us forward and out of the farm. To her credit, Katya didn't follow us, standing completely still in the center of the farm, her small hands tucked inside her apron as tears leaked down her face.

"She's a sweet girl," I said, turning away to face the front.

Brigit grunted, but didn't respond otherwise. Clearly, I was on yet another adventure with a taciturn Niemenian. I just hoped Brigit was better company than Sarala.

Chapter Seventeen

Once outside the village, the tall, white-barked trees crowded the thin path, giving ample opportunity for thieves and others to sneak out unnoticed. I kept my gaze to the front and my ears open, but I doubted we'd hit much trouble so close to civilization. There was a clear, gravel path before us, but the canopy blocked out the sky. Every so often, I'd get a glimpse of the looming mountains, and I couldn't help but wonder how this carriage would get over the rocky peaks.

Brigit was silent for most of the afternoon, except for the occasional soft coo to the horses. She was hearty enough to traverse the mountains by herself. Which made me all the more curious why she'd agreed to take a complete stranger with her on a trip into the isolated woods. Then again, she was twice my size, so perhaps she wasn't too concerned about it.

After we'd been traveling for a few hours, she finally spoke. "Can you see what my sister packed for food? Mind you don't get footprints on the furs."

I climbed down, careful to place my feet on wood and not the silky pelts, as I unwrapped the satchel. There, I found some small bread wrapped in wax paper, a few apples, and something that looked like fish in a jar.

"Hand me the jar," she said, eyeing me from above.

I did so and nearly gagged when she opened it. "That smells awful."

"Pickled fish," she said, pulling one out with her fingers and sliding it down her mouth. "Good for digestion."

"I'll pass," I said. Since Celia's camp, I hadn't really needed to eat more than once a day. And whatever hunger I might've felt had disappeared at the sight and smell of those fish.

"Did you bring any water?" Brigit asked. "Gonna need it when we get up higher."

I shook my head. "I'll just find a river and drink from that."

"Is this your first time in the mountains?"

"Yes."

She chuckled and handed me a long metal tube, sloshing with liquid. "You're going to need this. If you're going to help me fight off wolves, I can't have you sick from altitude."

"Is that a thing?"

She chuckled. "You'll find out soon enough."

"Wow."

We'd crested a hill, and suddenly, there were mountains everywhere. I'd seen them in the distance, of course, but now... now they seemed within striking distance. I craned my neck back to take them in, and my eyes swam, as if they couldn't believe such a thing existed either. At the tops of the mountains, a coating of white snow stretched far into the valleys, although it hadn't yet reached us. I hoped it wouldn't.

We followed the rocky path up then down then up, around, and down again. I was sure we weren't going anywhere but in circles, and yet with every new turn, the landscape continued to change. Large pine trees brimming with small birds and squirrels had slowly disappeared in favor of black rock that sloped on either side of us. Small white bushes waved in the whistling wind, but there wasn't much more out here.

"Whoa, whoa," Brigit said to the horse, stopping it short.

"What is it?" I went for my knife, realizing I hadn't been paying much attention to the surroundings. Then again, there wasn't much anyone could hide in around here.

"Path's narrow," she said, sliding off the carriage. "Get off and mind the stock. Careful of your feet."

I slid out of the carriage, realizing almost too late that the path was, indeed, *very* narrow. There was only a foot or so separating me from tumbling head-first over the cliffside.

"I said mind your feet." Brigit grunted, standing with the horse.

I swallowed my fear and proceeded to the back, but I held onto the carriage for dear life. Once I was in place, Brigit took the reins of the horse and led her forward slowly, cooing at her every so often to coax her to place her foot.

"Is it always this narrow?" I asked, keeping the carriage within grasping distance just in case.

"See there," Brigit said, nodding to the cliffside. "Rockslide. Took a chunk of the path with it. Happens from time to time."

"Could it happen to us on the path?" I asked.

She nodded. "Not much you can do about it if it does."

My breath, which puffed from my lips, was coming in shorter bursts now. More than once, I had to stop and catch it, glaring at the older woman who seemed to move with ease across the rough terrain.

"Drink that water," she called to me the fourth or fifth time.

"We can't be stopping this much if we want to make camp before dark."

I forced myself upright.

The path continued interminably, although I knew we were going up. I'd never felt so weak in my entire life, and coupled with the headache throbbing between my eyes, the cold seeping through my cloak, and my general exhaustion, I was miserable. More than once, I cast a longing look at the clean furs lining the bottom of the carriage. But I didn't want to show weakness to Brigit, and I had a feeling that even if I asked her if she could spare one for the trip, she'd refuse.

"If we're going to the capital city," I said resting my hand on the carriage, "where's everyone else? Shouldn't this road be packed with people?"

"They're on the royal road." Brigit kicked the rock. "Down there."

"Down...what?"

"Most of the roads leading into Linden go through the mountain, not above it. There's two roads from Aymar, both of which'll cost you more than I'll make in Linden to get past the first checkpoint."

"Checkpoint?"

"Cities in the mountain. Some are mining cities, others are just there to be a break in the darkness."

My foot slipped over another rock and I had to steady myself on the carriage. "Seems like it might be worthwhile to petition the queen to lower the tolls on the road, so people like you can get to and from the capital city easier."

"You'd think so, eh?" She shook her head. "Queens and kings have no use for people like me. All they care about is making themselves richer."

"Not all queens," I said quietly. "Brynna's a good person."

"Well, what did that get her?" The woman shook her head.

"Ain't nobody out there looking out for us, so we have to look out for ourselves. Your princess Brynna doesn't have a chance in hell of succeeding, and I think it'd just be suicide to return there to attempt anything. Kings and queens wage war, and the rest of us lowlifes suffer. That's the way of the world. Better to just stay out of it."

I stared at the landscape instead of responding.

"I'd keep your breath to yourself for a while. You need your strength," Brigit said, casting a wary glance overhead. "We'll be headed into wolves' country soon, and you need to be at your best if you have any hope of protecting yourself against them."

Protecting myself, not her. I nodded slowly. "So your plan is that when the wolves attack, you'll make a run for it and hope they stick around and kill me instead?"

She didn't bother to look at me. "Desperate times. And if we don't meet with the wolves, there'll be no issue."

"Don't want to tell me anything about them, because you hope they'll just kill me, right?" I said. "You could at least give me a heads up on where I should point my arrow. Your sister tells me they're as big as a barn."

She snorted. "My sister talks too much. They're people. Dangerous people. They use magic and witchcraft to fool you into thinking they're something different."

"M— They're Nestori?" I actually heaved a sigh of relief. Nestori, I could handle. Nothing but smoke and mirrors with powders.

"Don't be too happy about it. They're nothing like any Nestori you've met," she said. "The mountains made them evil creatures. The Nestori I've come across use the Mother's magic for good, not evil."

"Then you haven't met a lot of Nestori," I said. "I've met more than a few who've crossed the line."

She made a tutting sound. "It'll come back to bite them, then.

The Mother has ways of punishing people for using her magic for ill. It may not be now, it may not be next week, but it'll come."

Would it? I thought about Celia, and all the times she'd used magic for ill—and by extension, all the times I'd used knockout powder, flashbangs, and more to hurt people. But as The Veil, I'd been in pursuit of a loftier goal, trying to save people. It was a fine line to walk, and one I wasn't sure I hadn't crossed.

Brigit slowed the horse and went to the carriage, pulling out a small leather pouch, which she tossed at me. "If we happen upon the wolves, put some of that in your mouth."

I opened the bag and sniffed; it was some kind of pungent, minty leaf. "What will this do?"

"Keep your mind sharp." She returned to the front of the carriage. "You could try some now. Will help with the altitude sickness, too."

I was a little hesitant, but I pinched a bit out and stuck it in the front of my mouth, between my teeth and lip. The effect was immediate, the minty flavor exploding in my mouth and up to my eyes, making them water. I wasn't sure if it did anything other than wake me up, but my headache faded a little.

"Quit dawdling and come on," Brigit called from at least fifty feet ahead.

I pocketed the leaf pouch and followed her.

Dusk arrived with a beautiful rainbow of orange, pink, and purple, but Brigit kept pressing onward. I didn't ask if she thought we should continue in the pitch black of night, because I was afraid she might say yes. But just as soon as I couldn't see the path in front of me, we came into a small valley filled with pine trees, and it was there Brigit declared we'd be making camp.

"Stay here and guard the horse," she instructed, disappearing into the darkness.

I tilted my head back to look at the stars, finding nothing but dark gray sky. It had been overcast and cloudy all day, but I'd hoped the night would clear.

When Brigit returned, I helped her build a fire from kindling and logs I chopped with the axe. Brigit produced a bag filled with dried meat, and I took a little. My body hadn't stopped shaking since we'd left Forcadel, and my hunger had gone with it.

"Here," Brigit said, handing me a flask. "It'll warm you up."

"Aren't you worried about the wolves?" I asked, taking a small sip. It wasn't whiskey, but it sure sent a zing of heat through my body. It had a tangy, metallic taste that remained in my mouth for a few minutes after.

She chuckled. "Impending death will sober you."

"That it will," I said, handing the flask back to her. "I have to ask...why'd you let me come with you? You said I was a fierce warrior, so why aren't you worried that I'll rob you and leave you for dead?"

"You've got an honest face," she said, glancing at me. "And a desperate look about you. If I hadn't agreed to take you, I might've found you buried in my furs. At least this way, I get something out of it."

"Honest, hm?" I chuckled. "You'd trust a stranger based on a face?"

She didn't share my humor. "It's not as if I had a choice, really. I'm risking death every time I come into these mountains. If not the wolves then a landslide. Or bad weather. That's what killed my pa."

"Bad weather?" I asked.

She nodded. "He'd insisted on going out alone, as Katya was sick with a summer cold and couldn't be left. A month went by and we didn't hear from him. Some of the other travelers, they said they found his carriage at the bottom of a ravine." She took a long inhale on her pipe. "Never did find his body, and pretty sure the scavengers took all the pelts."

"I'm sorry," I said quietly.

"It's life on the mountains," she said with a shrug. "It's like I said, the queen don't care for us lowlifes. All they want is their gold and that's that."

I poked the fire with a stick to shift the logs around. "How many more days until we reach Linden?"

"We're moving along at a good clip," she said, looking at the sky. "We may hit a snowstorm in the upper ridges, but it's still early in the year. As long as the weather stays clear, perhaps tomorrow after—."

A twig snapped nearby, and I tensed, grabbing my knife hilt. As casually as I could, I scanned the shadows between the trees and the canopy. A shadow moved.

"Brigit," I said, my voice even. "We aren't alone."

Chapter Eighteen

The shadow fell from the trees, landing in our campsite. Her hair was like spun gold, her pale skin ruddy from the cold. Around her shoulders was the pelt of an animal—a wolf.

"Your cargo," she purred, walking to our fire. "Hand it over."

"Not this time, vermin," Brigit said, looking to me. "I came with reinforcements."

More movement in the trees—I counted at least five more. Slowly, I rose to my feet. "I don't want to hurt you. So just be on your way."

She chuckled and kicked the fire. Did she throw something into it? "I've been watching you, Forcadelian. The mountain's already half-defeated you. Besides," she grinned, "I, too, have reinforcements."

The others fell from the trees—I'd miscounted, there were ten. Or fifteen. I squinted but had a hard time distinguishing between person and tree.

"See? She can't even handle herself up here." The girl turned to Brigit. "I'll ask again. A third time and I'll take your life as punishment for your disrespect."

"Girl, get yourself together," Brigit spat at me. "And I would rather give up my life than willingly give anything to you creatures."

Katya's worried eyes flashed through my mind. "Don't test me," I said, trying to sound tough, but there was a burning sensation in my throat. I coughed roughly, rubbing my eyes and struggling to maintain my breath and sanity. This wasn't just altitude. There was something else. Something Nestori.

With heavy limbs, I stumbled over to the carriage to retrieve the bow and arrow, but I only had the two arrows. I'd planned on making more, but I'd left my mind back in the lowlands.

"Look out!"

I moved almost too late as a sword landed where my shoulder had been. I fell onto my back, the thrill of battle jarring me out of my stupor. The blade came for me again, and I batted it away with my knife, swinging my leg around and knocking the attacker onto their rear. Almost by instinct, I drove the knife into his shoulder, pinning him to the carriage for now.

"Now," I said, straightening and facing the girl who'd come for us. "Where were we?"

"You were surrendering," she said with a knowing smile. "Or do you want to experience pain like you've never felt before?"

I snorted. "You're going to have to do better than that."

And just like that, I was back in my element. With a smirk, I jumped into the carriage, grabbed the bow, nocked the arrow, and sent it flying into the tree. A cry of pain echoed, and a man fell from the tree, the arrow in his shoulder. Two were out, but more seemed to appear every second.

"What are you doing?" Brigit cried, holding onto the reins of the bucking horse. "*Kill them!*"

I didn't have time to respond as the first girl was back, livid and swinging wildly with her sword. I parried with my other knife, blocked, but couldn't get far enough away to land a disarming blow.

And then, suddenly, she stopped, giving me a knowing look. "You've got the look of someone who's made a few mistakes."

"What's that supposed to mean?" I said, gripping my sword and ready for whatever mind games she was playing.

"The Mother has a gift for you."

She pulled something out of her pocket—a powder—and blew hard, sending a cloud of white into my eyes and nose. I coughed, taking a step back. My eyes burned, my throat burned, and I rubbed my face as quickly as I could.

"What in the Mother was…"

My voice died in my throat. Before my eyes, the woman's face shifted—elongated. The trees grew dark—black as night and as tall as mountains. I fell backward, landing hard on my hands as I craned my neck, watching this giant wolf prowl amongst the trees.

But these trees were no longer Niemenian. They'd morphed. I was back in Celia's forest, the black sky flashing with lightning. Whistles echoed around me as I swung my sword wildly. It connected with a body, and when I turned to see who, my heart froze in my chest. Oleander, the royal guard I'd killed when I was fifteen, lay on the ground, an arrow in his chest. But as I fell to my knees beside him, he changed into Tasha, the butcher's son.

Someone was screaming, far away. "*The leaf, girl! Use the leaf!*"

A wolf stood between the two of us, cackling and taunting me. *Murderer. Murderer.* I looked around as more bodies lay before me, a battlefield full of death.

"Brynn."

Felix was walking toward me, his blue uniform dark with blood. He fell to his knees as a dark shadow approached from behind.

"Felix! Look out!" I screamed as the shadow raised her sword. She was me...

"Use the leaf!"

"What?"

"The *leaf!*" the shadow was screaming, but it wasn't my voice. It was Brigit's.

The leaf—the small satchel in my pocket. With thick fingers, I wrapped my fingers around the bag and yanked it from my belt. I turned it over and a sprinkle of dark green pieces fell out and I plucked one from the ground, clumsily sticking it in my mouth.

Immediately, a tart, bitter taste filled my mouth. My mind swam, but then cleared, as quickly as fog in the heat of a bright sun. Tears flooded my eyes and I blinked hard. The world faded from the dark, terrifying one of my dreams into the dull, cold world of the Niemenian forest. The wolf returned to a woman, and the dead bodies faded into nothing.

"No matter," the woman said, pulling out her sword. "We'll kill you by force."

I jumped to my feet, ready to engage. Then my eyes cleared more, revealing the woman to be no more than a girl. The others, five of them, were barely thirteen. There didn't seem to be an adult amongst them.

"They're kids," I said, looking to Brigit for confirmation.

"Don't let their youth fool you, Larissa," she said. "They're deadly."

"They aren't deadly. They're desperate," I said. "Using Nestori magic to trick us."

"You'll have more to worry about than us, then," Brigit snarled. "The Mother will punish you for using her magic to rob and steal."

The girl reared back, fear flashing across her face. I took her momentary distraction to pin her to the tree with an arrow. I took care to avoid her shoulder, but her pelt was big enough to keep her pinned to the tree.

"What's the meaning of this?" the girl wolf snarled, ripping at her pelt. She'd either have to lose the pelt or stay there, and I was fairly sure she wasn't going to give up her fur.

"Does your clan elder know you're using the Mother's magic this way?" I asked the girl softly.

Immediately, she reared back in fear but shook it off. "Who cares? I won't go back empty-handed."

I turned to Brigit, who was still snarling at the bleeding children as if they'd attack at any moment. There was a way for all parties to get out of this, but I had to be careful. "Can you spare one pelt?"

"W-what?" She shook her head violently. "No way."

"What's your game, Forcadelian?" the wolf asked.

"You won't go back empty-handed, but you're clearly outmatched," I said. "If you continue to fight, I'll have no choice but to kill you."

She swallowed, her pale face determined.

"But I'm willing to offer you a deal," I said. "I'll send you back to your clan with one pelt and your lives. And you will leave us be on the rest of the trip."

"What?" Brigit cried.

"I don't understand," the girl said, casting me a wary look. "Why would you let us live?"

I smiled. "Because you'll have to explain your wounds to your elders. Think of this as your comeuppance for using the Mother's magic for evil."

It was a roll of the dice, but I had a hunch these kids were operating outside their clan's rules. They knew they were outnumbered, but youthful ignorance would get them killed. Best to send them back to their elders with their tails between their legs and the fear of the Mother in their hearts.

I walked to the boy who was pinned to our carriage and pressed my hand to his shoulder. "This will hurt. One...two..."

I yanked the blade out and his screams echoed into the night. I caught him as he tumbled forward then carried him to the older girl, who watched me with a wild curiosity.

"I don't get it," she said. "Why won't you kill us?"

"Because," I said, pulling the arrow and freeing her from the tree, "that's not what I do." I looked to Brigit, whose face was a mask of fury. "Get the wagon together. We're going on."

We traveled by lamplight for another hour. Brigit's anger was palpable, even in the darkness, but perhaps she was too angry even to speak. Finally, when we'd put enough distance between ourselves and the wolves, we stopped and made a small fire.

"They'll be back," she said as I took my seat across from her. "And when they do return, they'll not only take my cargo, but my life."

"You're welcome for getting us both out of there unscathed tonight," I said, leaning back against the tree. "And they won't be back."

"How do you know?"

"The girl wouldn't speak the truth, but her actions were loud enough," I said. "She was afraid when I said she'd have to tell her elders what she'd been doing. And even more so when you said the Mother would punish her for her actions. My guess is that they've been tasked with retrieving pelts for their elders and have been picking off travelers instead of killing and skinning them themselves."

Brigit chewed on her pipe. "Did you learn that as the vigilante?"

"No," I said quietly. "I learned that when I was a thief just like them." I chuckled as I rubbed my eyes, which were still raw from the powder. "Though I've never seen that powder they used. What was it?"

"Hyblatha."

I did a double-take. "Hyblatha? As in the flower used in calming tea?"

"The flower is used in teas and tinctures, but the seed is more potent and poisonous," she said. "It causes hallucinations. The wolf idea was already planted in your mind, and the powder merely enhances that thought. That's why she asked you about mistakes. I'm sure whatever you saw in your hallucination was exactly what she wanted you to see."

I shivered, trying to erase Felix's bloody body from my mind. "Yeah, well, it worked. Thanks, by the way, for the antidote."

"That's tinneum," she said. "We use it to cure all kinds of ails, from fever dreams to illness and even the panics." She pulled down her upper lip to show me the small leaf pressed against her gum. "I'd be shaking in my skin if I didn't have this right now."

I pulled the bag from my belt and inhaled. "Is it okay if I keep this bag?"

She nodded. "What did you see that scared you so much?"

"A giant wolf."

"No," she said. "There was something else. Something that shook you to your core. Wolves are fearsome, but that was a soul-shattering terror on your face."

I exhaled, the image coming back into my mind. "A few years ago, when I was a thief, I was sent on my first mission alone. I killed a man. A royal guard."

"First time?"

I nodded. "I couldn't get his face out of my mind. So I returned to Forcadel to apologize to his family. I was going to turn myself in." I tilted my gaze upward. "Instead, the Mother saw fit to put a different path in front of me. I used the skills Celia taught me to help a woman. I decided that, instead of rotting away in a dungeon, I could use my skills to do good. Make Forcadel a safer place."

"And you saw that man?" Brigit said.

I nodded. "But he had a different face." Tasha had been the boy I'd been physical with for a few years, the son of the butcher where I'd swept during my Veil days. He and his parents had been killed when Ilara's bombs landed in their butchery. Their deaths were as much on my hands as Oleander's.

"Is that why you wouldn't kill those wolves?" she asked.

"I'm capable of resolving problems without taking a life," I said quietly. "It just takes patience."

"You know, one day you'll have to kill again, especially if you're going to war for your princess," Brigit said.

To that, I had still no good answers, so I looked at my hands. "Maybe I can just use some of that root on the kingdom. Make them hallucinate until I take over."

She made a small noise then said, "Perhaps. Or you can sprinkle them with a little bit of your optimism if you believe that the wolves are going to leave me alone."

I didn't respond; however, I'd seen our newfound friends following us in the trees. And they didn't bother us at all.

Chapter Nineteen

Felix

"Who in the Mother's name is letting people through?" Ilara bellowed from the golden throne.

A woman with gray hair was visibly trembling as she stood in front of Ilara. I'd been summoned to speak with the queen, but when I'd arrived, Ilara had barely gotten a word in before we'd been interrupted by this harried-looking messenger.

"I-I'm sorry, Y-your Majesty," the woman stammered, taking a step back.

Vernice placed a calming hand over Ilara's and whispered something to her. Ilara glared angrily at her councilor, but then seemed to relax a little.

"Tell me what you know," she snapped.

"T-there have been about fifty ships in the past week," the messenger said, twisting her hands together "Th-the gate master said that all of them had...well, they had your seal. A-apparently, it was stolen a few weeks ago and someone used it to..."

I tried not to smile. Brynna's handiwork, perhaps? But Ilara's fury was palpable, and I said a small prayer for whomever had allowed it to occur.

"Who's in charge there?" Ilara said. "In Skorsa?"

The messenger cowered before the queen, her gaze falling to the ground. "I believe, Your Majesty, that it was the local mayor, Kelsor—"

"Have him hanged," she snapped. "Or thrown into the river, I don't care. But I want him *gone*."

The messenger nodded.

"And I want it clear—explicitly—that the gates are to be opened for *no one*." She sniffed loudly, pacing in front of her chair. "Vernice, what about Neveri?"

She started. "What about Neveri?"

"Are ships coming and going from there?" she asked.

"I...I haven't heard they are," she said. "But I assume not—"

Ilara stopped in the middle of the room, and dread dripped down the back of my spine as I predicted what she would say next.

"Give the order, Lady Vernice. I would like the gate at Neveri *closed*. Permanently."

I said a silent prayer as Vernice gasped in horror.

"Close the gate at Neveri, Your Highness?" Vernice said with a nervous laugh. "I must object."

"Oh, of course you object," Ilara snapped, looking more like a toddler than a queen. "You're more loyal to Kulka than to me."

"I am Forcadelian first," Vernice said, her cheeks flaming. "But Neveri...those gates were never meant to be closed. I'm not even sure they can—"

"Then I suggest you find out," she said.

She licked her lips. "But more importantly, if you close the gates in Neveri, you will permanently cut off trade between Kulka and Forcadel. It could cause repercussions with our alliances—"

"What alliances?" she asked. "Neshua has not accepted me as queen. What do I care if I close my border to him?"

Vernice opened and closed her mouth, looking to me for help. But I was smarter than to get in the middle of this.

Ilara crossed her arms over her chest. "Prepare a trip to Neveri. I want to watch those gates close with my own eyes. Remind the people who's queen." She pointed her finger at the messenger. "Find Maarit and tell her to get a boat ready. We're leaving this afternoon."

"Of course," the woman said, clearly ecstatic to be released from the room. As she passed me, Ilara's attentions finally landed and I girded myself for more of her anger.

"Where were we, Felix?" she asked, her anger evaporating in the space of a few minutes. When a smile curled onto her face, my stomach dropped. "I had called you to discuss the number of soldiers we had in the city as of late. But...it appears a solution has dropped itself in my lap."

"Ma'am?" I said.

"You will reassign the newly graduated cadets to Neveri," she said, without missing a beat. "You and Lieutenant Kellis are to accompany me to the city to get them settled." She smiled. "Unless you have any objections?"

I hated to lose fifty soldiers, especially ones I'd had a close hand in training, but I couldn't see a better place for them. Out of sight, out of mind.

"No, Your Majesty. We'll make arrangements shortly."

Neveri was the one speck of dry land in a seemingly never-ending marsh. Its position close to the mouth of the Vanhoja river and nearness to the Kulkan border made it a strategic asset to Forcadel. Most ships from the farming country took their passage through the gates then to Neveri, before continuing down to the city of Forcadel.

Unlike Skorsa's gate, which was easily lifted and lowered,

Neveri's doors were only to be closed in times of great peril to Forcadel. In the six hundred years since they'd been built, there had been no peril so great.

Ilara, however, was using them to satisfy her own whims. It made me sick. Still, I could say nothing that the entire Council hadn't already attempted. Even Ilara's mild-mannered Severian aide had tried, but she wasn't to be dissuaded.

When her ship sidled up to the dock in Neveri, a crowd had already gathered—egged on, presumably, by the Severian guards who stood behind them. None of them seemed pleased to be there.

"Announcing Her Highness, Queen Ilara Hipolita Särkkä of the Kingdom of Severia," Maarit called to the crowd.

None of the Forcadelian crowed moved to bow.

"Is the custom in this nation not to bow before your queen?" Ilara bellowed. "Or are you just deaf?"

The Severian guards turned to the villagers, and some went for their swords. I gripped the ledge of the ship, knowing I was outnumbered, but I wouldn't let Ilara kill innocents because they wouldn't *bow* to her. But, after a tense moment, one by one, they showed deference.

"That's better," Ilara said, walking off the ship with her head held high. "Clearly, this city is in need of guidance," Ilara said to Maarit. "I look forward to seeing what you'll do here."

My eyes widened as hope surged through my veins. Maarit was being reassigned to Neveri? It was almost too good to be true.

"I plan to establish a real curfew," Maarit said. "And we will inspect every carriage that comes in and out of this city and document visitors and citizens alike. This city will become a model for what Forcadel could be."

"Hm." Ilara turned to me. "Are *you* mandating that visitors be documented, Captain Llobrega?"

"I am not," I replied. Mostly because I thought it to be illegal, immoral, and a complete disrespect of everything Forcadel stood for. "I don't believe it's an effective use of time. We get so many visitors, between the ships coming in and out, the travelers on foot —it would be a nightmare trying to keep it all straight."

"I see." Ilara turned back to the front. "I suppose I can understand that. This city is much smaller. But perhaps if Captain Maarit can get this city to behave, she might be able to help you with Forcadel."

With their backs turned, I chanced a look up to the Mother for help then over to Riya on the other side of the ship. As long as I maintained control of the guards in the castle, Maarit would never take over the city entirely. But I prayed for those souls in this city for what was about to come to them.

We rode into the city, the crowds of people lining the streets to see the queen, but nary a friendly face amongst them. I'd been to Neveri once, as a young cadet accompanying August and his father as they met with the Kulkan king. Then, my role had been as playmate and psuedo-chaperone to the young prince, although we'd managed to escape our guards and run around a bit before we'd gotten caught. The city was as unfamiliar to me now as it had been then, but even still, I could tell things were different.

"Felix, what do you think of Neveri?" Ilara asked, looking over her shoulder. "Is it not the most disgusting city you've ever laid eyes on?"

"It has its charms. Perhaps you just need to see more of it." I kept my gaze forward, looking for trouble, and somewhat hoping for it. I glanced to the rooftops, searching for a glimpse of a mask and a cloak. But she was on the other side of the country; she wouldn't be here in Neveri.

And yet...

My breath caught in my throat at the sight of Brynna staring back at me. It was one of those coronation posters that had been commissioned, but they'd turned it into a memorial. A hundred candles had been placed around the poster, hanging from the wall in the marketplace. Women passed by, bowing their heads in prayer, and a few wiping away tears.

"Maarit," Ilara said in a clipped tone.

"Of course," Maarit said, looking behind her to where Jorad stood. "You, take this down."

He hesitated, looking to me for guidance. Clenching my jaw, I nodded slightly. Still, he moved slower than he should have as he approached the memorial.

I watched the crowd instead of the destruction, feeling every flinch and angry cry in my gut. This town was already loosely in her grip; if she wasn't careful, she'd squeeze them right into mutiny.

"There," Ilara said, adjusting herself in the saddle. "Your new queen is here now. No need to mourn the old one."

Either she was stupid or oblivious, because the death glares she got in return were telling enough.

After making sure the local innkeeper at the Wicked Duck was well-versed in Ilara's tastes, Riya and I settled downstairs to drown our sorrows in a bottle of whiskey. After all, I wasn't going to take a break from my alcoholism just because I was traveling. Or so I'd tell them.

But seeing Brynna's memorial torn down—along with knowing what we'd witness tomorrow when the gates closed—had settled poorly in my stomach. My gaze caught on a painting of Neveri on the wall; open and free, the river filled with boats of all shapes and sizes.

"I can't believe she's really going to do it," Riya said. "Does she not know people are going to starve if we can't get food from Kulka?"

"Hopefully, this won't last very long," I said, but even I had my doubts. It had been weeks since I'd seen Brynna, and I had no idea where she was. I'd been debating whether to tell her that Brynna was alive, and hopefully amassing an army the likes of which had never been seen. But as much as I trusted Riya, the more people who knew, the more risk I would introduce. And Brynna needed all the help she could get.

"I hope Jo didn't go out under the mask," she said softly. "I'm worried about her back there with Coyle. You don't think he'll just arrest her without proof, do you?"

"Things aren't that bad yet," I said. "And if he did, I'd intervene. I'd rather her think it's me than pin it on any of you."

She sighed and shook her head. "I'm worried, though. Coyle might—"

"It'll be all right. The sun always rises," I said, looking at my hands. "Maybe if I'm lucky, Ilara will reassign me here, too."

"Don't say that," Riya replied, pouring herself another drink. "You may not see the writing on the wall, Felix, but I do. Assigning your guards here puts them out of your purview."

"There are still Forcadelians back home," I said.

"For how long?" Riya replied. "She's trying to isolate you so that when she *does* take you out, there'll be no one left in the city to give a crap."

I opened my mouth and poured the whiskey down, enjoying the burn. "Then I'll do what I can to protect the city until that day comes."

The next morning, nursing something of a hangover, I accompanied Ilara and Maarit on the riverboat toward the gates to witness their closing. Riya and I had commiserated as much as we could the night before, but as we departed the dock, I couldn't help the pang of sadness that echoed from my chest.

The river gates rose out of the dense fog, and a light drizzle fell on the deck. They were made of Niemenian iron, which didn't rust in the brackish water in which it sat. There were two gate houses and large, black chains that rested in the river on either side. Gearworks inside the fortresses used water to pull the chain either way—or so I read in a book once. Now, a long line of warships sat in the mouth of the river, preventing entry from the sea beyond.

"Close them," Ilara said with a smile.

Maarit waved her hand, and a loud blast of trumpet echoed toward the shore.

After a few moments of silence, there was a groaning in the distance, and the water rippled. The chains that had been hanging for generations tightened, rising out of the water as the hydraulics in the gate houses pulled them taut. Once they were straight, the gate itself moved, almost imperceptibly at first, and then the edges drifted toward the center. My heart pounded as the gap between the two sides grew smaller.

The edges of the gate met in the center, sending a ripple across the water that reverberated through my body. Forcadel was truly closed now, and I could only hope we weren't causing irreversible damage to what was once a proud, prosperous country.

A palpable exhalation echoed from those onboard the ship as the waves settled, and three of the Forcadelian guards looked away from the sight.

"There now," Ilara said with a triumphant smile. "Let's see any ships get past *that*."

"Very good, Your Majesty," Maarit said.

"I expect a weekly report," Ilara said. "Perhaps you can have Lieutenant Kellis pen it."

I started, sharing a look with Riya, who seemed as confused as I was. "I'm sorry, Your Majesty?" she asked.

"Oh, I suppose I forgot to mention it," Ilara said with a look that said she hadn't forgotten at all. "I'm reassigning you to Captain Maarit's command here in Neveri. Felix seems to have things under control in Forcadel." She smiled at me. "I hope you can spare her. I've sent your other lieutenant, Joella, to help in Skorsa."

At that, I couldn't mask my surprise. "When?"

"I assume she's already on a boat. Coyle recommended her," she said, a smile curling on her face. "After all, she's one of the best, because she's one of yours. Isn't that right?"

Fury shot through my veins, and it took everything inside me not to rip my sword out and fling it at her. Riya had gone pale, too, but maintained her cool. They'd been inseparable since childhood, and now they'd be on opposite sides of the country. There was no need for it, either. Just cruelty.

"Of course," I forced out. "Whatever you need, Your Majesty."

She quirked a brow, and with every inch of me on fire with disgust and hatred, I pressed my fist to my breast and bowed slightly.

The smile on Ilara's face was nothing but sadistic.

Chapter Twenty

Our journey continued for another three days—up mountains and through valleys—and after the first day, our wolf shadows stopped following us. I almost thought Brigit had a begrudging respect for the way I'd handled the situation, but I could've just been seeing things.

Midmorning on the fourth day, we crested a hill and came into a vast valley with houses, buildings, roads, and a tall, gray castle rising toward the sky in the center of the city. We joined a main road, paved with milled stone, and I let myself gawk as we entered Linden. There were more carriages with furs like ours, some much finer than the ones Brigit had. I was actually warmer than I'd been in days, so I pulled my gloves off and opened my cloak to let the cooler, dry air in.

"Three days in the mountains, and you're already acting like a Niemenian," Brigit said as I stashed my gloves in my bag.

"I may melt when I return to Forcadel," I said with a hearty laugh. *If I return...*

We passed a large, golden arch built into the mountainside, with three heavily-armed guards standing in front of it.

"What's that?" I asked.

"The underground road from Aymar," Brigit said, a little longingly, then shook her head. "People who pay to use it are morons."

I'd been around her long enough to read between the lines. "If I figure out a way to Ariadna's court, I'll see what I can do to get you passage onto the royal road."

"Don't hold your breath," she muttered.

Brigit drove the carriage into the center of town, to a bustling market. While she bartered with the man for a table to sell her wares, I fed and watered the horse using the last of our grain and a nearby trough. Out the corner of my eye, I saw Brigit hand over twenty gold coins—all she'd brought. It truly was do or die for them.

I patted the horse on the nose and acted like I hadn't seen when she walked back over.

"I can take it from here," Brigit said gruffly.

I thought I should stay and help but decided against it. "Do you know where the nearest mess hall is?"

"Mess hall?" She blinked as if I was speaking another language.

"Er...dining hall?" Another blank stare. "A place to purchase food to eat?"

"Oh, you mean the ruoka? It's down the street. Take two lefts then one right. On Upskala." She plucked a fox fur off the top and handed it to me. "Take this."

"I can't," I said, pushing it back into her arms. "You need this."

"You saved me more trouble by taking care of those wolves." She reached into her pocket. "At least take this silver. I'll make twice that with the pelts you helped me bring through the forest. It's the least I can do."

"Thank you," I said, clutching it to my chest. "And thanks for everything."

She grunted and took a pile of furs toward an empty table in the center of the market.

The mess hall was a black wooden building with a tall pitched roof, like all the others. When I walked inside, I was greeted by long tables and the stench of beer. Burly, fair-skinned men and women looked up at me as I stood in the doorway. I peeled myself away from the door, keeping my head down until I was ready to be seen. At the front of the room, a large pot of stew bubbled, so I joined the queue at the back, plucking a wooden bowl from the set.

"Long way from home, sweetheart," breathed a gravelly voice behind me.

"But it's a short distance from my knife to your gut, so back off," I snapped, not bothering to turn around. I'd learned my lesson in Aymar. Instead, I paid the remainder of my money to the woman at the front.

My new friend hovered behind me as I ladled stew into a bowl, his putrid breath clouding around my head. I turned my attention to the rest of the room, searching somewhere I could safely hide in plain sight, while still hearing enough conversation to be worth my while.

When a hand brushed my ass, I put the bowl down and pulled my knife from my hip. I pressed the blade into whatever soft part of him it had reached.

"I warned you once. This is twice. If there's a third time, you will lose it."

His hand disappeared.

I sheathed the knife and picked up my tray, continuing to the spot I'd picked out before I'd been rudely interrupted. I felt the eyes of a few diners on me, but I didn't look at them. I settled into my seat and stared into my stew. It didn't look all that appetizing —grouse and soggy potatoes—but it was warm.

"Forcadel?" the man across from me grunted.

I nodded, grateful the citizens of Linden were chattier than those back in Aymar. "Just in."

"Don't surprise me. Too much going on down there. You hear about that queen?"

Again, I nodded. "Shame, that. Ruined the whole country."

"That's what they do," he said. "The royal folk play chess with our lives and we all suffer, eh?"

I tried not to wince. This was the second time I'd heard this refrain, and it was hard to keep denying it. But perhaps it would be a good segue into the conversation I needed. "Yeah. Especially that Luard, right?"

"Luard!" He barked a laugh. "He's the worst of the bunch. Think he's trying to bed every woman in the city."

"Yeah?" I said, pushing a potato from one side of the bowl to another. "They let the prince out at night?"

"Can't cage him!" the man said, louder than I'd wanted. But he was already halfway done with his tankard, and based on his ruddy cheeks, it wasn't his first.

I chewed on a particularly tough bit of meat. "So, I'm new in town. Looking for a thrill, I guess. Know anywhere the women are pretty?"

He grinned, exposing his four missing teeth. "You'll want to avoid the Hanger, then. Girls there aren't much to look at."

I nodded. "I like my girls high quality. Where does your prince go?"

"Oh, for that, you'll be wanting to visit the Frille," he said. "But make sure to bring your coin. They cater to the royal family, so they don't come cheap." He made a face. "Heh."

I tried not to snort at the double entendre. "I would've thought they'd frown on that. Royal purity and all that."

"Ariadna does, but nobody can control Prince Luard. He's like a wildcat. A man with too much money and nothing to do, if you get my drift."

"The worst kind of person," I said. "Thanks for the tip."

Night had fallen and so had the temperature. It was a struggle to keep my teeth from chattering, so I pulled my gloves back on and my hood over my head. I tried not to think about what might happen if I didn't find Luard tonight—or worse, he didn't take me back to that frigid-looking castle in the distance.

I found the bar and waited in the alley across the street. After my toes had gone numb, a black carriage with fine white horses rolled up to the place. There were too many footmen dressed in what I assumed were the Niemenian royal colors to be a normal visitor. When the doors opened, Katarine's brother Luard stepped out, a bright smile on his face.

The two siblings shared some features—sharp cheekbones, pale blue eyes, blond hair—but that was where the similarities stopped. Where my Kat was calculating, prim, and very private, Luard seemed content to spread himself all over the world. His laugh carried in the alley; clearly, he wasn't worried about people knowing he was visiting a dance hall.

As he made his way inside, I unfroze my brain to develop a new plan to get inside. Back in Forcadel, I'd frequented a place called Titta's. I'd done a favor for her some years back, and so she'd let me prowl in her club for my criminals. I didn't have time to garner favor with the owner of the place, so I'd have to sneak in and hope for the best.

Or else my toes might just fall off.

The door was unlocked, and the space inside was dark, heavily perfumed, and filled with nearly-naked bodies. I kept to the outside of the room to avoid attention, making a beeline to one of the wicker baskets overflowing with clothes and grabbing the first thing I could get my hands on. There was a line of curtained changing spaces along the other wall, so I quickly crossed the room and closed the curtains behind me.

The space was barely big enough to stand, but a hanging mirror on the wall gave me my first good look at myself in a while.

My black hair frizzed around my face, pieces of my plait falling out in big chunks. I also had some hay and grass sticking to me, probably from sleeping in Brigit's barn. I hadn't taken a bath in... too long.

Princess, I surely was not. But perhaps I could make myself a little more appealing.

I undressed and folded the dirty tunic neatly. Then, carefully, I unbound my breasts. They were annoyingly large for what I needed most days—running with them was a veritable pain in the back— but when I needed to use my body to get what I wanted, they were up to the task.

The small gold coin around my neck glinted in the dim light. Felix's Forcadelian seal—I'd almost forgotten I was wearing it. I thought about removing it and leaving it with the rest of my things, but it was too precious to part with.

Leaving it be, I slipped on the garment I'd grabbed. It was more robe than dress, opening to the navel. The wide sleeves fell down to my hands, and there were two slits that came up to my hips. There would be no place to hide my weapons, so I stashed them behind the mirror with my old clothes.

Next, my hair. I undid the plait and brushed my fingers through it as best I could. Then quickly braided it back and stuck the tail under the robe. To complete the outfit, I wrapped a scarf around my head, hiding my dark hair somewhat. I was still obviously Forcadelian, but if I moved quickly, no one would stop me.

With my head down, I walked toward the main room.

"Hey, wait!"

I froze, steeled myself, then turned around. "Yes?"

"You can't go out there without a tray. You know that," the old woman said, thrusting a serving tray into my hands. "How are you going to bus drinks without it?"

"Right," I said with a bashful smile. "Thanks. Still learning."

It took me about three seconds to realize why the woman considered me wait staff and not a dancer. They were completely nude. All of them, men and women, waltzing and undulating without one speck of clothing on.

"Uh...huh."

I tore my eyes away from a particularly well-endowed man dancing on the table as Luard's laugh echoed in the space. I followed the source of the sound to the center table, where Luard had three naked women sitting next to him. It was truly a feat that he appeared to be giving them equal attention, bouncing from one to the other with a catty smile.

"Here." An older woman leaned onto my shoulder and slipped her hand across my bare ass. "Take this, sweetie."

I winced as she squeezed my ass but couldn't argue with the silver coin she placed on the tray. "Thanks."

Her hand went to my scarf, pulling it off. Suddenly, her drunk eyes widened. "You're one of them—"

"Gotta go." I spun on my heel, trying my best to disappear into the crowd. I'd wasted too much time already, and if they were looking for a strange Forcadelian, I was the only one matching that description. Luard's table was just a few feet away, but the crowd was thick around him.

"*Stop her!*"

Behind me, the woman was now been flanked by three guards. It was now or never.

Dropping the tray, I roughly elbowed my way through, nearly losing my robe in the process. With every person I pushed, another three took their place, laughing and talking without a care in the world. I doubled my efforts, pushing aside the dancing and imbibing clients with desperation.

Someone stepped on my robe, and I felt it slipping away. I yanked myself free and fell, face-first, into Luard's table.

"What in the Mother's name!" Luard cried, standing up as drinks and glass flew everywhere.

"Hey." I grinned at him. "Remember me?"

Luard's gaze was on my bare ass. "I don't know, sweetie, you got..." As his eyes traveled up to my face, the color drained from his. "Holy Mother..."

"Prince Luard, we're so sorry we let this—"

"Stand down, boys," Luard said, his grin growing with every passing moment. "And someone get this princess some clothes!"

"I mean..." He rubbed the back of his neck.

"I honestly don't believe this is the best idea, either," I said, crossing my arms over my chest as the black cloud of indecision came back with a vengeance. "If I do nothing, Ilara will continue to destroy the country. From what I've heard, it's about to erupt into anarchy." I sighed. "I can't let my people go through that."

"So you'd rather go to war?"

"If I can avoid it, no."

"And how do you plan to depose a queen without bloodshed?" He tilted his head to the side, as if I were speaking nonsense.

"I'm working on it," I said with an impatient wave. "Just... help me meet with your sister. That's all I'm asking for."

Luard sighed loudly. "What you need, my dear, is a plan. And aren't you so lucky that Kitty-Kat sent you to the most brilliant strategist in Niemen?" He rose to his feet and extended his hand. "Let's head back to the castle. I've already sent a messenger ahead to draw for a special bath for you. And perhaps a de-lousing."

"Ha-ha."

I had my doubts about Luard's self-proclaimed accolades, but I couldn't deny it felt better to be speeding through Niemen in a carriage covered in furs than walking through the unfamiliar streets. If I closed my eyes, I could almost imagine myself back in Forcadel. Save the freezing temperatures.

"How did you get out of Forcadel?" I asked. "When Ilara invaded."

"Kat and I were having a private dinner, per your request, and she helped me find a safe space in the castle before the guards came for her," he said grimly. "The Severians found me in some hidden room and kept me well fed until Katarine returned." He looked at me, all levity gone. "I refused to leave until I knew she was all right, but she insisted I get out as soon as Ilara would allow it. She told me she watched you bleed to death. She was devastated."

I nodded, shame bringing warmth to my face and tears to my eyes. "Katarine looked well, when I saw her. Surprised to see me alive, of course. I wish…" I sighed. "I wish she wasn't stuck there, playing tutor. I'd much rather she was as far away from Ilara as possible."

"Ilara wouldn't do anything to risk open war with Niemen. Katarine may be our youngest sister, but she's still royalty. And even if Ilara's being an absolute shit to her, there's still the possibility that Ilara and Ariadna might mend some fences."

I hoped that was a distant possibility.

We arrived at the castle, even more formidable and dark up close, but with Luard by my side, it seemed a little homey, especially when we were greeted by roaring fires in the main hall. Luard led me to his so-called "small" suite on the third floor, which was anything but.

"Ten bedrooms, a personal dining room, a small library I've never set foot in once, a lovely sauna and bath area that you're welcome to, and, of course, this sitting room."

I stood in the middle and took it all in. Vaulted ceilings with mahogany wood rafters. Beautiful crystal chandeliers with flickering candles. The dark wood theme extended to a hand-carved set of chairs, a mantle over a brick fireplace, and to the frames of the paintings on the wall, which were of very naked women.

"Well, at least you're consistent," I said, eyeing the one closest to me.

"I love a woman's body," he said with a satisfied smile. "But don't worry, I know better than to try anything with you. Even if you did serve yourself up to me."

"I'm sure," I said dryly. "Presumably because I smell like the inside of a barn?"

He pointed to the bathing room. "Be gone with you. Then perhaps we'll talk about your insane plan."

I took the most luxurious bath, filled with lavender-scented bubbles, and I washed weeks of grime and grit off. Luard's attendants even drained the bath after the first few minutes and allowed me to soak in clean water for another half hour. Finally, when my whole body was pruny, I dried off with the fluffiest towel and returned to the private bedroom Luard had given me. On the bed, fresh clothes were waiting, as well as a night shirt.

"Are you done yet?" Luard called.

"Coming," I said, pulling on the fresh clothes.

Luard was in the sitting room, his bare feet propped on the ottoman. There was a large dinner of chicken and vegetables waiting for me, and I unceremoniously dove in. I was halfway through my second chicken leg when I noticed the open letter sitting by Luard's side.

"Wasn't that addressed to your sister?" I asked nervously.

"Yes, and she was very happy to get it," he replied, turning over the page and reading the back of it. "Ariadna gets pissy when I keep things from her, so I ran upstairs and told her you'd arrived."

"And?" My heart pounded.

"And you're very lucky Katarine's an excellent writer." He half-smiled. "Ariadna wants to see you in the morning after breakfast."

I wasn't sure whether to be excited or terrified. "That's...great?"

"She wants to speak to you, but that doesn't mean she'll help." He rubbed his chin. "You might need to bring something more than just a request. What Forcadelian assets are you willing to give up? You'll need to dangle something truly juicy for her to bite."

"It didn't say in the letter?" I asked, plucking it off the table and scanning it. I caught brief mention of my intelligence and dedication to service, but no mention of Skorsa. "That's odd. Katarine told me to offer something, but I don't see it in here."

"Presumably, Katarine didn't feel it was her place to make concessions on your behalf," he said with a knowing smile. "Well, go on. What is it you want to give us? A new fleet of ships?

Another marriage for Kitty-Kat?" He gasped and clapped his hands. "Are you going to make that girlfriend of hers a lady and let the two of them get hitched?"

"Perhaps," I said, sitting back. "What would you offer?"

"Ah-hah," Luard said with a smile. "Well, seeing as you're on the other side of the negotiating table, I really shouldn't tell you how to win against my sister."

I fluttered my lashes, hoping I looked innocent enough. "But you said you'd help."

"I did, and for good reason, because you clearly have no mind for political strategy." He crossed his legs as he reclined in the chair. "I will say that the Severian queen has made a giant mess of things. There's a reason Forcadel is such an important trading partner. Almost all of our food comes via Forcadel, and now our ships can't get past Skorsa. Of course, our relationship with Kulka has always been strained, so that way's out. Ariadna's been worried about the cost of food for weeks now."

"So that's…good, right?" I asked with a little hope in my chest.

"For you, yes. For Niemen, no," Luard said. "Ilara closed all the borders because neither Ariadna nor King Neshua in Kulka will officially accept her as queen." He paused and leaned closer, lowering his voice. "Now, between you and me, Ariadna is wavering on that promise. But the way her eyes lit up when I told her you'd arrived…" He shrugged. "It may not be *impossible* that Ariadna sees a benefit to helping you."

I exhaled a little.

"She will, of course, want to know what you plan to *do* with those forces, should you get them." He tilted his head. "You can't honestly think you can get rid of Ilara without spilling some blood, do you?"

I looked away, deciding it was better to lie than to show my weakness. "No, of course not. I'll use whatever forces Ariadna gives me to take over the city, obviously."

"How?"

"...I don't know, march on it?" Military strategist, I was not.

Luard snorted. "You'd be the first, little princess. It's been tried by about a hundred Kulkan and Niemenian kings and all were thwarted by Forcadel's natural defenses. Even your Ilara had to sneak in."

"Then I'll sneak in, too," I said. "Felix mentioned there was discord. I'd use the extra forces to sow more of that."

"Discord is helpful." Luard nodded. "But you have to be careful you don't sow too much. Power vacuums are dangerous things, and the wrong person with the right sway can screw everything up." I didn't miss the short look he gave me. "How many soldiers do you bring to the fight?"

"There are still Forcadelian soldiers in the city who swear fealty to Felix, and they would return to my side," I said. "And perhaps... a hundred more in the forest."

"Well, that's not nothing, but you'll need more than just fomenting rebellion and marching on an impenetrable city by tomorrow." He rose and rested his hands on my shoulders. "I'm sure you're tired from the long journey, so why don't you run off to bed? You've got to lose those bags under your eyes before you meet the queen. Makeup will only do so much. And I'll call for my tailor, and maybe my jeweler can whip up a crown tonight."

"Actually," I said softly. "I'm not...technically royalty anymore, so there's no need for a crown."

"Oh, that's your first mistake," Luard said, tutting at me. "You are royalty, or else why are you asking Ariadna to help?"

I rested my hand against the door. "To be honest? I don't know. I've been asked that question more times than I can count, but I just can't come up with an answer that feels true." I shook my head. "Felix used to say that he'd rather have a queen who'd been protecting her kingdom from under a mask. He said I should do everything in my power to get my kingdom back, but..."

"All you'll be known as is a war-mongering princess who decided her crown was more important than people's lives."

Sarala's words came back to haunt me again. It had been easy to avoid thinking about the end of the road, especially as getting here had been in doubt for so long. But tomorrow I would be meeting with Ariadna, and I would have to decide what to do.

"Clearly, you've done above and beyond what was in your power to do," Luard said, rising to his feet. "But you're here now, so you might as well start acting like you *do* want the help you're asking for, or you won't get it."

I forced a smile onto my face. "I will."

But as I closed the door behind me, I hated that a small part of me hoped Ariadna would deny my request, relieving me of the decision I couldn't bring myself to make.

Chapter Twenty-Two

My anxiety was no match for the softest bed I'd slept on in weeks. I awoke to the sound of a servant placing a tray of breakfast food and a large carafe of coffee on the table in the corner. I was a little hesitant about to what the Niemenians considered good breakfast food—hopefully no more of that smelly fish Brigit ate—instead I found delicate pastries and a bowl of boiled, cold eggs. I ate my fill as the fire crackled in the hearth and enjoyed nearly the entire carafe before Luard came knocking.

"Good morning," he said, standing shirtless in front of the open window. "Appears you came on a good day."

He gestured to the window, and I could scarcely believe my eyes. The city had been blanketed by a sheet of white snow, giving it an ethereal, peaceful glow.

"I've never seen snow before," I breathed, pressing my hand to the cold glass.

"It'll last for a bit then all the horses and piss and shit will ruin it," he said. "But perhaps I'll take you out to the gardens to frolic after we meet with Ariadna." He looked at me. "If that's still what you want to do."

"Yes," I said with a firm nod that I still didn't feel. "You're right. What's the point of coming all this way if I don't finish what I started?"

"Excellent, because I've been up all morning thinking of the best way to use these forces you've spoken about. So get dressed and we'll chat."

Luard's tailor had sewn me a dress of light blue velvet and lace that was a little snug in the chest, but it would do for meeting the queen. It was paired with thick stockings and tall leather boots that I needed help lacing up. After I was dressed, two more ladies came in to do my hair and makeup.

"I'm afraid I don't have any foundation in your shade," she said, holding up a tray of lotions. "I'm sorry."

"It'll be fine," Luard said. "Just throw some red on her lips and we'll be on our way." He dipped his finger into one of the lotions and dabbed his nose, rubbing it in to hide some perceived blemish. "Oh, and one more thing."

He called out the open door to the receiving room, and one of his guards—Ivan was his name—came in with a black velvet box. Luard opened it, revealing a simple gold circlet, not unlike the one I'd worn back in Forcadel.

"You need this," he said, resting it gently on my head. "There, now you look like yourself."

As the women pinned it in place, I took in my appearance. I was a bit thinner than the last time I'd worn a crown, and the purple bags under my eyes were still present despite my long sleep. But Luard was right—the crown did make a difference. If only in how I carried myself.

"Well? Ariadna awaits," he said, holding out his arm.

Where the Forcadel castle was spread out across four levels, the

Linden castle was a maze with spiral staircases and what seemed like a thousand levels as we made our way toward Ariadna. I kept my sweaty palms pressed against the velvet.

"You're going to be fine," Luard said, looking over his shoulder. "I have prepped Ariadna, so she's already receptive. Just don't say anything stupid."

Saying something stupid wasn't what concerned me, but we'd arrived at a large set of doors with two Niemenian guards out front. They bowed to the royals then turned to open the doors. They scraped along the tile floor with a loud sound, making me wince and wonder if this whole castle could hear them.

The receiving room was actually quite small—smaller than the one I used to occupy. But there, in the center on a crystal throne, was Ariadna.

She was perhaps in her mid-forties, and carried a maternal swell in her lower stomach that she rested a pale, bejeweled hand on. Her bright blue eyes had focused on me the moment I'd walked into the room. I counted the steps until Luard stopped then raised my gaze to meet hers.

"My queen," Luard said, bowing from the hip.

I froze. Did I bow? Nod slightly? What was the protocol of one royal meeting another?

My heart thudded so loudly I was sure she heard it.

But she simply smiled with a kind look and pushed herself to stand. "Luard, I think I need to take a walk. Will you leave us for a bit?"

I didn't want him to go, but my tongue was stuck to the roof of my mouth. Luard walked away wordlessly, his soft footfalls echoing farther and farther away as I remained rooted to the spot. The doors behind me closed with a loud sound, and despite my best efforts, I jumped.

"You can exhale, you know," she said with a little chuckle. "I promise I won't behead you. After all, we are related through marriage."

I nodded, biting my tongue before the apology tumbled from it. "I suppose you're right."

She gingerly stepped off the dais and joined me in the center of the room. She rested her hands on my shoulders, pushing them down gently. "Brynna, please relax. I know why you're here and I'm willing to listen to you."

Something in her smile loosened the tension from the back of my mind. "All right. I'm...I guess I still don't know what I'm doing. Perhaps even less than when I sat on the throne."

"Oh, my love, none of us know what we're doing," she said, returning her hands to the swell of her stomach. "We just do the best we can with the information we have."

Much like with Luard, Ariadna's features and mannerisms reminded me of Katarine. The soft gaze, the quiet thinking, that slight pause before she spoke. It tugged at my heart. I hadn't even realized how much I missed my sister-in-law until just now.

"So, things are quite a mess down in Forcadel, aren't they?" Ariadna began as we walked down a long hallway.

"To put it lightly," I said. "How much do you know?"

"More than Ilara wants me to, I'm sure," she said. "And less than Katarine wants me to know, too. Most of her letters arrived already opened. What you provided me last night was the most enlightening I've received to date."

"The long and short of it is: Ilara came to my kingdom asking for help. I gave it to her, and she repaid me with a knife to the belly and the theft of my kingdom."

"And now you're here, asking me for help?" Ariadna asked lightly.

"I promise I won't stab you," I said with a nervous giggle.

"Well, that's good to hear," Ariadna said, rubbing her stomach with a soft smile. "Ilara informs me that she'll allow my ships entry when I accept her as queen of Forcadel."

"And..." I swallowed. "Why haven't you?"

"Because I don't like her, and I don't like being told what to do," she said. "The girl has a lot to learn if she wants to keep her position. Though from what Kitty-Kat tells me, she's not listening very well." She cast her gaze upon me. "Not that you did, either."

My face flushed. "I wasn't aware that you two spoke about me."

"Just idle chatter between sisters," Ariadna said. "She was, as you can imagine, devastated at the death of your brother. Even if they weren't romantically involved, she did care for him. From all her accounts, he was a good husband to her. And a better friend."

"I know," I replied softly. "And you have my word that if I reclaim the throne, Kat can continue to live as she pleases in my castle as my guest."

"*If* being the operative word," Ariadna replied. "What's your plan? What forces do you bring to the fight?"

I licked my lips, taking a breath to gather my thoughts and the information Luard had helped me prepare. "I have a hundred strong in the forest and Captain Llobrega promises the aid of the castle guard. My plan will be to use Niemenian forces to isolate the city through a blockade on the Ash river, and then use my forces to cut off the bay and the Vanhoja river on the other side."

"That sounds like a wonderful start to a plan," she said with a shake of her head. "But I still can't justify sending my ships down the river to help a foreign nation conduct a coup on a promise. After all, if I want the borders open, all I have to do is send a letter acknowledging Ilara's rightful ownership of Forcadel."

She could, but she hadn't. And I still had one ace up my sleeve, the city of Skorsa.

Yet, I hesitated. Up until now, this journey had been like being carried by a river, not resisting, but not helping myself along either. If I offered Skorsa, I'd be making a decision that this was the path I wanted.

Then again, I could offer and she could still refuse me.

"I am willing to allow you to take the city of Skorsa as thanks for your assistance," I said after a pause.

Ariadna tapped her bejeweled finger to her chin, deep in thought and I was actually relieved she didn't look too excited by the idea. "Even with Skorsa, it's a big ask. If you aren't successful, our alliance could jeopardize Niemen's relationship with Forcadel, perhaps permanently. It could result in all-out war between our countries."

I nodded, exhaling. "I understand."

"*However,*" Ariadna said, casting me a coy look over her shoulder. "If you get King Neshua on your side, and he agrees to provide half the forces you need, I'll send a fleet of ships to aid in your mission."

My mouth fell open, my emotions torn between that small glimmer of hope and complete dread. "Get Neshua on my side? As in, go to Kulka and beg him for help?"

"Yes," she said. "For you see, I may be biased because of our personal relationship through Kitty-Kat. But Neshua despises you for reneging on your marriage treaty. So if you convince him you have a shot then I'll believe helping you is worth the risk."

Convince Neshua? I was still convincing myself. But some part of me welcomed this new challenge. It was another delay, another distraction. Another leg to a journey I was rather hoping would never end.

"As a personal favor, I'll send Luard to accompany you to Delina," she said. "He needs some industry to keep him busy and I think this would be good for him. He's a brilliant man, but unfortunately, a little too wily when he's bored."

"I've noticed," I said with a dry laugh.

She smiled warmly, draping her arm over my shoulders. "Until you depart, I welcome you to enjoy Linden. Have Luard's guards take you on a tour around the city. We certainly have some of the best chocolates of the four countries."

I perked up, the memory of someone else telling me the same thing floating through my mind.

"Actually, Ariadna, I have…another small favor to ask."

It took Ariadna's people a few hours to locate Brigit. She had offloaded all her furs and spent the night in a boarding house. With two of Luard's guards escorting me, I rode in a carriage to the poorer side of the city, where I found Brigit preparing her wagon for departure.

I wiped the smile from my face as her eyebrows shot up. I stepped out, trying for an air of seriousness, but unable to keep the corners of my mouth from twitching. Luard insisted that I wear the gold circlet around town, and it was no surprise that Brigit's attention went to it.

"If you expect me to bow, I won't do it."

"I think we're way past bowing," I said, walking over to her. "Besides that, I'm not even royalty anymore. Although I do apologize for not telling you."

"It's understandable, considering the circumstances." She cast a look at my clothes, a new tunic and fine leather boots under a thick black cloak. "Did you have a chat with Ariadna?"

"I did," I said, deciding not to share any more, in case word got back to Forcadel. "And her brother Luard. He's one of those fancy princes who buys too many clothes. And it turns out, he's in need of a new fur supplier."

That was a lie. Luard said he had a great one out of the northern part of the country, but he didn't mind taking on another as a personal favor to me.

"Oh?" Brigit said with a look of surprise. "And so—"

I couldn't hold back the grin as I opened my palm, showing her a gold coin with Luard's seal on it. "This pass will allow you to use the royal road to Aymar for free, as many times as you need. He's partial to white fox fur, too. And...I've asked Ariadna to reconsider the tariffs on the road, especially for her own people. I don't know if she'll fix it, but..."

Her stoic eyes grew wet as she grasped the coin in her hand.

"I know you think the royals don't care about people, and maybe a lot of people get lost in the shuffle," I said. "But they do care. Or at least, I do. And if I get back on the throne, I'll do my best to make things better for everyone." I shrugged. "It won't really help you much but—"

She was no longer listening. Pressing the gold coin to her chest, she was silently praying, and a tear dropped down her weathered cheek.

"I'll ask the Mother to continue to look after you," she said, wiping her cheek. "Because if you show the people of Forcadel half the kindness you've shown me here, they would be lucky citizens indeed."

I swallowed the lump of emotion in my throat.

"Here," she said, pressing something into my hand. "Since I no longer need to travel the mountains, perhaps you can use this to keep your head."

I opened my palm—it was her bag of tinneum, the leaf that had helped clear my mind in the mountains.

"I can't take this," I whispered.

"I insist," she said, pushing it further into my hand. "There may be larger fears than wolves in your future. Best to approach them with a clear mind and heart."

Help one person. You will have made a difference to them, and perhaps that will settle the uncertainty in your heart.

I clutched the tinneum to my chest as I waved Brigit off. Perhaps that old priest back in Skorsa hadn't been too far off after all.

Chapter Twenty-Three

Felix

The trip back to Forcadel from Neveri was long, not the least because I was acutely aware that I was the only Forcadelian on board the ship. I'd never felt so unwelcome in my own country before.

It seemed Ilara was slowly chipping away at the fragments of my support network—perhaps to break me, perhaps just to watch me bleed. I could only imagine what fresh hell she had waiting for me when we returned. My only solace was that Katarine was too important to dispose of.

When my hometown appeared in the distance, I exhaled a breath. The spires of the castle were always constant. Katarine was still in the city, as were the rest of my youngest cadets. And no matter what Ilara threw at me, I could always don the mask and make things better for my people. It was those small bits of control that would keep me sane.

At the dock in Forcadel, Coyle wore his dress uniform and a smug grin. He, like Ilara, seemed triumphant over something. I half-expected him to have a pair of handcuffs, but he didn't.

"My queen," he said, bowing low. "Welcome back."

"Coyle, darling," she said, taking his arm as she departed the ship. "How has my city been in my absence? Have you captured that masked vigilante that's been terrorizing my streets?"

"We've narrowed it down," Coyle said, but I could hear the lie in his voice. "There have been more fires, though, and so I temporarily halted my investigation to focus on those."

"Good thing Captain Llobrega is back," she said, casting a look back at me. Was it a suspicious one, or merely relishing her cruel treatment of me? "How are my cadets, Lieutenant Coyle?"

"Very well, Your Majesty."

"Cadets?" I couldn't help myself. "What cadets?"

"I thought it best to remove some of your workload so you can focus on whoever's setting the fires in the city. After all, it's been weeks since you've started, and you've had very little progress."

I balled my fists and nodded curtly. "I'll do better, Your Majesty."

Coyle and I bowed in unison, and we remained silent until Ilara had climbed into her carriage and disappeared.

"I hope you don't mind," he began. "But Her Highness asked that your things be moved into Captain Mark's old rooms, so I took the liberty of doing it myself."

I quirked a brow, thankful I'd had the foresight to keep all traces of The Veil out of my closet. "How very kind of you. I hope this menial task didn't distract you from your all-important search for The Veil."

"As it turns out," he said under his breath, "The Veil hasn't been seen in a few nights."

"How convenient."

Coyle actually released a loud breath. "I know it's you, Felix. We can play this song and dance all day, but you and I both know the truth."

"If you're so sure," I said, tilting my chin up, "why am I not in shackles?"

He straightened his shoulders. "Because I'm giving you the chance to resign."

"I'm...sorry?" Resign? Was he mad?

"Resign and recommend me to take your place. You still have some sway, and now, with Maarit out of the way, there's no one else to take your spot but me."

"I'm not going to do that," I said with a smile. "You're on your own there."

"It's only a matter of time before I have proof that you've been masquerading," he said. "Ilara won't have any mercy."

"Then tell her." I stared directly into his eyes, perhaps the first time I'd been able to since he'd betrayed me.

Where I expected contempt and disgust, I found conflict.

"I don't think you can do it," I replied softly. "Because if you could, you wouldn't be here telling me. You'd have me in irons. You're just trying to play both sides again." I squinted at the blue sky. "But you know the problem with that? Eventually, people get tired of being played and you end up dead."

"I'm offering this to you as a friend," Coyle said.

I snorted and walked away from him. "You lost the ability to call me that when you betrayed my country."

That night, not wanting to be alone in my new quarters, which didn't feel like mine, I called upon Katarine and Beata in their private residence. Katarine ordered a small dinner for the three of us and we caught each other up on events in the castle and in Neveri. Despite the dark cloud over my mood, it was lightened somewhat by the soft looks and gentle touches they shared. Seeing Katarine so happy was worth, perhaps, some of this misery.

"Bea and I were out in the city today and, well...let's just say I think that's the last time I'm going to do that for a while," Katarine said, thumbing the rim of her wine glass. "I've never felt so unwelcome here."

I squeezed her hand. "I'm sorry."

"It's the bed I made," she said with a small shrug. "The people won't know that I stayed to protect them. I can't blame them for being angry."

"Things aren't looking good for either of us, it seems," I said, sitting back. "My cadets under Coyle's command, Jo and Riya in border cities. What's to say Ilara hasn't told one of her guards to throw them in the river and make it look like an accident?"

"Felix," Katarine said, tugging my arm. "You worry too much when you don't need to. Riya and Joella know to be on their guard and they can protect themselves just as well as you could."

"Perhaps even better," Beata said. "They may take some of the focus off you."

"I don't know how much Riya is going to be able to push back against Maarit, but—"

"She'll do her best," Katarine said with a smile.

"As long as it doesn't get her court-martialed," I said. "But the gates closing, that's going to mean big changes around here. We all know there was more product getting through than Ilara had wanted."

"Maybe when her own stores get so low that she can't eat her delicacies, she'll change her tune," Beata said with a snort.

Katarine reached across the table to take her hand with a soft smile. "And in the meantime, we'll have to send for our chocolates in the city."

Beata made a face. "They don't do it as well as I do."

"Speaking of which," Katarine said, sitting back. "Do you know where we put that present for Felix?"

"Oh, I think it's in the other room," Beata said, standing and placing her napkin on the table. "I'll be right back."

Katarine must've put it there strategically, because the moment Beata was out of earshot, Katarine leaned in. "Have you heard from...our other friend?"

I shook my head. "But I don't expect to. I expect to see her floating into the bay on a fiery ship of doom, ready to take on Ilara."

"Felix. Really?" Katarine snorted.

"She does have a flair for theatrics."

"That she does, but... It's been weeks," Katarine said softly. "I hope she's all right."

"I have faith that she is," I said.

"You may be the only one. Bea heard from her sources down in the dungeons—"

I blinked. "Since when does Bea have sources in the dungeons?"

"My love has sources all over the place," Katarine said with pursed lips. "I'll have you know."

Despite myself, I grinned. "Your *what*?"

"Bea," Katarine said, her pale face growing bright red. "My... whatever. Stop being an ass."

"So it's been said then?" I asked. "Finally, after so many years, and so many times of *her* saying it to *you,* you've confessed your love. August would've been so proud of you."

Katarine's face was now the color of a tomato as she stammered and played with the hem of the tablecloth. "I suppose it's all right now. Ilara already knows, so there's no benefit in hiding anymore."

I tilted my head to the side. "Do you think you'll marry her?"

"I'd like to," Katarine said, a small grin teasing the corners of her mouth. "But I don't know when or how. Things are so upside-down at the moment... But I think I'd want a small ceremony this time. Perhaps I'll send a missive to Luard and ask him to walk me. It was so dreadful to walk by myself."

I grinned, thinking back to Katarine and August's wedding. It had been a huge affair, a celebration lasting a whole week, with ad hoc celebrations the full month before and after. Katarine had been a gorgeous, if lonely, bride. Only her sister Erlina had been in attendance, as the second eldest, and she'd been more concerned about the treaty than Katarine's well-being.

"Do you remember sneaking out of the castle afterward?" Katarine asked, as if she were having the same memories. "Just the three of us, wearing cloaks and hoping no one would notice the newlyweds weren't making passionate love back at the castle."

"Well, one of you did," I said with a snort.

"Whatever happened to that girl?" Katarine asked, putting her chin in her hand. "August was quite fond of her, wasn't he?"

I nodded, taking another drink. "It's weird. I still expect to see him sometimes. Coming out of his room or playing tricks on the cadets. After he died, I was so focused on keeping the country together, I don't know if I ever..."

"He wouldn't have wanted you to mourn long," she said. "And I think he would've been thrilled to see Brynna give you more than enough distraction."

This time, I was the one to blush as Katarine cackled. "You know, with Joella and Riya gone, perhaps I could try my hand at The Veil."

I knew she was kidding, as she knew I'd never let her near a mask, but for her sake, I played along. "I think you'd do well. You'd need to work on your dramatics though."

"My swordsmanship needs a little work, too."

"Says the woman who bested August in every sparring match I ever saw."

She flushed, looking at her hands. "He wasn't a very skilled partner."

"Of course he wasn't. No one had the gumption to even try against him." I laughed. "Poor man thought he was the best swordsman in Forcadel and could barely even beat the youngest cadets."

We shared a smile that quickly faded into sadness. Just as I had a handle on my world, it slipped through my fingers, it seemed.

"Found it!" Beata chirped. "It was buried under a pile of clothes."

"Oh, my mistake," Katarine said with a wink to me. "I must've forgotten I put it there. I'm sorry."

Beata just kissed her forehead and sat down. "You've had a lot on your mind."

We shared the delicacies, some of the last that had been shipped in from Niemen before Skorsa had been closed, and descended into pensive silence.

"I'm still worried about my cadets," I said, picking up my goblet and washing the sweetness down. "I just hope Coyle doesn't do anything to hurt them... and that the cadets don't suffer from all this."

"Coyle's a traitor, but he's not cruel," Katarine said. "He won't torture them. Not if he wants them to swear fealty to him instead of you."

"Things are certainly aligning poorly for me lately," I said. "The only ally I have left in the castle is you. I don't know what I would do if she sent you away, too."

"Please, the bitch wouldn't know right from left without me."

I gawked—Katarine rarely cursed.

"It will be all right," she said, squeezing my hand. "As long as we have each other, it will be all right."

And as long as we kept the faith that Brynna would return, we'd survive.

Chapter Twenty-Four

Two days after I met with Ariadna, Luard and I were set to leave for Kulka. The Niemenian prince had given me strict orders to relax and enjoy a few days in the castle, so naturally I spent my time with his sister Erlina in the library, looking through military strategy for anything that might help convince Neshua to help. Much like the first time I'd tried to understand the complicated, interconnected politics of our three countries, I was hopelessly lost, but I did my best to absorb what I could.

I'd become familiar with Luard's guard Ivan, who'd been assigned to me when I went out into the city. He was a kind man, unaffected by any of Luard's antics but still amused by them.

"He really does talk more than he gets into trouble," Ivan said as we walked the stone hallways toward the waiting carriage. "He's quite brilliant when he wants to be, especially about politics. It's how he's managed to stay single for so long. And lucky for you, he's also well-versed in how to turn negative opinions around."

For my sake, I hoped he was right.

Another blanket of snow had fallen over the past few days, but the stones were clear and dry. A cold wind blew down the hall from the open door, and I stepped out into the winter day where Luard's carriage was surrounded by a flurry of activity. On second glance, it wasn't the carriage I'd been using the past few days, but a larger one, probably to carry more things. And Luard clearly needed it, as no less than five trunks rested at the back of the carriage, waiting to be loaded on.

"Doesn't travel light, does he?" I asked Ivan, who shook his head.

"The prince is used to a certain level of luxury, and we do our best to maintain that while he's on the road." He offered his hand. "May I take your bag? I'll put it inside with the rest of your things."

"My things?" I blinked. "I don't have anything other than this."

"Luard insisted on commissioning a few extra pieces of clothing," he said, taking the bag gingerly and frowning. "What's in here? Feels like weapons?"

I grinned. "A girl likes to be prepared."

"Ah, good, I haven't missed you." Ariadna came out of the open hallway, and immediately all the servants stopped and bowed. She waved her hand to acknowledge them, they returned to work, and she continued toward me.

"Thank you again for all your help," I said, still slightly nervous in her presence.

She rested her gloved hands on her swollen stomach. "Oh, to be young and travel again. Before my father died, I was quite the journeyer. Even made it down to Forcadel a few times to meet with your father."

A flitter of sadness came washing over me as I thought about how long it had been since I'd seen home. "If I make it back onto the throne, I would love for you to come visit. And Kat would as well, I know."

"I would love to see the ocean again," she said with a warm smile that faded slightly. "However, you might want to plan for what could happen if you're unsuccessful with Neshua."

"I prefer to plan for the known problems and solve the unknowns as they come up," I said with a nervous laugh. "Habit of being a vigilante, I guess."

"My point is that you're welcome to return to Niemen and live here in the castle," she said, taking my hands in hers. "I might have an advantageous marriage ready for you if you can stomach traveling with him."

I caught Ivan's eye, and we shared a grin. "Thank you, Ariadna, for your graciousness. As much as I've enjoyed my stay in Niemen, it's entirely too cold up here for me. My place is in Forcadel, with or without a crown."

"Very well," she said, releasing me. "When you've received approval from Neshua, send Luard back. I'll commission a fleet of ships to take the port city of Skorsa and then continue down to the bay, where we will assist you in whatever capacity."

"Ah, my favorite women," Luard said, walking up to the carriage, smelling of perfume and sporting a few red spots on his neck. "Are we ready to depart?"

Ariadna gave him a once-over, disgust clear on her face. "Please keep it in your pants, Luard. You are royalty."

"I *wear* protection," he said, walking up to her and taking her hands. "Believe me, the last thing I want is to saddle some poor woman with my child. Could you only imagine the gray hairs she'd get?"

"Yes, because I have a few of them myself." Ariadna pressed her hand to Luard's face softly. "Take care of yourself, brother."

"I will." He kissed her hand. "Please tell my newest nephew or niece not to arrive until I've returned."

They shared another quiet moment, and I took the opportunity to disappear into the carriage to give them their privacy. Perhaps one day Katarine and I might be so close as to share such familiarity, but the concept of sibling love was as foreign to me as this country.

Luard's carriage was more tasteful than I would've figured for such an ostentatious man, and it was a comfortable ride. I settled in on the velvet cushion and folded my hands in my lap. The door opened, and Luard ducked his head as he climbed inside, taking the seat across from me. Out the window, Ariadna stood in the alcove, wearing a look of concern and amusement.

"The worst part of leaving home," Luard said, waving at her as the coach moved.

"I can't understand why Kat left all this," I replied, watching them disappear into the darkness of the castle. "Your family seems very...loving."

"Kat understood that it was what was best for her," Luard replied, sitting back. "And luckily for her, she made herself a new family in Forcadel that loves her as much as we do."

I smiled, thinking about her and Felix, but didn't respond.

We hadn't ridden for more than ten minutes when the carriage came to a halt, nearly throwing me off my seat. Luard clapped his hands together and went to the window, pulling down the glass and offering me the chance to poke my head out. Our carriage was in a queue of them, each one being inspected by a uniformed guard.

"So this is the underground road, hm?" I asked, craning my neck to see beyond the line of carriages. A golden arch bordered the opening, but beyond that, there was nothing but darkness. I tilted my gaze upward to take in the mountain, that familiar dizzy sensation coming back. The mountain was enormous, and the hole before us not so much.

"It's much nicer than traipsing through the valleys," he said.

"Not as cold, and the accommodations are always friendly. We may even stop in at the mines while we're there."

I nodded, but all I could think about was the mountain, the rock, and what might happen if the tunnel should crumble. "When was the last time there was a cave-in?"

"Oh, sweet Brynna, are you nervous about going underground?" He laughed when I nodded. "It's been centuries. The Niemenian engineers who built this road knew what they were doing, I promise you. How do you think we get all those delicious meals into the castle? It's clear we can't grow anything at this altitude."

Still, my panicked heart wouldn't stop pounding as the carriage door opened. "Afternoon, Your Highness," greeted the guard outside.

"Claud, very nice to see you," Luard said with a grin. "How's the family?"

"Very well, sire." He bowed. "Have a pleasant journey."

"We'll certainly try," Luard said, casting me a look as the door closed. "Are you sure you're ready for this?"

I pulled the bag of tinneum Brigit had given me from my belt and placed a small pinch under my bottom lip. The herb filled my mouth with a tangy sensation, and slowly, my panic faded into the background.

"Let's do this," I said.

The carriage lurched forward, and we were bathed in darkness.

The herb continued to work its magic, and my curiosity grew instead of my fear. The tunnel was spacious, and every so often, another carriage or wagon would roll by. The farmers and fur traders onboard didn't look concerned about traveling underground, and I tried to take my cues from them.

Luard did his best to be an effective distraction, regaling me with stories of his conquests and adventures as a young prince on the prowl. How he got away with most of his antics, I had no idea. But when I shared my greatest victories as The Veil, it was his turn to be impressed.

"You can certainly take care of yourself," Luard said after I told him the story of how I sank a Kulkan ship full of vegetables but made everyone think it was an expensive Niemenian vessel. "I'm glad to have you with me. You'll be good protection."

"From what?" I asked, gesturing to the empty darkness around us. "Isn't this the royal road?"

"True, but once we get out of the mountain and onto the trade roads, it gets a bit dicier."

"How long until we get there?" I asked.

"Four days, usually. Three if we hurry."

I peered out the dark window. "We'll be traveling overnight? Non-stop?"

"Oh, of course not," Luard said. "The road intersects with some mining villages along the way, and we stop there to sleep and eat. Some are more luxurious than others." He sighed. "It's been a few weeks since I've been to the hot springs. Perhaps we'll pay them a visit."

"You do remember that I'm on a mission to get my kingdom back, don't you?" I asked.

"Doesn't mean we can't spend an evening covering ourselves with volcanic mud," Luard replied with a haughty look. "And speaking of this all-important mission... Have you given any thought to how you'll approach Neshua?"

"Maybe I'll just strip naked and throw myself at him," I said, looking out the carriage window as another wagon rolled by.

"While I would certainly enjoy seeing that, I think you should come up with a secondary plan. What is it that you need from him? What are you willing to give up?"

"Your sister said—"

"Forget Ariadna." Luard waved his hand. "You don't want to tell Neshua that her help is dependent on his. You should approach him as if he's the only one you're asking. Why should he listen to you?"

I sank back into the cushions, my gaze returning out the window. "Because I'm a better queen than Ilara?"

"Try again."

"Because I can renegotiate treaties and open the gates?"

"Better, but still not good enough," Luard said. "You've got to start thinking outside of yourself if you want people to listen." He paused. "Are you willing to give up another border city?"

I chewed my lip. "Neveri could be an option."

"One you're willing to exercise?"

"I don't know," I said. "Yes, if it means I could get Neshua's support. But...I really don't like screwing with people's lives like this. I've already bartered away Skorsa. Never mind that I'd be losing a strategic advantage on both fronts." I exhaled. "Unless... it's the right choice to make."

"Unfortunately, there are no right answers here," Luard said gently. "Being a queen means making hard decisions and hoping that you're doing what's right for the majority of people, even if it means screwing over a few." He patted my knee. "But if it makes you feel any better, Ariadna is a great queen, and the people of Skorsa will be well taken care of."

"It doesn't matter. I've already agreed to it." I chewed my lip as another carriage passed. "And I'm not willing to make a decision about giving up more border cities until I have all the information. I want to see what Neshua is thinking, gauge his reaction to my arrival." I sank back in the seat. "I'm afraid I'll need something more than a border city to convince Neshua to help me."

"Good thing I'm well-versed in persuasion," he said. "The trick is to strike a delicate balance between letting them have the upper hand and still remaining desirable enough to listen to. Neshua obviously has the upper hand. What we need to work on is making you desirable enough for the favor we're asking."

"And how do we do that?"

"Well, first, you need to lose that dejected look on your face," Luard said, poking me with his foot. "Look like you're a winner and the rest will follow."

I hadn't even realized I had a losing look. "Fine, what else?"

"You'll need to watch that silver tongue of yours," he said. "People will say things that will goad you into responding, and you need to temper that response. Don't let them see your weakness, and don't let them see you mad. *Especially* someone like Neshua, with whom you have a prior history."

Based on the behavior of the lord who'd come to my coronation, I couldn't argue with that. They, unlike me, had seemed very interested in making sure there was resolution.

"If it helps, pretend you're that vigilante again," Luard said, nodding to the bag at my side. "Make your face your new mask."

I snorted. "It's a lot easier to temper your responses under black fabric."

"You'll need to learn how to do without it when you're queen. Best to get into the habit now."

Chapter Twenty-Five

Without the sun overhead, it was difficult to tell how much time had passed. We stopped midday in a cavern to eat some of that disgusting pickled fish along with some dried meat. Afterward, we set off again, and Luard took a long nap. Instead of sitting inside, I braved a spot next to Ivan on the bench and got to know the rest of the guards as they rode on horseback in front of and behind the carriage. Each had come from a noble family, but too far down in the heirs list to be of any value. So they'd joined on as royal guards to be useful and travel the world.

"Truly," Ivan said beside me, "I think I'd be bored to tears if I was in Erlina's detail. All she does is read books in the library."

"With Luard, we're never in Linden for very long," said Hagan, a tall, young man with broad shoulders and a blond mustache. He and his husband Nils, another guard about a head taller with dark brown hair and a sweet smile, had been married about six months.

"Must be nice for the two of you to be able to be together all the time," I said.

"It has its moments," Nils said with a shrug. "My mother would prefer it if we were back in town more, though."

"In any case, I'm glad to have you for company," I said. "I couldn't imagine Luard traveling with boring guards. I think he'd send them to an early retirement." I looked to the sole female guard, Asdis, Ivan's sister. "And I'm surprised you put up with him."

"Someone has to make sure he wipes his ass," she said with a grin.

"It takes a special kind of person to handle Luard," Ivan said.

"Oh, Ivan," Luard said, poking his head out of the carriage. "I only trust you to handle me. You do it so gently."

The guards whooped with laugher, and I joined in as it echoed off the tunnel walls.

Along our journey, we passed several secondary paths and signs indicating that villages lay at the end of them. But finally, after a few hours on the road, Ivan turned the carriage off the road toward a sign marked *Utvonnet Springs*.

The secondary tunnel was smaller, but there was a pinprick of light in the distance. It grew to an opening, with a few buildings visible, and then, as we exited the tunnel, we came into a cavern nearly the size of Forcadel.

"Wow," I breathed, tilting my head back to take it in. This was no sad, dark place—it was a bustling and vibrant city. Wooden houses were organized on a neat grid, each with a nearly identical thatched roof. On the other side of the cavern, a gravel road wound up the side, leveling off at entryways.

"Other roads?" I asked Ivan, pointing at them.

"No, that's the ore mines," he said. "Maybe Luard can arrange a tour."

I chewed my lip. "I'm not really here to sightsee—"

"You'll want to see these," he said with a knowing smile.

We continued down into the village, and a small crowd gathered as they recognized the royal seal on the door. Children trailed behind, laughing and calling out to Luard and the guards. Several young women had undone the top buttons on their dresses, leaning over the picket fences and waving as we went by. Our stop for the evening was a small, two-story inn, complete with an older couple standing outside.

"Welcome back, Prince Luard!" the woman said, as her husband stepped forward to start unloading the carriage. "I trust your journey was pleasant."

"As always," he said, extending his hand to help me out of the carriage. For appearances, I took it and stepped out. "May I present my traveling companion, Brynna?"

Inside, the inn was pleasantly furnished, with leather chairs in front of a hearth. But to my surprise, there was no fire—just a warm, red piece of metal glowing.

"No fires in the caverns, by royal decree and common sense," the woman—Dagmar—said, coming to stand next to me. "That is pure Niemenian metal, heated from the steam of the hot springs. Keeps things toasty!"

I knelt closer, the warmth from the pipe hotter than any fire I'd seen. "Fascinating."

"It's been a while since we've had a Forcadelian in our midst," she said, handing me a steaming mug of something spicy and sweet. "Are we to expect a wedding announcement soon?"

I caught Luard's gaze as he walked into the room, and he winked. "Dagmar, you know I can't be tamed by any woman."

"Yes, but Queen Ariadna might have other plans for you!"

"She's smarter than that."

They got into it, quibbling like a mother and son, and Dagmar even gave Luard a friendly swat on the rear after he made an off-color joke. She left the room, her cheeks flushed and a giggle on her lips, and Luard joined me at the hearth.

"You make friends everywhere, don't you?" I asked, taking a sip of the drink.

"Someone has to," he said. "So, dear Brynna, we have several options for entertainment tonight. There's a traveling theater troupe in town, or we could visit the mud room. Your skin will glow after, I promise. Or—"

"Luard," I said, gently. "On a mission, remember?" I didn't feel right pampering myself when my people were suffering.

"And the horses need to rest," he said, taking the cup from me and placing it on the mantel. "As do you."

There really was no arguing with him, so I swapped my traveling tunic for one of the velvet dresses Luard had brought for me, we set out into the small underground village with Asdis and Ivan.

"The two lovers are really quite boring now," Luard said with a roll of his eyes. "But Hagan has the best taste in wine, so I suppose they're a package deal. Please, do me a favor and never get married, you two."

Asdis crossed her heart, but Ivan just shook his head. "I think you're the longest relationship I've ever had, Luard."

"Ah, likewise," Luard said, blowing him a kiss.

Their back-and-forth continued, much to Asdis' annoyance and my amusement, as we came into the main square of the town. There, we found the one dining hall in the town, already filled with diners young and old. Luard paid a gold coin for all of us ("The lovers decided to stay at the inn and snuggle, they don't get a free dinner") and we were served a bowl of stew and given a tankard.

Luard drank half his in one gulp then belched loudly.

"You are a prince," Asdis said with a dry look. "You know Queen Ariadna asks me to report on your behavior, right?"

He flashed a charming grin. "And I assume you lie admirably."

"I stretch the truth," Asdis said with a sly look. "You're lucky I do, too."

"Asdis, when, oh, when are we going to put aside this silly front and finally fall into bed together?" Luard asked, batting his eyes.

She lifted her finger in an offensive gesture, and Ivan howled with laughter. Eventually, Luard did, too.

"So, Forcadelian," Ivan said. "How are you liking all this Niemenian food?"

"It needs more salt," I said, although I kept my voice low. In truth, I was grateful for anything that wasn't pickled fish. "And I'm dreaming of apples and berries and fresh fish."

"You'll get your fill of that in Kulka," Asdis said. "Delina has some of the best dining halls in the world, in my opinion. Grapes and vegetables and game…" She took a large bite of stew and made a satisfied noise. "But this is pretty good, too."

"Asdis doesn't like to admit that anything is better than what she can find in Niemen," Ivan said, nudging his sister. "I think she secretly hates it there, but won't admit it to herself."

Addis scowled and flung a carrot at him.

"I understand loyalty," I said. "I've never appreciated my home more than these past few weeks. Everything is so different—and cold, too."

"This is your first time out of the country?" Ivan asked.

I nodded. "When I left the castle at thirteen, I spent a few years in a forest near the border with Kulka. But that was the farthest I'd ever been from Forcadel." I allowed a little sadness to tug at my chest.

"Wait, what?" Asdis asked. "You left the castle at thirteen and lived in a *forest*?"

"How much did you share with your guards?" I asked Luard, and he put down the tankard.

"Only that you're royalty and we're going to Delina. I figured the rest would be up to you to explain to them. Not my story to tell."

For what felt like the millionth time, I regaled them with the story of my past, Celia, The Veil, and everything else that had happened up until this point. They were a rapt audience, with Asdis' bright blue eyes growing wide with every twist and turn to the story.

"And so here we are," I finished, gesturing at the room around us. "I'm on a mission to get help from Neshua and pray that he takes me seriously."

"If he doesn't," Ivan said, "you are welcome to join us on our traveling caravan."

"Yes, please," Asdis said. "None of the other female soldiers want anything to do with Luard."

"I can't imagine why," I drawled with a look at him.

"Oh, poking so much fun at me," Luard said, sitting back. "Perhaps it's time to poke some fun at you, little princess."

"Go for it," I said, leaning back. "Do your worst."

He smiled with something calculating in his eyes. "What scares you?"

"What?" I said with a laugh. "What kind of a question is that?"

"I like to know how people tick, and I haven't figured you out yet." He rested his hands at the nape of his neck. "What kind of a woman willingly gives up her royal seat and becomes a vigilante? What's driving her? What's she afraid of?"

I took a long sip. "She's afraid of being told what to do by her overbearing father."

"But how would one even begin to become a vigilante?" he pressed. "You didn't just walk out the door and put on a mask?"

"I told you," I said, taking a long sip of my beer. "One day I decided I'd had enough of robbing people and returned to Forcadel."

Luard's eyes had taken on a different look, almost like he was peering beneath my skin. "What made you decide you'd had enough?"

"Why are you so interested?"

"Because I think it's germane."

"To what?"

"To what you're accomplishing," Luard said. "By all accounts, including Katarine's, you were a reluctant queen, which makes me question why you're really doing this—and how far you're willing to go to get what you want."

I had no response to that, or none that I was willing to share. My own indecision still rested in the back of my mind, and I was sure Luard didn't want to hear about that. "As far as it takes."

"Not an answer. You have to quantify it to yourself. At what point do you decide the stakes are too high, the risk isn't worth it?" He bit off a piece of bread. "Because I think that point might be closer than you think."

"Oh yeah?" I crossed my arms over my chest, my heart fluttering with nerves. "Are you so familiar with me now?"

"I know you won't tell me why you made a complete reversal from being a thief to a vigilante, which means that whatever happened still haunts you." He sat back. "That, I think, is just the tip of the mountain."

"Oh, leave her alone," Ivan said, breaking the tension. "Luard, you're drunk."

"I have had exactly two beers, and you know I only start getting handsy at four."

They got into it, and I took the opportunity to down more of my own drink. Somehow I had a feeling I hadn't heard the last of this conversation.

Chapter Twenty-Six

The clocks on the wall said it was nearing midnight, but I was wide awake. Luard expressed a desire to visit some of the women in the village, so Ivan followed him, grumbling all the way. That left Asdis and me to stroll the streets.

"I can't believe all of this lies beneath the mountain," I said, as we passed a sign for a mineral bath. "When I was traveling over from Aymar, it seemed like there was no one in this country."

"The mountain trails are hard, and I don't envy the people who pass through them." She paused and pointed at a small clothing shop. "I'm in need of some new shoes. Do you mind if we stop in?"

I didn't, but as I had no coin of my own, I browsed while Asdis looked for a sensible pair of boots to wear. In the corner there was a small cotton loom, a sewing machine, and several bundles of already-made fabric. It seemed this village had everything it needed.

"Two gold coins for a single pair?" Asdis said, blowing air out from between her lips. "Fine. Put it on the prince's tab." She cast a look at me. "Are you sure you don't want anything?"

"I already owe Luard enough," I said, although I cast a longing look at a black velvet tunic and leggings. Mine were becoming threadbare. But Luard had already provided several tunics to me in varying colors, so I would have to pass.

With new boots purchased, Asdis and I continued our walk through the city. A gaggle of children ran by us, laughing and shoving one another. I thought they might be runaways or orphans, but they queued up outside a small schoolhouse.

"There really is no sleeping here, huh?" I asked.

"Oh, of course people sleep. They're just on a different timetable," Asdis said. "The mines run all day and all night, and since there's no sunrise or sunset, families just live their lives according to the mines' schedule. Some children go to school at night, others during the day."

She pointed to a window with dark curtains to block out the light, and although I supposed I understood, it still made for a curious situation.

"I could never be The Veil here," I said idly. "I did most of my hunting by moonlight."

"I think it's fascinating, this life you had," she said, casting me a look. "A princess vigilante."

"To be fair, up until four months ago, I was perfectly fine leaving off the princess part," I said, looking up at the cave ceiling. We'd been underground for about a day, and I was starting to miss the sun and the stars. "I hope Luard is only planning to stay here a night."

"I believe so," she said. "Despite how he acts, he's quite serious when he wants to be. He knows the importance of getting you to Delina quickly."

"He's out getting laid," I said dryly.

"I am *not!*" Luard and Ivan had found us, the former having something of a satisfied smirk on his face. "For your information, I've just been to see the mine's foreman. And you, little princess, are in for a treat tonight."

I had several thousand theories for what Luard was going to show me, including perhaps, finally trying to bed me. He and Ivan led me through the streets, pausing only briefly to say hello to passersby. Our destination was the maze of pathways and doors on the other side—the mine.

"Now, what I'm showing you is a closely guarded Niemenian secret," Luard said over his shoulder. "I trust that you'll respect our country's lifeblood and not try to, you know, invade and steal it."

"I doubt that the Forcadelian Council would approve of sending soldiers into the mountains," I drawled. "And besides that, we have enough on our hands with trade routes."

"Well, your ancestors felt differently," Luard said as we came up to the first door where two heavily armed guards stood.

"Evening," Luard said, flashing a coin. "I'm here to inspect our stores on behalf of the queen."

"Who's she?" the guard asked.

"Who are you?" Ivan snapped. "Do you know who you're addressing?"

The guard gave Ivan a once-over, then glanced at Luard. He then stepped out of the way, although I felt his lingering gaze on me as we disappeared into the torchlit tunnel.

"Like I said, closely guarded secret," Luard said with a smile. "Ivan, be sure to talk to the foreman about that man and give him a raise for being so cautious."

"Will do, Sire."

We were checked for identification three more times as we descended into the mines. The air smelled faintly metallic and musty. Every so often, vibrations would echo through the rock, some faint, some loud, but Luard and Ivan seemed unbothered. Still, the old fear that the mountain would collapse on top of me came back, and I kept close to the men.

We passed through another checkpoint and the dim light took on a green hue. I glanced behind me—up until this checkpoint, we'd been illuminated by the Niemenian metal pipes, heated using natural hot spring water so they'd glow. But in here, light was given by mushrooms growing in the corners of the tunnel.

"Pardon, Your Highness," the guard said. "I'll need your cloaks."

"Why?" I asked. It wasn't as cold as the surface, but there was still a damp chill in the air.

"The wool can cause a fire," Luard said, pulling off his cloak and handing it to the guard. "Trust me when I say you don't want anything that could cause a spark where we're going."

Nervously, I undid the clasp on my cloak and handed it to the guard. "Where are you taking me, Luard?"

"You'll see," he said cryptically.

We continued along the green-lit tunnel until finally arriving at a pair of double doors and two guards. They took one look at Luard then bowed low and went to the doors. Each had their own key, and together, they unlocked the door. With great effort, they pulled them open, and I held my breath.

It was sand—black sand. Mounds of it stacked high in this cave. Those green mushrooms had been placed on columns every twenty feet or so, illuminating the space and showing just how much was there.

"Well?" Luard said, his voice echoing off the walls. "What do you think?"

"What am I looking at?" I asked.

"This is a special kind of Niemenian ore called ond," he said. "Only found here in this mountain. The old Nestori believed it was buried deep by the Mother because it was concentrated evil. But of course, we know better now."

"Do we?" I said, inching away from it. "What does it do?"

"Here in the cool cave, absolutely nothing," he said. "But put it anywhere near to a spark and..." He made an explosion noise.

"So you're telling me we're standing in a cave full of explosive sand buried deep in a mountain?" My voice had gone up, but I didn't care. I wished I'd brought the tinneum with me.

"We've taken all the necessary precautions," Luard said. "Both for ourselves and the villagers. Niemenians have a healthy respect for the stuff, and we don't use it lightly. Mostly to quickly blast through rock to tunnel through the mountain. That road we came in on? We used ond for that."

"And why are you showing it to me?" I asked.

"Well, in the first place, we're taking some of it with us," Luard said. "I received special permission from Ariadna. I thought you could use it."

"What, like in Kulka? To blow something up? To threaten them?" I asked, stepping back further. "Luard, I'm not going to use this as a weapon. I don't know if I was clear about this, but I have a lot of issues with murder."

"I'm not saying you lob it at Neshua's face, silly," Luard said with an exasperated sigh. "But I'm sure you could find some use for it. Especially considering you don't have a whole lot of firepower against Ilara. This could help put you on an even footing."

I shook my head, thinking about what Ilara had done to Forcadel. "I'm not going to stoop to Ilara's level and use it against my own people."

He cleared his throat and crossed his arms over his chest, leveling his calculating gaze at me. "Why did you leave the forest thief's den?"

"That has nothing to do with this," I said, throwing my hands in the air.

"I think it does, and I think you agree with me, which is why you're getting angry right now." There was nothing friendly in his stance, and I didn't like it.

"I'm not discussing it with you," I said darkly. "And you can just stop prying."

He shrugged. "Then turn back around and be a vigilante. You're obviously not ready to be a queen."

"I am," I said weakly, but even I had to admit it was half-hearted. I stared at him for a long time, waiting for him to look away. But he kept my gaze, searching for all the secrets I'd locked away. The room was hot now, and I wanted to climb out of my skin.

Finally, I broke.

"Three years ago, I killed a man," I said evenly. "A contingent of Forcadelian royal guards were carrying jewels for Kat's crown. Celia ordered us to take it out. A Forcadelian soldier was about to kill one of ours, so I...I shot him." It was hard not to see it in my mind's eye, especially after the wolves in the mountains had refreshed my memory. "I couldn't live with myself, so I decided to return to Forcadel to turn myself in. Instead...well, the Mother seemed to have different plans. I dedicated my life in service to others, protecting the city and the people in it. I hadn't killed a single person until...until Ilara invaded."

"You didn't kill anyone during the invasion," Luard said.

"Every death that day is my fault," I said as a tear rolled down my cheek. "Every death since she came onto the throne is my fault, too."

"So why are you struggling?"

I swallowed, shaking my head. "Because if I challenge Ilara, more deaths will be in my ledger."

"But if you don't challenge her, the same will happen," Luard said. "She doesn't care about your people. All she cares about is herself."

"Trust me, I know," I said, running a hand through my hair. This argument had been circling through my mind for weeks now, and I had no resolution.

"You aren't tussling with street thugs anymore, you're going to war. Yes, Brynna," he said when I opened my mouth to argue, "war. The kind where cities get destroyed and people die. You're going to have to come to terms with that sooner or later."

"Maybe Ilara will get better," I whispered.

"I think we both know you don't believe that," Luard said. "If you did, you'd be back in Forcadel or out in some faraway city, running around under a mask and happy in retirement. But you've traveled over mountains and through rivers to get to this point. Why are you doing it if you aren't fully invested?"

I stared at the ground with no good answers.

"I know you're scared." Luard rested a hand on my shoulder. "But you can't let your fear cloud your judgment. Your people need saving, and you're the only one who can do it."

"I just want to save everyone without bloodshed."

"I'm sorry to say it, but that isn't going to be possible," he said, a little more gently. "What you can do instead is strive to save the *most* people. With this sand, with this weapon, you can do that. Instead of sending a hundred soldiers to die, you could send five and have the same effect. Five would still die, but the other ninety-five would be safe. Isn't that the best possible outcome? Keyword being *possible*."

Despite the unease in my stomach, I nodded.

"Nobody said this job was easy," he continued with a soft smile as he squeezed my shoulder. "Which is why I thank the Mother every day that I was born so far down the line, there'd have to be a coordinated attempt to get me on the throne. However, I do think, more than anyone I've ever met, you have the right mindset for this. If I had to pick a queen—"

"You'd pick the one who'd been protecting her country wearing a mask," I said quietly.

"Even if she has a lot of hang-ups about killing people." He grinned, and some of the tension left his face. "So how about it? Can we take the ond?"

I exhaled, loosening some of the tension that had kept a vise grip on my heart since setting out on this journey. Luard was right; I wouldn't have come this far if I hadn't thought I was on the right path. All my unease had been fear of the truth, not fear of the mission. It was time to let go of the fantasies of saving everyone as I'd done as The Veil. I would have to prepare myself to make decisions I wasn't comfortable with. Starting with accepting this volatile weapon.

"Yes," I whispered. "We can take it."

"Excellent choice," he said, throwing his arm around my shoulder. "And now that we've got that soul-baring conversation out of the way, let's get out of this dank mine. I am *dying* to pay a visit to the mud spa. My skin is so clogged."

Chapter Twenty-Seven

Felix

As the days drew on, the consequences of Ilara's decision to fully close the borders became more apparent. The signs were visible every time I left the castle to patrol with my new guards—from the dwindling produce available in the town square to the way even the friendliest faces had soured in our direction. Worse still, I'd received the first resignation in what I assumed would be many more. The soldier—Greene—had three young children at home and couldn't take the pressure of worrying if she'd be home that night.

"If the queen doesn't take me out, the townsfolk surely will," she said, casting a wary look onto the streets.

"I understand," I said. "Thank you for your service to Forcadel."

It wasn't going to be the last time I had this conversation, especially as I had nothing to offer in the way of hope. Even with guards stationed at Ilara's favorite businesses, more had gone up in flames. Every night, there were more reports of people breaking curfew, of vandalism and property destruction, and whispers that the city was about to explode.

But I was starting to get tired of spending my long nights patrolling the city just to come across the crimes after the fact. If I didn't find something soon, Ilara would grow weary of me, and perhaps do something drastic.

To complicate matters further, Coyle continued to stalk my movements, and now, being in the castle, it was harder for me to slip from my room unnoticed. He also must've tipped some of his Severian counterparts off to his suspicions, because I found myself with two new escorts and their smug-faced Severian lieutenant when I tried to leave through the front gates that night.

"It's unsafe for you to be out there alone, what with all the fires happening." The look on the lieutenant's face as he spoke to me would be enough for me to order a flogging.

"I believe I can handle myself on a simple patrol," I replied.

"We can't take too many chances while Captain Maarit is gone," he said. "Her Majesty insists that you be protected."

I'm sure she'd cry a river if I wound up dead. "Are you ignoring a direct order?"

The lieutenant opened his mouth, but thankfully, I was saved by someone calling my name. Zuriel was crossing the green, holding his hands nervously. He, like Coyle, was a man I would've preferred to see in the stocks or in jail, but he would serve as a convenient cover for me to lose my supposed babysitters.

"Captain," Zuriel said, nodding slightly. "Might I have a word?"

I glanced at the Severian lieutenant and dared him to contradict me. "Dismissed."

He and his two guards hesitated, but only for a moment, then continued walking the green. Once they were out of earshot, I turned to Zuriel, staring him down with all the disgust I could muster.

"What do you want?"

"Oh, well." He cleared his throat. "I wondered if you had a chance to consider the request I'd sent to you, for protection?"

I quirked a brow. I'd seen his letter on my desk but tossed it in the trash without reading it. "Protection? From whom?"

"The city is in a state of upheaval," he said. "No fault of your own, of course. I know you're doing the best you can with what you've been given."

"No, but fault of yours," I replied without missing a beat. "If you want an armed guard, you should hire one yourself."

"See, that seems to be a bit of a problem," he said with a bashful smile. "As all of the trained security forces are either here with you in the castle or—"

"Or think you're a traitor," I said.

He sighed. "I want you to know that I had nothing to do with the death of Maurice or August. Or even the attempted poisoning of Princess Brynna."

"Mm." I can't say I believed it.

"My involvement in the conspiracy came very late in its execution," he continued, looking out onto the city. "I'm not completely blameless, as I didn't tell anyone, but by the time I became involved, there was no stopping it."

I glared at him. "Really? No stopping it? Are you sure about that?"

"I became aware of the plot during the summer festival," he said. "By then, the city was already filled with Severians. The only thing there was to do was to—"

"Protect your city and your princess, instead of saving your own ass," I replied. "I fail to see how your security problem is mine."

He smiled thinly. "Because if the mayor of Forcadel should be injured or, Mother forbid, killed—"

"Then perhaps the citizenry would see it as justice," I replied.

"If you're looking for sympathy, you won't get it from me. I am loyal to Forcadel, not to those who would betray it to the highest bidder."

"But you, yourself, are serving the queen."

"Because I have no choice," I replied. "Unlike you, I consider the needs of others, like my guard. But you…you smiled at Brynna as you stabbed her in the back. That, I'll never forgive."

As my guards returned, I decided to kill two birds with one edict. "Under the circumstances, perhaps I can see fit to give you an escort home." I snapped my fingers at the Severians, who scowled. "You two, you're now to walk Mayor Zuriel back to his house."

"But—"

I quirked a brow and the one on the left quieted. Perhaps without their lieutenant there, they were less willing to break rank.

"Thank you," Zuriel said.

"It's more than you deserve," I muttered as I turned to leave.

There was something devilishly satisfying thinking about Zuriel succumbing to a riot in the city. I wasn't sure I'd lift a finger to help him if things came down to it. After all, it was his fault the city was in upheaval. I was surprised someone hadn't targeted him sooner.

But if his house went up in flames, I wouldn't shed a tear. I had other things to worry about.

Unlike in Zuriel's cushy neighborhood, in Haymaker's Corner, the Severian guards were plentiful and all the shops were closed thanks to the curfew. Even the inns and bars were dark, perhaps too nervous because of what had happened to Stank's to remain open. Or, more realistically, they just didn't have enough patrons.

One cafe still had a few lights burning, although it appeared they were merely cleaning. A flash of red hair caught my attention and I smiled. It was a woman named Ruby—one of Brynna's informants. Brynna gave her large sums of money and Ruby provided what intel she could.

She'd been largely missing from the city these past few weeks, but the other night, her fiery red hair had caught my eye. Then, I hadn't had any coin on me. Now, I'd come prepared with a bag of gold.

Inside the small cafe, there were three other people, including what looked like security, so I kept my distance on the rooftop nearby. They didn't seem to be in a great hurry to get home, as they all had tankards sitting on the bar while sweeping and mopping the floor. But then one of the girls disappeared to the back with the bodyguard and didn't return. About half an hour later, he came back and the man and woman left with him, leaving Ruby by herself.

Knowing my time was short, I crept off the rooftop and waited in the shadows. I didn't see any Severian guards, so I dashed across the open street into the alley between the cafe and its neighbor. Pressing myself against the wall, I slid toward the back of the cafe, testing the door to see if it was unlocked. Quietly, I pulled it open, revealing the back kitchen, a large table, and a cold hearth.

"Daniel? Is that you?"

Ruby walked into the kitchen and took me in, her eyes growing three sizes. "W-who are you? What are you doing here?" She pulled a knife from beneath her apron. "Don't you dare think about robbing me."

"I'm not here to rob you," I said, staying near the door anyway. "I'm a friend. You can call me...The Veil."

She straightened and quirked one perfectly-shaped brow. "*You* are not The Veil."

"Fine, I'm a temporary substitute," I said, staying in the shadows. "Can I trust you like she did?"

Ruby pursed her lips. "Can I trust *you* is the question?"

"I don't have anything to offer you, other than my word that I won't speak of your involvement, much like The Veil didn't when you told her where to find those contracts."

"She promised not to speak of that," Ruby said with a glare.

"She didn't," I said with a half-smile. "I was there when she made the deal. She was…training me to take her place while she left to travel the world for a few months."

"The rumors I heard said that she was back in town," Ruby said, crossing her arms and leaning against the doorframe.

I hesitated. Did I confirm them? Did I trust this woman enough to keep Brynna's secret? "I can't say I've seen her lately."

Ruby shrugged. "What if I said she came to see me before she left? Told me that she was hanging up her mask and leaving for good?"

"I'd call you a liar."

Ruby smirked. "Fair enough. What is it that you want from me, Man-Veil?"

"I'm looking for information about who's behind all these fires in Haymaker's Square recently," I replied.

"The only people looking for information about that are royal guards," she said with a quirked brow. "Did you switch sides, Man-Veil?"

"I'm not looking to turn them in," I said, holding my hands up. "I'd like to make a deal. I may have information on people who can help them achieve their goals."

"There's nothing to talk about," Ruby said. "Nobody in charge. Just a bunch of pissed-off people."

"I know that's not true," I said, inching closer to her. "I know that there's someone pulling the strings. The fires aren't random—they're targeted. Someone has a list of targets, and they're going through them one by one. Sending a message."

"You seem to know a lot about this. Don't see why you're bothering me with questions," she replied, averting her gaze.

"I just need a name."

"No, you want a meeting," she said. "A name is just that—a word. Useless." She scoffed. "Didn't the real Veil teach you anything?"

"Fine, arrange a meeting, then," I said. "Can you help me?"

A smile curled onto her red lips. "How about this? If you can bring me a name, I'll set up a meeting. But first, I'd get the hell out of my cafe before Daniel gets back."

Chapter Twenty-Eight

"Achoo!"

"Ugh," Luard said, wiping his nose with an embroidered handkerchief. "I forgot how much I hate grass."

After another two days in the mountain, we finally reached the end of the tunnel. The soft light became blinding, and I took refuge inside the dark carriage with Luard until my eyes adjusted. Although we traveled on a main gravel road, it was flanked on either side by large swaths of farmland, some with wheat, some with fruit trees, and others with produce I didn't recognize from far away. There seemed to be few people, but perhaps that was just the nature of things here.

"Are we in Kulka yet?" I asked.

"No," he said, blowing into the cloth. "About half a day's ride until we get there—and trust me, you'll know when we reach it." He leaned back on his hands, sniffing loudly. "This Mother-forsaken land is the one part of Niemen that actually produces food for the country. It's our most treasured possession. And something the Kulkans desperately want."

"I can only handle one country's turmoil," I said with a laugh. "So don't ask me to negotiate that, too."

He reached across the carriage and patted my knee. The journey out of the mountain had also given me time to ponder the breakthrough we'd had in the mines. I wasn't ready to stomach the idea of killing, so I put that in the back of my mind. I would continue on to Kulka and give Neshua my best attempt.

And if he denied me, so be it. But at least I'd know I gave it my all.

As the day drew on, we saw more Niemenian guards encamped along the road. Then, a long line of tents and a makeshift wall of wooden posts that stretched as far as the eye could see. I glanced at Luard, who seemed more preoccupied with his draining nose than with the guards.

The carriage rolled to a stop, and raised voices drew me outside. There, two Kulkan guards dressed in forest green uniforms stood with their swords drawn, preventing us from going any further. There was also a large pike in the center of the road, and more Kulkan guards behind it.

"What's going on?" I asked Hagan.

"Just the usual," he said, hopping down. "Good afternoon, we're seeking passage into Kulka."

The guard on the left put his sword down. "You got papers?"

"Of course we do," Ivan said, plucking an envelope from behind the top cushion along with a bag of coins. "Prince Luard from the kingdom of Niemen."

The guard read the letter and picked through the coins. Then he spotted me. "And who's the girl? She don't look Niemenian."

"Lady Larissa," Luard said, poking his head out and pressing his hand to the small of my back. "We're newly married. She's the daughter of a Forcadelian shipping magnate. Super rich. Great in the sack. We're on our honeymoon."

I craned my neck up at him with narrowed eyes. "Really?"

"All right," the guard said, folding up the letter and handing it back to Ivan. "Where are you headed?"

"Delina," Luard said with a grin. "I want to show my new lady the vineyards and see how frisky she gets when she's drunk."

The guard was grinning at me like I was naked, but he gave the word to clear the road so we could pass. Luard and I clambered back inside, and the carriage moved forward.

"Really? Great in the sack, huh?" I crossed my arms.

"I have a reputation," he said, wiping his nose. "They wouldn't believe I would willingly be married. I had to make it seem like you're worth the hassle. And I'd prefer to keep your real identity a secret here in Kulka, at least until we know how Neshua will receive you."

"Thanks," I said, leaning back. "I suppose it worked, though."

"Of course it did." He sat back and closed his eyes. "Offer's still open if you want to consummate—"

"I think I'm good."

I'd thought the farmlands of Niemen were impressive, but Kulka truly was worthy of its reputation as a farming nation. Green, rolling hills extended as far as the eye could see. We passed every kind of produce, from fruit trees to low vegetable patches to blooming vineyards. At night, we stopped in small villages of maybe fifty people, eating our fill of sweet peaches and succulent lamb and sleeping on beds filled with goose down.

The more I saw of the nation, the more I thought about how all of this could've been mine had I not run away. At the time, the notion of leaving Forcadel, of being alone in a foreign land, had been terrifying. Now, I didn't find the prospect so scary. I'd been to nearly every country in this continent in the past few weeks, and

I'd managed just fine. Perhaps there was something to everyone's faith in me.

On the second day of travel, we passed by a mound of what appeared to be perfectly ripe apples by the side of the road.

"What is this nonsense?" Luard asked as the carriage rolled to a stop.

"Maybe they need help," I said, climbing out of the carriage.

In the distance, a middle-aged woman was walking toward us with a wagonful of apples. She didn't look in danger, but I still wanted to investigate. I hopped the low fence and walked toward her.

"Good afternoon," I called to her. "Are you well?"

"As well as anyone in this country," she barked back. "Are you looking for food? Ten gold coins for this bushel."

I released a short laugh. "I mean…there's a perfectly edible pile by the road. Did you mean to do that?"

"'Course," she said. "And you can take that pile if you want, I guess. You just looked like fancy rich people who have money to spend on an old woman."

She wasn't old, but I didn't want to argue the point. "Why are you throwing out all this food?"

"Ain't got nowhere to sell it anymore," she said with a shake of her head. "With all the borders closed with Forcadel, we can't get our goods down there. There's no point in even going to market here in Kulka. Too many other vendors in competition with each other."

"Surely, there's someone who could eat that food," Luard said.

"They can eat off the side of the road, I guess." She picked up the wagon and walked back down the dusty road toward her farmhouse.

"I'm sure Neshua will love to hear that his people have nowhere to sell their goods," Luard said with a knowing look. "And I'm sure the people of Forcadel are missing their fresh food.

More ammunition for your meeting."

We had no need for the food, so we carried on, although I kept the woman's dejected face in my mind's eye. All that food would've gone to Forcadel. Were people starving in my country now?

And more importantly, did Ilara care about them?

The answer was clear—if she did, she wouldn't keep the gates closed out of some petty, vindictive need for people to acknowledge her.

My fists balled as hot anger surged through me. Katarine had spoken at length about the delicate trade balance between Kulka, Forcadel, and Niemen. Then, I'd thought it was easy to simply give up and shift pieces to make things more equal. Ilara had proven just how much we relied on these other countries—and how much they relied on us.

"You look like you're about to deck someone," Luard said.

"Maybe I am."

He chuckled. "Keep that righteous fire alive. You'll need it when you meet with Neshua."

Four days after we left the border, we arrived in Delina. It was a quaint city, perhaps the most sprawling of the three capital cities I'd been to in the past few weeks. It was dirtier, too, with clay-colored roads and patches of grass growing from beneath whatever stones had been laid. Still, the people were well-dressed and well-fed, and seemed not to care that a Niemenian entourage had rolled into their capital city.

"Where's the castle?" I asked, peering out of the window. I expected to see it rising somewhere among the low buildings.

"Oh, it's an ugly thing," he said. "Takes up a large footprint, but not very tall. Over near the water."

"That's right, we're near the water again, aren't we?" I said. "How long would it take for a ship from Delina to get to

Forcadel?"

He dabbed his nose. Now that we were out of the grass, his allergies seemed to have calmed somewhat. "Ships usually hug the coastline from here to Neveri, then cut through the Vanhoja river down to Forcadel Bay. But, of course, there's a blockade on both the bay and the river, so..."

The carriage stopped abruptly, and Luard and I shared a look when we heard Ivan shouting. With my hand on my knives, I opened the door, Luard right behind me. Preventing us from moving any further was a gaggle of Kulkan guards, all of whom had their swords pointed at us.

"What is the meaning of this?" Luard said, climbing out of the carriage. "Do you not see the... Oh."

"Oh?" I looked over his shoulder, then I caught who he was looking at. "Oh."

"Do they not teach you manners in Niemen? When one enters a foreign country, one must announce his presence to the royal family."

Ammon, Crown Prince of Kulka and my former fiancé, stood in front of ten guards. I only recognized him due to the gold crown on his head, as he looked nothing like the frog-faced boy who'd come to Forcadel to sign the peace treaty between our nations. The man before me now was roguishly handsome, with thick lips and large, green eyes that seemed to look straight through me. I wasn't in the market for a husband anymore, but I probably could've grown to love him if he'd turned out like this.

"Well, considering we haven't actually made it three feet inside the capital city, I don't see how we could've announced ourselves before now," Luard said, an easy smile on his face. "I've visited your fair country many times, Ammon. You've never paid me a personal visit before."

His eyes darted to me. Did he recognize me? "My guards informed me you'd taken a wife. I knew that to be false, so I wanted to see for myself what kind of Forcadelian whore you were dragging into my country."

"I'm not sure which offends me more, that you think it was a lie that I'm married or my choice in bride," Luard said with a glance at me. "Prince Ammon, may I introduce Princess Brynna-Larissa Archer Rhodes Lonsdale."

I gawked at Luard. Clearly, he was no longer concerned about keeping my identity a secret.

"W... Aren't you supposed to be dead?" Ammon's eyes bulged, reminding me of the boy he'd been, and his hand slid off his pommel.

"That's what they keep telling me," I said with a hesitant smile. Luard nudged me softly and I cleared my throat, stepping out of the carriage. "I'm here to speak with your father. Would you mind giving us an escort?"

His sharp eyes narrowed and he lost whatever surprise had captured him. A cruel smile twisted onto his thin lips, giving him something of a ratlike expression. "Please tell me you're here to ask for asylum from the Severian queen."

"No, I'm not," I said slowly. "Why?"

"Because I'd love the pleasure of denying it to you," he said, resting his hand on his sword once more. "Whatever issue you may have, I'm afraid you'll have to deal with it alone. My father won't want to speak with you, and, frankly, neither do I."

I couldn't believe my ears. "Don't be petty, Ammon. I'm sorry I didn't marry you, but—"

"Brynn, not a wise choice," Luard muttered beside me.

"From what I hear, I came out on the better end of things." Ammon sniffed, his gaze dropping to my muddy boots. "After all, I'm still a prince and you're...well, a ghost."

I opened my mouth to continue our repartee, but Luard caught my eye. I wiped the annoyance off my face. "From what *I* hear, Ammon, the Kulkans aren't too pleased with Ilara, either. Iron gates closed, trade routes disrupted." I paused and shrugged. "Only so much food you can produce and eat without shipping it to the other countries, right?"

"It's not an ideal situation," he said, after a long pause. "Our envoys aren't having much luck with her. But I have faith the logjam will end, and we'll be back to an amicable solution. Better, perhaps, than when the Lonsdales ruled."

"I hear all it takes is for you to accept her as the rightful queen of Forcadel," I said, crossing my arms over my chest. "Which begs the question, if you hate me so much, why hasn't your father accepted her?"

He cleared his throat, a little pink appearing on the tops of his cheeks. "My father isn't convinced her reign will last. But I am."

"Such a fan of Ilara, are you?" I asked.

"More a fan of her than you."

I barked a laugh. "Oh, get over yourself. Aren't you already married with two kids? Little desperate to be so mad over someone you barely knew."

"You *ran out* on an official treaty," he snarled. "And, to date, Forcadel's end of the bargain remains unfulfilled. In my eyes, that makes you untrustworthy."

I took a step toward him. "You and I both know that Ilara's ruining Forcadel, and when Forcadel's ruined, so is the Kulkan economy, so quit being such a little sh—"

"*Brynna*," Luard snapped, reminding me that I was in a foreign country and addressing the crown prince.

I straightened, embarrassment warming my cheeks. "Listen, all I need is an audience with your father. Then we will be on our way."

"It's common courtesy," Luard added. "As one royal to another."

Ammon was silent for a long time, chewing on his ample lips and thinking. Then he straightened, another ominous smile curling onto his face. "Fine, I'll take you to my father."

My mouth fell open in surprise. "R-really?"

"Oh, of course." That cruel smile widened, and my hope disappeared like a candle blowing out. "He's been in such a morose mood lately. It will be nice to give him a good laugh. And you, dear former fiancé, are quite the joke."

Chapter Twenty-Nine

My stomach churned uncomfortably as Luard's carriage rattled toward the castle, flanked on all sides by guards both Niemenian and Kulkan. I'd hoped to have more time to think about how I'd approach Neshua, but now my time was up. And based on Ammon's response, I was already at a major disadvantage with his father.

Luard was seemingly more put out with our treatment than with my impending meeting with the king. "I should have Ariadna send his father a strongly worded letter. I am a prince. This is uncalled for."

"You can't blame him," I said, looking at the ceiling. "Things are upended since Ilara took over. Maybe he thought you were bringing a Severian into his country to take over."

"Nobody's stupid enough to do that."

I glared at him. "Har har."

He nudged me gently. "You seem a bit spooked. Don't tell me

you're getting cold feet again?"

"Not cold feet, but..." I sank back into the cushions and allowed the worry to envelop me fully. "Anger I can handle. Distrust, sure. But laughing at me? I have no idea how to combat that. I've never been *laughed* at before."

"Not even when you showed up in Forcadel wearing a mask?"

"No," I snapped. "Because I showed up in Forcadel and beat the shit out of a bunch of criminals. I earned my respect."

"Then you'll just have to earn Neshua's respect," he said. "What do you know about Kulka so far that could help you?"

"It's...odd that Ammon was there to meet us at the outskirts of the city," I began, glancing out the window. "Neshua must be spooked by Ilara, so any foreigner in the city is under suspicion."

"Which means..."

"Maybe he'll be eager to have me back?" I said, hopefully. "But I don't know, Ammon—"

"People who don't sit on the throne don't always know what's best for it," Luard said.

"Fair enough. But I still can't figure why Neshua hasn't accepted Ilara yet. Of all the trading partners, they have the most to lose. Forcadel takes a lot of their food off their hands."

"Might be a good question to ask Neshua," Luard said. "You never know, he might just tell you. Or, if you're even luckier, he won't and you'll be able to read it on his face." He chuckled. "I do so love palace intrigue."

We turned a corner and came through a pair of iron gates at the front of the castle. Thick-trunked oak trees lined the gravel road, and even here on the royal grounds, there were orchards and groves to provide food for the country. My heart pounded as I rubbed my sweaty hands on my pants. I was in no shape to meet with Neshua, and yet, there I was.

"You look like you're about to hurl." Luard reached into my bag and pulled out the small leather pouch of tinneum. "Take some of this and calm the hell down."

I took the bag from him and pinched out a small amount, pressing it into the bottom of my lip. The tangy, metallic taste filled my mouth. At once, the cacophony of nervous voices in my mind echoed into silence, leaving nothing but the sound of horse hooves on gravel. As the carriage rolled to a stop, I inhaled deeply, grabbing hold of my confidence and allowing my worries to fall to the side—at least temporarily.

"Feel better?" Luard asked as I released a loud breath, slumping back into the cushion.

I nodded, pushing the small bit of greenery to the back of my mouth to chew.

"Remember what I said about masks. You need to wear one of stone when you go in there. Don't show anything on your face, don't even hint about your indecision. Go in strong, be confident, and get what you want from them." He reached under the seat again, this time taking the gold circlet out of its carrying case and handing it to me. "You're a queen. So act like it."

The carriage rolled to a stop, and some of the butterflies returned, but not nearly as badly. I rested the gold crown on my head, letting the weight of it be a reminder. The door opened to Ivan's sympathetic face, and Ammon's annoyed one just beyond. "Well? I don't have all day."

"Be nice to him," Luard muttered under his breath. "It'll throw him for a loop."

I stepped out of the carriage, Ivan squeezing my hand as I settled on the ground. I straightened my shoulders and walked forward with purpose. I was in enemy territory, and this was my one and only chance to prove to them I was worth my salt. And above all else, I tried not to think about how if I failed in the next ten minutes, my entire journey would be for naught.

The carriage had come into a large circle with a bubbling fountain bearing a statue of some long-ago Kulkan king, holding a sword and a bushel of grapes.

"You smell atrocious," Ammon said as I fell into step beside him.

I wanted to match your charming personality. The words were on the tip of my tongue, but Luard's warning echoed in my ears. The tinneum leaf had made me calmer, but I wasn't out of the woods yet.

"Awfully presumptuous of you to show up here, asking for help," Ammon scoffed. "I can't wait to hear my father deny it to you."

"You know," I said, as we came to a stop in front of two large double doors, "I would love to meet your wife. I'm sure she's absolutely lovely."

"She is," he said, lifting his chin in protest. "As I said, I think I came out on the better end of things."

I forced a smile onto my face as I recognized the uncertainty on his face. "I'm sure you did. And for what it's worth, finding you a suitable replacement to uphold my end of the treaty will be first on my list once I'm back in power."

He pursed his lips then made a gesture for the guards to open the doors. With his back turned, I allowed myself a smirk of victory.

It was short-lived, however, as I walked into the throne room and came face to face with the king of Kulka. Neshua sat on a golden throne at the front of the receiving room. Here, as in Niemen, there were small differences from Forcadel. Instead of paintings of conquests, there were tapestries depicting harvests and garden parties. Fresh cut flowers in vases sat atop marble columns behind the king. There was a bowl of half-eaten green grapes beside him, which he plucked from and popped into his mouth. He was much older than I remembered, grayer around the temples. But his sharp green eyes were the same. I held my chin high as I walked into the room.

"Well, well," he said, his mouth full. "Look who's come on bended knee, asking for help from the great nation of Kulka. Please, tell me what I might do for a disgraced princess of Forcadel."

I pushed the tinneum leaf around in my mouth, allowing my thoughts to slow down. I forgot the stakes, forgot what would happen if I failed, and just believed that I wouldn't.

A smile curled onto my face as I slipped into The Veil's lower octave. "I should be asking what I might do for you, Neshua."

His sharp eyes looked up when I declined to use his honorific, as Luard had suggested. "I don't *need* anything you can provide."

"Are you sure?" I asked, clasping my hands in front of me while making sure not to tilt my head too far and lose my crown. "I just got an up close and personal look at your country on the way in. Seems like you're suffering from the same problems as the Niemenians. Closed borders mean you can't sell your goods to the Forcadelians and points beyond. Your relationship with Niemen is still strained, so you've got nowhere to sell your goods. It seems everyone would be better served if the Forcadelian queen simply returned to the previous agreements."

"Yes, they would," he said with something of a grimace. "I should ask the current queen to do that."

I smiled. "I'm sure she'd be happy to, just as soon as you declare her the rightful sovereign of Forcadel."

His eyes flashed, if only for a second, and I understood what Luard meant about palace intrigue. Neshua wasn't ready to accept Ilara, which meant I had a leg up.

"I don't understand why it's any business of yours what happens between Forcadel and Kulka," he said.

"Well, believe it or not, my loyalty to my country doesn't require me to sit on a throne," I said. "Or did word not reach you about how I spent the last three years in Forcadel as a masked vigilante called The Veil?"

It was a gamble, but I hoped, perhaps, it might prove something to him. My hands began to sweat as he turned to his bowl of grapes and pulled another off the vine.

After a pause that lasted for ages, he swallowed and lifted a shoulder. "I might've heard something like that from Lady Vernice in her last letter. She indicated you'd nearly killed her."

"It was knockout powder and she was fine," I said with a wave of my hand. "The point is, I don't want my country back because of some ego trip. I want it back because my people are suffering, and as long as I draw breath, I'll do whatever I can to help them. Whether it's as queen or a vigilante."

"That's all well and good," he said. "But you are one woman—and barely a woman at that. What chance do you have against Ilara's forces?"

My pulse skipped, but I couldn't back down now. "I already have the assurances of Queen Ariadna that if I launch an offensive, she will provide forces to assist me in taking back Forcadel from the Severians." *It's just dependent on you.*

"Oh, do you?" he said with a raised eyebrow. "Why would she give such a promise to you?"

"Perhaps she believes in what I can do," I said. "And while the Niemenians would be enough, I think it might send a better message if I had the blessing of the Kulkan king as well."

He plucked his goblet off the table and took a long sip. "Blessing and, I would assume, some artillery."

"If you see fit to provide it," I replied evenly, "it would be welcome."

"And how do you plan to take this artillery and support and turn it into a coup?"

I told him the same thing I'd told Ariadna, about Ilara's tenuous grip, and about the forces I could count on when I returned. As before, I embellished Celia's numbers and also added a few hopeful figures from Ariadna's side, all the while, watching

Neshua's reaction for any sign I might be making headway. The tinneum in my mouth was starting to fade, and my fears were creeping toward the front of my mind again.

"I must confess," he said, popping another grape into his mouth, "you seem much more capable than Vernice indicated. Perhaps all that time away from the throne did you some good."

My hopes dared to lift. "Does that mean you'll help me?"

"Well, what you're asking for is a lot," he said, examining the nail on his left thumb. "And while it's clear you can speak to kings and queens and bend them to your will, what isn't clear is if you can deliver on your promises. I have nothing to prove that you're even capable of leading an offensive, let alone succeeding."

"I can. I—"

"Words are meaningless," he said. "Show me you can do what you say, and I'll agree to your terms."

"Show you what?" My heart pounded in my chest; I had no idea how to do what he asked. "That I can take back a kingdom? I'll show you when I do it."

He cracked a humorless smile. "I'm thinking more a test. Prove to me that you can do what you say, and you will have your forces."

I forced my mouth to remain closed as I ran through a thousand different scenarios. How could I prove to him I could take over a kingdom? There was no comparable action—perhaps conquering a city, but what city? A Kulkan city? A Forcadelian one?

"I've just received word that Queen Ilara has closed those infernal gates in Neveri," Neshua said. "It's now downright impossible to get anything past the border."

"You want me to get the gates back open?" I shrugged. "Sure."

"Oh, no, that's just a temporary solution," he said. "Neveri has long been a missing jewel on the Kulkan map, and I'm eager to get it back. So to prove to me that you're capable of conquering

Forcadel, you will conquer Neveri."

I chewed the tinneum, which now had no flavor, to buy myself some time. I'd had one card, and Neshua had played it before I had a chance to. I still wasn't wholly convinced it was the best option, but now, it was either give him Neveri or nothing.

Scratch that—it was *conquer* Neveri or nothing.

"If you'll provide me passage to the city and some forces to assist," I said slowly. "I accept."

"I have a better idea." Neshua's calculating smile sent chills down my spine. "I'll have Ammon take you down to a port near the border—we'll send our fastest ship laden with our best guns."

I actually smiled.

"But you will be responsible for taking the city by yourself, with whatever forces you already have," he finished, sending a dagger into my heart. "Once you've done that, we will consider helping you."

It took everything in me to keep my jaw from falling to the floor. "You want me to accomplish this *alone*?"

He plucked his goblet off the table and waved it at me. "You accomplished much as The Veil, so you've indicated. You have forces back in Forcadel you could call on. Unless, of course, you were lying about them."

"Of course not," I said, scrambling to keep my cool as sweat broke out behind my neck.

This seemed like a bad decision, but I had nothing else. If I wanted Forcadel back, I would have to meet his terms. And even though every inch of me wanted me to resist, to find some other option, my gut knew this was as good as I would get from the farmer king.

"Deal."

Chapter Thirty

"So, it's not the best outcome, but it's not the worst..."

Luard had been waiting for me with the carriage, and as we rode toward the city center, I filled him in on what had happened. As I spoke, all the panic that the tinneum leaf had kept at bay threatened to sweep me into darkness.

I groaned and buried my head in my hands, not even bothering to pick up the circlet as it slid off my head. "I'm so screwed."

"You aren't screwed," he said, swiping the crown from the floor and replacing it in its box. "Yes, things are a bit more complicated. But you aren't completely defenseless. You have me. You have Ivan and the rest of the guards. You have the ond."

"I'm not using that now," I snapped. "It's bad enough I'm betraying my country—"

He sighed, annoyed. "You aren't betraying it. You're merely moving some pieces around the board to place yourself in a better strategic position." He tilted his head to the side. "I would think a challenge like this would be something you'd welcome. This sounds like something a vigilante would do."

"I never did anything on this scale," I said. "Sinking ships and causing trouble for Beswick is nothing compared to capturing an entire city. I don't even know where I'd begin."

"How did you accomplish things as The Veil?"

"I learned what I could about the target," I said. "Listened. Found his weaknesses. Exploited them where I could, and where I couldn't, I hit them where it hurt." I made a face. "I don't see—"

"Learn what you can about Neveri," Luard said, rolling his eyes. "Find the weaknesses and exploit them."

"It's easier to exploit the weakness of a crime boss than a city."

"I have faith you'll figure it out," he said with a grin. "Besides that, you aren't on your own. We're going to join you in Neveri."

"That's very kind of you." I shook my head slowly "But I don't think that's a good idea. This…is gonna be dangerous."

"So?"

"I'm probably going to be sleeping in places you might not enjoy. And to be honest…" I swallowed. "While I appreciate your help up until this point, I don't know how I'd use you going forward. I have enough to worry about without trying to keep you safe."

He pressed a hand over his chest in mock surprise. "Princess Brynna, you wound me. I'm very helpful."

I knew he was kidding, but I wasn't. "This isn't going to be like in Linden, or even Delina. I'm going to be in full-on vigilante mode."

"I am well aware. But you can't do it all, Brynna," he said, all the levity gone from his voice. "Perhaps I'm not good with a sword, but you don't have a lot of allies right now. You could use all the help you can get."

Luard paid for a couple of rooms at the nicest inn in the city. As I was unable to sit still, Nils and Asdis escorted me on a walk around to stretch my legs and prepare as best I could for this next leg of my journey. They were as comfortable here as they'd been under the mountain, and seemed as eager as Luard to help me.

"If I were you, I'd find a mapmaker to sketch the city for you," Nils said as we walked through the streets of the capital. "You said you've been there, but it's always easier to visualize things when it's written down."

"You should probably get a compass, too," Asdis said. "There's a nasty swamp down there, and if you ever need a quick escape, you might need to hide in it."

"I need new weapons too," I said, adjusting my slingbag against my chest. "I'm out of arrows. I doubt they've got any Nestori potions here, but they may." I cast a longing glance at the sea in the distance, wishing it looked more like home. "I wish Kieran would float into town. He always has the best stuff." To their confused faces, I clarified, "He's a pirate."

"You certainly associate with all kinds, don't you?" Nils said. "Princes and pirates, thieves and soldiers."

"Gives me a complete picture of the world," I said. "Although the princes and soldiers tend to have limited information."

Nils got directions to a local mapmaker and paid two gold coins to commission a drawing of Neveri to be completed by the end of the day. While he haggled on the time of delivery, I gazed longingly at a drawing of Forcadel, walking through the streets in my memory and trying not to get too homesick. I ran my finger along the cross-section where Tasha's butchery—and my home— had been. Was the pile of rubble still there?

"Brynna?" Nils asked, getting my attention. "Ready to go?"

I tore my gaze away from Forcadel and memories and followed the two Niemenians out the door.

Asdis declared our next stop would be a weaponsmaker, as the

Kulkans always had something new in terms of design and aesthetic.

"Why?" I asked.

"Lot of spread-out land," Nils said. "More lawlessness in Kulka than in other countries just because there's more space to cover, so they have to be more creative with their defenses."

"And offenses, too," Asdis said. "Oh, that one looks great!"

She pulled me inside the large shop, and I was at a loss for words. Swords of all sizes and shapes hung in rows, each with a sign denoting the style. Asdis made a beeline for a curved scimitar, while Nils browsed through the broadswords. I casually examined a pair of knives that were as long as my forearm and a club-like weapon that released spikes at the press of a button, but neither were really my style.

In the corner was a display of crossbows and arrows promising deadly accurate aim, and a target leaning against the wall to test it. My crossbow was an old favorite, but the one I picked up was light as a feather. I aimed and shot it at the target, earning a whistle of approval from Nils.

"You didn't even aim."

"I did, just very quickly," I replied, looking closely at the springs and gears. It was fancy, but probably not very practical. The more pieces a weapon had, the more likely it was to fail. "Years of practice."

"I've had years of practice and I'm not that good," he said.

"You've had years of practice in a controlled environment," I said, placing the crossbow back and gathering a set of arrows. "It's different in combat. You've got to improvise."

"Ooh, look at this," Asdis said, handing me an arrow with a long rope attached to it. "See, the arrowhead is weighted. It's supposed to be good for climbing walls." She handed it to me. "Could come in handy with that gate."

I held the arrow for a minute, chewing my lip. "Is there any way I can convince Luard to stay behind?"

"Do you think we can convince him of anything?" Asdis asked. "And besides that, it sounds like you'll need our help. We may not be able to hit a target without aiming, but we have swords and hands, eyes and ears."

I opened my mouth to argue, but I had the peculiar sensation that I was being watched. Outside, a Kulkan guard had appeared, and based on the scowl on his face, he was none too pleased to find me in a weapons shop.

"Would you mind paying for these?" I said, handing the bundle of arrows to Asdis. "And maybe a whetstone if they have it. I'm going to go see what he wants."

I walked out of the store, a chill skittering down my spine at his stare. "Can I help you?"

"Be ready to leave at sundown," he said. "And tell the Niemenians they are no longer welcome in this city."

"No longer welcome, we'll see about that," Luard muttered.

As the sky turned pink and purple over the horizon, he and his guards escorted me down to the docks. My pulse was throbbing in quick rhythm, but outwardly I was calm. I had replenished my weapons and Luard had given me a full coin purse of gold.

I was dressed in one of my older, black tunics and leggings, and instead of the thick, black wool cloak I'd been wearing since Linden, I returned to my leather vigilante cloak. It had been too thin to wear in the northern climates, but now that I was returning south, it would be plenty.

"You were planning on leaving anyway," I said with a smile. "How long will it take you to get to Neveri by land?"

"Two weeks, maybe," Ivan said. "Depends on what we find at the Kulkan-Forcadel border."

"If they don't let you through," I said nervously, "don't push it.

If it comes down to you being arrested or—"

"Don't worry your pretty little crowned head," Luard said, patting our joined arms. "Do you know how many times I've been nearly arrested?"

"Ten," Ivan mouthed behind Luard's back.

"Nine, you bastard," Luard said. "That last one her father only threatened to arrest me."

"What's the difference?" Ivan asked.

I smiled, but I couldn't shake my nerves. Up until now, I'd been in the company of friends—or strangers who became friends. Ammon's ship was full of hostile actors, and no manner of cajoling or favors would change their mind.

The smell of the salt water and the sloshing of the water against the dock posts brought me back home, and my nerves calmed somewhat.

"If I were you," Luard said as he gazed at the ship that would be my passage on the open ocean, "I would establish your dominance early. Your energy is very nervous—they'll pick up on that. And what's to say they don't toss you overboard?" He pulled something from his pocket—a new mask. This one with gold thread. "If you're going to wear a mask, you might as well have some royal markings."

With care, I thumbed the embroidery. "Where did you get this?"

"I made it," Ivan said. "I'm quite good with a needle. We all thought it would be helpful."

Shaking my head, I placed the mask in my slingbag and turned to them, sadness tugging at my heart. "So this is goodbye for now, I suppose."

"We'll be in Niemen before you know it," Luard said.

I hugged each of them individually, lingering with Asdis, Luard, and Ivan. And then, with my new mask in hand, I marched up the plank to the boat.

Chapter Thirty-One

Felix

"Give me his name, and I'll set up a meeting."

Just when I thought I'd cleared a mountain, another popped up to block my path.

It was ingenious, really. The person who was leading the rebellion had been careful not to let his name slip except to those he trusted. And only those he trusted got a meeting with him. Ergo, I would have to prove I could be trusted in order to get his name to get a meeting.

Chicken, meet egg.

Back at the castle, Ilara was reveling in her decision to close the gates. She blissfully ignored reports that food imports had grown scarce; in fact, she cared very little about anything except showing off her wealth and status. But my blood pounded in my ears whenever I received that small card signaling she wanted to see me.

"Felix, dear. It seems like forever since we've spoken," she said, offering me a warm smile that I knew was completely fake. "Have you made any progress on the one thing I've asked you to do?"

"Unfortunately, no," I said, forcing myself not to see the look of pity on Katarine's face and girding myself for the fury that would radiate from Ilara at my failure.

"Oh, well," she said, pushing herself to stand. She wasn't angry. But why? Had Coyle told her he suspected me? Was she about to put me in irons? I couldn't believe I was hoping for her mood to snap, but at least I'd know where I stood with her.

What in the Mother's name are you playing at? She looked like the docile princess who'd come on bended knee to ask for help, not the raging monarch she'd been over the past few months. I didn't trust this new-old version of her, so I kept my thoughts short.

"I'm frustrated with my lack of progress," I said to the silence. "And I don't want to disappoint you."

To that, she chuckled. "I daresay this challenge has flummoxed you. You know, Brynna spoke very highly of you, which was why I'd allowed you to stay on."

I couldn't help the hitch in my breath, and I struggled to come up with a response that wasn't to scold her for using Brynna's name.

My silence was met with a coy smile. "I think you're still distracted, Felix. You say you're loyal, but I don't see it. Not in your eyes, not in your actions. For Brynna, you followed her around as a masked vigilante. But for me, you won't even try to find who's responsible for hurting your own people."

My heart was beating faster now. Was she testing me to see my reaction or was she merely making conversation? Ilara may have had irrational tendencies, but she wasn't idiotic.

"Indeed," I said, after a long pause. "But I'll redouble my efforts and bring them to justice."

"See that you do," she said with a smile.

I pressed my fist to my chest and bowed. "Of course, Your Majesty. Was that all you needed today?" *Please, Mother, let it be all.*

"No, actually, Lieutenant Coyle informs me that we've got a new crop of graduates ready," she said, offering her arm. "I'd love it if you'd accompany me."

"G-graduation?" I couldn't help my surprise. "But we just graduated a class less than a month ago."

"Yes, but we've had some...newer recruits?" She offered me her arm. "Come, let's see what Lieutenant Coyle has done with his men."

I had no idea what I might find during this graduation, but I readied myself to offer words of support to my cadets. I hadn't seen any of them in weeks. They were probably scared, confused, and the more I could show a unified front, the less chance they might make a wrong move and end up in Ilara's crosshairs.

What was left of the cadets stood at attention against the back wall. They wore their dress uniforms, a dark blue jacket and white pants with brown boots. The oldest ones—only sixteen—had small rapiers at their hips.

As we drew closer, their gazes swept toward me, and I saw relief reflected on several of their faces. Ilara made sure to walk the length of them, smiling and holding my arm as if she owned me. Which, I supposed, she did.

Coyle stood at the front of the green. He bowed low to Ilara and nodded slightly to me.

"Your Majesty, I think you'll be happy with what's been going on out here. These cadets are truly ready to take their next steps."

I couldn't resist a small jab. "You must truly be impressive if these kids have been under your care for a matter of days."

His smile widened. "Happily, they were under Captain Maarit's control. I merely continued what she had started."

My unease grew but I didn't respond. Instead, I kept my eyes on the green where the doors had opened and another squad of cadets exited, walking two-by-two. All Severian, all with a steely-eyed focus. I counted nearly sixty—more than had just graduated.

"Who are they?" I asked.

"It's as I said," Coyle said. "The cadets that have been under Captain Maarit's tutelage. I think they'll make a fine addition to the forces already in the city. I'm sure they'll do their best to quell the brewing rebellion."

I wasn't sure why these young kids made me nervous—perhaps it was that there was nothing kind in their faces. And perhaps they wouldn't have the same love of country that my cadets did. I chanced a look at my former charges; the oldest ones hadn't flinched. The younger ones, though, had gone pale. Did they see their future here slipping away, as I did?

"They are quite obedient," Coyle said, raising his sword to signal them to begin their sparring match. The Severians faced each other with unflinching ferocity, and it made my stomach turn to think about what might happen if those kids were set on mine. How Coyle could stand there and be their leader was beyond me.

"Very well done," Ilara said, clapping her hands together. "Coyle, I must say, I wasn't convinced you were the right man for the job. But seeing how quickly these children have taken to you, well..." She grinned, and for a moment, she wasn't a cruel mistress. "I'm pleased I picked you for this job." Her gaze left him, and her cruelty returned. "Wouldn't you say, Felix?"

"I can hardly tell the difference between Forcadelian and Severian." I should have held my tongue more, but I couldn't tear my eyes away from my youngest cadets, pale with terror.

"You look put out, my dear," Ilara said, turning to me with a pout. "It appears Coyle can handle things from here. Why don't you escort me back?"

Despite the rising disgust in my mouth, I allowed her to take my arm and I walked her back to the castle. She said nothing, but wore a look of superiority on her face, which told me she was plotting something.

When we reached her throne room, she pressed a hand lightly on my arm. "Katarine has been asking for someone to go speak to Lord Garwood. I wonder if you could go down there today?"

I couldn't hide my surprise. The former Councilor had been stuck in the dungeons since Ilara had taken over, and no one had been allowed to speak with him. Was she truly in a generous mood, or was there something else going on?

"I would be happy to," I said.

"I can be merciful," she said, almost as an afterthought. "*If* he accepts me as queen. See if you can convince him."

Even though I had the queen's permission, I was still leery about walking down to the dungeons. Ilara might've been warning me about what would happen if I continued defying her. Especially with this new crop of Severian soldiers. I couldn't be sure, but I feared the Severians outnumbered the Forcadelians. It would be that much harder to break Ilara's iron grip when Brynna returned.

I continued into the depths of the dungeons, assaulted by the scent of death and decay. I came to the front guard and he narrowed his eyes at me.

"Do you have permission to be down here, Captain?"

I could've had him court-martialed, but I nodded. "From the queen herself."

He hesitated for a moment, but when I showed him I had no weapons, he allowed me to pass. I continued down the dark hallway of the dungeon, inwardly flinching as the cries of the prisoners reached my ears. There were more innocents in here than criminals, of that I was certain, including the man I was sent to speak with.

The guard at the other end of the hall questioned me as his partner had, but eventually turned to unlock the cell door behind him. I stepped into the darkness, my gaze adjusting to the form of a man sitting against the wall.

"Lord Garwood?" I called.

He chuckled. "I'm not a lord anymore, Felix."

I knelt beside him, noting the gauntness of his dirty cheeks and how the spark had left his gaze.

"You'll always be a lord," I said softly.

"What are you doing here?" he asked. "Here to seal my fate, finally?"

"Ilara won't have you hanged," I said. "Optics look bad."

"She could just poison me, the way she did Maurice and August." He kicked the bowl at his feet. "I'm surprised she hasn't already."

"She's keeping you alive in case she needs you," I replied then shook my head. "You know why I'm here, and I'm sorry to have to ask it. But are you ready to swear fealty to Ilara?"

"I'm loyal to the crown of Forcadel," he said, closing his eyes. "And those who share the Lonsdale blood. Even if they no longer exist."

I sighed, closing my hand over his. "Don't be so sure of that."

He cracked open an eye, then smiled. "My sister has come to visit me in my dreams, warning me not to give up hope yet. Perhaps she knew something about her daughter."

"I don't know what other hope I can offer you," I whispered. "But I know she would be very disappointed if you were to pass before she saw you again."

The corners of his cracked lips turned upward. "How is my husband?"

"Safe in Niemen," I replied. "Katarine corresponds with him regularly with updates on your health."

"Hope she's lying to him," Garwood said with a weak, wet cough. "He'll never forgive me for putting the crown above all else."

"I can understand his frustration," I replied. "Ilara isn't going to let up any time soon. But I wanted to let you know...well, to give you a little hope that things might be changing soon."

"I have all the hope I need. The Mother protects me," he whispered, more a prayer than a statement. "And my niece is alive and on her way to reclaim her kingdom..."

If he had something else to say, it was lost as he slipped into unconsciousness. I straightened, wishing I had the power to do more for him—or to at least send a healer to his aid. Brynna would've figured out a way to do it.

Unfortunately, I wasn't Brynna, and so I left him and carried my guilt with me.

⊃————•

"How was Garwood?"

Ilara was waiting for me at the top of the dungeons; clearly she'd had me followed down here.

"Unwilling to submit," I said. "Although it doesn't appear he has much time left."

She cast me a look. "Perhaps not. But I would remember what happens to people who disappoint me. My patience is running thin, and when it wears out," she met my gaze, "you will be disposed of. Am I clear?"

"Yes, Your Majesty."

Chapter Thirty-Two

"Get up!"

I opened my eyes to shadows standing in the sunlight. Disembodied hands hoisted me upright and threw me onto the deck. Now wide awake, I scrambled to my feet and yanked my knives from my belt, seething.

"What in the Mother's name do you think you're doing?" I snapped.

"I needed that," Ammon said, sipping on something warm in a china cup. "You were sleeping on my supply of biscuits."

Slowly, my sleep-deprived brain sped back up. I was on a ship headed toward a southern port in Kulka. My esteemed hosts hadn't found a space for me, so I'd cuddled up in what I thought was an out-of-the-way nook. Turned out I'd been laying on Ammon's breakfast stash.

Once he'd retrieved his precious biscuits, the Kulkan prince retreated to the quarterdeck, and I was left to wander amongst a ship of Kulkan mariners. It was fairly clear to me that he wasn't going to want to have any long, engaging chats, so I made my way to the bow of the ship. I leaned over the railing and watched the blue waves splash up against the hull.

We were moving at a fast clip—even faster than Kieran's riverboat. As Luard had predicted, we would be hugging the coastline until we reached Neveri, or, I supposed, some port city north of it. Along the shore, small fishing villages dotted the landscape. More than once, we zoomed by a fishing vessel, out trolling for the catch of the day.

"I take it fishing is a large part of your economy, too?" I asked a sailor who came up beside me.

She gave me a look like I was dirt then picked up the rope by my feet and walked back to the middle of the boat.

"Guess you guys aren't going to be warm and hospitable either," I muttered.

After a few hours of watching the shore, I grew restless. I found an out-of-the-way spot at the front of the ship to take stock of my weapons—and try to figure out my next move once we returned to land. Of the things I'd brought from Forcadel, all I had left were my listening cups, one flashbang grenade, and some gloves that could be used to scale a building easier. That, plus the new crossbow and arrows that Luard had insisted I buy, and the map and compass was everything I had available to capture the city.

I laid the map out on the deck, placing a knife on two corners and my sword on the other to keep it still. In my youth, I'd been to Neveri a handful of times. It was the closest major city to Celia's camp, and sometimes she'd send us to fetch things she either couldn't or didn't want to steal. I was usually accompanying an older person who'd known their way around, so I hadn't taken the time to learn the street names. Still, some of the words on the map looked familiar, and if Celia could get her thieves into the city, I could sneak in as well.

Neveri was technically a river town, situated around five miles south of the mouth of the Vanhoja river. But between the ocean and Neveri, there was nothing but thick swamps and uninhabitable land that stretched all the way north toward the Kulkan border.

If the gates were truly closed, it would take some creativity to get into the city unnoticed.

I got the feeling someone was watching me and I glanced up from beneath my eyelids. One of the younger sailors stood about ten steps away, holding his hands behind his back and staring at me with wide-eyed fear.

"Yes?" I asked.

"P-Prince Ammon has asked to see you," he said. "Are you gonna kill us?"

"No," I said, sitting up. "But if you'd like a shiny gold coin, you can sit here and watch my things while I go meet with him."

The boy swallowed and looked behind him at the sailors. "I don't know—I have a lot of work—"

"Fine, fine," I said with a growl. With care, I carefully rolled the map and repacked my slingbag. "Can't bribe anyone around here, it seems."

I walked the length of the ship, feeling the gaze of the sailors on me as I went. Perhaps they were all curious about the mysterious woman who was cleaning weapons and looking over a map, too.

"I need to speak with Ammon," I said to his guards in front of the door.

"Ammon has nothing to say to you."

"Well, he summoned me," I replied sweetly. "So unless you want to disobey his direct order..."

They collectively rolled their eyes and moved out of the way. I thanked them with a saccharine smile and pushed the door open, almost immediately reveling in the shade and lack of blistering sunlight.

Inside, Ammon had clearly made this ship his own. His

princely crest adorned nearly everything, from the tapestry on the wall to the bedsheets to the wine goblet at his hand. I wouldn't have been surprised if he had the symbol tattooed on his manhood.

"You've made my crew afraid with your weapons sharpening and general appearance," he said, turning the page of his book. "Please keep your things to yourself."

"Well, considering you made me sleep outside last night, I had to make sure the weapons I'm using to take over Neveri were still on my person."

"Temper, temper," Ammon said. "If you're mean to me, I may not help you at all."

"A thousand apologies, Prince Ammon. But you see, I'm wet, cold, and hungry. And I'm on a ship where everyone thinks I'm going to murder them, apparently." I paused, Luard's voice in my mind. "But I understand that they're afraid, so I'll keep my weapons out of sight."

"Very well, that is all."

Instead of responding, I just rolled my eyes and left him. If I spent another moment in his presence, I might do something stupid.

"Oh, and Brynna?"

"Yes?" I drawled, turning around.

"The Nestori on board believes we're due for a nasty storm." He glanced up at me. "Take care not to fall overboard."

As predicted, around mid-afternoon, the energy on the ship changed. The crew began shouting more to one another and running across the deck with purpose. A looming gray cloud had formed, reaching high into the heavens, and we seemed headed straight for it. A gust of wind sent my cloak flapping behind me and shortly after, a wave crashed over the bow where I'd been sitting. The ominous storm was creeping closer—and we seemed pointed right at it.

I turned back around to rejoin Ammon—after all, I wasn't about to get tossed overboard in a storm—but his guards had reappeared to block the door.

"Go bother someone else," one said.

I released a growl of frustration and stormed away from them, but didn't get very far. The crew was moving quickly to trim the sails and tie down whatever was loose, and there seemed nowhere I could go that wasn't in the way.

"*Move!*" cried a sailor, running after a rope that had gotten free from him.

A flash of lightning streaked down to the water and the crack of thunder made me wince, both from the volume and from how close it sounded.

The ship dipped low in the valley of a wave, and another wave crashed over the side of the ship, drenching me completely, and nearly taking me with it. Luckily, my slingbag had been strapped on my back, or else it and all my weapons would have gone overboard. I said another quick prayer of thanks to Nicolasa for the foresight to make it waterproof.

Still, it didn't seem smart to remain close to the edge of the ship, so I teetered my way toward the center as the waves picked up. But it was harder now that rain began to pelt the deck, and the sun had vanished behind the dark cloud.

"*Out of the way,*" one of the sailors barked at me as I fell into him. He practically threw me against the railing, and I was drenched by a cresting wave. I wiped the salt from my eyes and coughed out the water as I spotted the quarterdeck. Prince Perfect was still seated at his desk, blissfully unbothered by the ship rocking and rolling.

Another sailor cursed as she ran into me, and I screwed up my face and wiped the wet hair from my eyes. This was ridiculous— Ammon had to let me inside. I was a guest, and he may not have agreed that I was royal, but what good would it do him if I fell overboard?

A lot, a nasty voice answered, but I brushed it out of the way. With great effort, I pulled myself the rest of the distance to the captain's quarters. But before I could knock, two guards materialized in the darkness, barring me entry.

"Oh, *come on,*" I barked at them.

They shook their heads and remained steady, a feat considering the ship was being tossed about as it was.

I released a growl of frustration and turned away, searching the deck for shelter. Now the rain was coming in sheets, and lightning kept cracking the sky. I feared it would hit one of the tall masts and the whole ship would be alight. Then we'd all be doomed.

With my heart beating wildly, and my mind racing through the terrible scenarios, I remembered the tinneum in my bag. With trembling, cold fingers, I found the small pouch and gave myself a small taste. Immediately, the fear in my mind began to loosen, even as the ship still rocked in the waves.

I was pressed up against the main mast, and seemed to be mostly out of the way. The sailors didn't seem scared—just harried as they tied down things that had become loose. Inside the quarterdeck, Ammon was casually sipping on his wine. I seemed to be the only one on board who was fearful.

I closed my eyes and focused on that fact—if they weren't afraid, I wouldn't be either. Or at least, I would try very hard to convince myself not to be.

Weather was weird. One minute, I was hoping I wouldn't drown in a tempestuous black sea, the next we were sailing along a glittering ocean. If my boots weren't squelching with every step, and my hands weren't still shaking from cold and fear, I wouldn't have known we'd been caught in a ferocious storm at all.

We must've made excellent time, because the Kulkan port city came into view as the sun began to set in the distance. I was ready to be off this stupid boat and continuing my journey. If all went according to plan, tonight I'd finally be back on Forcadelian soil for the first time in weeks. It wasn't home, but it would be closer than I'd been.

I let that lovely thought bolster me as Ammon finally graced me with his presence and the ship prepared to dock.

"Well? You've been looking at that map for ages. Surely you have a plan for capturing the city?" he asked.

"My style is more flexible," I replied with a dry look.

"Fair enough," he said, surprising me. "I'll be embarking to the closest Kulkan military outpost. It's about two hours' fast ride from the border, and half a day from Neveri."

I nodded, grateful that he was offering to help me further. "If you'll get me a horse, I should be able to sneak past the border—"

He laughed. "Oh, dear Brynna. I'm merely telling you *my* plan. How you get to Neveri from here is up to you."

There it is. Of course he wasn't helping. Our agreement had been that he'd take me to this port, and nothing else.

"Don't dawdle," he said, turning away. "I'll be inspecting the outpost and when I am finished, I'll return to Delina. If I don't receive a message from you before I depart, well…" He cracked a grin over his shoulder. "Good luck."

"And how long will you be at the outpost?" I asked.

He shrugged. "My style is more flexible. It depends on what I'm dealing with."

"Walk out on one wedding and suddenly nobody likes you," I grumbled.

Chapter Thirty-Three

As soon as the ship's plank touched the dock, I was off. My legs wobbled from being on solid land for the first time in a few days, but I carried on, determined to show all the Kulkans that I wasn't a weakling.

The town itself was fairly small for a port city, with flat-roofed houses that would make a vigilante's work easy. The citizenry had gathered in clumps around the dock to see their prince arrive, and I didn't miss their star-struck gazes. Ammon was beloved in his country.

My stomach, however, made it very clear that before I tackled Neveri, I would need to eat. So I headed into the first mess hall I found, welcomed by the smell of freshly baked bread and roasted vegetables. I paid the woman one silver for a large plate and a tankard of mead, and settled in. The food was gone in minutes, earning me a chuckle from the man who was clearing the plates.

"We don't normally get people that eager to eat," he said,

giving me a look. "Especially ones who've been in from sea."

"Let's just say my traveling companions weren't the best," I said, sitting back and growing tired from a full belly. "Speaking of, how do I get to Neveri from here?"

"It's southeast. There's a road you can take that'll get you there in about five or six hours. Three if you can get a horse," the man replied. "But you'll only get so far before they stop you. Ain't nobody crossing these days."

"I'm sure a few people are getting by—"

"Not for the past few weeks. Used to be that you could sneak across. Now they guard the road like it's precious gold or something." He blew air out between his lips. "It's getting bad over there. The border towns were used to getting fruit from this side of things—soil's a bit better. And we can't eat all that we produce, either."

"Yeah, I heard," I said with a grimace. "So no one's getting through? Not even with money?"

"Maybe with money. But none of us have enough to give up to cross."

I nodded. Luard would be able to pass, that was good. As for me, I'd have to figure something else out.

After finishing my meal, I set out onto the darkening streets, taking the route the man had given me. There was a chill in the air, but it was nice, and the wind had a salty taste. Children still played outside. Although they didn't seem to have a care, their parents all wore a look of uncertainty.

"Nervousness spreads." Nicolasa's words seemed appropriate even in Kulka.

I left the city, following a main road with signs pointing to Neveri. All of them had another sign pinned on top of them—*border closed.* My feet had begun to ache, but I strengthened my resolve every time I passed those signs, and the miles to reach the border ticked lower.

In the distance, a small city was visible—whether it was Neveri or not, I had no idea. Based on the last sign I passed, there were still ten miles to the city, so probably not. I checked my compass, which still pointed in a southeasterly direction, so I was going the right way. Perhaps it was another border city on the way—and perhaps, my swollen feet would get a reprieve and I could purchase an evening at the inn.

Hoofbeats pounded in the distance behind me. There was a group of riders coming on me fast. Kulkan soldiers, perhaps? Either way, I didn't want to chance anything, so I found a nearby bush to hide behind. I hoped the moonlight wouldn't give me away, but even with it shining fully, it was still difficult to see out on the empty road.

I held my breath as the riders passed by—four horsemen and... Ammon's carriage.

I didn't have the energy to scowl; if Ammon was headed toward the smattering of lights in the distance, that meant it was the Kulkan encampment. I would surely find a heavy contingent of Forcadelian soldiers on the other side of the border. Crossing there might not be the best option.

So, hoping the Mother and my compass would guide me, I turned on my heel and headed south, hoping I'd come across something better.

It didn't take me long to realize why the road was the best way to go. For a few miles, the ground was hard and grassy, an easy trek. But the smell of a swamp reached my nose, and soon my pace was slowed as my boots sank into wet ground with every step. Mosquitoes nipped at every bit of exposed skin and the cool air was now uncomfortably wet.

Thoughts of what might be lurking in the darkness of the swamp kept my heart rate up, but I forced myself to put one foot in front of the other. By now, I was too far into it to turn back, and eventually—eventually I would hit something. Either the Vanhoja river or Neveri. Or I'd be eaten alive by some monster swimming in the depths.

Every so often, my foot would land in a deep puddle, and cold, salty water would splash up onto my pants. So I'd edge my way around until I found solid ground.

"Well, Mother," I said, wiping grime off my pants for the umpteenth time. "If You were curious if I really wanted my crown back, I think You have Your answer."

As if to prove a point, a cold wind blew and the clouds obscured the moon, bathing me and the endless swamp in pitch-black darkness. I pulled out my compass, squinting in the dark to make sure I was still going in the right direction. But my hands, slippery from muck and water, couldn't hold it and the small piece fell into the murky depths.

"Perfect."

I closed my eyes to keep my temper from causing me more problems, and kept walking in the same direction.

By now, my tongue was dry and my eyes drooped. There was no relief in sight—no light in the distance, nothing that might indicate I was close to anywhere I could safely lay my head. I thought about the pounds of food lying in the road back in Kulka, about the uncertainty on the faces, and about the people in Forcadel who needed saving. They needed me to complete this mission, not collapse into the welcoming mud and die.

Although that did sound tempting.

In my distraction, I tripped over something and fell forward, landing in a stream. I pushed myself up out of the wetness, spitting the salty, dirty water and blinking. The clouds had moved, and the moon brightened the land with light once more.

I'd stumbled into a large river, and based on the size and my general location, I had a strong suspicion it was the Vanhoja river.

In the distance, to the east, the faintest sunlight was creeping over the horizon, so I headed in that direction. The path was still slow and muddy, but with the improving light, I could at least keep a better eye on where I placed my feet.

Almost as soon as the sun broke the horizon, I spotted the city —or at least the church spire. Tears fell freely from my eyes as I breathed in the air of my homeland, and I collapsed to my knees when I reached the first gravel road. I pressed my forehead to the ground, thanking the Mother for keeping me alive, for allowing me to see Forcadel once more.

I wasn't sure how long I lay there, and I must've fallen asleep because the next thing I knew, something was poking me in the back. Groaning, I blinked in the sunlight to see a form surrounded by light.

"Mother?" I rasped, my throat in dire need of water.

"Are you all right?" It wasn't the Mother, but a teenage girl. She placed a basket by my side and rolled me onto my back. "You look frightful. Did you walk through the swamp?"

I nodded, squinting and running a hand over my salt-crusted face.

"I thought you might be dead," she said. "Can you walk? My house is just up the road. I've got water and food there."

Although my body protested mightily, I pulled myself to sit then stand, and gingerly followed the girl back to her house. It wasn't lost on me that this girl was allowing a complete stranger, one covered in mud, into her house simply because I needed help.

With cracked lips, I smiled. Finally, I was back amongst my people.

The girl, whose name was Norah, took me back to a small house on the outskirts of town. She provided me with a fresh tunic and leggings, and allowed me access to her water pump to clean my boots and myself. When I returned to gather my things and thank her, she had set out a large breakfast for me.

"This is...too much," I said, but sat down at the table anyway. "Thank you for your generosity."

"We have to do what we can to take care of each other in these troubling times," she said, looking out the window. "How did you come to this town? Through the swamps?"

I nodded and took another large bite of food. "The border's closed, so I had to improvise."

"Make sure you don't advertise that fact," she said, coming to sit at the table. "The new captain in the city doesn't take kindly to trespassers from Kulka."

"I'm Forcadelian," I said, taking a large bite of the sweet roll and savoring the taste. It had been too long since I'd had one of Bea's amazing rolls. I'd almost forgotten they existed.

"To the Severians and those who swear fealty to them, it doesn't matter," Norah said. "The queen herself was in Neveri a few weeks ago to close the gates. She left one of her monster captains to oversee us, and things haven't been the same since. Our food supplies are dwindling, and no one cares."

My heart leapt when she'd said "captain," but I doubted Felix would be called a monster. I chewed slowly, noting the bowl of berries on the table weren't as bright as the ones I'd eaten the night before in Kulka. "What's the captain's name?"

"Maarit. She's Severian," Norah said. "Things were bad before she arrived, but now they're worse. They used to at least let people out through the roads. Searched and approved with heavy tariffs, of course. But now, they'll stick an arrow in anyone who dares pass." She cast a look at me. "You're lucky you didn't run into any of them."

"I took my luck in the swamps," I said.

"And lucky you were. Surprised you didn't get eaten by a river dragon."

I swallowed the berry before it got stuck in my throat and decided to change the subject away from all the things that could've eaten me the night before. "So this Maarit, what's her deal? Why did they close the borders?"

"Probably the incident in Skorsa, if the rumors are to be believed."

"What Skorsa incident?" I asked, a sinking suspicion in my stomach.

"Apparently, the mayor there let some ship through. Or a bunch of ships, he was getting paid off. So Ilara had him strung up in the city square and put a captain in both border cities."

My stomach rose into my throat. Kelsor's death wasn't on my hands. Ilara had made that call, could have very well have just thrown him in jail. But it was hard not to feel culpable.

"How far is the city from here?" I asked.

"Not far. Maybe thirty minutes south along the road," she said. "But they're checking everyone coming in or out. If you don't have papers—that is, if you can't prove you're Forcadelian—they won't let you inside the city."

I'd never heard of anyone having to have any kind of registration. It smacked of something dangerous and un-Forcadelian. "What kind of papers are we talking about?"

"It depends on the person who's checking entry that day, so I've heard," she said. "Last week, they let me in with my mother's discharge papers—she was in the Forcadelian army. But my neighbors were turned away with their annual tax receipts."

I nodded. "I'll figure something out, I'm sure." Even if it meant sneaking into the city.

"I'm sure you will, Your Majesty."

My head snapped up. "I'm sorry?"

She slid a crinkled-up piece of paper across the table. My likeness stared up at me, pronouncing my coronation three months before. It wasn't an exact match, but anyone who saw the poster might make the connection.

"I'm flattered," I said, slowly, looking up at her. "It's not the first time I've been mistaken for Brynna. But I assure you, I'm not her. Her nose is too big. And she's too…" I gestured to the poster. "Delicate."

"Ah, well, hope does spring eternal," she said with a heavy sigh, as she pulled the paper back to her with a forlorn look. "I've been praying to the Mother that she'd send the princess back to save us all."

"You hope the princess is alive?" I asked. "Why?"

"There's been precious little to be optimistic about. I've lit more candles in the church than there are stars in the sky, it seems." She sat back. "Maarit thinks if she squeezes hard enough, she can choke the life out of this city. But what she doesn't know is that the harder you hold, the more people resist." She shrugged. "And the harder it is to keep them in place. People are angry, and something is going to burst soon."

I glanced at my face again, oscillating between giving her that hope and keeping my cards close to my chest. For now, I decided to keep them close.

"For your hospitality," I said, placing a few gold coins on the table. "I wish I could give you more, but—"

"It is as the Mother wants," she said, pushing the coins back to me. "I hope you are successful in whatever you're here to do. If I can help at all, please allow me the honor."

I glanced up at her. Perhaps there *was* something. "Can you get me into the city?"

She beamed. "I can certainly try."

Chapter Thirty-Four

About an hour later, Norah and I were on our way into town. She insisted I ride on her old mare while she guided the reins, and I was too grateful for her help to argue. We didn't get very far down the road when we came upon a long queue of carriages, lined up all the way into the city.

"That's where they're checking papers," Norah said, resting her hand on the horse's nose.

I craned my neck to look ahead, spying two guards inspecting a carriage. I chewed my lip—would they check my slingbag, and, if so, would they let me inside the city with all my weapons? My mind spun through scenarios until I saw a woman with small children.

As casually as I could, I pulled my slingbag off my back and snuck it under the hem of my tunic. Then I adjusted the cloth so that it looked smooth and settled back in the saddle. The only one who'd noticed my movement was Norah, and she nodded once, turning toward the front.

I kept my head down as we approached the guards at the gate. There were a pair of young Forcadelian guards there—barely older than I was.

"Just me and my sister," Norah said, handing them papers. "Be careful of the baby when you search her."

"Okay, dear, come on down." A Forcadelian guard stood to my right. His voice was kind as he held out his hand. "This won't take long."

I took his hand, thinking quickly. "It's been such a long journey." I whimpered. "I'm a little faint." Then, with a sigh, I fell forward into his arms, making sure to keep my "belly" away from him. "I'm so sorry."

"It's quite all right," he said. "You can get back on the horse."

"Thank you, kind sir," I said as he almost picked me up and seated me. I chanced a look at his face and my heart stopped in my chest—he looked so much like Felix. Before he met my gaze, I averted my eyes, covering my face with my hands in mock embarrassment.

"Oi," his partner barked. She was Severian. "You can't do that. She needs to be inspected."

"I inspected her and she's fine," he barked back. "And if you got a problem with that, you can go talk to Maarit."

Once we were given the all clear to go, and we were out of earshot, Norah chuckled. "You might not be the princess, but I'm glad the Mother told me to help you. You have a look of hope about you."

I merely smiled. I had a sinking suspicion that she still considered me to be the lost princess, but I hoped that she would keep that.

Norah and I parted ways once I was safely inside the city, and she promised that her house would be available if I ever needed a place to sleep or hide.

"Just up the northern road," she said. "Turn left at the patch of yellow flowers. It will always be open for you."

Once she was out of sight, I turned my attentions on the city at large. Aware that I might be recognized, I kept my face down as I perused the vendors in the central town square—or lack thereof. More than one booth was completely empty, with a sign that indicated the owner would be back when the blockade ended. I thought about the bushels of apples rotting on the side of the road in Kulka, and a fresh surge of anger coursed through me. I stopped at a booth proudly displaying baskets full of root vegetables and made a show of poking through the produce.

"It's a silver per pound," the woman said, chewing on what appeared to be a stick.

"A silver?" I quirked a brow. "Seems high. And you don't have a lot of produce."

"My family's gotta eat," she said. "My sister usually brings her produce from Kulka, and since that blockade, things have been tight."

I nodded, picking up a potato and examining it. There were spots on it—it wasn't even fresh. "When do you think the blockade will be lifted?"

"Who knows," she said with a shake of her head. "But if you ain't going to buy anything, move along."

I thanked her, even though she was rude, and continued along the promenade. Out of the corner of my eye, I spotted three Severian guards entering the market. With light footfalls, I kept close behind them, pretending to stop at a booth nearby when they stopped.

"Need to see your papers," the older one said, picking up a rhubarb from a nearby vendor's booth. "These look a little too much like Kulkan produce."

I made a face. How could he tell that? But everything from the strawberries to the lettuce seemed a few shades greener than anything else around it.

The old man paled but handed over a weathered document. "It's all on the up and up. Just had a nice harvest this year. We're right on the border, you see, so—"

"I don't buy it," the head Severian said. "You're under arrest for selling illegal wares from the nation of Kulka."

My jaw fell open as the other two guards grabbed the man by his frail arms and yanked him over the booth, clapping thick irons on his wrists and dragging him down the street. The senior officer tore up the paper and let the pieces float to the dirt floor.

"Let that be a lesson to the rest of you," he barked. "There's no fooling the royal guard of Forcadel."

In the first place, neither guard was Forcadelian, and something scratched inside my mind at the thought of them declaring themselves as such. I cast a look around at the neighbors who wore similar looks of loathing their faces. Yet none of them had done anything to save their friend. They were angry, not stupid.

"Does that happen a lot?" I asked the man at the booth.

"More often now," he said. "Maarit, she's got this place on lockdown. Curfews every night, random inspections. Some of the farmers have taken to leaving their best-looking produce at home so that it doesn't get mistaken for Kulkan produce."

I glanced down the line of vendors, noting more than a few empty tables. "Is there enough to go around?"

"Well, since we can't get the Kulkans in the city, we've lost about half our customers. If we don't make money, we can't buy from our neighbors." He sighed wearily. "It's a mess."

Mess, indeed. I placed a gold coin on his table. "Thanks for the info."

I didn't see any more incidents like the one in the farmer's market, but there was clearly a simmering resentment of the occupiers in the town. That was good—I could use that. But whether I could twist that from disliking the Severians to accepting the Kulkans was another story.

When dusk fell on the city, the Severian guards began to bark about curfew, and the vendors and shopowners closed their doors. The soldier presence would probably double around dusk as they herded villagers into their homes for the night, so I scaled a two-story building and settled in on the roof.

My plan was to stay there for the duration of dusk, but exhaustion finally caught up with me, and I fell right to sleep.

When I awoke next, it was dark and there was a nasty crick in my neck. I lay there for a little while, resting my body, but my mind swam with eagerness. I only had a few days to get an idea of the city before I had to get word back to Ammon.

I slid my cloak over my shoulders and put the slingbag in its place. Finally, I pulled out my mask, tying it around my head with a satisfied smile. Cracking my neck, I set off into the dark city.

The rooftops here were similar to Forcadel, and I was almost immediately back in my element. The Severians moved at a leisurely pace, but they spoke very little. When they'd pause to take a break, I'd whip out my map and orient myself.

Voices echoed up from one of the alleys, and I turned my head to listen, mostly out of habit.

"You! Boy! Stop!"

The boy dashed into the open street then froze as the two Severians surrounded him. He was barely thirteen and carrying a bag in his hand. Silently, I slid my bag off my back and crept to the ledge. I didn't want to intervene, but I'd be ready if I had to.

"You know the rules," the female Severian—she had a beak nose, so I'd call her Beaky—said. "Nobody out after dark. Means you, too."

"I wasn't doing nothing wrong," the boy said. "I had to stay late at the smithery. Couldn't leave until now. Please, I'm just trying to get back home."

"What do you have in the bag?" Beaky said, pulling it from him and dumping out the contents. A loaf of bread, some fruit, and a coin purse.

"P-please, that's all we got for the week," he said.

"Where'd you get this apple?" the male Severian guard—he had a mole on his right cheek, he was now Mole—asked, plucking the fruit from the ground. "You know Kulkan produce is strictly outlawed."

"I didn't know it was Kulkan," their supposed victim said. "I just bought it from a vendor today. Thought it was a Forcadelian apple, honest."

Beaky snatched the coin purse from the ground and dug through it. "Suppose we could let you off with a warning. We'll take this, though."

I chewed my lip as the boy begged, crying about his sick mother and younger siblings. He couldn't have been older than fourteen, and the ash smudges on his face told me he was telling the truth about coming home from work.

I rose, gathering the edges of my cloak in my hands as I prepared to jump. With a loud breath, I leaped off the building, comforted as the air gathered in the pockets around me. Landing softly in the alley between the guards and the boy, I stood slowly, giving the Severians my most terrifying glare.

"Is there a problem here?" I asked, lowering my voice.

Mole snorted. "And who are you?"

"Some freak walking around in a mask and cloak, huh?" Beaky chuckled. "Forcadelians are idiots."

"I'll give you one last chance," I drawled, flashing them the two knives at my side. "Let him go, or you'll bleed."

They barked a laugh as they ambled toward me. As Mole

swung, I ducked, and his fist landed square in his partner's face. I swung my leg around to kick him in the back with my knee, sending him flying forward. Beaky was screaming, furious and bleeding from her nose, as she came for me again. My right fist connected with her stomach, my left into her cheek, and I grabbed her by the scruff of her neck and tossed her over my shoulder into the brick wall.

Mole had recovered and came for me, so I grabbed my weighted twine from my belt, swung it around to gain momentum then released it. The balls wrapped themselves around his arms, and again, he fell forward. With a kick to the face, he was out as well.

"Holy Mother…"

The boy had pressed himself against the wall, eyes wide and mouth open.

I walked over to him and held out my hand. "Are you okay?"

He nodded. "T-thank you."

"Get home," I said, handing his coin purse and bag to him. "And try not to stay out after hours, mmkay?"

He dashed out into the alley just as a set of hoofbeats approached. With the boy safely disappeared into the darkness, I made a break for the rooftops, scampering out of the way just as the first three guards arrived. I tried to avoid feeling too good about what I'd done.

The night was still young, but I was tired and not in the mood to sleep on the roof again. So I found a small inn, The Wicked Duck, and palmed the few precious coins I had. Inside, there was a single woman at the counter who gave me a curious look when I entered.

"How much for a night and a meal?" I asked.

She surveyed me suspiciously. "Are you visiting?"

Remembering what Norah had said, I forced a smile onto my

face. "Just need a night, then I'll be on my way."

She sighed and pulled out a thick book. "I gotta know where you came from, how you got here, and what your business is in town. For Captain Maarit."

"Really?" I frowned, as if this was new information to me. "Why does the captain want to know who's staying in the inns?"

"Who knows? But if I don't report every stay to her, she'll take ten gold coins from my coffers. So, again," she picked up a quill and leaned over the paper, "where'd you come from, how'd you get here, and what's your business?"

"Wow," I replied with a shake of my head. Luckily, I had a ready-made story. "Name's Larissa. Coming from the village of Kutei. Here to fetch some produce for my ma and I lost track of time."

Kutei was the small village outside Celia's fortress, and the produce line was one she'd told us to use if the guards were getting too curious. I supposed some things were just ingrained.

The woman wrote down all the lies I fed her. "That'll be one silver," she said. I handed her the gold and she quirked a brow. "Farm girls don't usually carry this much gold around on them."

"It was a good day," I replied with a smile.

She handed me a key and a bowl and directed me toward the back room where an old pot of stew was bubbling. I ate my fill and drank so much water it sloshed unhappily in my stomach as I climbed the stairs to my room for the night. It was a modest place, with a single bed in the corner and the dying sunlight streaming onto the covers. Without even removing my boots, I flopped into bed.

Sleep tugged at my consciousness, but just as I was drifting off, the hairs on the back of my neck stood up. Voices, footsteps—it was too late (or early) for either.

My things were still in a bag by the door, so I climbed out the window, hanging by the sticky gloves and waiting to hear if I'd just been paranoid, or if someone was really coming to my room.

The door opened and I cursed silently.

"I promise you, there was someone here," the innkeeper said. "I did as you told me. Anyone from Kutei, call the guards."

He grunted, and I wrapped my hand around my knife, readying myself to come to the woman's aid. I didn't fault her for giving me up.

"The Veil was seen tonight," he said.

"The...Veil? The actual Veil?" The woman sounded shocked. "Where?"

"Two of Maarit's guards said she interfered with an arrest."

"Why would she do that?" the woman wondered.

"No idea. All I know is that if I bring her to Maarit, I can retire from the service and get outta this country before the Mother burns it to the ground."

"If I see her again, I'll tell you."

Silently, I climbed up to the roof and sat on the ledge, cursing myself and my inability to let anything go. I should've let that boy...what? Get his money stolen and his food ruined? All because he was out too late? It wasn't fair.

But if I didn't change my mindset, I would get caught. Already, my cover had been blown. If Maarit knew The Veil was in town, Ilara would know as well, and then everything would be much worse for me.

And now, I was out one coin and still had to sleep on the roof again.

Chapter Thirty-Five

Felix

I didn't want to admit that seeing Garwood in such a state had spooked me, but I couldn't quite get rid of the scent of death and dismay from my nose. I had joked about going to jail before, but seeing it—and realizing I would be absolutely useless to Brynna in there—spurred me to action.

I'd spent the morning in my office—not the one I was used to, but the one I'd been forced into by Coyle—drafting a timeline of events. At my left hand was a list of every merchant who provided goods or services to the castle, where I'd added the dates and locations of fires. On a fresh sheet of parchment, I jotted down each of the fires in sequential order, including their connection to the castle.

Ilara's furrier in Merchant's Quarter was first, followed by the dressmaker. But the next three had been food-related. After that, a couple more fires in that same quadrant, to include a tailor, a fabric importer, and a shoemaker. Then the target had returned to those providing food to the castle, and even the townhouse of a merchant marine. All connected to Ilara, but other than that, no obvious thread.

On the back of the parchment, I jotted down each of the merchants who hadn't been torched yet—still more than I could handle by myself, but a smaller list than before. Tonight, I would narrow my search there, and hope I got lucky.

A soft rap at the door jolted me from the jumbled thoughts. "Enter," I called.

Katarine walked inside, a warm smile on her face. "I got your message. But I also had to pass through two Severian guards on my way in. What's that about?"

"They said something about increased security threats," I said, looking down at my list again. "Odd, considering I'm their captain and should've been the one assigning security details."

"Felix, I'm worried," she said softly. "I've been hearing your name more and more from Ilara's lips, and none of it is good. Tell me you've made progress."

"No, but that's why you're here," I said with a hopeful smile. I briefly told her about my encounter with Ruby, and she agreed it wasn't very promising. "At least I know there's someone in charge. I can keep pulling at that thread."

"She might've been lying to you," Katarine said.

"There was something about that bodyguard," I said. "Guarding the three of them past curfew? Escorting them home? Something's amiss there. And these fires haven't been random. I just can't find a pattern." I slid the paper I'd been working on over to her. "Can you?"

Her brows knitted together as she studied the page. "No, other than they're serving the castle."

"These last five," I pointed to the bottom of the list. "I had guards stationed there, but somehow the fires started anyway." I flipped over the page to show her the remaining vendors. "I'm going to go out tonight and hope one of these goes up in flames."

"Perhaps I can help narrow your search," she said. "Ilara's passed down a new edict, not sure if you've heard."

"No," I said with a shake of my head. "What is it?"

"The Forcadelian merchants will now be wholly dedicated to transporting Forcadelian food to the western ports and returning with…well, with Severian glass." She crossed her arms over her chest and shook her head. "In Ilara's mind, she thinks it's a concession to the merchants for closing the other borders. Severia is still open, she says, so we'll just trade with them."

"That sounds like an utter disaster. Any chance of talking her out of this idiotic scheme?"

"I've been trying, but I'm afraid my sway over her is diminishing. I'm here because there's a chance Ariadna could change her mind, and Ilara isn't dumb enough to draw her wrath. But I've been invited to fewer meetings, been consulted half as much as before. Soon, I might be relegated to sitting in my study and penning letters to my sister."

"I'm probably not far behind you," I said. "What with my babysitters and Coyle taking my guards, I'm surprised I'm still allowed to walk around."

"Then perhaps you should use this new information to your benefit," Katarine said. She flipped through the list I'd given her and pointed to five names on it. "These are the merchants who've agreed to her terms, at least for now." She handed the paper back to me. "The probability is that they'll be next."

"You're amazing, have I told you that lately?" I said with a grin.

"Just find something, Felix," she said, not sharing my levity. "It's already bad enough around here. I don't know what I'd do if you left me, too."

That night, it took me nearly two hours to lose my Severian guards. Sooner or later, I wouldn't be able to leave at all. Much like

Ilara's patience, my time was running out.

As sailors, the merchant marines conducted most of their business at sea, and thus didn't have businesses to torch. But they all maintained residences in Sailor's Row, and all within a few blocks of each other. It was convenient, and, I hoped, a good sign for the evening.

I settled across the street from one of the larger houses, watching the crescent moon overhead and listening to the water nearby. Every so often, there would be snippets of conversations from the Severian guards, but nothing worth getting up over. Around midnight, I changed positions, visiting the other four houses in turn, finding much the same thing.

I was almost back to the first house when a woman's scream pierced the night. The two Severians on the streets below jumped to their feet and ran toward the sound, and I was in hot pursuit. I wasn't going to get involved, but I didn't trust that the Severians wouldn't make a bad situation worse.

When we arrived at the source of the screaming, a young girl was being held down by four larger men.

"Let the girl go!" the Severian called.

The goons turned, and I frowned. The supposed victim wore a smirk and had no bruises on her. In fact, she wasn't even bound.

"What the—"

All four thugs pulled out large knives and my heart sank into my stomach. It was a trap. I had no love for the Severians, but I couldn't let the citizenry kill a pair of guards. Ilara's wrath would be unending, and she wouldn't stop until every Forcadelian suffered.

So I gathered the edges of the cloak and leapt off the rooftop, landing between the thugs and the guards. I didn't know if the rebels would come after me the way they were going after the Severians, but I hoped, at least, I could buy them some time to get backup.

"What's the big idea?" asked the man in the front. "Thought you were supposed to be on our side?"

"That ain't The Veil?" the girl spat, wiping her mouth and producing a large knife. "That's some imposter. I told you, the real Veil is dead."

"It doesn't matter if I'm the real Veil or not," I said. "You can't go around killing royal guards."

"They're *desert-dwelling scum*," the girl, clearly the ringleader, snarled. "And you should be ashamed of yourself, protecting them like this."

I held up my sword. I doubted she'd tell me anything, but I still had to try. "Who are you working for?"

The girl snorted then burst into laughter. "I ain't working for nobody."

She didn't strike me as the sort of criminal mastermind who'd come up with something like this, but she certainly seemed to have an ego.

"Awfully complex plot here," I said, although it wasn't really. "You come up with it all on your own?"

"'Course I did," she said. "Boss just said—"

There it is. "Boss?" I smiled. "Who's your boss?"

More voices, footsteps. Perhaps the next patrol was coming around.

"Please, all I need is his name," I said.

"You ain't getting *shit* from me," the girl said. "Let's go!"

They dashed past me into the main street, and I followed them. If they didn't tell me their boss's name, perhaps they'd lead me to him.

"Stop! Vigilante!"

I spun on my heel, face-to-face with a crowd of Severian soldiers. They'd come to help their fellow soldier, but when they saw me, sheer glee appeared on their faces.

"Look what we have here," the first one—a rat-faced Severian who'd been assigned to me a few times—said. "A vigilante."

They didn't recognize my face under the mask, but they'd surely recognize my voice, so I opted against speaking. I was a few blocks from the water, too far from anywhere to hide. I lacked Brynna's ability to twist herself out of bad situations and I had no backup.

Water it was.

I spun on my heel and took off, surprising them only momentarily.

"*Get him!*

I ran as hard as my legs would move, but with every step I took, more guards seemed to appear out of nowhere. I prayed to the Mother above that she might clear my path.

My boots clacked against the wood of the docks not a moment too soon, and with a deep breath, I dove head-first into the water. The cold seeped down to my bones, but I kept myself calm as I swam through the murky depths. My fingers made purchase on a barnacle-covered post, so I quietly broached the surface.

"Where'd he go?"

"Are you sure it was a he? I thought The Veil was a woman?"

"Who knows?"

"I know Coyle's going to be furious with us for letting him go."

"The Forcadelian? He won't be around much longer. Maarit's going to fire him as soon as she gets back from the border."

"And not a moment too soon. I'm tired of answering to Forcadelians."

Their footsteps echoed away, but just to be sure, I waited an extra few minutes before pulling myself from the water. Tonight had been a disaster on all fronts, and I could only guess what trouble revealing myself to the guards would cause in the coming days.

Chapter Thirty-Six

The next morning, I blended in with the Neveri farmer's market, hoping to hear more news about The Veil, and what trouble I'd gotten myself into. But conversations were at a minimum—there seemed to be more guards than people, and none of the vendors even responded when I wished them good morning.

Clearly, The Veil's appearance had made things worse for the town, but at least I was able to move without being stopped without my mask. I planned to take full advantage of my freedom and revisit some of the places I'd seen following the Severian guards the night before.

A twitter of laughter reached my ears, and a gaggle of women wearing tall boots and carrying baskets of laundry waltzed by, clearly headed for the river. They seemed blissfully unaware of the unease that had settled on the town; after all, even if the Forcadelians were starving to death, the Severians would still need clean clothes.

To wit, one of them had a basket full of Severian uniforms.

I kept enough distance so that it wouldn't appear I was following them. My mind ran rampant with ideas how I might use them—steal a uniform? Impersonate one of the women to gain access to the heavily guarded soldiers' barracks?

Instead, I settled for listening to their idle chatter about the weather and who was pregnant and who was cheating on whom until they brought me something I could work with.

"Did you hear about that masked woman?"

I nearly tripped over my feet, but recovered before anyone noticed me, busying myself with adjusting my boot, as if it had come off.

"They say she's from Forcadel City, but who knows?" said one of the older women with a pinched nose and stringy black hair. With the way she carried herself, she seemed to be the leader of the group.

One of the younger women with cherubic cheeks grinned excitedly. "They say she took out twenty guards."

"Twenty? I heard fifty."

"Do you think it's the real Veil?"

"Wouldn't surprise me," said the leader with a lift of her shoulder. "But it also wouldn't surprise me if it was a Kulkan, either."

"Don't be daft, a Kulkan?" One laughed. "Why would the Kulkans want to help us?"

"And they say Ammon's brought a thousand men with him to an outpost just beyond the border," said the girl to my right. "I think that's why there've been more soldiers in the city lately, or why they've been so terrible."

"Girl, don't gossip. The Severians have been bad since Maarit arrived, and they'll be bad until Ilara gets whatever bee is up her butt dislodged."

The washers shared a giggle and I ducked my head to pretend

like I was laughing as well.

"Oh, don't say that too loud," a mousy woman said. "Maarit will come down here and throw you in jail."

A tall woman in the back leaned into the group. "I heard Simone say The Veil had a mind to put that queen's head on a pike."

"Don't you know anything? The Veil doesn't kill."

I craned my neck to look at the woman who'd spoken so clearly. She was maybe twenty, but she wore a dreamy expression on her face.

"You know so much?"

"I used to live in Forcadel," she said, picking up the tunic she was washing and flinging it in the wind. "And I saw her, once. Saved my life. She beat back ten men who were trying to rob my father's store. She had all this Nestori magic at her fingertips too."

I snorted but then rubbed my nose as if I'd sneezed. Ten was a stretch—the most I'd ever taken was four or five. Maybe.

"She's amazing," the woman continued. "So if she's in the city, I have faith that we'll be okay."

"Or we're all screwed," the leader said. "I heard from my cousin back in Forcadel City that there are riots in the streets. A whole rebellion is brewing there."

"Don't say things like that." One of the middle-aged women shook her head. "If it spreads, we'd have to take up arms against our own people."

The women shivered, as if the real world had suddenly intruded on their happy little bubble. But the cherubic-cheeked woman brushed it off with a happy sigh.

"Well, I heard she gave it to a couple of the guards last night," she said, putting her basket down and miming some punches in the air. She clapped her hands together. "Oh, what I wouldn't give to see all those desert-dwellers bloody and tossed on their asses."

They laughed together, and I broke into a smile, but the sound of pounding hooves quieted the conversation. I turned to look over my shoulder as a contingent of Severian guards came riding up, surrounding the group of women where they stood in the streets. The women's faces had paled considerably, especially as the main rider, a Severian in her mid-forties, dismounted and walked up to the group.

Based on the crest on her uniform, she was probably Captain Maarit. She wore impeccable brown boots and what appeared to be a freshly pressed uniform. Her black hair was cropped short and slicked back behind her ears, and her dark eyes surveyed the women who'd all gone stick straight. Her eyes grazed over me, but as I wasn't dressed as a washerwoman, I pretended to be in the wrong place at the wrong time.

"Ladies," Maarit said quietly. "Having a good day?"

"Yes, Captain," the eldest replied. "Is there a problem?"

"Did I hear conversation about The Veil?" she asked, her boots scuffing against the dirt. "You've no doubt heard about the new edict in the city?"

"N-no?"

Maarit's smile wasn't friendly. "Anyone with information on the vigilante is to report it directly to the royal guards, and anyone found in violation of this law will be sent to the stocks for one day."

They nodded. "We don't know anything, Captain. Just that... she's here."

"And how did you find that out?"

I gripped my knives, which were strapped to my legs under my dress. There was a sinister tone to her voice, as if she were looking for examples of insubordination, but would make do with whatever came along. I didn't want to announce my presence, especially without my mask and cloak, but these women were innocent.

"Maarit, enough."

My jaw dropped before I could stop myself as a familiar figure came riding up on a brown horse. Riya, one of Felix's most trusted lieutenants, halted her horse between Maarit and the trembling launderers. There was a fierceness on her face that was at once comforting and terrifying. But she was wearing a Severian officer's uniform, too. I ducked my head further to hide myself.

"Lieutenant," Maarit said, and the unsaid conversation hung in the air. Riya had addressed a superior officer by her last name—and a Severian, too. I chanced a look up at them and saw nothing but animosity there.

"This isn't necessary," Riya said, breaking her gaze first. "I'll take care of them. If there's even a problem. Not worth involving the captain of the city."

"It appears leaving things up to my lieutenant hasn't worked out very well," Maarit replied, icily. "Have you found that masked woman yet?"

I snuck a look at Riya; she hadn't even noticed me. "No, I haven't. But I've stepped up patrols."

Maarit took a step backward, victory clear on her face. "Very well. I expect a report at the end of your shift. There's a troublemaker in the village, and I want her found."

"Yes, ma'am," Riya said, pressing her fist to her chest in salute.

Maarit mounted her horse and whistled at the other Severians. They took off in a cloud of dust, missing Riya's annoyed head shaking.

"So." She turned on the women. "What really happened here?"

"N-nothing," the mousy woman said. "We were just here talking."

"About?"

"T-The Veil," she admitted shyly. "Just talking about what she did in Forcadel. I can't imagine that would garner her attention. I don't even know how she heard us."

"She's got bat ears," Riya said with a soft smile. "Listen, I don't want to come back here. So try to keep The Veil conversations to a minimum, okay? Please, as a favor to me."

They nodded and turned their backs on her, grabbing their baskets and hurrying away, whispering to themselves despite her warning. I didn't miss the look of dismay on Riya's face, or the way she mounted her horse and took off in the opposite direction.

Seeing Riya protect those washerwomen had been a double-edged sword. On the one hand, I was glad to see a familiar face, and one who might be loyal to me if I revealed myself to her. But on the other hand, I couldn't understand why she'd be in Neveri instead of helping Felix back in Forcadel. And until I knew which side she'd landed on, I didn't want to make contact just yet.

Tonight, the moon was hidden by a layer of clouds, and the city was thick with fog. Fall was rolling in from the north, and a chill was trying to press in with it. Under cover of darkness, I found the soldiers' barracks and waited on a rooftop nearby. It was a bit risky to be so close to the enemy, but sometimes that was the safest place to be.

Riya walked out of the barracks, flanked by a group of ten Severian guards. They followed in lock-step, but there was something off about the way they faced her. She was leader in name only, and once she left them, they'd do whatever they wanted.

"If I hear anything about you abusing the townsfolk again, I'll be passing out suspensions, is that clear?" she said, her trademark no-nonsense voice falling flat on her subordinates. "Whether you were born in this country or not, you will respect the people of this city. You're all Forcadelians now."

I doubted that, especially as half her troops were Severian.

"Dismissed," Riya said, sounding exasperated.

She watched her soldiers dissipate into the dark streets and her shoulders slumped. A whispered prayer to the Mother went to the sky, then she continued down the road.

I turned the other way, toward where her guards had disappeared, to conduct my own search of the city. Or rather, to keep an eye on Riya's guards, who most assuredly would not heed her directions on leaving the townsfolk alone.

But as the afternoon turned to dusk, it seemed to be the people who weren't leaving the guards alone. There was a definite new feeling; more shadows darting in the alleys. More hushed conversations as people took their time walking home.

A few times, I thought I might have to intervene with the guards, but even they seemed hesitant to do more than bark. One or two people were easy to bully and intimidate. But groups of four or five, confidently strolling down the street—that was harder to tamp down.

"Hey, you!" a Severian guard called. "You guys better get home or else we'll arrest you."

The man in the group made an offensive gesture, and his friends laughed. "Didn't you hear? The Veil's in town. You all need to be careful or else you'll end up on the pointy end of her sword."

"If you know where The Veil is hiding, you must tell us, on penalty of death," the Severian bellowed.

But his anger only caused the Forcadelians to laugh harder. "Listen to him! He's scared out of his wits!"

"The Veil's coming for you all."

"What's going on here?" Riya said, walking into the middle of the fray. I hadn't even seen her come back. "Why are you out? There's a curfew."

"We don't answer to you, *traitor*," the loudmouth said. "You're one of Llobrega's. He let the princess die, and all the other ones, and that's why we're stuck with that bitch queen."

I winced as the Severians collectively gasped in horror.

"How *dare* you disparage your queen!"

"Traitor!"

"Hang on, everyone just take a breath," Riya tried, but even her formidable voice was drowned out in the fracas. The Severians had drawn their weapons, and the Forcadelian townsfolk had as well. If someone didn't intervene soon, there would be blood on the streets.

"Fine," I muttered, swinging myself off the roof and landing in the center of the fracas.

Cheers rose from those on the Forcadelian side, and a hushed shock descended on the other side.

"The Veil!"

"I knew she was here!"

"She's come to save us!"

"H-holy Mother."

Riya had all but dropped her sword, her mouth hanging open as if she'd seen a ghost. And I supposed, perhaps, she had. Felix must've kept his word not to tell anyone I was alive. I didn't want to give either of us away, but I winked and hoped she could see it in the dark.

I straightened and pulled my sword, pointing it at the guards. "Enough of this. You go on your way." I looked at the group behind me. "And you five get home and sleep it off. Leave the troublemaking to me."

"W-we have orders," Riya said, as if she wasn't quite sure she was believed what she was seeing. "Orders to take you in, V-Veil..."

I grinned wider. "Do you, now?"

"She ain't the real Veil," said the tall, thin guard to Riya's right. Severian. "Too young."

"Oh, well." I shrugged. "I suppose you should come arrest me and find out if I am, in fact, the *real* Veil."

I'd hoped the townsfolk would take the hint and dissipate, but they remained fixed in place—and if I wasn't mistaken, more were arriving to watch me fight. I didn't have time for this—the longer I stayed, the more chance Riya might get in trouble.

I reached into my slingbag, feeling for anything that would help me. I found a small pouch and, praying it was something useful, I lobbed it toward the guards. The world exploded in a bright light—a flashbang grenade! I slammed my eyes shut and turned, making a break for the open street as the soldiers cried out in confusion.

I skipped over one alley, finding a stack of crates and scaling them quickly. Once on the roof, I crept low on the tiles, hiding myself with my dark cloak and mask and waiting. The soldiers— including Riya—assembled in the center of the street. Some of them still rubbed their eyes and blinked wildly from the flashbang, while the others just looked angry.

"Where'd she go?"

"I missed it, what was that explosion?"

"Fan out," Riya said. "I've seen this before. You three go check out that explosion. You three go down that street, you three go down that one. I'll take this corner. We are capturing only—but use deadly force if you must."

They looked like they wanted to argue, but instead followed orders. I didn't miss how they didn't salute or address her; perhaps she wasn't as integrated as I thought.

My heart leapt into my throat as she turned and looked up at the roof. It could have been the darkness, or my eyes still adjusting from the brightness of the flashbang, but I thought she smiled in my direction. But almost as quickly, she turned on her heel and walked in the opposite direction.

And after a moment, I peeled myself off the roof and followed her.

Chapter Thirty-Seven

I kept a close distance from the rooftops, catching wisps of her conversations with the guards and trying to determine if she was purposefully throwing them off or if she was incompetent. When one of them asked if they should check the rooftops, she dismissed them entirely.

"That's a myth," she said. "The real Veil, if it is her, usually kept to the streets."

I chewed my lip; clearly, she was up to something. I needed to get her alone, but it was hard with her soldiers appearing out of the woodwork every other block to provide a status update. I didn't want to get her in trouble by being seen with her. If she could be trusted, she could potentially be a powerful ally.

Unfortunately, her destination seemed to be the soldiers' barracks on the west side of town, and I could no longer follow her. I waited on top of the building across the street, weighing my options. Was she going to report to Maarit? Was she going to bed?

Either way, I didn't want to lose her.

A pair of Severian guards walked by, one of them about my size. Riya would recognize my face, but in the dark and fog, she might be the only one. I could be in and out before anyone recognized me.

I shimmied down the building and followed my Severian targets. Silently, I crept up behind them and knocked the first out with my conjoined hands then swung the other way and knocked out the other. After glancing around to make sure no one had seen, I dragged both their bodies into a nearby alley and set to work disrobing the smaller of the two. Then, I searched for a place to dispose of them.

I picked the lock on the back door of the nearest building and poked my head in—it was a smithery. But more importantly, there appeared to be a closet big enough to hold the two soldiers. I pulled them inside the room and into the closet, closing the door and propping a chair against the knob.

"Sorry about your headaches," I mumbled, walking over to the uniform piled in the corner. The overcoat was big enough to fit over my tunic, as were the pants, but it made me ill to put the Severian seal at my left breast.

"Just temporary," I whispered to myself. "Temporary and then you can burn it."

Fully dressed, I left the smithery as casually as possible, my slingbag hidden under my overcoat. A pair of soldiers walked toward me, and I steeled my face as they came closer.

"Halt!" they called. "Where's your partner?"

"That drunk," I said, crossing my arms. "Never showed up to work today."

The one on the left—a Severian—eyed me. "No Severian would do that."

"Don't know what to tell you," I said, looking at the Forcadelian and hoping he'd back me up. "Maybe he's sick or hungover. I don't know. But I reported it to Kellis."

"Kellis won't be in charge much longer," the Severian replied. "Maarit's about to fire her."

"Shame," I said, although inwardly, my concern grew. "Anyway, I'm headed back up. I've checked this street. Had to give two citations to some old women. Wish people would just listen."

"C'mon," the Forcadelian said, brushing past me. "I don't want to be out here all night."

Although the Severian was still wary, he followed his partner. And I continued on toward the barracks.

Seeing how they'd reacted, perhaps a drunk partner wasn't the best option. So when I came to the gates, which were closed, I tried a different tactic.

"Help! Help!" I cried, banging the gates. "My partner was attacked!"

"What's going on?" Another Severian guard came to the gate. "Where's your partner?"

"We got jumped by some kids—a lot of them. He told me to go get help." I cast a worried look behind me. "Please! I'm worried they're going to kill him!"

"Why didn't you stay?" he grumbled. "Let him get help?"

"They had him pinned down, I don't know why they let me go!" I cried. "Please, you have to help!"

He grimaced and put a whistle to his lips. Almost immediately, five more guards appeared out of from the darkness, and the gate opened.

"He's down the street!" I said, pointing the way I'd come. "Please!"

"Go with them, you stupid girl," the Severian guard barked at me.

I turned to him, putting as much fear and terror into my eyes as I could. "Please don't make me go back there. I'm so scared. They're going to kill me."

He narrowed his eyes. "What's your name? I'm writing you up for dereliction of duty. You'll be lucky if you don't get court-martialed for this."

I sniffed and wiped my eyes as I checked the surrounding area for other guards. "It's—" I reared back and punched him in the face. "None of your business."

I stuffed the guard in his box near the gate and hurried inside.

I canvassed the building, finding most of the lights off except for a set on the northwest corner. Maarit's office? Probably. The security here was light, with only a few passing guards keeping tabs on things. They paid me little notice as I finished my circle of the building. Once the patrol was out of sight, I hid in the darkness and yanked the Severian uniform off, leaving it in a pile under a bush. It might've come in handy later, but I wasn't sure I could stomach wearing it again.

Instead, I unfurled my cape, glad to be back in my own clothes again. The walls of the barracks were smooth, but I'd packed gloves that could help in this situation. They stuck to the brick, allowing me to ascend the side of the building slowly but surely. When I reached the light of the window, I slipped my hand out of the glove and dug in my bag for my listening cups. With care and balance, I used the small hand-cranked drill to create a tiny hole in the wooden window pane, then slipped the tiny metal tube attached to a long string through to capture the sound. On the other end of the string was a larger metal cup, which I stuck in my mouth as I returned my hand to the glove.

I continued scaling the wall until I reached a small overhang, and pulled myself to sit on the edge. I replaced the gloves in my bag, then pressed the cup to my ear to listen.

"...have sounded the alarm. If she's still in the city, we'll find her." Riya was speaking, and if I hadn't known better, I would've thought her a loyal soldier.

"How in the Mother's name did she get inside the city?"

"I have no idea, but I'm having the border patrol review their protocols," Riya said. "She's slippery, though. It's hard to prevent one person from coming in and out."

"And this woman who appeared tonight," Maarit said. "Are you sure it's her?"

Riya hesitated then her chin dropped. "I know her voice. That was her."

"Convenient."

I nearly fell off the roof. That wasn't the response I was expecting.

"Convenient, how?"

"Because you're the only one who says it's actually her. And you're also the prime suspect in being The Veil of Forcadel," Maarit said, her chair creaking.

"You know as well as I do that Princess Brynna was The Veil," Riya said.

"She was, until she died," Maarit said. "But there have been reports of people picking up where she left off. Queen Ilara told me to keep an eye on you and let her know if The Veil should show up on my streets."

"It's rather hard for me to be The Veil when I have ten soldiers who'll swear that I fought her," Riya said, but the nerves hadn't left her voice.

"Could've been a woman you hired to play the part in your absence. I don't know, Lieutenant Kellis. But what I do know is that the queen will be glad to hear that I've taken care of this new iteration." She placed her glass down. "You are under arrest for crimes against the crown."

Riya's face paled and she snapped to her feet. "What evidence do you have?"

"I don't need evidence," Maarit said. "All I need is a mask and a dead body and Queen Ilara will be more than satisfied."

"Over my dead body," I muttered. It was more important that Riya remain in Maarit's pocket than to hide in the shadows. I pulled the listening cups from the window and dropped myself to hang from the roof. I lurched myself back and forth until I got enough momentum. Then with a heave, I positioned my boots toward the window and swung hard.

The glass shattered beneath my feet, and I landed on the ground, spraying glass everywhere. Maarit's eyes had grown three sizes; perhaps she really had suspected Riya. And to her credit, Riya reached for her sword.

"What are you doing here?" Riya demanded.

"Saving your ass, Lieutenant," I replied, relishing the feeling of control. "It appears you've been mistakenly identified." I laughed and gestured at her. "You're too stocky to climb on rooftops."

Maarit rose from her desk. "Are you...really The Veil? The one from the city of Forcadel?"

She knew exactly who I was. I swept my cloak behind me and bowed. "The one and only. I'm here to make some changes in town. So I suggest you remind your soldiers that they are merely guests in Forcadel. And they have overstayed their welcome."

"Fancy words," Maarit replied, showing no signs of fear. "You've got magic tricks, but you're just one person. And right now, you're in my territory."

"Ah, that's where you're wrong," I said, narrowing my eyes. "This is *my* territory. And as I said, you've overstayed your welcome."

Maarit cried for guards as Riya rushed toward me. I yanked out my knives and clashed with her. I didn't dare look her in the eyes, not sure if she was quite skilled to hide her emotions if I did. In the interest of time, I pushed her back, then fell to a crouch, swinging my leg around to knock her over. Before she could get up, I flung one of my knives at her, slicing her shoulder and pinning her to the ground.

"I don't take kindly to traitors," I spat, hoping she'd see through it.

Three guards shoved their way through the door, and it was time to make my exit. I backed up to the window and blew a kiss at Maarit. Then with my hands curled around my cloak, I fell backwards and out into the night air. My cloak broke my fall, but not well, and I landed hard on the gravel below. There wasn't any time to think about it, though, as more soldiers would be assembling as soon as Maarit raised the alarm.

I scrambled to my feet and made a run for the open gate, bypassing the guard I'd knocked out and two others who called out in confusion. I made sure to take dark side streets and alleys until I was sure I hadn't been followed. There, I caught my breath, leaning against a wall and wiping sweat from my forehead. Twice now, I'd revealed myself and twice I'd had to make a run for it. Still, both times I'd been trying to help. Whether or not it would come back to bite me remained to be seen.

Two Severian guards ran by, and I pressed myself against the wall. I'd have to find a place to rest for the night, and potentially think about my escape. Maarit knew I was Brynna, which potentially meant that both my masked and unmasked faces would be on wanted posters tomorrow. Things had certainly become more complicated.

But that was tomorrow. Tonight, I needed sleep.

I retrieved my sticky gloves from my bag, not willing to risk walking out onto the street now. And with my arms aching, I climbed the building until I reached the roof—a flat-top with a tall ledge that would hide me. Unless, of course, the Severians got wise to my habits.

I landed in a heap against the ledge and exhaled loudly. My eyes were just about closed when a voice called out.

"Hey."

Chapter Thirty-Eight

My eyes snapped open. Riya sat on the other side of the roof, her bandaged shoulder in a small sling.

"Had a feeling if I waited on a rooftop long enough, I might come across a ghost." She tossed my knife on the roof. "Do you want that back?"

"Thanks," I said, unsure if I should trust this or not. "Are you badly hurt?"

She shook her head, pointing at the bloody uniform. "Just a flesh wound. And it certainly convinced Maarit that we weren't working together."

"Oh, really?" I said, standing gingerly. "Because if I were her, that's exactly what I would've thought. I would've stabbed you in something vital if I hated you."

"The Veil doesn't kill," Riya said, coming to her feet and walking toward me. "And you are, in fact, the real Veil."

I stared at her, unsure what would happen next. But with her uninjured arm, she yanked me into a hug, squeezing me with all her might. I returned her hug a little more carefully, but with no less relief. Even though she'd seemingly been helping me all this time, I couldn't help the small grain of worry that I'd been misreading her signals. But now, I had no doubts.

"Thank the Mother," she whispered, her eyes shining with tears as she gripped my face. "Are you really here? Are you really alive?"

I nodded, unable to find it within me to be sarcastic in the face of Riya's emotion. "I'm really alive, I promise."

"Does Felix know?" she asked. "How did you survive? What are you even doing here?"

"Yes, Felix knows. Long story on survival and I'm here to..." I swallowed. "Well, I'm here right now."

She gave me a look. "What does that mean?"

I told her about returning to Forcadel, about the letter Katarine had given me to deliver to Ariadna and how that had led me into Kulka and Neshua. But as I drew closer to my purpose in Neveri, nerves began to edge into my voice.

"The truth is..." I swallowed hard. "The truth is that Neshua said he'll only help if I prove to him I can take back the city. This city. He wants me to take Neveri for the Kulkans."

"Oh," Riya said, her eyebrows raised. "Well, that's going to be tough. There are three hundred soldiers in the city now—mostly Severian, with about a third Forcadelian. How many soldiers is Neshua giving you?"

I winced. "In debate. Prince Ammon is sitting in an army fort up north, and he promised if I give him a plan worth aiding, he would help."

"And do you have such a plan?"

"No," I said heavily. "I've spent the past few days getting the layout of the city, and so far, there's just a bunch of soldiers, a big swamp, and a gate that can't be opened. Against just me, that's..."

"There are those in the city who'd take up arms against the

Severians," Riya said. "When we arrived in Neveri, there were monuments to you all over the place. Nobody wants them here."

Norah had had one of those very posters. No wonder she'd been so eager to help me. "I don't want to get the citizenry involved, if I can help it."

"The citizenry would get involved, whether you like it or not. But I'm also talking about the royal guard from Forcadel," Riya said. "About fifty of Felix's most recently graduated cadets were assigned here with me because Ilara was concerned they were more loyal to him than to her. They would surely turn for you."

"I think I saw them when I came into the city," I replied. "Was one of them Felix's...?"

"Cousin," she said with a hidden smile. "Jorad. Good kid."

"Do you think he recognized me? I'd rather not reveal myself just yet." But then, I winced. "Except I just revealed myself to Maarit."

"She won't tell anyone," Riya said.

"Really? I would've thought Maarit would want to use this knowledge to her advantage," I said with a doubtful glance. "She could put my face on wanted posters and kill my ability to walk around in broad daylight."

"Yeah, but..." Riya chuckled. "The problem is that Ilara's touchy when it comes to you. She can't stand that everyone liked you better."

I snorted. "That's idiotic."

"Nobody said Ilara was smart," Riya said with a smile. "But Maarit is. If Ilara caught wind you were alive, and Maarit didn't immediately put a stop to it, the good general would be swinging from the gallows before the day was over. She won't breathe a word until you're dead."

"That's actually good news," I said, sitting back. "I was afraid I'd have to watch myself in the daylight."

"I'd still watch yourself," Riya said. "Maarit may know the

truth, but you still look like the girl on those memorial posters. Things have gotten even worse for us guards. Seeing The Veil, it's given the people something to hope for. Like a savior has come to deliver them. If someone saw you and recognized you..." She shivered.

"I hadn't realized The Veil had become so renowned outside of Forcadel City," I said, rubbing the back of my neck. I'd thought my antics were well-contained. "Didn't Felix say nobody noticed?"

"And you believed him?" She snorted. "He was trying to get you to focus on being queen."

I had to laugh, thinking about the slow dance we'd performed during those three months. "He didn't do a good job of that, unfortunately."

She grinned and nudged me. "How did Felix take it when he saw you? He was absolutely distraught after he thought you'd died. Inconsolable. Cried, even. He didn't even cry when August died."

"He took it well," I said, grateful that the night hid my flushing cheeks.

"Did he kiss you? Confess he loved you?"

"Riya!" I said, probably a little louder than I should have. We sat in silence for a moment, listening for footsteps, but the night remained quiet. "That is *none* of your business."

"Of course it's my business," she said, nudging me again. "I'm one-third of the trio who was out on the streets finishing what you started."

"Thank you for that," I said, running my hands together. "I'm surprised. I thought...well, I thought you guys didn't like me that much."

"Well, after you tried to reassign our captain..."

I sighed. "He told me to."

"Yes, I know," Riya said with an exasperated smile. "I know that was just him being an idiot. Falling in love with his queen scared the piss out of him."

My face warmed again, thinking about the way the proclamation had rolled off his lips all those weeks ago. I wondered if he still felt the same after my absence. "So you guys...talked about that?"

"Didn't have to," she said smugly. "I can read Felix like a book. He likes to control his world, and you represent absolute chaos."

"I could use some of that control right about now," I said, gazing at the stars above. "I feel like every move I make results in more consequences than I could've intended. And now this? Taking over a city just to hand it to the Kulkans? It seems wrong, and yet...it's the only way I can bring peace to the country. And at the same time, it's so impossible that I don't even know where to begin."

"It's not like you to be so unsettled," Riya said, nudging me.

"Well, it's been hard to trust my gut since Ilara put a knife in it," I said with a dry laugh. "Luard told me to do what I normally do: observe, find a weakness, and then exploit it. But I can't seem to find any weaknesses."

"If you could get the gate open, that might be a glaring weakness," she said. "But you can't just open and close it, like in Skorsa. You've got to have some manpower. The gear works are under two fortresses on either side of the river, and from what I remember as a girl, they are massive."

"How do I get there?" I asked.

"The fortresses themselves aren't that heavily fortified, but they're hard to get to," she said. "You can only go there by boat, and the only boats going that way now are military vessels. Anything else would get blown out of the water." She screwed up her face. "But I'll see what I can find out."

"Thank you," I said, offering her a smile. "It's really nice to have an ally in the city. I can't tell you how happy I am to see you."

She reached under her tunic to reveal a small coin—the Forcadelian seal. The same one I carried around my neck. "To whatever end, Your Majesty."

$$\Rightarrow\!\!\!-\!\!\!-\!\!\!\rightarrow$$

As the sun rose over the city on my second full day in Neveri, I considered my next move. Things were still dire, but thanks to Riya, I now had more information about the city. A third of the guards in the city were Forcadelian, and some of those were Felix's. That meshed with what I'd seen so far, especially the young faces of the kindest soldiers. Riya had said they would ally themselves with me, but I wasn't convinced. And I didn't want to think about what I might be forced to do if they didn't.

For now, my hopes were pinned on Riya being able to find out more about the gate. Around midday, I found her patrolling the farmer's market. She caught my eye but didn't immediately come to speak with me. Instead, I loitered around one of the booths, eyeing the molding strawberries as if I were trying to decide if they were worth my gold.

"Afternoon." Riya's voice was soft, and her mouth barely moved as she brushed by me, sliding a piece of paper into my hand. I quickly hid it up my sleeve, making sure to linger over the berries for a few minutes before moving along

Heart pounding, I found my way into an alley and pulled out the hastily written note, my hopes sinking with every word. There was one ship that took soldiers to the gate—it left at midday and the Severian lieutenant took a headcount of every soldier coming on and off. Riya noted they were almost exclusively Severian, which meant sneaking on was a no-go. But the military vessel was the only way; they had heavy patrols watching the river now that the gate was closed.

I leaned against the wall, crumpling the paper as my mind spun through alternatives but landing on none. I uncrumpled the paper, reading it a few times, looking for something I might've missed in her words. I flipped the page over, finding a small postscript.

You might find another ally at the Wicked Duck.

I furrowed my brow; I'd purposefully steered clear of that place since the girl had sold me out. But Riya wouldn't lead me astray, so I stuffed the paper into my bag to burn later and headed toward the other side of town.

There, behind the stables at the inn, I found a Niemenian royal carriage.

Chapter Thirty-Nine

Felix

It had been a miracle that I'd made it back to the castle without being seen, dripping wet as I'd been. The Severian guards had been quick to report to Coyle that they'd seen the masked vigilante in person, and combed the city for the masked vigilante.

And while they'd focused on me, eight houses went up in flames—every one a merchant who had agreed to Ilara's new edict on moving food directly to Severia. In my mind, someone had laid one exceptional trap, and I'd played an unwitting accomplice to it all. But more importantly, my one lead had gone cold.

If that weren't bad enough, I now had two permanent Severian shadows wherever I went. Coyle said they were a precaution, but they were nothing more than babysitters. Perhaps he was hoping to catch me in the act. Still, I wasn't about to let adversity get me down. If they wanted to babysit me, they'd have to do it out on the town.

Because with no other leads, I settled for knocking on doors and asking questions. Unfortunately, it was starting to look like a large waste of time.

"I got nothing for you, Captain."

"Get off my stoop."

Most of them just slammed the door in my face. It was hard to be a hated man in my hometown.

Three days of nonstop searching, and I'd crossed off every house in Mariner's Row. No one had given me anything of value, but I had circled the homes that seemed more terrified than disgusted. Those would be ones to revisit, perhaps at night under a mask when I could lose these shadows. Brynna had found success breaking into houses and threatening people; perhaps it was time I tried the same.

We crossed the main street separating Mariner's Row from Sailor's Corner, and something new caught my eye. A riverboat that hadn't been there the day before was in the docks. We were still receiving ocean-faring ships, but the riverboats were mostly dry-docked now that the borders were closed. So where had this one come from?

And why did it look familiar?

"Change of plans," I said to the two Severians behind me. "We're going down to the docks."

The dock master met me at the on-ramp, pulling his hat off his bald head and wearing a sheen of sweat on his upper lip.

"Afternoon, Captain," he said. "Suppose you're here about this new ship, hm?"

"I am," I said. "What do you know about it?"

"Just a cargo ship, here from Skorsa, they say." The way his voice shook, I knew he was lying. But my Severian guards weren't listening, so I let him ramble. "They were one of the last ships that got through before the new order took over, know what I'm saying?"

"I do," I said. "Thank you."

So as to not arouse suspicion, I made a show of meeting with the other ocean-faring ships in port, even though I had other guards assigned to that duty. The first ship looked Kulkan, but upon inspection of her papers, she had come from a port out west.

"Queen Ilara's having us take vegetables to the ports out west, close to Severia," she said. "Bring back all this glass. We ain't seen a gold coin in weeks, but if we don't do it..." She looked behind me at the guards. "Just a tough situation. But I'm lucky, I don't have a house for them to torch."

"I understand," I said, wishing I could do more for her. But she seemed relieved when I disembarked.

The other two ships were the same—bringing glass from Severia in exchange for food that was worth twice what the glass was. Like the first ship, they hadn't been able to turn a profit, and one was saying he was about to sell his ship and try his luck in another industry.

"But what other industry is there?" he asked.

I had no good answers, so again, I left without offering any advice.

Finally, as we came to the last dock, I got a good look at the ship that had come in from Skorsa...and my pulse quickened as my memory snapped into place.

This ship belonged to Kieran—the pirate that had been Brynna's contact. I hadn't seen him in months, but it couldn't have been a coincidence that he'd come from Skorsa. My heart skipped in my chest, igniting the hope that I might see Brynna again. I prayed the pirate was smart enough to be prepared for an inspection, especially arriving in such a noticeable vessel.

"Captain?" I called to the ship as we boarded.

The woman who walked out of the ship wasn't Brynna, but I recognized her as one of Kieran's. "Good afternoon, Captain Llobrega. Is there something I can help you with?"

"Inspection," the Severian guard barked. "Where are your papers? What port did you come from?"

"Ah, lovely to be back from chilly Skorsa." The pirate himself appeared from his quarters, wearing a fine tunic and shiny black boots. A pang of jealousy ricocheted through my mind as I thought about him and Brynna, but I stuffed it down. "Captain Llobrega, this is truly an honor. I didn't think you lowered yourself to spend time amongst the peons."

"With so few ships coming and going, it's important to make sure that the right ones come to port," I replied easily. "What was your business in Skorsa?"

He wagged his eyebrows at me. "Carrying precious cargo to the border."

"And did you bring that precious cargo back?" I pressed.

"Sadly, said cargo was destined for another location, so my job was just to get it to the border." He gestured around at the rest of the ship. "But please, feel free to search the place for anything you might find unsavory. I doubt you'll find anything."

I nodded to the two Severians, and they pushed past me to examine the rest of the ship. Once they were gone, I turned my attention back to Kieran.

"May we speak in your office?" I asked.

"By all means!" He gestured for me to follow him, and once we were inside the safety of his quarters, I lost the remainder of my patience.

"Cut the crap. Where is she?" I demanded, marching toward him.

"I don't know," he replied with an unnatural ease. "I assume she's fine."

"What do you mean, *you assume?*" I moved closer, poking my finger into his chest. "I need some answers, pirate, or I'm going to start breaking out the irons."

"Calm yourself, lover boy," he said, pushing my finger away. "Our fair Veil asked me to provide her passage to Niemen, which I did. She went off on her merry way into the mountains and that's the last I heard from her."

Disappointment settled in my chest. "How long ago?"

"Three weeks, maybe four," he replied, adjusting his tunic. "I daresay I'm offended on her behalf that you're so worried about her. The Veil is a highly capable woman. She's handled me more times than I can count."

I narrowed my eyes at him. "So I heard."

He chuckled and wrapped his hands behind his head. "Oh, don't be jealous. She was practically mooning over you the whole trip. Warmed my cold, salty heart." He cast me a lazy look over his shoulder as he walked back to his desk. "I suppose I can see what she likes about you. You both have an admirable loyalty to your country."

"And you, it seems, are loyal to the highest bidder."

"Um, pirate?" He pointed at himself. "But I do happen to admire The Veil and all her spunk. Which is why I'm offering *you* my services, for a small charge."

"I don't need your services," I snapped.

"Oh, don't you?" he chuckled, shuffling papers around. "Word in the underbelly of Forcadel is that there's a Man-Veil wandering around, asking dumb questions and getting no answers." He tilted his head in my direction. "Wouldn't you like it if I could find you those answers?"

"The issue is, of course, whether they're the right answers," I replied, not letting myself fall for his easy words. "To the questions I need answering."

"Oh, pssh, I won't lead you astray," he said with a shake of his head.

"Pardon me if I don't trust you."

"Is this about our little Veil?" Kieran said, leaning on his desk. "Are you reluctant to accept my help because of our wild, sexual past?"

I couldn't help the growl vibrating in my chest. "I don't trust you because you're a pirate."

"The Veil did," he replied softly. "And I kept my word to her not to speak of her real identity to any of the crew." He raised his gaze to meet mine. "You can ask them yourself whether they've seen Princess Brynna. All of them would say she's dead."

I straightened, crossing my arms. "You didn't tell a soul?"

"Not a single one," he said. "Had to tell the crew she and I were banging our way to—"

"All right, all right," I said, waving my hand. "Fine. I need the name of the man who's been leading the rebellion in the city."

Kieran whistled. "Unfortunately, I don't know the answer to that question, as I've been out of the country for a while," he said, running his hands along the desk. "But I can take you to my contact who's telling me all the juicy details from the underworld and get you acquainted with him. If I were to stake my reputation on you, it might help grease some more wheels and open some more doors."

I carefully considered his proposal. "What do you want in return?"

"What any man wants, really..." He grinned as I balled my fists in preparation for another crude pass at Brynna. "Calm yourself, Captain. In a nutshell: I want to leave, and your queen is making that difficult. You're a man in power. So help me and my ship get out of here."

I licked my lips. "You'll need clearance, and Ilara is..." The Severians opened the door behind me to continue their inspection. "Very particular these days."

"So I've heard," Kieran said. "Well, Captain, I'd be honored if you'd give your best to your wonderful new queen."

I nodded instead of answering and beckoned the two Severians off the ship with me.

"Do you know that guy?" one of them asked me.

"Yes," I said with a glare. "And he isn't to be trusted."

But unfortunately, he was the only option I had.

⇒————→

"Well, getting out of port is going to be difficult," Katarine said from her desk.

After speaking with Kieran, I returned to the castle with my babysitters. Even though it was well before midnight, I still slept poorly, tossing and turning with the worry about what might happen if I wasn't successful. And at dawn's first light, I was waiting for Katarine in her office to discuss strategy.

"How did Kieran get in, then?" I asked, resting my chin on my hand.

"Gold, I'd wager. He is a pirate," she said, reading a sheet of paper before signing it. "Ilara's now personally reviewing all requests and it's her signature and seal that permits ships to come and go. So whatever he paid, I'm sure it was sizable. Which is probably why he wants a cheap solution out. Can't be good for business to give away all his profits."

I nodded and paced the length of her office. "So what do I do? Kieran's my only hope for getting any information."

She tapped her finger against the desk. "I could forge Ilara's signature."

"No way." I shook my head firmly. "I'm not letting you get tangled up in this. If Ilara finds out—"

"There's no way she could know it was me," Katarine said. "We'll break into her office, I'll sign and seal passage papers, and you can deliver them to Kieran. Easy."

"You're mad," I said with a small laugh. "There's guards all over the place, especially at night. How would we even get into her office? How would I get out?"

"Unless Coyle's changed the schedule, they run on fifteen-minute shifts. Ilara usually leaves her office around four in the afternoon, so you'll join me back here after she leaves. We should be able to get in and out in five minutes."

I ran a hand through my hair. "And what about getting out of the castle? I can't shake my Severian guards."

"We'll leave from my office to my residence," she said, returning to the letter at her desk. "Obviously, with your well-known drinking problem, you'll be too soused to leave. There's a servants' staircase three doors down from my room which I believe connects to one of your secret passageways. Beata will help you get out unseen. They've been guarding the garden gate but haven't been as strict about the servants' exit."

I turned around, hearing that same clear-headed strategy she'd shown time and time again. "You sound like you've thought this through, Kat."

She exhaled. "If things continued to deteriorate, or if I caught wind that you or Beata would be in harm's way, I wanted to know that I could get you across the border." She looked up at me. "What?"

"Always have a plan brewing, don't you?" I smiled warmly.

"It helps me feel in control," she said with a small sigh. "But up until now, it was mostly flights of fancy. My forgery isn't very good yet, but if I practice today, I can surely manage." She pulled out a sheet of paper and began to trace.

I watched her for a moment. "Kat. I can't ask you to do this."

"Felix, we're all treading on thin ice," she said, exasperation creeping into her voice. "And I'm the only one who's safe in the castle. I want to do this—you *will* let me do this for you."

"Just…make sure you burn the evidence of all that tracing," I said, walking to the door.

"Oh, Felix." She rolled her eyes. "I wasn't born yesterday."

Chapter Forty

I wasn't sure whether to be pleased or worried about Luard's arrival in Neveri. On the one hand, it was more allies and soldiers, but also…he had a habit of inserting himself in places where he didn't belong. And with my nightly activities under heavy scrutiny, I would have to be careful how I allowed myself to be seen with him.

I spent most of the day hiding my face and avoiding attention from the local soldiers. I didn't want to approach Luard or his team until I had them alone, and unfortunately, they spent most of their first day in town in the middle of taverns and whatever shops were open. As the afternoon drew on, they returned to their inn. I had a good vantage point from the rooftop across the street, but since the caretaker at the Wicked Duck knew my face, I couldn't just walk in the front door.

When dusk started to settle, and Ivan rose from his nap, I dug around on the roof until I found something big enough to throw. I lobbed it at the window. But, of course, Luard's boisterous laughter echoed at the same time.

I threw another—same thing.

"Mother damn it all, shut up, Luard." I grunted as I scrounged around for another stone. I listened for the laughter then threw the rock once it had subsided.

Ivan came to the window and pulled it open.

I waved frantically.

"What are you—"

"Ssh!" I hissed, glancing at the alley and putting my finger to my mouth. I motioned for him to move out of the way then popped up and walked to the other edge. With a running start, I leapt over the alley, my fingers connecting with the overhang of the roof. And with a heave, I swung myself through the open window, landing in a crouch.

"Well," Luard said, his eyes wide. "That was quite an entrance. You've certainly taken to vigilantism again, haven't you?"

I walked to the window and closed the curtains. "It's been difficult to move around here. How did you guys get past the guards at the city limits?"

"My charm," Luard said, with a knowing glance. "Though they still searched our entire carriage. I made sure to file an official complaint. Maarit should be paying me a visit."

My eyes bulged. "Are you serious? She could—"

"Relax, Brynna," he said, holding up his hands. "It's merely a tactic. If I act like a spoiled prince, offended that I was treated like an enemy combatant, she's less likely to assume I am, in fact, an enemy combatant."

I relaxed, but only a little. "She's a real piece of work. You'd better be careful about pissing her off."

"Duly noted," he said. "So? How goes it?"

I wished I had more to share with him. "The good news is that Riya is here—she's one of Felix's lieutenants and she's promising to find me a way to the gates so I can get a closer look. But from what I've seen so far, it'll be tough."

I heard voices outside the room, and Ivan and I shared a look. Someone knocked loudly on the door. "City of Neveri guards. Open up."

One quick look out the window told me I'd be unable to escape that way, so I opted to dive under one of the beds and hope they didn't look there. No sooner had my feet disappeared from the light than the door opened and black boots walked inside.

"When we knock, you open. Or are things different in Niemen?"

Maarit had made a personal visit, as expected, along with four other guards. I couldn't tell if Riya was one of them, but I assumed not. I might've given her a reprieve, but not enough to fully restore trust.

"Things must be different, because the last time I visited Forcadel, I wasn't barged in on," Luard replied casually, leaning on the bed I was under. "Good thing I wasn't in here with a woman, or else I would've been really cross."

Maarit walked to the window, opening the curtains. "I am curious why a prince of Niemen decided to enter our city. On your way to visit your sister in Forcadel?"

"Oh, I'm a wild stallion," he said, his weight crashing down on the bed. "But I do think I might write to my dear sister in Forcadel and tell her just how I was welcomed into the country. She does have the ear of that new queen now, and I know she'll be most interested to hear how visitors are received in the border city."

There was a pregnant pause, then Maarit cleared her throat. "We have a lot of unrest in the city as of late, and I'm merely concerned about your wellbeing. I would be happy to leave an extra guard here."

"Oh, there's no need for that," Luard said. "My men are quite adept at keeping my nose clean, as it were. But I would love it if you'd give me a personal tour of your great city. I like to know where I should spend my money—and where I shouldn't."

"Of course." Her shadow moved, perhaps into a half-bow appropriate for a prince of a foreign nation. "Anything else I can do for you during your short visit?"

He made a noise. "I confess, I would like to see these great gates I've heard so much about. They're closed now, aren't they?"

I bit my lip, curiosity and fear zipping down my back.

"I'm afraid I can't do that," Maarit said, predictably. "Ferrying a prince isn't something I want to allot resources to right now."

"No resources necessary," Luard said. "I'm well-equipped with guards of my own. I'm sure we can commission a ferry—"

"Only military vessels are allowed west of the city." Maarit's tone had grown terse, and I closed my eyes as I willed Luard to tread carefully. It wouldn't do him any good to arouse suspicion.

"And when is the next vessel leaving?" Luard asked, sounding oblivious to everything except his own ego.

"Why so interested?"

"Silly reason. Ariadna is curious to know if the Niemenian steel used to construct the gates is still strong. Apparently, there's something in the old treaty that dictates if the steel rusts or deteriorates, Niemen will replace it. She received a note from Her Majesty, Queen Ilara, some time ago asking her to inspect it. And so I got the short end of the stick and was sent all the way here."

I craned my neck upward, knowing he couldn't see the look of disbelief on my face.

Above me, paper rustled, and I heard the telltale sigh from Maarit's nose. "I see. Why not mention it when I asked you why you were here?"

"I didn't think it was any of your concern," Luard said. "After all, I'm not a prisoner. I can move freely in the city, can I not? I thought the same would go for the gates. Silly me, I forgot we're in a war."

"We aren't in a war," Maarit said, rustling the papers more. "Let me see what I can do for you, Prince Luard. I'll send a messenger in the morning with an update."

"Not too early," Luard said lightly.

The footsteps shuffled out of the room and after a few minutes, the door closed. I waited even longer for the echoes on the stairs to disappear, and Luard poked his head under the bed with a smile.

"Still alive down there?" he said in a quiet voice.

"What in the Mother's name?" I breathed, sliding out. "How did you come up with all that?"

"Easy," Luard said, handing me the paper he'd given to Maarit. It was written in a loopy scrawl I recognized as Ilara's from the few letters we'd exchanged. It was exactly as Luard had said—a request to Ariadna to send someone to inspect the gates, as per the treaty.

"This... What...?"

"Obviously, it's a forgery," Luard said, snatching it from me. "Asdis used a couple of letters Ariadna received from the queen as a practice guide."

"We used it to get past the border," Ivan said. "And to get into the city, as well. It's a convenient excuse for a Niemenian prince to be traveling to the city—especially since the gates were recently closed."

"I didn't want to play it unless I had to," Luard said. "Since Maarit was one of Ilara's, it would be harder to fool her. But it appears to have worked. So now we have a way to the gate, and you have one problem solved."

"Do you actually think there's an issue with the gate?" I asked.

"Of course not," Luard scoffed. "Niemenian steel is good for thousands of years. But... it's incredibly combustible with the ore from the mines. The very same ore we have in our carriage down below. Which we should—"

"No," I said with a shake of my head. "Not yet."

Luard sighed and sank onto the bed. "And why not? We've got

the opening."

"Because if the gate explodes, Maarit will point a finger at you," I said. "And besides that, if it is as combustible as you say, you might get caught up in it. I said I wanted to understand the layout before I took action, and I meant it."

Luard looked at Ivan, who thankfully nodded. "I agree with Brynna. As unstable as ond is, it's best to be more cautious."

"Fine," Luard said. "It's your schedule."

"There's still the problem of getting inside the fortress," I said. "I can't just waltz in with you guys."

"You leave that to us," Luard said. "For now, you should probably rest. You look terrible. Look at those bags under your eyes. What've you been doing? Acting like some kind of vigilante all night?"

"There's no way this is going to work," I said with a roll of my eyes. "I look nothing like a Niemenian."

"Nobody ever looks at my guards," Luard said, adjusting the white sash across my chest.

When I'd awoken this morning, Luard had filled me in on his insane plan. I was to dress like a Niemenian, complete with white powder on my face and blond wig, and pose as one of Luard's guards on the trip today. I thought it was quite possibly the dumbest thing I'd heard to date—and I was trying to take back a kingdom without an army.

"You look fantastic," Asdis said. "Luard came with four guards. Three men and a woman. He'll leave with the same number."

"See, Asdis, I knew you were useful for something," Luard said.

She pursed her lips at him, but I still wasn't convinced. "The innkeeper saw my face."

"Then we'll make sure to avoid her," Luard said, placing the cap atop my head. "Don't pout. It's a great honor to be one of my guards."

I stared at the ceiling. "If you say so."

There was a knock at the door, and I tensed. But Luard casually strode to the door, opening it without a care in the world.

"Good morning, Prince Luard." Riya was on the other side of the door, her face stoic and her stance tense. "Captain Maarit sends her sincerest apologies, but she's unable to take you on a tour today. So she's sent me in her place. My name is Lieutenant Riya Kellis. I have a contingent of guards waiting downstairs and a horse ready to take you."

"Oh, Lieutenant, don't stand in the hall like that," Luard said. "Please, do come in. I'm just putting my shoes on."

She walked inside, standing stiffly in the door as she watched him. "We really must get going. The ship will be leaving at the top of the hour."

"Perfect," Luard said, looking over at me. "I'll be taking two guards with me. Ivan and Asdis."

Riya nodded us, then did a double take. She stepped fully inside the room, shut the door, and pointed a very angry finger at Luard.

"What in the *Mother's* name are you playing at?"

"Oh, come now, nobody else will recognize her," Luard said, gently pushing her finger down. "Because nobody will be looking at her. I'm more than enough to draw attention, and you'll vouch for her."

"They're all Severians down there," Riya said. "They don't trust me. And they definitely don't trust you."

"Then we'll have to tread carefully. Asdis, dear, are you ready?" Luard asked me.

Riya exhaled loudly. "I have to protest, on behalf of Lady Katarine *and* Felix. If Brynna is caught as a spy, or at any point of this ill-thought-out plan, Luard, you could be in serious trouble. I'm not sure if even your connections to Niemen would save you then."

"Brynna won't get caught, will she?" Luard said, resting a hand on my shoulder.

"That's not—"

"I appreciate your concern, as I heard quite enough of it from Brynna on the way from Linden, and more from Ivan and the rest of them on the way down here," Luard said, some of his casual veneer disappearing again. "But I made a promise that I would help, and Mother willing, I'll help." He grinned tightly. "I am certain she can pull this off. I've seen what she's capable of. And there's no way she can get on the ship otherwise, hm?"

Riya sighed. "No, all the guards on the ship will be Severian—and on a roll call. But this is...this is a lot."

"Well, if it fails, we'll just all just jump overboard and swim to shore!" Luard said with an overly cheery smile.

Chapter Forty-One

We descended the stairs of the Wicked Duck, leaving the real Asdis behind in the room with a good book to read. My heart throbbed as we passed the innkeeper, but she waved us on without a second glance. The second test, of course, would be the Severian soldiers out front.

"We'll need a few minutes to ready the carriage," Luard said as we came into view. "We'd be more than happy to meet you at the docks in a few moments."

"No," said a Severian to Riya's right. "Maarit's orders are not to let you out of our sight."

Riya pursed her lips but said nothing to the insubordination. "Please hurry."

Hagan, Nils, and I turned to ready the carriage, although the latter two would be staying behind on this journey. "Don't worry," Hagan said. "Luard knows what he's doing. He's snuck more people into more places than I can count."

"So he's done this before?" I whispered back.

Nils winked. "It's usually a woman he's sleeping with, but yeah."

They helped me settle onto the back of the carriage as Hagan drove it to the front. There, he passed the reins to Ivan, and Luard climbed inside. He rapped on the window behind me, perhaps to remind me to wipe the nervous look from my face. The carriage rolled forward, and Hagan and Nils waved as we left them behind. Two Severians fell into step behind the carriage, but they took no notice of me sitting on the back. Still, I kept my face averted just in case any of the citizens recognized me.

The ride to the docks was a short one. Already there was a queue of Severian soldiers lining up to board, standing next to a sour-faced Severian with a clipboard. He didn't look any nicer when Luard stepped out of the carriage and made his way toward the boat.

"Lieutenant," the Severian commander said to Riya as she walked up to him. "What's the meaning of this?"

"Morning, Illsey. We're here under orders from Maarit," Riya said, handing him an envelope. "The prince of Niemen has been ordered by Queen Ilara to inspect the gate."

He read through the letter three times, clearly looking for a sign of forgery, then tossed the letter aside. "Fine. Just keep them out of the way."

"Of this glorified carriage? Absolutely." Riya turned to Luard. "Come, let's get to the front of the ship so we don't interfere with Lieutenant Illsey's important work of transporting soldiers half an hour up-and-down river."

We were the last to board, and once Illsey had counted the number, the boat pushed off from the dock and headed upstream. From here, I got a look at the city of Neveri from afar, overlaying it with the map in my mind. The swamps extended as far as I could see, a natural defense from Kulka and invasions beyond. I could scarcely believe I'd managed to walk so far without any idea where I was going.

"The gate is made of Niemenian steel, as you know, Prince Luard," Riya said. "The finest Forcadelian engineers built it six hundred years ago with help from the Niemenians and it's passed the test of time."

"Lieutenant, perhaps it's not wise to share the specifics of our armaments with our northern neighbors," Illsey said, coming to stand next to her.

"Considering that we helped build said armaments," Luard said with a look, "I think I'm well aware of all the intricacies of its construction."

I cast a curious look at Luard. Clearly, he didn't know the intricacies, or we wouldn't be on this ship. But it was a nice lie that Illsey probably couldn't argue with—and one that might get us passage into the fortress.

Illsey, however, wasn't amused. "You should watch your tongue, Niemenian. Or else you might find yourself off this ship."

"Oh, calm yourself, Lieutenant Illsey," Luard said, patting the Severian on the shoulder. "I'm the fifth son of a dead Niemenian king, and my country is on the other side of Forcadel. I have no desire to get in the middle of Forcadel and Kulka's border dispute."

"What border dispute?" Illsey said, narrowing his eyes.

"Isn't there one?" Luard asked lightly. "I assume there's always a dispute with Forcadel. They're just so eager to grab as much land as possible."

"Fortunately," Riya said, interrupting whatever Illsey was going to say, "we've been a little preoccupied of late. All borders remain as they've been for the past twenty years."

"Except, of course, the one between Forcadel and Severia," Luard said. "Tell me, do you guys consider yourself Severians or Forcadelians?"

Riya, wisely, didn't answer, so Illsey did for her. "This is now the border of Queen Ilara's domain. That's all you need to concern yourself with."

"Mm...six hundred years," Luard said, shaking his head as he picked the conversation right back up. "Has it really been so long since Neveri belonged to Kulka?"

Riya coughed. "Actually, it fell briefly to Kulka about fifty years ago, for about ten years, but was reclaimed."

"That sounds about right." Luard looked at Illsey, whose jaw twitched every time Riya spoke. "See what I said about borders in dispute? It's so hard to keep everything straight."

After the first bend in the river, the gate became visible. It was, as Riya had said, much larger than the one in Skorsa and constructed differently—more like a massive, iron garden gate with a river running through the pickets. In the center, where the garden gate lock might be, there were chains with links the size of horses that dropped into the river water, then reappeared on the banks and continued inside the two brick fortresses.

It certainly looked immovable.

"How close can we get to complete the inspection?" Luard asked. "My sister will want a detailed report to send back to Queen Ilara."

"You'll be able to see them from afar," Illsey replied with a firm tone. "That should be plenty."

"Oh, no, my dear sir, that won't do at all," Luard said with a frown. "I'll need to get up close and personal with the gate. Really get my hands on the iron. And I'll need to inspect your gear works as well."

Illsey opened his mouth to argue, but Riya held her hand up. "I have to agree with him. Maarit said to allow them full access." She half-smiled. "After all, he's just the fifth son of a dead king. How much trouble can he be?"

Half an hour later, the riverboat sidled up to the fortress on the western side of the river. There was another Severian lieutenant waiting for us on the dock, and his disdain matched Illsey's once he caught sight of the interlopers onboard.

"What's the meaning of this?" he demanded from Illsey as he walked down the gangway.

"By Maarit's orders," he said with a look. "They're to be escorted into the fortress and be allowed to see the gear works to test for...imperfections."

"Yes, yes, we won't be long," Luard said, beckoning myself and Ivan to follow. But Illsey held up his hand.

"Only you, prince," he said. "Your guards stay."

"My two guards must go," Luard replied, a steely note in his voice. "They're my metalworks experts, after all. You can't expect a prince to know everything."

Illsey surveyed him for a moment, and I almost thought we would be denied, but he nodded. "Fine. They may go."

I followed Luard off the ship, hoping the extra scrutiny wouldn't result in them looking too closely at my powdered skin. But as before, Luard's boisterous voice drew all the attention away from me.

"Marvelous, isn't it?" he said, pointing to the chain that extended from the center of the gate in the river all the way to this fortress. "Look at the size of them. Just masterful craftsmanship by the Niemenians, don't you think, Illsey?"

"It's all right," he grumbled. "Come along, we don't have all day."

The fortress had walls about twenty feet high, with close-in trees that would've been easy to scale—a reminder that up until three weeks ago, these fortresses had been mostly empty, the open gate merely a symbol that flanked the opening of the river.

Illsey led us through the front entrance, secured by two knotted wooden doors. I wasn't sure what I'd expected to find, but...the empty courtyard wasn't it. The only thing of interest was a massive, spiked wheel. The chain that originated in the center of the gate was wrapped around it, each spike poking through the center of the link.

I nodded in understanding; turn the wheel one way, move the chain, open the gates, and presumably the other way closed them. But turning the wheel at all…that looked difficult.

"Where is everything?" Luard asked.

"Surely, someone who knows the specifics of the gate's construction would know," Illsey said with a curious look.

"I know how they were designed, not where you stash them," Luard replied with an easy smile.

Illsey sighed. "C'mon."

We crossed the empty courtyard filled with dry, parched-looking grasses. On the opposite side of the fortress was another door, which was guarded by two soldiers. They gave Illsey a salute and moved out of the way, but their eyes remained on the back of my neck as we passed them and walked down a stone staircase.

"Oh, this is an adventure," Luard said, winking at me. "Or they're about to murder us. I'm not sure which."

I gave him a look as Illsey snorted. "Calm yourself, Prince. I'm merely taking you to the gear works as requested."

We came to another door at the bottom of the staircase, and as Illsey pushed it open, I was hit by the smell of musty, muggy air and the distinct tang of metal. My jaw dropped as I took in the sight of the cavernous space filled with soldiers. In the center of the room was a spindle—presumably connected to the wheel above, also seemingly made of Niemenian ore.

"Mm-hm," Luard said, walking into the room. He cast a long look at the soldiers who'd stopped to stand at attention. There were Severians, but more than a few Forcadelians in the group. "Do you really need so many soldiers to stand guard? Or are you waiting for Her Highness to give the word to open the gates again?"

"Our security protocols aren't your concern," Illsey said. "You said you were here to inspect the gear works. Inspect it."

"Well, Ivan, Asdis," Luard said, waving us forward. "Get to inspecting."

I followed Ivan to the center of the room, and he made a show of running his hands along the spindle. He squinted at the machine, tilting his head backward, and following a series of tubes that fed to the walls and beyond. "It's water powered," he murmured.

"What?" I asked.

"What are you two talking about over there?" Illsey barked.

"Merely observing the water intake," Ivan said, waving me toward the other end of the fortress where one of the largest tubes terminated. He smiled at the three Forcadelian guards standing at attention. "If you'll allow us access."

They glanced at each other, then at Illsey behind us, and he begrudgingly gave them the order to move. Once they were out of the way, Ivan pressed his hand against the tube and smiled.

"See, there's the valve up there. I bet that this wall leads toward the river and ocean," he murmured. "Yes, very clever, very clever."

"So it's possible to turn on without a hundred men?" I asked, hopeful.

"Possible, yes. Realistic?" He cast a look around the room. "There are fifty guards in this room, by my count. You're going to have to come up with something spectacular to get past all these people."

Behind us, Luard was eyeing the spindle with something sinister in his eyes; no doubt thinking about the ond. But there were too many Forcadelians in here. I couldn't risk killing them with the Severians.

"I just need a little time," I whispered to Ivan. "But now that I know it's possible, that may be all I need."

Chapter Forty-Two

Illsey allowed us a short inspection of the southern fortress, which we found to be exactly the same as the northern one. Ivan and I didn't linger long, making sure to loudly announce that we saw no defects in the iron, and that we would be providing our queen—and Ilara—with a glowing report.

The ride downriver to Neveri was much quicker, and since most of the soldiers had been awake all night on their shift, the deck was quiet. I leaned over the railing, watching the landscape slide by and thinking through the loosely connected ideas that would eventually form a plan.

It was possible to open the gates, but I would have to subdue a literal boatload of soldiers to do it. I twisted through all kinds of scenarios, from trying to move the wheel from above to infiltrating as a soldier and turning it on when no one was looking. Each plan was more ridiculous than the last, until I was contemplating asking the Nestori if they'd invented anything for invisibility.

Once in the city proper, we returned to the Wicked Duck, where we met with Asdis and swapped clothes. Luard and Ivan disappeared into the city with her in search of food and drink, leaving me alone with my thoughts. I washed the makeup from my skin, sliding my dark tunic and pants back on and feeling more like myself.

Around dusk, Luard reappeared with a napkin full of bread, dried meat, and soft cheeses. "Dinner, since I assume you'll be going out under the mask tonight."

"Perhaps," I said, taking the food and chewing on it. "Both times I've revealed myself to Maarit haven't worked out well for me."

"Then perhaps you should quit playing around and start executing some kind of a plan," he said, sitting down on the other side of the bed. "Ammon won't wait around forever, you know."

"I know," I said, swallowing hard. "I just can't figure the best way to break into the fortress."

"Can't you?" he asked with a look. "Use the ond. Problem immediately solved."

I didn't want to dismiss him immediately, as I could tell he was growing tired of my delay tactics. "What happens if we do that?"

"So glad you asked," Luard said, kicking his feet off the bed and sitting up. He pulled a small piece of parchment out from his back pants pocket. Spreading it out on the bed, it revealed a detailed sketch of the gate, including the gatehouses and the underground spindles we'd seen.

"Ivan's handiwork, I had him work on it this afternoon," he said, by way of explanation. "The ond is potent, but that's a lot of iron to work through. Basically, we'll need to place it at strategic points on the gate to get the maximum effect." He drew his finger down one of the chains to the gatehouse. "And even better, by the time the ond works through all that iron, it'll have enough energy to take out both gate houses. Especially with that giant spindle in the center of the room made of ore."

The faces of the Forcadelians I'd seen underground flashed in my mind. "Is there any way we can destroy the gate without destroying the gatehouses?"

"And why would you want to do that?" Luard asked.

I gave him a look. "Because there are people down there, Luard."

"Mother, now is not the time for this nonsense," he said, running his hand through his hair. "Listen, you have to level the playing field. It's the only way this harebrained scheme is going to work. You can take out a hundred soldiers of the *three hundred* we have to contend with."

"The soldiers who'll die...they won't only be Severians," I said. "There'll be Forcadelians amongst the dead. You're asking me to sign a death warrant on my own countrymen."

"Then what do you suggest?" Luard asked, sitting back. "Do you have some magical powder that will suddenly make them fall asleep?"

"Actually, I do," I said slowly. I couldn't believe I hadn't thought about it already. "I use knockout powder all the time. And it's an enclosed space, so with enough of it..." Just as quickly, I shook my head. "But then we'd be susceptible."

"Can't you use that foul-smelling herb?" Luard asked. "That smells bad enough to wake the dead."

A smile curled onto my face as my brain tumbled over thoughts. "No, but...maybe... Luard, you're a genius."

"That was never in debate, my dear, but for what this time?"

I couldn't find it within me to react snidely. "When I was in the mountains with the fur trader, we were attacked by a group of kids who used this herb—hyblatha—to give me vivid hallucinations. It's pretty common, but up until recently, I hadn't known it could be used for that. But more importantly, tinneum, that foul-smelling herb, dulls the effects. Which means that if we can get enough hyblatha inside the fortresses, we can use the tinneum to keep our heads and effectively take out all the guards for an extended period. Turn on the water, open the gates, and then return to the city!"

I grinned at Luard, but his expression was only mildly interested. "And where will you get this powder?"

My smile grew. "Celia has a ton of hyblatha—she uses it as a calming tea. They've got rows of it growing at the camp. And the stuff is so potent, much more than the knockout powder, only a little goes a long way..."

"I suppose that could work," he said. "But there will still be at least two hundred soldiers in the city to deal with."

"When I'm at Celia's, I'll ask her for more help," I said. "And with those soldiers, and with this plan, Ammon is sure to find that worth aiding. I don't think we'll be looking at two hundred either. Riya said there are about fifty from Felix's old guard here who would back me when they find out." I couldn't help the flutter of excitement in my chest. "Luard, this is it. This is the plan I've been waiting for. We can get what we want and no one has to die."

He surveyed me for a long time before nodding. "Fine. I suppose I can let you play this out a little longer. Where is this Celia woman?"

"About a day's ride from here," I said, looking out the window. "I'll see if Riya can get me out of the city tonight. From there, I'll continue to Ammon's to get more forces. I should be back within two days and ready to execute this plan."

"Fine," Luard said, coming to sit up. "But just remember: Ammon's not the only one who's risking a lot to be here. If you dawdle too long, you might just find yourself without any allies at all."

I didn't miss the steely-eyed glare he sent my way as I left. I was granted a reprieve for now, but soon Luard's unending patience would run out.

With the setting sun, I moved quickly to locate Riya. I found her in the farmer's market, giving stern lectures to the citizens about staying out too late and receiving more than her fair share of dirty looks.

"Hey," I said softly.

"You need to get out of here," she said. "Maarit's on the warpath tonight, especially as The Veil hasn't been seen in a night."

"Well, The Veil won't be seen much longer because I'm headed out of the city," I whispered.

"Where to?"

"Going to get some reinforcements," I said. "Think you can help me sneak out?"

She shook her head. "I already used up whatever goodwill I had with Maarit taking Luard to the gates. And right now, she's pulled all the Forcadelians off border patrol since they apparently let a wanted criminal into the city. You'll have to go through a very unfriendly Severian border patrol."

I blew air out from my lips. "So what do I need in order to pass muster?"

"Papers proving you're a citizen," Riya said. "Or a good bribe."

"Bribe, probably not." I had no coin left, and I doubted Luard would give me any, not after the way we'd parted. "But I can figure something out."

"When you come back, try to come in on the northern road, during the day," Riya said. "If you're not seen for a few days, I'll pressure Maarit to reassign the Forcadelians to patrol that route again. And if worst comes to worst," she grinned devilishly, "I'll leave a present for you in the forest so you can sneak in easier."

"Better to leave it with a woman named Norah," I said with a nod. "She helped me get into the city the first time, and I'm sure she'll be willing to help again. She lives on a farm up that way."

"Will do," Riya said. "Good luck, with whatever you're doing. And hurry back. I don't know how much longer the people can stand things as they are. If you don't do something, someone else might."

Chapter Forty-Three

Felix

It was impossible to sit still, as I waited for the hours to wind down until our mission. I still wasn't convinced Katarine could pull off Ilara's forgery—nor was I convinced we could get in and out of her office without being seen. There were so many variables, so many things that could go wrong. What if the guards were early? What if Ilara came back?

Katarine would be risking a lot—her position, her alliance with Ilara, and potentially Beata's safety. I would've rather kept both of them far from danger, but my preferences were clearly not being honored lately.

I fidgeted, watching the clock on the wall and counting down the minutes until four. Out my window, Kieran's ship was a small white dot, but it was still there. For how much longer, I didn't know. I didn't have any illusions. If he found a way out, he'd take it.

There was a soft knock at my door, and I turned, hoping to see Katarine or even Beata. Instead, it was Mayor Zuriel, who seemed a little bit less put-together than usual.

"Good afternoon, Captain," he said, ducking his head in a rare show of deference. "I wonder if I could speak with you about something?"

My instinct was to kick him out, but I waved him in. "What?"

"I thought I might ask you to increase my security detail again," Zuriel asked, the worry clear around his eyes as he sat in the chair.

"And why would I do that?" I drawled.

"Because I received this note this morning," he said, thrusting a paper at me. I unfurled it, my brows furrowing as I read through the hastily scrawled handwriting.

Traitors to Forcadel beware.

"How did this come to you?" I asked, my pulse quickening. "Did you see anyone?"

"No, it was just wrapped around a stone and laid on my doorstep," he said, running a hand through his slicked-back hair. "Have you seen anything like this before?"

"No," I said, rolling it up and handing it back to him. "Didn't you say you were threatened a few weeks ago? The guards are still stationed at your house."

"Yes, but... This is different. I don't know why, but I feel like whoever is doing this is going to strike."

I surveyed him. He was a lot thinner without his pearly smile and fancy jackets. Far from being the cheerful man I'd seen with his family, he looked close to death.

He sighed softly. "I know you have no love for me, Captain, but I do fear for my family's lives. Surely that means something to you."

"I'm sure Brynna feared for her life when she was bleeding to death on the forest floor," I replied coolly.

"I have a wife," he said, his voice cracking. "And two children. Please, if not for me, then perhaps just...for them."

The pleading in his voice moved me, but only a little. "If you're so concerned, I would have them stay with family. Somewhere far from your house. At least then, you'll be the only one hurt."

He opened his mouth to speak but decided against it. "Thank you for your time."

⇒————→

Zuriel's distraction was short-lived, and soon I was back to watching the clock. There was really nothing I could do for him now anyway. Kieran was my best shot at finding the name of the rebel leader.

Around three, Katarine sent an official, written invitation to dine with her and Beata. It was rather formal, but it was also a paper trail and would help build an alibi should Ilara get suspicious. And it was the signal for me to join her. The queen must've taken an early day.

I rose, stretching and moving slowly as I stacked my papers on the desk. The messenger had left the door ajar, and my two Severian guards had their eyes on me. Best not to look too eager, or too nervous.

With the invitation left on my desk, I exited my office and strolled down the hall, stuffing my hands in my pocket. Out of the corner of my eye, I watched my escorts for any sign of suspicion, because if they thought something was amiss, they surely wouldn't allow Katarine to send them away.

I ascended the stairs to the third level, walking down the hallway toward Katarine's office. But when her door opened, I nearly lost my carefully constructed mask.

"Afternoon, Felix," Ilara said. "What are you doing here?"

"We're dining tonight," Katarine replied from her desk. She wore a warm smile that betrayed nothing of tonight's mission. "It's so hard to pin him down, I had to practically send him a missive."

Ilara turned back to her and grinned. "Well, he has been quite busy of late. Perhaps the two of you can find out who's blowing holes in my city, hm?"

"It is certainly on the agenda," Katarine said with a sad sigh.

Our ruse seemed to have worked, because Ilara bid us both farewell and continued out into the hall. But there, she stopped. "Felix, why are there two guards out here?"

"I believe Lieutenant Coyle has assigned them," Katarine said, resting her joined hands on her desk. "There have been some threats to Felix's life, what with all the discord in the city. I think he's just being extra cautious."

Ilara, clearly unaware of this, turned back to them with a snide look on her face. "I don't know why Lieutenant Coyle made such a decision, but perhaps their talents would be better suited to protecting *my city* from harm, don't you think?"

"Couldn't agree more," I said, turning to the two Severians. "If you would, find Lieutenant Haarkan at the front of the castle and tell him to assign you a patrol for the evening."

The guards stared at each other but were smart enough not to disagree with me while their monarch was staring daggers at them. Once they'd disappeared, Ilara pursed her lips and turned back to us.

"Curious," she said, looking at Katarine. "I'll have to have a word with Coyle about this."

"As will I," I said. "Have a pleasant evening, Your Majesty."

Katarine rose and bowed, and I saluted. Then, finally, she left us in peace.

I waited until the door at the end of the hall had closed before I collapsed onto the spare chair. "What in the Mother's name...?"

"We don't have long," Katarine said, rising. "I assume those guards will go to Coyle instead of Haarkan, so he'll be sending a replacement up as soon as he can. By my count, we have twenty minutes to get in and out."

"But how did you—"

"Ilara asked me a few weeks ago why you always seemed to have guards by your side," Katarine said, walking out the door toward Ilara's office. "Clearly, Coyle hadn't gone through her, so I reasoned that she might help us lose them for the next few minutes."

"We can't do this now. Beata isn't here yet," I said, glancing down the hall.

"I'm here." Katarine's girlfriend appeared in the library doorway, wiping her hands on her apron. "I had to hide when Ilara showed up."

"Beata, are you sure you can do this?" Katarine asked, showing the first signs of nerves all day. "I can be the lookout if—"

"No, no," Beata said with a firm nod to me. "I'm ready."

"Did you get the key?"

Beata nodded and reached into a secret pocket in her dress. "They're all having supper now, so I have to get it back before they return and find it missing."

"We'll be quick," I said, leading the three of them to the door. Ilara's office was five doors down. Normally, it was a few steps. But now, it seemed interminable.

"Let's do this," Katarine said, brushing past me to walk down the hall. Beata went in the opposite direction to stand lookout at the intersection of the hall with the main one.

"Not too late to turn back," I said.

She firmed her smile. "I would never."

"Wait," I said to Katarine, pressing my ear to the door and listening, just in case. When I heard nothing, I nodded to her and she used the key, opening the door with a soft click and letting us both into the dark office.

It looked no different than when it had been Brynna's, except for the large Severian crest where the Lonsdale one had hung. I resisted the urge to take my knife to it and followed Katarine to the desk.

"There has to be one of these forms in here somewhere," she said, flipping hastily through the stacks of papers. The two stacks on the desk held nothing of value, so she started going through each of the drawers. Every pull seemed louder than a cannon blast, but perhaps it was just amplified by the pounding of my heart. I didn't care if I was caught; if Katarine or Beata were swept up in this, I'd never forgive myself.

"Hurry," I muttered.

"Ah!" she cried then covered her mouth and stared at the door. After a breath, she spread the form out on the desk and picked up the pen beside the largest stack. Carefully, she filled out the form, using a nearby signed paper of Ilara's for reference.

"Kat," I whispered.

"Calm down," she said, finishing the flourish on the ship number. "I need to concentrate."

With precision, she dipped the pen into the ink and pressed it to the paper. Her tongue stuck in the corner of her mouth, she carefully drew the I and then the rest of the name. I had to admit, it was almost dead-on.

"There," Katarine said, standing and blowing on the paper. "Get me the wax seal."

I searched the room for something to light under the wax to melt it, finally finding a match and a candle that would have to do. I could practically hear my heartbeat as the candle flickered under the wax pot, and Katarine snaked her hand through mine and squeezed.

We both jumped when a voice echoed in the hall.

"Coyle," I mouthed to Katarine. It hadn't been twenty minutes yet—clearly his guards had moved faster than we'd anticipated. Quietly, I crept to the door and pressed my ear against it to listen.

"What in the Mother's name are you doing up here?" he asked. "And where are Katarine and Felix?"

"We've been so worried about Felix lately that Kat insisted on inviting him to dine with us," she said. "She promised him a fine bottle of whiskey, just to sweeten the deal. If you ask me, he's drinking—"

"You didn't answer my question," Coyle barked. "What are *you* doing up here?"

"Oh, Kat forgot some papers she wanted to look over," Beata said, the lies running easily off her tongue. "She would have come herself, but Mother bless her, she already took down her hair. You know how she is." Beata laughed. "Wouldn't be caught dead with a strand out of place."

"All right, Bea," Katarine grumbled beside me. "Ease off a little."

"But where is the lie?" I whispered with a smirk, which earned me an icy death glare.

"Anyway, if you're concerned, you can escort me," Beata said, holding out her arm. "I don't like walking the castle alone. Too many unfamiliar faces."

"Fine." Coyle sounded annoyed. "Get what you need from her office and I'll walk you back to your room."

"Such a sweetheart," Beata said.

I looked back at Katarine, who was pressing the waxed seal to the paper, wincing as the paper crinkled and cracked in the silent room. But she replaced the set and blew out the candle, closing the pot and leaving it exactly as we'd found it.

In the hall, Beata's voice echoed as she and Coyle walked away. When there was silence, I chanced a look out into the hallway. It was empty, but I was sure Coyle would send a replacement to check it out.

"C'mon," I said, casting one final look at Ilara's office to make sure we hadn't left any traces of ourselves. And with Katarine's sweaty hand in mine, we dashed across the hall to the library and its secret entrance. It would take longer for Coyle to get to Katarine's suite, but not by much.

We ran through the dark passages, Katarine just ahead of me, until she stopped abruptly. On the wall, there was a small chalk mark. And with a small push, what I'd thought was the wall was actually a door.

"Hurry, this is a servants' hall," she said. When I closed it behind me, it practically melted into the stone behind it. No one would've known it was there. To my curious look, she blushed. "It's how Bea and I used to...well, it was our secret."

Voices echoed down the hall behind us and we quieted. Katarine again led the way, pulling pins out of her hair and tucking them into the bodice of her dress. She stopped at a door at the end of the hall and pressed her ear against it.

"All clear," she whispered, cracking it open to reveal the hall outside her bedroom. She dashed across it, slamming her key into the doorway and allowing me inside. There was a dinner already set out, complete with a large bottle of whiskey. She bypassed the dinner and grabbed the bottle, running to the window to pour out half of it.

"Get on the couch."

I did as instructed, and she unbuttoned my shirt, messing my clothes and taking off my boots. Then she stuck the half-empty bottle in my mouth and forced me to drink, before finally placing it in my hand as the knob on the door turned over. I closed my eyes and allowed my mouth to drop open.

"Pathetic."

"Coyle, if you don't have anything nice to say, don't say it at all," Katarine chided. "Now get the hell out of my room."

The door remained open for a moment longer, but I didn't chance opening my eyes to see his expression. Finally, when the lock clicked, Katarine exhaled loudly.

"That was close," Beata whispered. "Were you successful?"

Katarine pulled the sealed envelope from her dress pocket, which she slapped onto my chest. Then she took the bottle from my hands and drank three gulps.

"I take it back," she said with a bit of a pant. "I don't want to be a vigilante after all."

Chapter Forty-Four

To get out of Neveri, I hid under one of the queued carriages leaving the city. It was a bit nerve-wracking, especially as they started feeling around the bottom, but eventually, we were on our way. I held on as long as I could, then dropped onto the dusty road.

And with a smile on my face, I continued toward the east, away from the setting sun.

My estimation of the distance had been a bit skewed; on foot, I didn't see the forest in the distance until midday. By the time I reached the shade, I was exhausted and miserable. Whistles greeted me signaling my arrival, but none of them seemed to indicate I was an enemy. I wasn't sure what welcome I was expecting, but the small girl who'd bounded in my direction surely wasn't it. Her light brown hair and eyes were familiar, but it could've been that she had the same starved appearance as all the other kids in the camp.

"Elisha," she said after a moment. "Remember? You trained me once?"

"I trained a lot of kids," I said, turning to walk to the Nestori hut. Celia hadn't come to greet me, I wasn't sure if that was a good or bad thing.

The girl wasn't deterred. "So what are you doing here? Did you finish your mission? Are you back for good?"

I ignored her. I hadn't thought I'd be given a parade, but Celia usually knew I was coming the moment I set foot in the forest, and, in the past, had come to speak to me in person. Making me come to her seemed like a bad sign for the favor I was about to ask.

"Are you leaving again? Can I go with you?"

"Look, kid," I said, spinning around, "I have a lot on my mind. So can you just run along and annoy somebody else?"

"Be nice to the little girl," came a sultry voice. "She's merely excited to see you. As are we all."

I looked up to see Celia standing in the doorway of her hut. Something about her scrutiny made me want to stand between her and Elisha.

"That will be all, Elisha," Celia said to the girl.

Elisha bowed at the hip and scampered out, clearly proud of herself for getting noticed. I had a feeling she wouldn't be too far away, and that I might have to find a way to keep her off my back.

"Are you queen yet?" Celia announced.

"Do I look like I'm queen?" I said with a scowl. I would've preferred she not announce it to the entire camp. "I'm working on it."

"You were working on it weeks ago. I hope your progress is better than that."

I sighed and motioned to her house. "May we talk?"

"Do you have anything of value to say?"

I swallowed, thinking quickly. I wouldn't tell her about the ond, but she might have some use for the hyblatha. "I have a new weapon for you."

My heart leapt when she tilted her head in agreement and walked back inside her hut. Calmly, I followed.

"I hear you've been on quite a trek," Celia began, settling down and surveying me as if I were a misbehaving child.

I sat on the edge of the chair, ready to pounce or run if things didn't go well. "Oh yeah? And where do you hear that?"

"My spies in the city report you boarded a ship with the pirate Kieran. They say a Forcadelian woman who bent the gates in Skorsa with her own two hands."

"I bribed the mayor," I replied dryly.

"And now you arrive in my camp from the west and Neveri, which tells me you've made a full circle." She caught my gaze. "Am I wrong?"

"No, you aren't wrong." I gave her the short version of my trek, from Ariadna's conditional help to Neshua's task. I left out Luard's involvement, not wanting to show my hand too much. I also didn't mention the Niemenian ore, partially out of respect to Luard, but also because I didn't want to have to give Celia any of it.

"And so now you're here to…what? Get twenty thieves to help you conduct a wildly outrageous mission?" She shook her head with a twitter of laughter. "Oh, dear Brynna. I told you a long time ago that you needed to lose your soft heart. And now here you are twisting and turning to make a complex solution to an easy problem to save yourself pain."

"What other solution do you have?" I asked, the back of my neck warm with nerves. She couldn't know about the ond, could she?

"Hm." Celia sat back and surveyed me. "Tell me about this new weapon."

"It's not new, per se," I said. "It's hyblatha. Apparently, you can use the seeds to cause hallucinations that last. Better than knockout powder."

"I already have something like that," she said.

"Yeah, but..." I tossed the small bag onto her desk. "This inoculates us from the effects."

She inhaled the scent and wiped a tear from her eyes. "Potent."

"Well?"

"It is certainly clever," she said, sliding the pouch back to me. "But before I agree to help you, I'm going to need a demonstration of this new combination. Make sure this weapon is as powerful as you say."

I would've rather just taken my herbs and soldiers and gone, but I would get nothing if I didn't play her game. I wasn't looking forward to feeling the effects again, but if it meant I would have help, I would.

"Of course."

⇨————→

Elisha had been loitering around the house, and so she was sent to gather the people and materials for our test. As she bounded away wearing an excited grin, I buried the unease I felt watching Celia speak to the young girl.

"You know, she reminds me a lot of you," Celia said, catching my gaze.

"I wasn't that much of an ass-kisser," I said, crossing my arms over my chest.

"You were eager," Celia said. "I've never seen a child throw herself at so many trainers in such a short amount of time. You, of course, were worried I might return you to your father. Elisha is driven by the fear I might cast her from the camp."

Perhaps someone should tell her there are worse fates. I kept my comments to myself, as I still needed Celia's approval.

Elisha returned shortly after with Nicolasa in tow. She carried with her two small leather pouches and wore a confused look on her face. Behind them, Jax, and Locke, a tall goon who'd been at the camp nearly as long as I had, were ambling toward the training rings.

"I was sure the child was mistaken," Nicolasa said, handing Celia the bags. "But you did want hyblatha pulverized into powder, correct?"

"I did," Celia said, nodding once to Jax, who barely cast me a second look, and the rest. "Larissa has brought us a new use for the plant. One of you will inhale the powder to test its effects. Another will inhale the powder with the antidote."

"What's supposed to happen?" Jax asked.

"Well, one of you will have intense hallucinations," Celia said with a small shrug. "And the other, we hope, won't."

Unsurprisingly, none of the men stepped forward. But Elisha did. "I'll test it."

"Your funeral," Jax muttered. "What's to say that's not poison?"

"Then you do it," Elisha said, casting him a scathing look that said exactly how she felt about him.

"Why don't we let Larissa do it?" Locke said. "She's the one who brought it in. Why's she so special?"

Celia held up her hand to silence everyone. "Larissa will test the antidote. Locke, since you've got an opinion, you'll take the other sample."

I pinched a bit of the tinneum out of the bag and stuck it in my mouth. The bitter taste brought tears to my eyes and softened some of the nerves I couldn't shake here. I took my place in the center of the training ring next to Locke, who was grumbling.

"Quiet," Celia barked at him. "Nicolasa."

The Nestori walked up to us and poured a little into her hand. She inhaled deeply and blew a pile into my eyes, causing me to cough as the sweet and salty taste melded with the bitter herb in my mouth. I chewed harder, forcing more of the sharp tang from the herb.

"Well?" Celia asked.

Before I could answer, Locke released a blood-curdling scream and fell to his knees. Elisha jumped back, scrambling away as if he would rip her face off. But whatever hell Locke was trapped in was his own. Tears dribbled down his face as he begged a faceless, nameless person for forgiveness and other things I couldn't make out.

Without missing a beat, I grabbed more of the tinneum out of my bag. "Jax, get your ass over here and help me fix him."

"Wait." Celia watched Locke with a cruel sort of look. "I want to see how long this lasts."

"Celia, you can't be serious," I snapped, stepping forward. Before I could get to him, Jax grabbed my arm and pulled me back.

Locke writhed on the floor, his voice echoing into the ring and drawing the attentions of everyone in the camp. Before long, a crowd had gathered, murmuring conversations about what was going on. Locke rocked himself in a fetal position, his face red and his body shaking with tears. His pants grew wet as he soiled himself, but he was too far gone to notice.

The minutes passed slowly as he continued to writhe on the ground. Those gathered looked on with a mix of horror and fear. Only Celia, with her greedy, calculating eyes, seemed not to care that a man was slowly going insane.

Finally, the rocking stopped, and Celia nodded to Jax to release me. I ran to Locke and pried his mouth open, pressing the tinneum into his mouth. His watering eyes blinked.

"Chew," I whispered, running a soothing hand over his sweaty head. "It'll pass. Just chew."

Slowly, my words got through to him, and the redness subsided. His eyes still bore the wild fear that had gripped him, but he was able to sit up. The more he chewed, the more he came back to himself. Finally, he realized who was holding him and pushed me away.

"Get off," he grumbled. "'m fine."

"What did you see?" Celia ordered.

"That's not important," I snapped, remembering my own visions. "You saw it worked. Now hold up your end of the bargain."

"Locke."

"I saw my parents," he said. "The day they sold me."

A collective hush descended on the group and my heart wrenched in my chest. Celia, however, didn't notice or didn't care.

"Excellent," she said. "Nicolasa, I want you to plant several new gardens of the hyblatha. Whatever we can spare will be diverted to this new weapon." She looked to me. "Whatever we have on hand, prepare and give to Larissa."

Nicolasa opened her mouth as if to argue but nodded. "Yes, ma'am."

"I want you to find tinneum—if we can't grow it here, we'll find a supplier."

"Yes, ma'am."

Celia cast a look around at the rest of those gathered, still shell-shocked at what this herb had done to one of the toughest in the camp.

"Get back to work," she barked. "Or there will be no dinner tonight."

Slowly, the crowd dissipated, casting nervous looks at Locke, who was blushing bright red with embarrassment. He rose to his feet and stumbled to the edge of the camp, refusing all overtures from those he passed. I watched him in silence until he disappeared through the front gates of the camp and into the darkness.

"Now, then," Celia said, drawing my attention back to her. "Jax, you will go with Larissa. Take the hyblatha with you and report back on its effectiveness."

"Jax is all I get?" I said, stepping forward. "I told you, I need at least twenty thieves. There are a hundred soldiers in there—"

"Well, you're going to fail, so I'm not wasting my time."

Her words echoed in my ears. "I'm sorry, *what?*"

"If you were serious, you would be asking me for twenty swords, not twenty thieves." She crossed her arms over her chest. "You're still afraid to get any blood on your hands. Even if it's the enemy's blood."

"It's not that I'm afraid," I spat, but my voice shook with uncertainty. "I'm walking a fine line—the people in this city won't be too happy to find out that I sold them for strategic advantage. So the fewer lives I take, the less trouble I'll have winning them over."

She cast me a long look that said she could see right through me. Even if she didn't know about the ond, she clearly knew I was hiding something from her. My voice cracked as I took a step toward her. "Please, Celia. I need more than one person."

"Fine, take two." She cast a gaze over to the young girl. "Elisha, you will accompany them as well."

She left the three of us in the training ring, and it was all I could do not to kick something.

"So...*Boss*," Jax drawled, crossing his arms over his chest. "What's the plan?"

I gave Jax the abridged version, not wanting to share it all until we were back in Neveri. He seemed as enthused at the idea as Luard had been, but since Celia had ordered him to help, he could do nothing but nod and agree. Elisha, on the other hand, gaped at me as if she'd never seen me before.

I patted her on the head. "Breathe. I'm still the same person."

"B-but you're a princess."

"Well, kind of."

"And a vigilante."

"Yes, I am that."

"You're a princess vigilante."

"Yes, I am," I said with a "please help me" look at Jax. Our third, however, was uninterested in doing more than the bare minimum. So I knelt down to Elisha's level. "Listen, I'm not really thrilled that you're coming."

That snapped her out of her reverie. "But I can help!"

"I know you can." I waved my hand to silence her. "However, you're just a kid. And what we're doing is going to be very dangerous."

"I know it is. That's why I want to help."

I pursed my lips. "You will help, if you'll let me finish. Your job will be to be our eyes. We'll need to know where the enemy is, and in order to do that, we'll need you in the trees to scout. Understand?"

She seemed to see through my ruse but nodded anyway.

"Also," I straightened, "you'll probably have to protect a prince, since I'm sure he'll want to come."

Her eyes grew three sizes. "A *prince?* Is he handsome? Is he charming?"

"He's neither, but I'm sure you'll find out sooner or later."

Things weren't looking up, but at least I had the hyblatha and some help. Jax wasn't wholly worthless, and Elisha could serve as a scout. Small blessings were still blessings, even if they scowled and smirked at me.

In the interest of time, I suggested we split up—I'd continue on to Ammon and Kulka and Jax and Elisha would get familiar with the city. At least, that's what I told Jax. In truth, I didn't want to mix Jax's clear disdain for me with Ammon's. I could only handle one smirking face at a time.

After leaving them to prepare for their journey, I stopped in the weapons hut to replenish my arrows and other trinkets that might be of use, like my weighted twine that could trip up an incoming soldier. I couldn't help but feel woefully underarmed, but I tried not to let it bother me. With my slingbag laden with what I could carry, I made one final stop before I would head north toward Ammon, to retrieve the hyblatha from Nicolasa.

The Nestori looked up at me from her mortar and pestle. She wore a mask, but the scent of hyblatha was thick in the air. I chewed the small piece of tinneum I still had in my mouth to stave off the effects.

"I had a feeling you'd be back," she said. "The winds have been shifting."

"I'm sure the winds are very concerned with my movements," I said with a laugh as I walked to their powder stores, shelves of woven baskets with small name tags.

"You're a force of nature," she replied softly. "And the Mother knows a queen in the making."

Celia's words came whistling back through my mind and I turned to the basket, pulling down one marked *knockout powder* and grabbing a few small leather bags.

"You've certainly become well-versed in Nestori magic," she said softly. "I'd hoped to keep the hyblatha secret from Celia for as long as possible."

I stopped, looking at her over my shoulder. It had never occurred to me that she might have known about it. "I had to give her something."

"I know," she said. "The knockout powder is more humane. Unfortunately, the hyblatha is more plentiful. And once we obtain the tinneum plant..."

I stared at the ground, remembering how real it had seemed to see Oleander's body. To smell Felix's blood as he stumbled forward. "I'm sorry."

"The Mother doesn't like Her magic used to hurt others, but sometimes...sometimes we must make the hard choices." The grinding sound stopped, and she caught me with her gaze. "And just hope the Mother judges us fairly for doing the best we can under the circumstances."

Chapter Forty-Five

Nicolasa's words hung in the back of my mind as I left the camp, headed north toward the border. Part of me knew I'd always been skirting a line as The Veil, but another part knew that my intentions were pure. If I was using the magic to help people, perhaps that was good enough for the Mother.

Celia's forest ended right at the border to Kulka and I only supposed Celia had run the Severians out of the forest, or perhaps they were too afraid of her to step inside her domain, because there wasn't a single guard—Forcadelian, Severian, or Kulkan— manning the border fence that stretched across the entrance to the forest.

The problem, though, was that I didn't quite know how to get back to Ammon's fortress. Walking westward was a good bet, but at some point, I might need to veer south, if the map in my mind was to be trusted. The darkness, which had been a blessing at the border, was now a hindrance, slowing me as I fumbled through dark fields and farms.

Worse still, as the hours drew on, my stomach began to growl. Along this long stretch, there were farms, to be sure, but no inns or taverns. Not that I had any coin to purchase, but some sign of civilization would've been welcome.

Kulka is fairly spread out. Truer words, Asdis. My kingdom for a horse.

Midnight came and went, and I finally found a sign that said I was going in the right direction. A few more hours later, as the sun rose, I happened upon a kind farmer who gave me directions to that road, and also a few apples to take with me.

"I can't sell them in Neveri," he said with a sad shake of his head. "It's a shame to waste the Mother's bounty."

I thanked him, wishing I could give him money, and continued on my way.

Once I hit the main road, I was joined by a couple of wagons and men on horseback every so often. There were Kulkan soldiers in the bunch, too, but I didn't give them a second glance. Out here, I was just another peasant.

Finally, as a headache pounded at my temples, I found refuge under a tree out of the way and catnapped for a few hours, sleeping on my slingbag to protect it from poachers. I awoke still hungry and thirsty, but no longer completely miserable. I packed my things on my back and continued along the road, praying Ammon would provide food and water once I arrived.

The sun was high in the sky when I spotted a line of waving flags in the distance. It could've been the encampment, or it could've been a city. Either way, I picked up my pace and headed toward it, every step a silent plea to the Mother for a reprieve.

I nearly cried when I saw the Kulkan flags and made out the white tents. I tightened my slingbag against my back and broke out into a run. Perhaps it was my delirious mind, but I thought I smelled succulent pheasant and roasted vegetables. Oh, but I might kiss that prince if he gave me even a piece of moldy bread.

But before I could dash through the fence, I was met with two spears in my face.

"State your business," they snapped in unison.

"I'm here to see the prince," I replied, putting all the energy I had left into a confident gaze. "Surely he mentioned he'd be expecting me. Brynna."

They hesitated then dropped their spears and lunged for me.

"Just get Ammon," I said as the two Kulkans locked me inside a makeshift jail.

I paced in the cell for a few minutes then picked a stick off the ground and banged it against the bars.

The flap opened and a young Kulkan soldier said, "Quiet down in here."

"Did you get Ammon?" I asked, leaning my face against the bars. "It's time-sensitive."

"No, I didn't. Because we don't trouble the prince with little insects who try to break into the camp." She smirked. "Not too bright, are you?"

"Very bright, considering Ammon's expecting me," I said. "Also, while I wait, can I get some water and some food? Nothing fancy."

She rolled her eyes and walked out.

I waited, keeping my face pressed against the bars for another few minutes, then realized she wasn't coming back.

I sighed. "Hello? Anyone going to help me out here?"

This time, another soldier came in—this one an officer. "Quit making noise in here or we'll have you executed."

"Ammon might not like that, because then he won't get his city," I drawled. "So go get him, bring me some water and some food."

The officer eyed me. "What do you want with His Highness?"

"His Highness is expecting me. Brynna." I paused. "Princess Brynna-Larissa Archer Rhodes Lonsdale. Of Forcadel."

He didn't show any sign of recognition. "So not only are you an annoying little peasant, now I find out you're Forcadelian."

I blew air out of my nose. "Just tell Ammon that Brynna is here with an update on his little quest. You won't regret it."

He rested his hand on his pommel then turned and walked out. Again, I was left with my thirst, my hunger, and an increasingly nervous feeling. Maybe getting myself arrested wasn't the brightest plan—especially since Ammon hadn't let anyone know I was returning. Probably for the best, as word might seep into Neveri, but still... It didn't make for an easy explanation.

Finally, the flap opened and the prince himself strode in with two guards. If he cared about me or my predicament, he didn't show it.

"Well? Do I have a city yet?" Ammon asked.

"Kind of hard to do that when I'm stuck in a prison," I replied with a flick of my wrist. "You should've told your guards to expect me."

"I expected you days ago. Thought you were dead."

"You gave me a week."

He released a tired sigh. "I only assume you're here for something."

"Let me out of this jail cell, give me some food and water, and I'll tell you what you want to know." I flashed him a grin. "Please? I've been walking for a while and it's hard to talk."

He grimaced and motioned to one of the two guards behind him. The guard disappeared for a moment then returned with a small cup of water.

"Thanks," I replied, tossing the infinitesimal water down. "So, here's the thing: There's a gate."

"If that's all you're here to tell me—"

"I have a plan to get it open," I finished with a dirty look. I gave him the synopsis—fudging my numbers on how many Celia had kicked in—after all, when I'd rehearsed this speech, I'd had more than one-and-a-half thieves with me.

"It seems you have it all thought out," Ammon drawled. "I fail to see how or why you need my help."

"Well, things are a bit dicier than I anticipated," I said, hoping he didn't see through my bluff. "The point is we both want this, so —"

"Correction, *you* want this," Ammon said. "I could go my entire life without getting the city of Neveri back under Kulkan control. Our agreement was that you would deliver me a city already taken, not that I would help you do it."

I gripped the bars. "You have hundreds of soldiers here. You can spare twenty."

"I don't think I can. Because I've yet to hear a plan that sounds in any way feasible. Drugging and rousing soldiers. Using water to move metal." He sniffed. "You must think me a fool. Or you are."

"Ammon, I swear to you, I can give you a demonstration—"

"Enough!" He held up his hand and damn if it didn't silence me. He surveyed me for a long time, and I wasn't sure if he was going to agree or order my execution. Finally, he broke his gaze and turned it out toward the camp.

"I've completed my inspection of this encampment and we will be setting sail for Delina in two days. At that time, I'll take a short detour down to Neveri's gates. If they're still closed, we will return to Delina and this very idiotic exercise will be completed."

My jaw dropped. "I can't do this in two days."

"Then I suppose we'll be returning to Delina, and your efforts have all been in vain."

He turned to go, and I cried, "Wait!" He stopped. "Just wait a second. Fine. Just give me a horse to get back to Neveri quickly and I'll see what I can do. But what about when you get to Neveri and the gates are open? Will you help me then?"

"We'll just have to see what shape things are in, won't we?" Ammon flicked his wrists and the guards went to open the gate. "Two days, dear Brynna. Better hurry."

Ammon's timeline pressed like a weight on my neck, but at least I was moving faster than on foot. The horse he'd given me was a beautiful mare, and she was more than willing to keep up a brisk pace as I dashed back toward Neveri. Although it took more time, I doubled back to the forest and Celia's camp to cross the border. It was a weak spot, and I didn't have time to try to outsmart the border patrol somewhere else.

With the dawn rising behind me, my heartbeat pounded with the mare's hooves. I was woefully under-equipped for this plan—a plan that, even if I'd gotten everything I wanted, would've been far-fetched. Luard was surely not going to be pleased that neither Ammon nor Celia had offered any support. Did that mean he'd walk away? I didn't want to think about it. I was running out of time, I was out of ideas, and I just prayed I was returning to a city that would give me a break.

Almost at the last minute, I remembered that Riya had left me something at Norah's house, so I pointed my horse toward the northern side of the city. But when I arrived at the small farm, she was nowhere to be found. I left Ammon's horse in her paddock with some hay and walked up to the house.

"Hello?" I knocked. "Norah?"

When she didn't answer, I picked the lock on her door. Inside, her kitchen was as immaculate as it had been when she'd fed and watered me the first day I'd been in Neveri. On the kitchen table, however, was a folded-up Severian uniform.

"Ah, Riya," I said softly, running my fingers along the fabric. I didn't want to wear one of these again, but the timeline made me desperate.

After I dressed, I left Norah a note thanking her and explaining the new horse in her paddock then continued toward the city. But when I reached the main road, the queue of carriages I'd expected to see wasn't there. There was nothing but soldiers, standing idly with their swords and talking with one another. I was relieved to see that more than half were Forcadelians. Perhaps Riya had been able to work her magic on Maarit after all.

Pulling down my uniform, I marched toward them, as if I was absolutely supposed to be there. But before I even reached the border, two spears crossed in front of me, blocking my path. A pair of young Forcadelian soldiers—Felix's cousin one of them—stood at attention.

"Halt," his partner, a light-skinned Forcadelian with high cheekbones, said. "Name and rank."

I froze, looking down at my uniform for any identification. But I didn't recognize Severia's officer rank badges, and there was no name tag on the uniform.

"I...uh..." I said, taking another step toward them. "Kellis sent me."

"And?" the female guard said, clearly not impressed. "Kellis sends you without a name and a rank?"

"Aline." Felix's cousin—Jorad, I think his name was, gave his partner a look. "What did Kellis send you to do?" he asked me.

I sighed, looking up at the sky again and wondering how much I could trust him. Time was of the essence, and if I didn't do something soon, it wouldn't matter if they knew who I was.

So I pulled the Forcadelian seal from beneath my tunic and flashed it in the sunlight. "She said I should come on this road if I needed to get inside. That there were those here who could help... help a disgraced princess."

Jorad's eyes widened and his partner lost her scowl. "Are you... serious?"

"Listen, it's imperative that I get inside the city," I whispered. "Or I need to find Riya and talk with her. Is there anything you can do for me?"

Aline shook her head. "They don't let us do anything, unfortunately."

One of the Severians caught her eye and marched over. "Oi! What are you three doing talking? Should you be working? Who is this person?"

"Yes, sir," Jorad said, saluting him. "There was some miscommunication. Guard Rodilla here should've been at the southern gate."

The lieutenant eyed me, but clearly had some semblance of trust for Jorad and Aline because he nodded. "Fine. But if I hear of you running late to your position again, I'll have you written up and demoted."

"Yes, sir," I said, saluting him as Aline had done. And with a final smile back at the two of them, I hurried toward the town.

Chapter Forty-Six

Neveri was eerily silent, especially for this time of day. The farmer's market was almost completely empty, and the blinds were drawn on all the houses. Those who'd ventured out wore haunted looks and kept their heads down. Even the soldiers seemed quieter than usual as they maintained their posts on the corners.

While I wore this uniform, they took no notice of me. I would have to thank Riya for her forethought. But she wasn't amongst the guards, and it made me a little worried for her. Surely, the two at the border would've mentioned it if something had happened to her. And surely the Forcadelians wouldn't be back on border security if Maarit thought they weren't to be trusted.

As soon as I came into the city square, I found the reason for the odd energy in the town, and my stomach rose into my throat.

Five people were hanging from a makeshift gallows in the center of town. Three men and two women, all wearing signs. As much as I didn't want to, I forced myself to walk up to them, as they each had a scroll pinned to their body.

Executed for selling illegal wares.

Executed for breaking curfew.

Executed for disrespect of a soldier.

Executed for breaking curfew.

Executed for vigilantism.

I covered my mouth with my hand, closing my eyes as I took several steps back. I stared at the last one. It was a boy, a makeshift black mask pinned to his chest.

A tear rolled down my face as I forced myself to look at every one of their disfigured faces. These weren't criminals—they were just innocent people. The man who'd been hanged for selling illegal goods was the same one I'd seen taken away the week before.

The woman who'd disrespected a soldier...my heart released a sob. It was Norah. Sweet Norah who'd lied and helped me get into the city. Had Riya's overture of the uniform been the catalyst for this? I was sick at the thought.

I felt a presence behind me and turned, too shocked to stop myself. Jax and Elisha had found me, the younger girl looking paler and more scared than she'd been in the comfort of Celia's care.

"Elisha, I need you to get a message to someone," I said, skipping over the pleasantries. "Find a man named Ivan at the Wicked Duck. Tell him there's an empty house outside town where we can convene. Leave on the northern road, turn left at the patch of yellow flowers. Jax, find Lieutenant Riya, tell her the same. Ask her to gather everyone she thinks will be loyal to me."

Jax followed my gaze to the bodies in the breeze, then nodded solemnly. For once, he didn't have a sarcastic response.

"Thanks," I said, turning on my heel. "And be careful."

Numbly, I left down via the northern road, nodding to Jorad and Aline. Their Severian lieutenant hadn't noticed me this time, which was a blessing. I might've run him through with my knives had he spoken to me.

Once I was back on Norah's farm, I pulled the Severian uniform off and burned it to a crisp.

I tended to Norah's few animals, feeding the chickens and giving an apple to her old mare. It was a welcome distraction from all my failures. Soon, Luard would arrive with the rest of my thinly populated team. And soon they would all know the truth—and I would finally know if I'd reached the end of my luck.

As the sun began to set, I heard the sound of light conversation and footsteps down the path. My heavy heart lightened when Riya and the two young soldiers, all in plainclothes, opened the front gate.

"Your Majesty," Jorad said, pressing his hand to his chest and bowing. "It's an honor to serve you once again."

His partner, Aline, did the same. "My apologies for treating you so gruffly earlier today. Had I known—"

"It's fine," I said, waving my hands. "Are these...all the soldiers who would come to my aid?"

"All the soldiers I trusted with this information," Riya said with a half-smile. "Are your reinforcements inside?"

I didn't have the heart to tell her the truth, so I forced myself to smile. "They'll be arriving later tonight."

"Already here," Jax said, walking up the path with Elisha in tow. "We passed the information onto your friends. They're understandably going to need a little time to get out of the city."

In all, it was well past dark before the Niemenians arrived—and it was just Luard and Ivan. Both were all smiles to see me, promising that it had only cost them a few gold coins to bribe the guards at the border.

"A few?" Riya said with a snort. "Our kingdom's security is worth more than that."

"Erm..." Luard began as he walked into Norah's house.

"Brynna, dear. Where is everybody?"

"This is everybody," I said darkly. "Ammon gave me a horse, Celia gave me Jax and this kid, and that's…it."

I held my breath as I waited for his response. But while he didn't look pleased, he still patted me on the shoulder. "Well, let's see what you've got."

The small group gathered around the large, circular dining room table. The only one without a seat was Elisha, who perched on a crate in the corner. I didn't like my odds of attempting this with so few people, but it was what I had.

"So, here's the plan," I began, and told them what I'd told Ammon. I kept my eyes on the center of the table as I spoke, unwilling to watch their reactions. What I was saying was pure lunacy. When I got to the part about the hyblatha in the gatehouses, Luard released a loud snort.

"So you want us to barge into a heavily fortified outpost, blow some powder at them, and hope we have enough to cover all the soldiers?" Aline asked. She glanced at Riya. "What do you think, Lieutenant?"

"I think she's our queen and we should listen to her," Riya retorted, but the dismay on her face was clear. She'd expected more from me.

"I think it's lunacy," Jax said. "First of all, they—" he pointed at the Niemenians, "ain't soldiers. They're royal guards. Second of all, unless the gatehouse is about twenty feet wide, we're suicidally outnumbered, even with your pants-pissing powder."

I licked my lips, nerves fluttering in my chest. "It's not the best option, but it's the only one—"

"No," Luard said with a heavy sigh. "It's not. We can use the ond to destroy the gate. We only need enough bodies to scale the gate and place small bags of powder in strategic locations. All that requires is the ability to climb and balance, something my guards are more than capable of doing."

"I'm confused," Riya said. "What's he talking about?"

"There's an ore, a secret weapon from Niemen," Ivan said. "When mixed with Niemenian steel and fire, it causes a chain reaction that basically..."

Luard made an explosive sound.

"Excellent!" Jax said, clapping his hands. "So why aren't we doing that?"

"Because it would also destroy the forts beside it, including all the soldiers that currently reside underground," I finished, with a dirty look at him. "And I'm not willing to risk that much life. Especially when some of it is Forcadelian."

"Or any lives at all," Jax drawled. "Still carrying that death with you, aren't you?"

My face warmed. "Shut up, Jax. Now's not the time—"

"She absolutely is still carrying that death," Luard said, casting him a look. I suddenly regretted putting them in the same room together. "She won't make the hard decisions she needs to. Which means that my guards and I will be returning to Niemen."

"Returning to Niemen?" Riya said, jumping to her feet. "Why would you abandon my queen like that?"

"Because your queen isn't doing what needs to be done," Luard shot back. "She's got the solution, and yet refuses to use it."

"Because she's being cautious!" Riya barked.

"Because she's a coward," Jax said.

My chest tightened as the factions in the room turned from friendly to ferocious in a matter of seconds. I searched for a place to cut in, to calm the rising timbre of voices, but there was nothing I could say. They were all speaking the truth.

"She's no coward," Riya snarled. "She's risked her life for this kingdom—"

"And she refuses to risk anyone else's," Ivan barked. "Great for a vigilante, terrible for a kingdom."

"Well, maybe I agree with her that blowing up her own soldiers isn't the best option," Jorad said, jumping into the discussion. "Some of those men and women are my friends. They could be our allies as well!"

"Is it any better than the entire kingdom falling to pieces?" Luard asked. "Because if we don't do this, Ilara will continue her reign. And we've all seen what—"

"Enough."

My voice broke out clear and calm, startling all those arguing. I stared at the table, their voices ringing in my ears as I absorbed every truth they spoke—and the consequences if I didn't step up and do what needed to be done.

I'd grown weary of my song and dance, of the back and forth. I'd crossed this entire continent to find a solution that would do the least amount of harm without ever considering that my inaction was causing the *most* harm. I'd chalked my success so far up to luck, but that wasn't the truth. I'd made the decision to continue every step of the way. I hadn't turned around in Skorsa. I'd willingly joined Brigit in the treacherous mountains. I'd agreed to travel to Kulka. I'd offered Neveri to Neshua and then agreed to have a hand in its conquering.

But now, here at the end, I was wavering on this final step. One that required me to make a sacrifice I wasn't strong enough to make—to take lives that were, by all accounts, innocent, in order to make things better for the rest of my countrymen.

"Sometimes we must make the hard choices and just hope the Mother judges us fairly for doing the best we can under the circumstances."

Luard was right. It was time to make the hard choice.

"Luard, we will use your ore on the gate," I began slowly. "You're right, it's the best option. We'll do our best to save whomever we can, but if we move forward, loss of life is unavoidable."

I chanced a look at Riya, whose jaw was clenched. But to my

surprise, she nodded. "And more importantly," she said, "the explosion should draw Maarit from the city, along with a contingent of her forces. That way, the bulk of the fighting will be away from the city and we can minimize impact to the citizenry."

I shared a small smile with her. "How many soldiers do you think she can assemble?"

"Fifty can fit on the barge we sailed on, and there are two of those," she said, tapping her fingers on the table. "I don't know if she'll be able to rouse that many in a short amount of time, but we should estimate high."

"So a hundred soldiers?" Jax said with a wince.

"Can we be sure that those numbers will all be Severian?" I asked, nodding to Jorad and Aline. "What about their contingent?"

"Maarit would have to be idiotic to use them," Riya said, looking behind her. "She already relegates them to border patrol with one Severian for every two Forcadelians."

"We can try to get onto the barge," Jorad said, looking at Aline who didn't look convinced.

"But," Aline said, "we're the only soldiers who know who you are. And I don't know...I'm not sure if the rest of them will turn as quickly as we did. Some probably would."

"I have faith in them," Jorad said.

"But if you don't," I said slowly, "we're still looking at a hundred hostile soldiers."

"We could use that hyblatha," Jax offered, leaning on his elbows. "That could take some of them down."

"Do we have enough?" I asked.

He shrugged. "Do you have any other ideas?"

"What does it do again?" Riya asked.

"Makes you piss your pants," Jax said.

"Hallucinations," I corrected, looking at Elisha, who was watching the conversation intently. She jumped when I caught her attention. "How good are you with a crossbow?"

"The best," she said proudly. I looked to Jax for confirmation and he shrugged—the most approval I'd get from him. "Fine, you'll be in the trees with Luard and you'll be responsible for dispersing the hyblatha. Those of us on the ground will use this tinneum to inoculate ourselves. If they're on the barge, we could take a large number of them out at once. Once they're under the influence, we'll—"

"Kill them?" Aline asked quietly.

"Tie them up," I said softly. "Some of them may be Forcadelians willing to return to our side. I meant what I said about trying to save as many lives as possible."

She actually smiled, as did Jorad.

"I don't know," Luard said, scratching his chin. "This all seems like a bit of a long shot, you know? Sure would've been nice if Ammon had given you some help."

"I know. This isn't the way I planned on this going," I said, pressing my hands to the table. "But unfortunately, this is the best we have. Still..." I swallowed hard. "I understand if any of you want to walk away now."

I gazed out at the room, from the Niemenian royal guards to the young Forcadelian soldiers to Jax and Elisha. It wasn't much of a rousing speech, but I wasn't one for inspiring people to my cause.

"To whatever end, Your Majesty," Riya said, coming to her feet. She covered her left breast with her fist and bowed.

Jorad and Aline jumped to their feet, following suit. A ripple of warmth slithered through my stomach as the Niemenian guards stood and performed the same motion. Luard merely stood and covered his breast. Finally, Elisha rose and covered her right breast with her fist—and was then guided to the left by nearby Riya.

The only one not on his feet scoffed. "I still ain't bowing to you," Jax said. "But I'm coming."

Perhaps I would've liked to have had more bodies in the room, but at least I knew these bodies were loyal. And that was worth its weight in gold.

"Very well," I said. "Let's take a city."

Chapter Forty-Seven

Felix

"Here," I said, throwing the letter down on Kieran's desk. "Will this suffice?"

It had taken me three days to finally ditch my guards at night, and with all the new Severians roaming the streets, it was damned near impossible to get back down to the docks unseen.

Kieran's brows rose as he gingerly lifted the envelope. With the expertise of a pirate, he slid a knife underneath the seal, keeping it intact and reading the letter. "Oh, very well done. You've got the makings of an excellent vigilante if the whole captain thing doesn't work out for you."

I sniffed. "Will you help me, then?"

"As it turns out, I have some things that need delivering tonight," he said, rising to his feet. "And you've got two arms to help."

I didn't have much space to argue, and soon I was lugging two large bags over my shoulder. The pirate, of course, carried nothing except his ego.

"This isn't smart," I said. "You know there are people patrolling the streets, right?"

"I would assume you know their routes," he said. "As you're their boss."

I rolled my eyes. "Sadly, I don't have as much power in the castle as you might think. There's a man aiming for my job. Coyle," I replied. "And he'd love nothing more than to catch me wearing a mask."

"Ah, well...why don't you take care of him?" Kieran asked, running his hand along his throat. "Surely the man leaves the castle. Could be sucked into a horrible situation. Muggings happen, you know."

"The Veil doesn't kill," I replied softly.

"And *you* aren't The Veil," Kieran said. "What the real one doesn't know won't hurt her. Besides that, doesn't he deserve what's coming to him?"

He did, but not by my hand. No matter how far away I'd strayed under the mask, I still had faith in the justice system. One day, Coyle would receive his punishment for what he'd done, and those he'd killed. But if it was by my hand, under the mask, then I would be no better than him.

"Fine, fine. You two really are made for one another," he said with a sigh. "She had funny ideas about killing people, too. Too noble for my blood."

Luckily, we avoided capture or being seen by any of the patrols, but my arms were starting to hurt from carrying the metallic-smelling bags. I didn't ask what was inside them—it felt like sand of some kind. Just when I was about to complain, Kieran announced that we'd arrived.

"Finally," I said, throwing the bags to the ground.

"Who's this?" There was a man in the alley.

"Man-Veil, this is John," Kieran said. "John, this is the Man-Veil. He used to keep shop at Stank's bar, until, of course, our fair queen decided to ransack the place."

John appeared in the moonlight—an older man with a withered face and a grizzled beard. His name was familiar; perhaps he'd been one of Brynna's informants.

"You aren't The Veil," he replied, eyeing me.

"That's why I said *Man*-Veil," Kieran said. "He's here in her stead. She's out of the country taking care of some business and causing some trouble."

John nodded slowly. "She said she was headed out. But nothing about leaving anyone in her place. How can I be sure I can trust him?"

"Because I'm telling you to," Kieran said.

The other man waited then slowly nodded. "You're terrible at what you do, by the way. Nobody wants to talk to you."

"Thanks," I drawled. "I'm looking for the leader of whoever's causing trouble around here. Make contact before B—The Veil returns and takes back the country."

"Takes back the country?" he snorted. "For whom?"

I hesitated. "The people."

He barked a laugh. "And is The Veil going to sit herself on the throne? She's going to have some competition for that."

"What do you mean?" I asked with a look at Kieran. He seemed just as confused.

"Listen, I can't help you," he said. "Except to tell you that The Veil should probably stay gone. This city's about to erupt, and those who sleep in the castle had better prepare themselves for war. The people have had enough of that Severian brat and her minions, and they're about to do something about it." He turned to Kieran. "Which reminds me... did you hold up your end of the bargain?"

"Bargain?" I furrowed my brow. "What bargain?"

"Your stock is being offloaded as we speak," Kieran said. "I just had to make sure I was able to get out tonight before I could give it to you." He pointed to the bags at my feet. "A sampling of my inventory."

"What stock?" I said to Kieran. "What are you planning?"

"Giving Ilara a taste of her own medicine," John replied with a smile.

"Her own..."

Kieran made an explosive sound and my jaw dropped. "You brought more of those...those death bombs into this city?"

"Not the Severian kind, no," Kieran said. "But something just as good from our friendly neighbors to the north."

I licked my lips, sensing that *any* explosives in the city boded nothing well for it. "This isn't a good idea. There has to be another way—"

"Well, while you two converse on finding a peaceful way to end the conflict," John said, picking up the bag, "I'll be taking these to my boss. With his thanks."

"Wait," I said. "Just give me his name. That's all I want."

John smirked. "I'll do you one better. You tell *me* his name, and I'll set up a meeting."

I licked my lips as John disappeared down the street, furious that yet again, all that work, all that risk to myself, to Katarine, to Beata, had been for absolutely nothing. I was right back where I'd started—I needed a name, and I had nothing but wasted time.

"Oh, come now," Kieran said, clapping me on the shoulder. "It's not entirely for naught. You had a little bit of an adventure and stole from the queen. And now you helped a dear friend get out of her clutches before the storm hits."

I stared at his hand and brushed it off. "Or, I could just arrest you for treason. I am still captain and whatever you imported into the city is probably cause enough to hang you."

"Oh!" He put his hand over his heart. "You wound me. And after I got you an audience with John."

"Who made it very clear he didn't want to help me." I flexed my hand for a moment, still imagining wrapping it around his thin, Kulkan neck. "Time is running out and if what he says is true —if the people in this city won't accept Brynna returning..."

"The people might, but the people leading the people..." He shrugged. "Power vacuums do that. But I wouldn't worry. Our Veil has a way of making herself known. Especially if she has the backing of the Niemenian forces."

Something twinged in my gut, as I allowed despair to take root. "If she convinced Ariadna to help. If she even reached Linden at all."

"Don't do that," Kieran said. "You know Veil as well as I do. She's too stubborn to die. Especially in a mountain. She'll die in a blaze of glory, fighting off twenty men."

I surveyed him curiously. "Why are you helping me?"

"Because our little Veil might never speak to me again if I didn't," he said with a dramatic sigh. "And I'm still angling to be a pirate king, or at least to receive a statue made out of gold for all my help to the Lonsdale line."

My brows lifted. "Pirate...*king*?"

"Has a nice ring to it, don't you think?" He flashed me a roguish smile and I had an urge to knock a few teeth out.

Instead, I turned to the city beyond as the sky grew pink. "So... do you think she's all right?"

"I'd like to think she is," he replied softly. "It doesn't do to dwell on the future—it'll happen whether you're ready or not. Best we can do is focus on the here and now."

"True, but I won't breathe easy until she's back home—and back on the throne where she belongs."

"I never breathe easy when she's around," he said, shaking his shoulders. "Too slippery and wily for my tastes. Always thinking about her next move. But..." He grinned. "I do hope that in my travels, I'll cross paths with her soon. I'm honestly interested to see what she's been up to since we parted."

"Can you...do me a favor, then?" I asked. "If you see her

before I do, tell her..."

"I'd be happy to give her that kiss if you—"

A loud explosion echoed behind me, and I jumped to my feet. In the distance, an orange light flickered—fire. Was it Zuriel? Or someone else? But before I could question further, another explosion echoed from somewhere far away.

"Well, it appears things have already gotten started," Kieran said, rubbing his hands together. "If you'll excuse me, I've got to get out of the city before anyone decides to arrest me. Good luck on your vigilante mission!"

I let Kieran leave—I had more important things to worry about. Namely, the fireballs that continued to explode every few minutes from all corners of the city. It was as if Ilara was invading again, and like last time, I had no idea who was responsible. Scenarios flooded my mind as I came across the first scene—a three-story building in Sailor's Row that was flickering in orange fury. A crowd had gathered nearby, gasping and pointing at the angry flames rising into the dark sky.

Another explosion rocked the building, spraying splinters and glass everywhere.

"Help! Help!"

My heart leapt into my throat as I heard the soft sound of a cry from inside the building. And despite my better judgment, I threw the cloak hood on top of my head and dashed through the fiery entrance.

"Who's in here?" I called.

"*Help!*"

The voice was coming from a set of burning stairs. I darted up two-by-two, hoping that they—and the building—would stay intact long enough for the both of us to get out. The heat was already unbearable, and it grew worse so as I climbed higher. I put my cloak over my mouth and ventured onto the second floor, testing my weight with every step before placing it fully.

"Where are you?" I called.

"Over here!" the man cried, waving at me from underneath a beam. I ran over to him and with a kick, knocked the burning beam off his leg.

It was Zuriel.

I stared at him for a moment, torn between letting the man who'd betrayed his country burn and the pressing need to do my job.

"M-my wife," he choked. "Where is she? And my kids, they're here, too—"

"I haven't heard anyone but you," I replied, hoping that just meant she was already outside. "C'mon."

I yanked him up by his collar and tossed him over my shoulder, carrying him down the stairs. The floor creaked and gave way behind me, but we made it out the front door just as the house collapsed.

"No!" Zuriel cried, trying to push himself out of my grip. "They're still in there!"

I threw him to the ground, coughing the smoke from my lungs and rubbing my eyes. Some part of me thought he deserved this, but...his family didn't. Behind me, the building was unrecognizable now.

"I thought they'd be safe here," he whispered. "But I was coming to visit them, and the explosion..."

So he hadn't even been in the building when it had happened. This wasn't an attempt on his life, it was an attempt on his family —perhaps a fate worse than death. This went beyond just intimidation. This was the mark of someone with great experience dealing with those who'd crossed him.

And at that moment, I knew exactly who was leading the rebellion in the city.

Down the street, the Severian guards were riding up on horseback, and some of the neighbors had come bearing buckets of water. So before I was captured by my own guards, I turned and ran down the street.

Chapter Forty-Eight

"There's another riot on the western side of the city," Riya said. "I need all available soldiers to convene at the corner of Perrit and Finch to help calm things down."

The five soldiers—all Forcadelian—seemed confused, especially as Riya had another four soldiers behind her that could've also helped with this supposed riot, but didn't disobey, turning and jogging toward the city without another word. Their sour-faced Severian lieutenant, however, didn't budge.

"I haven't heard anything about this," he said. "And I don't believe that—"

His words died on his tongue as he fell forward, victim of a swift punch to the back of the head.

"Jax!" I hissed at him.

"We don't have time for this," he said. "Those soldiers are going to know there isn't a riot pretty quickly."

"Nor do we have time for arguments," Luard said behind me as he and his guards appeared from the darkness. "Onward!"

Once we were clear of the border, we formed a perimeter around the Niemenians as if we were escorting them. A heavy fog had rolled into the city, obscuring the moon and casting a halo around the few torchlights. Our first stop was the Wicked Duck, where the Niemenians quickly readied their carriage for departure —or more importantly, the large trunk of Niemenian ore that sat beneath Luard's seat.

"This is where we leave you," Jorad said, casting a nervous look around before bowing to me. "We will do our best to rouse the forces."

"Wait until you see the explosion," I said, adding, "Just in case."

"Will do." He bowed once more, and Aline did as well.

"Good luck, Your Highness," she said with a soft smile.

They disappeared around the corner, and I couldn't help but feel a little worried. I didn't like giving up resources. What if their entire contingent turned on them? What if they weren't believed? What if—

"Don't fret," Luard said, coming to drape an arm around me. "If this fails, we'll all be dead."

"Thanks…"

Every second they took to pack and prepare was agony. The border guards Riya had sent away would soon realize they'd been sent to the wrong place and Maarit might sound the alarm. The sooner we were on the boat, the better.

A whistle echoed in the night, and fear slid down my back.

"We have company," I said to the Niemenians.

"And what in the Mother's name is this?"

Maarit appeared in the alley, flanked by five soldiers who were blocking us from leaving. I ducked my face behind the Niemenians, my fingers closing around the knives hidden under my Severian jacket.

"I've grown tired of this sticky city," Luard said, his voice loud and obnoxious. "I want to continue my journey down to Forcadel to see my sister."

"We have a curfew, Prince," Maarit said. "It's for your own safety."

He released a loud sigh, and Ivan stepped forward. "Captain, my sincerest apologies. But I also think it's a good idea for the prince to leave. With all the riots in the city, and with his penchants for nightly prowls, it's a recipe for disaster. We'd like your blessing to take a vessel out of the city tonight."

Maarit surveyed him for a long time, as if she were trying to figure out what the game was.

"Captain, I have to agree with him," Riya said. "It'll be one less thing to worry about while we try to calm the city down. I think there's a fishing boat or two still in port."

Finally, the Severian nodded. "Fine. Tell the commanding officer I said to allow the prince and his staff onboard and to take them down to the city. Pay them a sum of fifty gold coins for their trouble."

"Of course," Riya said, saluting Maarit before turning to Luard. "Your Highness, if you please, it's just a short ride in the carriage."

Maarit stayed to watch the final preparations of the carriage. Jax and I climbed onto the back while Riya sat up front with Ivan. Hagan and Nils rode behind on their horses, and Asdis sat inside with Luard. Elisha, I hoped, had enough sense to follow behind us and stay out of sight.

Finally, after an eternity, Ivan snapped the reins and we moved forward.

Once we were in the open street, Luard opened his window and poked his head out to wink at me.

"See? I told you I'd be useful."

As the carriage rolled through the empty streets, Luard set to divvying up the ond into individual bags. Every torchlight we passed outside the carriage set my heart aflutter, but we weren't bothered at all, especially with Riya sitting on the front bench with Ivan.

We left the Niemenian carriage in an alley as Luard finished with the ond. Riya, Jax, and I continued onto the docks where we found one small fishing vessel—a schooner with two masts already converted for upriver travel. Riya marched toward the captain's quarters and banged loudly on the door.

"Open up!"

The light flared inside, and the door opened. "What's the meaning of...oh..." The captain, a short, squatty woman with more wrinkles than smooth skin, opened the door. "What can I do for you, Lieutenant?"

"I'm here on behalf of Captain Maarit," Riya said. "We've gotten reports that this ship has been harboring known fugitives." She nodded behind her to the rest of us. "Team, take prisoners."

Jax and I went downstairs to wake and round up the crew. They cried out in protest, but once they saw our uniforms, they quieted almost immediately. I didn't like how easily Maarit's fear-based regime had taken over this city, but I also couldn't argue that it was useful in this case.

While we distracted the crew with a series of inane questions about their mates, cargo, and past, the Niemenians and Elisha snuck on board with the ore.

The captain, sitting amongst her bewildered sailors, crossed her arms in fury as she stared down Riya. "We ain't got nothing illegal. I promise your boss that."

"I have my orders," she said, waiting on the gangway.

Elisha's curt whistle pierced the night air and I nodded to Riya.

"We'll just see what we find during our search of the vessel," she said.

The Niemenians were out of sight when we re-boarded the ship, but Nils was waiting by the ship's engine to kick it off. I did a quick scan of the boat to make sure the rest of my small crew was onboard, then ducked behind a stack of crates. From my slingbag, I found my mask and wrapped it around my face.

With a smirk, I walked to the gangplank then kicked it into the water.

"Oi!" the captain called from the dock as the engines rumbled to life. "What's the big idea?"

I stood on the edge of the ship, hanging onto the nearby rigging, then bowed with a flourish. "The Veil thanks you for your contribution."

In unison, the sailors' jaws fell open and the captain began to sputter wildly. Whether she was pleased or not, I had no idea, as her words were lost on the wind.

"And you're sure you wanted to do that?" Riya asked as I jumped down.

"The boat captain will tell Maarit that The Veil stole her boat," I said, glancing behind me. "If we're lucky, maybe Maarit will already be on her way when the gate explodes. Then she'll either have to double back, or she'll engage us with fewer soldiers. If we capture Maarit, we should be able to force the surrender of everyone else."

"That's a lot of ifs," Riya said with a look.

"But it's a smart risk," Luard said, walking out of the captain's quarters with a wine goblet. "Look who's suddenly become a strategic thinker."

I tried not to look too pleased with myself.

⇀————•

The thick fog made it difficult to see more than a few feet in front of us, so Jax and I sat on the bow of the ship, listening for the sound of the water against the gates. We moved slower than I wanted to, but it was the safer option with our limited visibility.

"There," Jax said, pointing to a faint light in the distance. "That's probably one of the gatehouses, so we must be close."

Finally, the gate materialized, large and foreboding and hundreds of feet tall. I just hoped we'd brought enough to destroy it all.

Behind me, Luard had his makeshift schematic of the gate unfurled on the deck of the ship. "Set the charges at each of the main hinge points. And for the Mother's sake, don't light up a smoke nearby. This stuff is highly flammable."

"How do we plan to climb the gate?" Jax asked.

Asdis procured a set of arrows that had ropes attached to the back of them—the ones I'd seen in Kulka. "These. We shoot them at the bars and then use the rope to climb up. It's supposed to be for scaling fortresses, but it should work on a gate, too."

"Let me see that," Jax said, a note of interest in his voice. "Where'd you get this and how can I get more?"

At the bow of the ship, Hagan caught the gate and Nils shut off the engines. Jax walked to the bow and aimed his crossbow upward, firing toward the first join of the iron bar to the pegs of the gate. The arrow cleared the bar then circled back down, and the specially-designed head connected with the rope, securing it against the bar. Jax tugged on the rope, then put his whole weight on it.

"I need one of these," he said, pulling himself to walk up the rope. "Oh yes, I need one of these."

Asdis joined him, and the three split up across the three levels of the gate, with Jax taking the top level. As soon as they were clear, Nils maneuvered the boat toward the other side of the gate, where Riya, Hagan, and I would place the other set of ond bags.

Riya whistled from her position at the back of the boat, and I followed her gaze. In the distance, there was a pinprick of light on the docks—perhaps a sign that Maarit was gathering her forces.

"Great," I said, swallowing my nerves.

We came to the other gate hinge, and as Riya used the special crossbow to attach to the nearest connecting point, I turned to Luard. "We shouldn't be long, but if that line of torches gets too close—"

"Quit flapping your jaw and get to work," he said with a look.

I smiled and pulled out my special climbing gloves. They stuck to the Niemenian ore as well as brick, allowing me to slowly walk up the length of the post. Riya and Hagan would take care of the lower rungs and the chains leading to the gatehouses, but I delegated myself to handle the highest.

With my gloves, I scaled the gate quicker than Jax had. When I reached the top, I stuck my gloves in my back pocket and stared out at Neveri in the distance. The gaggle of torchlights was now floating down the river. They'd be here within the hour.

I couldn't focus on that, though. The ond was in small leather pouches in my slingbag, tied together by a string that Nils had doused in oil. I was to place a bag every ten feet or so, securing the bag to iron with a little tack. Once I'd reached the end of the gate, I turned around and walked back to the center, using my sticky gloves to climb back down. There, Riya and Hagan were already with Luard on the boat, having picked up Jax's team from the other side.

"All good?" Riya asked.

"Hope so," I replied with a smile. "Let's get moving."

The boat's gears churned into action as they started moving with the current away from the gate. Luard handed me a bow and arrow with a special, flammable tip, a flint, and gave me a reassuring smile as he lit the arrow. I walked to the front of the ship and stood at the bow, aiming my arrow at the gate as we backed away from it.

Time, which had been running so quickly, slowed down, as the full weight of what I was doing resonated in my mind. If I shot this arrow, I would be most likely dooming everyone in both forts to death. There would be no warning, no escape. A hundred souls would be added to my tally.

"Brynna." Riya rested her hand on my shoulder. "It's okay. This is the right thing to do."

I lifted the burning arrow, aimed at the center of the gate, and released it. It soared through the night sky, and for a brief, terrifying moment, I thought I might've aimed too short.

Then the world exploded.

Chapter Forty-Nine

The next thing I knew, I was staring up at an orange sky, wondering if I'd slept through the night. My body was shivering—or perhaps it was just the way the ground under my body rocked and swayed. Something was burning, perhaps myself. No, the rain was on fire.

That doesn't make any sense.

Finally, my brain sped up. I wasn't staring at the daylight; it was fire reflected on the dark clouds. My body was lying flat on a boat that was reeling from the waves. The rain coming down was...

I lifted my aching head, and my heart fell into my stomach.

The wreckage was absolute and severe. All that was left of the massive, immovable gate was twisted metal fragments. Both fortresses were gone—nothing but white flames flying through the dry grasses nearby. There were probably no survivors.

"Brynna?" Riya's voice was far away. "Are you okay?"

She appeared in my line of sight, her face a sooty mess. She cupped my cheeks, calling my name once more. I shook my head, finally noticing the ringing in my ears then nodded to her.

"I'm fine," I croaked.

She helped me stand, and I took stock of my crew, holding my breath until I saw every one of their faces. We'd made it out all right.

"That was certainly a vigilante explosion," Luard said, coming to stand next to me. "Ammon'll see that from a mile away, I'm sure."

"And—" Riya's voice cut off abruptly. I turned to her, confused, my gaze dropping to the arrowhead sticking out of her chest.

In slow motion, she fell backward. The last thing I saw was her shocked expression before she disappeared over the edge of the ship.

"*Riya!*" someone screamed, perhaps me. I tried to run to her, to save her from the water, but something hard stopped me.

"We have to *move*," Luard said, waving his hand at something.

Another arrow landed in the center of the ship. Then another. Then a whole rainstorm of them. The crew ducked for cover, Jax using his knives to bat away one that had come for Elisha.

The ship stopped abruptly, and all onboard fell forward.

"We've run aground!" Hagan called.

"No shit," Jax groused, rubbing his head.

"Everybody off!" Luard called, grabbing me by the collar and pulling me off with him. My feet landed in thick mud—we were in marsh. The fire had illuminated the swamp, but so far, the grass hadn't lit, even with the raining debris from the explosion.

"We've got company," Jax called out.

I spun to the back, nerves fluttering in my stomach. Maarit had been more successful in gathering her forces than we'd thought. There were five ships in total—including two fishing vessels—each filled with Severian soldiers.

I grabbed Luard's shirt. "Go hide."

"What? No, I'm not—"

"Luard," I said, looking him in the eye. "I need you hidden. Elisha as well. Please…"

He swallowed then nodded. He grabbed the two large bags of hyblatha and the crossbow and smiled at me.

"Don't die, okay?" And with that, he dashed into the cattails. A moment later, Elisha followed, and I was grateful I wouldn't have to argue with them.

"You okay?" Jax's voice was clear and I looked up at him in surprise. "With your friend dying?"

Riya's face flashed before my eyes. "As I can be."

"Well, you'd better get okay, because I'm not doing this by myself," Jax said.

I snorted. Good ol' Jax.

I looked around at the others—Hagan, Nils, Ivan, Asdis—and gave them a nod. They pulled their swords and nodded back. And together, we climbed back on the ship to face our enemy.

Maarit stood at the front of the first boat, watching us with a sadistic sort of glee. She didn't care that she'd just lost a hundred soldiers; she was more concerned about getting my head on a silver platter.

I scanned the faces of the Severians on board and my heart sank. Jorad and Aline weren't among them—no Forcadelians were. We were on our own.

"Well, well," she called. "This was certainly a well-thought-out suicide mission. You've destroyed our gate. Queen Ilara will be displeased at this egregious act of war on behalf of the Niemenians."

"I'd say that closing the borders was act enough," Ivan barked back.

"But perhaps she'd be willing to overlook this grievance if you handed The Veil over to us," Maarit said.

"You'd really overlook all this destruction for me?" I said, resting my hands on my hips. "I must be a pretty high value target."

"The highest," Maarit said. She cast a look amongst my group. "Ah, and I was sure that I'd find Kellis in your little gang. Perhaps she died."

I took one step forward, before Jax put a hand on my shoulder.

Maarit just laughed. "Oh well, she was a terrible lieutenant anyway," she said with a disinterested shrug. "It doesn't matter. I'll bring your masked head to Queen Ilara and—"

"You seem to think you're going to win this," I said, channeling my anger into cool fury.

"I think you're outnumbered five-to-one," she said. "I think your only means of transport is marooned on this swamp. And I think you're stalling so your prince can make his escape."

"You must not know a lot about me," I said, as a whistle echoed in the air.

"Don't I?" Maarit said, pulling her sword.

"Because if you did," I said, tilting my chin upward, "you'd know that I always have an exit strategy."

Twin arrows sailed through the air, landing on the rim of the boat, and a cloud puffed in front of Maarit's face.

"Now!" I cried.

From my soaked pocket, I pulled the small bit of tinneum leaf and stuck it in my mouth. The hyblatha powder, carried by the blowing wind, dissipated around us and I held my breath as Maarit began to laugh.

"What is this?" she said, waving the dust around her. "Another one of your tricks? I daresay I'm growing..."

Her eyes widened and she blinked two, three times. To my left, a female soldier screamed and pointed at the fire. To my right, two men jumped into the water.

"What are they seeing?" Ivan asked.

"Whatever they fear most," I said, pulling my crossbow from my wet slingbag as an arrow landed at my feet. "We're not out of the woods yet. Jax, let's go. Niemenians, you stay here and bind them. Guard Maarit at all costs."

I tossed my wet cloak to the ground and took off toward the nearest boat, where I was met with three guards and their swords. I parried them with my knives then used my crossbow to pin one to the nearest mast. The other two went flying into the river with a kick.

"Stand down, traitor!" A sword blade came within a hair's breadth from my nose, and I only just moved out of the way.

The soldier was a Forcadelian, so I smashed a bag of knockout powder into his face and let him fall forward. I took the remaining bag and jumped to the next nearest ship, throwing it onto another man while I dealt with the others. But I'd miscounted—there were at least ten waiting for me. And I had nothing to use against them.

I turned to jump off, but they grabbed the back of my slingbag and wrested me to the ground. One of them pointed his sword at me, ready for the final blow.

"Here!" Jax cried from the next ships over.

He was bleeding from the cheek and holding three bags. With a heave, he tossed them into the air above the ship. I wrestled my crossbow free and shot toward at the bags, releasing the white powder into the air around us. The soldiers on the ship blinked, staring at each other in confusion. Then, one by one, they dropped their swords and ran to opposite corners of the ship, trembling in fear.

"Thanks for that," I said, stuffing another leaf in my mouth. "What's left?"

"Veil, look!"

In the distance, a new ship was sailing through the fire—Ammon's schooner. I could scarcely believe that he'd come, or that we'd managed to meet his deadline.

A loud boom echoed, and something black sailed through the air toward the nearest ship.

"Jax, get out of there!"

Jax tilted his head up, knocked out the soldier he was tussling with, and dove into the water just as the cannonball landed. A precious few seconds later, the ship exploded into timber and fire, sending debris flying.

"I thought he wasn't going to help?" Ivan asked.

"Everybody to shore!" I barked, jumping off the boat before another cannonball tore through the deck. I landed with a splash and pushed my way to shore through the muck. Jax joined me shortly thereafter, wiping soot from his face.

"What in the Mother's name...?" he asked.

"I knew you were working with the Kulkans," came Maarit's voice behind me. I turned to look at her—surprisingly clear-eyed, but bound.

"I gave her some leaf," Luard said, standing next to her. The bottom half of him was covered in mud, but he looked more pleased with himself than when he was showing me around his castle rooms. "Thought she might want to watch her pretty little soldiers fall one by one."

"This won't stand," she said, adjusting herself on the wet sand. "Ilara won't allow you to keep this city. She will reclaim it, the same way she claimed Forcadel."

"She got lucky in Forcadel," I said, wiping the sweat off my brow as Ammon's ship floated through the wreckage they'd wrought. "Now shut up while I deal with this asshole."

The schooner came ashore on the soft sand. A Kulkan sailor appeared, pointing his sword at me. "Surrender, or else!"

"Tell your prince to lay off the cannon fire," I called as loudly as I could.

"Oh, goodness." Ammon appeared over the bow. "Are you really alive? I thought for sure you would've perished." He tilted his head at me. "And what is with that ridiculous mask? Are you playing at some kind of secret identity?"

"I appreciate the assist," I said with an even smirk. "I thought you weren't going to provide any help?"

"Has the city been taken yet?"

"Not yet," I said, uncrossing my arms and pointing at the person behind me. "But all I have to do is return to town with their fearless leader in tow, and it's as good as mine."

"Or," Ammon said with a cruel smile, "I shall take her, and use my considerable firepower to take over the city myself." He squinted at the city in the distance. "I find I don't need you anymore."

Luard made a noise. "That was *not* your agreement, Ammon."

"Stay out of this, Niemenian," Ammon said. "But as it stands, you're merely one girl with a laughably small group of soldiers. How you managed to subdue all these people is beyond me, but it's clear you can't take them *and* my forces."

My mind spun. He certainly had more forces than we did, and our hyblatha powder was all but gone. There was nothing stopping him from taking Maarit prisoner and waltzing into the city with her.

"Forcadelians are well-versed in reneging on agreements, so I'm surprised you didn't see this coming," Ammon said. "But that just goes to show that you are—"

An arrow landed in front of him, and he jumped back five feet. "What the—?"

Another halo of arrows rained down, and I spun to the east. Was it more of Maarit's soldiers?

"Stand down, Kulkan," Jorad's clear voice echoed out from the darkness.

My heart leapt in my chest. Fifty Forcadelians—dressed in dark blue, a beautiful color, *my color*—stood on a boat that had snuck up in the dense fog. The archers who'd let their arrows fly had reloaded, and the others stood ready with swords.

"What's this?" Maarit cried. "You're pointing your swords at the wrong person, you fools. *She's* the traitor!"

"The only traitors are those who take up arms against our queen," Jorad said, nodding to me. "Our *rightful* queen. Brynna-Larissa Archer Rhodes Lonsdale."

A murmuring echoed from the captured soldiers behind me. "Hey, Brynna," Luard said, tossing me something gold and circular. It was a little muddy, but my circlet shone in the fire of the gate.

"Really?" I said with a look. "You brought this here?"

He shrugged. "Thought it might come in handy."

With care, I slipped the black mask from my face, the cool night air refreshing on my sweaty skin. And with little fanfare, I set the gold circlet on my head.

At once, the Forcadelian guards rested their hands on their left breasts, and bowed. Some of the captured who had their wits about them jumped to their feet and bowed as well, although they couldn't salute with their hands bound. Luard and his guards stood reverently, and the Severians gaped, most of them seemingly without a clue of what was happening.

But more importantly, Ammon had lost his confident smirk. He'd thought he'd be coming into a city in chaos, and his soldiers would quickly take the town. Instead, he found himself evenly matched with a queen. Not one who'd been shoved into the position because of her blood or circumstance. But one who'd truly earned the title.

"Ammon," I said, turning to the scowling prince. "I'll be sailing to the city with my soldiers. I'll honor the specifics of our agreement within three days."

"That was not—"

"I don't think you want to be broaching that subject right now, what with all these arrows pointed at you and your ship," I said, allowing Jorad to help me onboard the ship. "Three days. I'm sure you can find some way to amuse yourself."

Chapter Fifty

By morning, the Forcadelian flag had replaced the Severian one in the Neveri town square.

A loud cheer rose from the townsfolk nearby, and it disgusted me to know that there would be another flag coming soon. For now, though, there was peace.

The Severian soldiers surrendered with little fight, especially as word of who had led the charge to destroy the gate had spread amongst the Forcadelians. Jorad had taken the mantle left by Riya to rally the Forcadelian soldiers. Even though I didn't have the ability to do so, I promoted him and Aline to lieutenants. The others were imprisoned in the barracks, although I offered freedom to any who swore fealty to me. Unsurprisingly, most declined.

"What will we do with them?" Jorad asked as we walked through the town.

"I'll let Ammon decide their fate," I said. "And heavily suggest he ship them back to Severia."

"Are you really going to surrender the city to him?" he asked. "After you spent so much to take it?"

I pulled a scroll from my pocket and unrolled a long list of names. At the top was Riya's, but there were other Forcadelians amongst the dead. I wore her pendant on the chain on my neck, next to Felix's. Now, there really was no looking back. I would see this journey to the end to honor her sacrifice.

"It is what I had to do," I said after a long pause. "For the greater good of the country."

"I don't envy you, my queen." He rested his hand on his pommel, looking surprisingly like Felix in his steely gaze.

"You can call me Brynna," I replied, shaking myself from my memories. "I'm not queen yet."

"My cousin would flog me within an inch of my life if I disrespected you like that," he said with a half-smile. Then, with a hand to his chest and a bow, he turned to walk away, leaving me to continue the trek to Ammon's ship alone.

The Kulkan prince hadn't been seen in the three days since we'd arrived in the city, but one of his guards had found me and told me he was tired of waiting. So with an uneasy stomach, I stepped onto the boat. His guards took one look at me then let me pass without a fuss. With my hand on my pommel, I crossed the deck to the captain's quarters, throwing open the door.

Ammon sat behind a desk, a glass of wine perched next to him and his traditional golden circlet resting on his brown hair. His tunic was a fine red velvet, trimmed with gold. Even in my fresh tunic, I felt woefully underdressed compared to him. Even so, I strode toward him with shoulders back and chin high. Because now, at least in my mind, we were equals.

"Well," he said, looking up at me. "Are you done settling the city yet?"

"Almost," I said. "I've asked the citizenry to gather, and I'll announce it this afternoon. Then the city is yours."

"I have to say, I'm a bit underwhelmed." He picked up his goblet and took a sip. "You've taken a border city that was only mildly protected by destroying a gate and making friends with the population who were already mostly Kulkan anyway."

"Doesn't matter how I did it," I grumbled. "It's done. And you'll hold up your end of the bargain."

He chuckled. "My concern, Brynna, is that if you think taking back the city of Forcadel will be as easy as what you've accomplished here, you are sorely mistaken. This town was only half in Ilara's grip—all it needed was one small nudge. In Forcadel, she's implanted her forces deep into the city, brought in her own people. You'll need much more than the...well, laughable group of individuals you had with you."

"I'll have more," I said. "Because I'll have the forces of Niemen and Kulka at my back."

He rose up, meeting me with the same intensity I gave to him. "Fair enough. I'll grant you this—we will send a fleet of ships to blockade Forcadel Bay."

It wasn't exactly what I was hoping for, but it would have to do. "Fine." I turned to go then stopped and looked over my shoulder. "And one more thing, princeling. If I hear one whisper that you're treating these people inhumanely, that you've changed their lives any more than the flag they salute, I'll return and I'll reclaim it. Is that understood?"

"I hardly think you're in a position to be making threats," Ammon drawled.

"All right." I turned to face him fully. "How about this: if I hear one whisper, I'll sneak into Delina, climb the castle walls, and cut off your manhood. You already have two heirs. It won't be like you're missing anything vital to your country's survival." I rested my hands on my hips. "And if you don't think I can, let me remind you that I climbed an iron gate last night and blew it to smithereens in addition to sneaking in and out of a heavily guarded city for the past three weeks. Breaking into your pathetic castle would be easy."

Ammon licked his lips, crossing his legs ever so slightly.

I smiled. "Pleasure doing business with you."

That afternoon, I prepared to give away the city I'd just conquered.

There was a quiet murmur as I walked toward the dais. Not a week ago, five souls had lost their lives here. And now, I was announcing the surrender of the city. As I settled myself, I gazed into the crowd at the faces of the people who would no longer be mine. I recognized a few of them from my time in the village, and I tried not to dwell on the number of soldiers amongst them.

Behind me, Jorad, Luard, and the Niemenians stood at attention. And Ammon had sent one of his highly decorated majors to complete the transaction. I only supposed he couldn't be bothered to see it himself.

I'd thought a lot about what I might say to my people. It was a tricky subject, and I didn't really know how this news would be received. But in the end, all I had was the truth and my heart, and so it was from those two places I spoke.

"My fellow Forcadelians—" I barely got the word out before the crowd erupted in cheers and a lump formed in my throat. I swallowed it, composing myself as the roar quieted. "It's been a tough few weeks. The turmoil in this city has been unimaginable. People have died. Friends, family, loved ones. And now, we have freedom once again."

Another cheer. My stomach was threatening to come up, and I pressed a hand to it to keep myself grounded as I took deep breaths.

"But sadly, I come with...news that you may not like," I said. "Because this city...now falls under the Kulkan flag."

A hush descended on the crowd, and the jubilance turned into confusion and shock.

"I have received assurances from Prince Ammon that the borders will remain open," I said. "You will return to lives of prosperity and peace—"

"What if we don't want Ammon here?" cried a woman in the back.

"We want to be Forcadelian!"

"Ilara remains on the throne in the capital," I said, holding up my hands to quiet them. Shockingly, it worked. "I won't lie to you," I said, clasping my hands behind my back. "This was not an easy decision. Giving up this city and its people inside wasn't something I ever wanted to do—or planned on doing. And destroying the gate..." I glanced down at the list of names. Forty-two Forcadelian deaths, including Riya. "To those who lost friends and loved ones...I am truly sorry." I swallowed and fought the tears. "I wish that turning the city over to the Kulkans wasn't part of that deal, but..." I squared my shoulders and stared out into the stony faces of my countrymen. "But I know that no matter what flag flies above our heads, we will always be Forcadelians. And I will forever be your servant by the Mother."

I cleared my throat as the silence stretched out. "I am continuing to Forcadel to take back the throne. To return Forcadel to open borders and free trade, to put right what Ilara has made wrong. Now that we have the backing of Neshua and Ariadna, we have a fighting chance," I said. "Forcadel is a much different city than Neveri, and the stakes will be much higher. But I know, with you by my side, and the Mother above, we will be victorious. We will reclaim our land for ourselves."

Silence rang out through the crowd. I didn't know what I expected—applause? Thanks? Cheering? Instead, I got the confused murmuring of a crowd unsure of their future.

"Your turn," I said to Ammon's second-in-command. As he

opened his mouth, I grabbed him by the front of his shirt. "And you'd damn well better make them feel good about this, or I will throw you into the river."

I released him and walked off the dais, flanked by the Niemenians and Jorad.

"That was an impressive speech," Luard said, falling into step beside me. "Didn't get the applause I expected, but I'd give it a passing grade."

"I'm handing them over to another king, what did you expect?" I said with a longing look behind me. There was nothing more I could do here. "After I killed..."

"You will lose a lot more people in the coming weeks," Ivan said. "Best to learn how to deal with it now, before the numbers increase."

"I don't want to learn to deal with it," I said as we came to Luard's carriage in front of the Wicked Duck. "Because then I'll make callous decisions with people's lives. I want to know the name of every person who dies because of me. Even if they do so willingly."

Luard nodded. "You will make a good queen, Brynna."

"I've gotten the assurances from the Kulkans," I said after a long pause. "Now it's time for Ariadna to send her forces as well. I need you to return to Niemen and tell her what you've seen."

"I'll send—"

"No, Luard," I replied firmly. "I have soldiers under Jorad's command, and I'm sure I can wrestle more from Celia now that I've proven myself. What I need from you is to tell your sister. Because those ships she'll be sending through Skorsa are the most important thing right now."

"Fine," he said with a dramatic sigh. "I suppose I can return home for a brief stint. But rest assured, I'll be back. I want to see how this adventure ends for you."

I looked to Ivan for help, but he shrugged. "I can only do what my prince commands."

Luard hugged me. "It has been a pleasure getting into trouble with you, Brynna. Be sure to give my best to my sister when you see her."

I opened my mouth but was struck with the uncomfortable knowledge that I wouldn't be able to see Katarine until I found a way inside the castle. I had the support of Kulka and Niemen, but there was still so far to go.

Chapter Fifty-One

Felix

There had been twenty explosions in all—every one of the remaining merchants on my list had gone up in flames. But unlike before, where there'd been one at a time, they'd gone off in near-perfect precision. Fifty lives had been lost, including Zuriel's wife and children. Then, yesterday, Zuriel himself had been found hanging in his office. It might've been poetic justice, but it sure didn't feel like it.

Ilara had been furious—both because she now found herself without anyone to make her clothes and jewels, but also because the attack had been a complete surprise. I was waiting for her to point the finger at me, yet surprisingly, she kept her temper around me and allowed me to conduct an investigation.

Of course, I knew who'd brought it to the city. Katarine gave me a name for the stuff—ond. Supposedly it was a Niemenian state secret, and it unnerved her to see it used so widely. But I wasn't surprised that our rebel leader had been able to procure it. He was a man who knew how to get things.

After the furor had died down somewhat, and the citizens shifted from shock to clean-up, I finally returned to Ruby's shop—this time as myself. I wanted it to be the first branch of trust in what I hoped would be a long, fruitful relationship.

Ruby wasn't at the counter, but the man I'd seen cleaning with her the other day was.

I walked up and rested my hand on the glass. "Afternoon."

The man nodded. "What can I do for you, Captain?"

"Tell your boss I'm ready to see him," I said, leveling my gaze at him. "I know who brought the ond into the city, and unless he agrees to meet with me tonight, I—"

Whatever else I had to say died on my lips as the world went black.

I awoke in a quiet room with my hands bound and an aching head. It took a few minutes for my wits to come back to me, but finally I remembered where I'd been, and who I'd been talking to. My next questions were why my Severian guards hadn't come to my aid or noticed that I'd been captured. Never thought I'd miss those assholes.

The lock turned over on the door, and I smiled as the door opened.

"I thought it might be you," I said.

Johann Beswick, the slumlord crime boss who'd been Brynna's target as The Veil, smiled at me from across the room. He looked much less healthy than the last time we'd crossed paths—he'd lost a lot of weight in his cheeks, and his hair was thinning. But based on what I'd seen these last few weeks, he still retained that cold-blooded grip that had caused so much pain to so many.

"So, Captain," he said. "Or should I say, Man-Veil." He tossed something at my feet—the mask that had been hidden under my tunic.

I narrowed my eyes. "Who else did you tell?"

"Don't worry, I trust my people," he said with a wave of his hand. "The better question is, of course, what are *you* doing under the mask, instead of sitting at the right hand of that desert-dwelling bitch? I thought you'd turned tail on our fair nation."

"And I thought you'd run away to Niemen," I countered. "Instead you're here, fomenting rebellion and playing hero. Doesn't seem like the kind of thing you'd get your hands dirty with."

"I'm offended you're so shocked." He walked from behind the desk to cut through the bindings at my wrists. "This is my city, and that bitch queen has no right to sit on that throne."

"Well, yes, but..." I rubbed my red wrists. "You're a criminal."

"So? Criminals can be patriotic." He sat down on the edge of the desk. "But again, you haven't answered my question. What are you doing out here?"

I looked behind me at the two guards standing at attention. "Tell them to get lost."

Beswick considered for a moment then waved his hands. The two guards nodded and left, closing the door behind them.

"I'm here because Brynna asked me to help her find allies in the city," I said.

Beswick's eyes widened and he actually looked shocked. *So he doesn't know.* Good, that meant Kieran could still be trusted.

"This does not leave this room," I said. "But she's in Niemen, hopefully convincing Queen Ariadna to help us. To...I suppose, help you." I could only imagine the look on her face when she found out. "When Brynn gets back, we're removing Ilara from power. And we'd like your help."

"If she gets back," Beswick replied with a shrug. "What's to say she doesn't just disappear into Niemen? Or what's to say Ariadna will even agree to help us at all?"

"Because I have faith in her," I said. "You should know. She nearly took down your entire operation."

"She didn't even get close," Beswick said. "Which is why I *don't* have any faith in her. Sure, she found evidence, but she didn't take into account the safeguards I'd put into place and had to resort to...well, what she did."

"She made a mistake," I said. "She won't make it again."

"I daresay she won't get the chance to make it again," he said, coming to stand in front of me. "I'm going to make you a deal, *Captain.* You can walk out of here and not speak another word to anyone about my operation. Or, if you choose to cross me, I'll have my people sneak through the servants' quarters and kill your little Niemenian friend and her maid girlfriend."

It was the same as it had been—all this trouble, all this effort, and I was still hitting a brick wall. "You don't have to turn me away. We can work together. Brynna will come back. I made a promise to her that I would find the rebels and convince them to join her. And you aren't going to make me break a promise." I rose to my feet. "You're a businessman. Let's do business."

"I used to be a businessman," he replied with a casual wave of his hands. "Now I'm a rebel leader. I don't make deals with royals."

"Good thing she's not a royal," I said. "She's The Veil. And if anyone can figure it out, she can."

Loud noises echoed in the room behind us, and Beswick jumped to his feet. Without another word, he dashed through a secret door behind him—one I hadn't even noticed was there.

"W-wait a second!" I said, jumping to my feet. But before I could get very far, the door behind me opened and Coyle walked into the room, flanked by two of his favorite Severian lieutenants. He shook his head as he glanced at the mask on the floor.

"Oh, Felix," he said softly. "I'd held out hope it wasn't you."

"Thank you for rescuing me," I said, but I knew lying would be in vain. The time had run out and I was just delaying the inevitable. "When those guards took me, I—"

"Don't play dumb with me," he said, continuing to stare at the mask on the floor. "You've been parading as The Veil for months now. Several witnesses down at the docks name you as the man carrying ond into the city. Unless...of course there was someone else." His eyes practically begged me to give a name.

And I did consider it. But if I allowed myself to be arrested instead of selling Beswick out, perhaps that would prove to the slumlord that I, too, could be trusted. And when Brynna returned...perhaps she'd find him in a better humor. It could be one last sacrifice I would make for her.

"No, it was me," I said, sitting back.

"I know that's a lie," Coyle said, walking toward me. "Who was it? Where did they go?"

I grinned. "You're going to have to ask nicer than that."

"Was this you, too?" He pulled something out of his back pocket and flung it on top of the mask. My heart sank when I saw what it was—Katarine's forged passage papers for Kieran. "I don't think either of us wants to cause an international incident," he said, his meaning clear as day.

"Of course," I said, without missing a beat. After all, I was the one Coyle wanted out of the way, not Katarine. I would gladly take the fall to keep Ilara away from her.

Coyle smirked as he walked in closer. "Sloppy, sloppy work, Felix. I thought you were smarter than this."

I crossed my arms over my chest. "I'm surprised it took you this long to figure it out."

He glanced behind him at the waiting lieutenants, who'd been a rapt audience at our repartee. "Search this place for anyone else who might be hiding."

"But, sir—"

"*Now*," Coyle snapped.

They saluted and disappeared, and he shook his head.

"Doesn't feel great to have your subordinates disobey you, does it?" I said. "I hear you're a man who's about to lose his job."

"And you're a man about to lose his head," Coyle said. "Don't you understand that I was trying to protect you from Ilara?"

My brows rose to my forehead. "In what way?"

"The moment a masked vigilante appeared on the streets, she wanted me to have you, Jo, and Riya strung up for treason. But I persuaded her that you were loyal, and that I would personally oversee the investigation." He shook his head. "I tried to warn you, Felix."

"You also put babysitters on me—"

"To prove that you *couldn't* be The Veil, because you had eyes on you at all times." He smiled thinly. "But now I have no choice but to arrest you. I can't get you out of this."

"Then perhaps you shouldn't have betrayed Brynna," I said, rising and holding out my wrists for irons. "Because unlike you, I know where my loyalties lie. And they aren't with that desert-dwelling bitch. You betrayed our country, Coyle."

"I did what I had to do to survive. I just wish I could've saved you, too," he replied as his lieutenants reappeared. "Cuff him and take him to the dungeons. We will have him brought up on treason charges. Her Highness will be most pleased that we've finally caught the dangerous rebel leader."

I let them bind me, rough me up, and leave me bleeding as they threw me in the back of the prison carriage. But I looked out into the curious faces of nearby onlookers, and I didn't see fear. I saw determination. The citizens of Forcadel weren't giving up, and neither would I.

I had faith that Brynna would come for me.

Brynna's adventures continue in

THE VEIL OF TRUST

Acknowlegments

Thanks to my parents, who continue to show faith and support for my work and my crazy schemes, and for letting me crash at their house between home purchases. Extra special thanks to my mom for listening to me gripe and moan about how difficult this cursed book was to write.

Thank you to my bevy of beta readers: Kristin and Alice, for helping me get out of my own head.

Thank you to Dani, my magnificent line editor, who took on this book even though she was going through a hellish month.

Thank you to my QA checker, Lisa, who always manages to find the small little details that I miss.

Thank you to my final typo checkers, Bettina, Elizabeth, and Jessica, for plowing through this book so quickly.

And finally, thank you to all the challenges that came up during the drafting of this book. I can now say that this was the toughest book I've ever written and every other book from now on will be a breeze in comparison.

Also By the Author

THE SEOD CROI CHRONICLES

After her father's murder, princess Ayla is set to take the throne —
but to succeed, she needs the magical stone her evil stepmother
stole. Fortunately, wizard apprentice Cade and knight Ward are
both eager to win Ayla's favor.

A Quest of Blood and Stone is the first book in the *Seod Croi*
chronicles and is available now in eBook, paperback, and
hardcover.

Lexie Carrigan Chronicles

Lexie Carrigan thought she was weird enough until her family
drops a bomb on her—she's magical. Now the girl who's never
made waves is blowing up her nightstand and no one seems to
want to help her. That is, until a kind gentleman shows up with all
the answers. But Lexie finds out being magical is the least weird
thing about her.

Spells and Sorcery is the first book in the Lexie Carrigan
Chronicles, and is available now in eBook, paperback, audiobook,
and hardcover.

Also By the Author

THE MADION WAR TRILOGY

He's a prince, she's a pilot, they're at war. But when they are marooned on a deserted island hundreds of miles from either nation, they must set aside their differences and work together if they want to survive.

The Madion War Trilogy is a fantasy romance available now in eBook, Paperback, and Hardcover.

empath

Lauren Dailey is in break-up hell, but if you ask her she's doing just great. She hears a mysterious voice promising an easy escape from her problems and finds herself in a brand new world where she has the power to feel what others are feeling. Just one problem —there's a dragon in the mountains that happens to eat Empaths. And it might be the source of the mysterious voice tempting her deeper into her own darkness.

Empath is a stand-alone fantasy that is available now in eBook, Paperback, and Hardcover.

About the Author

S. Usher Evans was born and raised in Pensacola, Florida. After a decade of fighting bureaucratic battles as an IT consultant in Washington, DC, she suffered a massive quarter-life-crisis. She decided fighting dragons was more fun than writing policy, so she moved back to Pensacola to write books full-time. She currently resides there with her husband, daughter, and two dogs, Zoe and Mr. Biscuit, and frequently can be found plotting on the beach.

Visit S. Usher Evans online at:
http://www.susherevans.com/

Twitter: www.twitter.com/susherevans
Facebook: www.facebook.com/susherevans
Instagram: www.instagram.com/susherevans

9 781945 438264